"Evie Dunmore's debut is a marvel. Set against the backdrop of the British suffrage movement, *Bringing Down the Duke* is a witty, richly detailed, historically significant, and achingly romantic celebration of the power of love and the passionate fight for women's rights. A stunning blend of history and romance that will enchant readers."

—Chanel Cleeton, *New York Times* bestselling author

"Evie Dunmore's *Bringing Down the Duke* dazzles and reminds us all why we fell in love with historical romance."

—Julia London, *New York Times* bestselling author

"Miss Dunmore is a literary force to be reckoned with. She's single-handedly forging a new historical romance era and I am here. For. It."

—Rachel Van Dyken, #1 *New York Times* bestselling author

"Simply superb! Evie Dunmore will wow you."

—Gaelen Foley, *New York Times* bestselling author

"One of my all-time favorite historicals."

—Maisey Yates, *New York Times* bestselling author

"*Bringing Down the Duke* was one of the best books I've ever read—absolutely adored it. Dunmore had me in tears, had me holding my breath . . . the emotion and passion made the book ache and sing."

—Jane Porter, *New York Times* bestselling author

"Charming, sexy, and thoroughly transportive, this is historical romance done right."

—*Publishers Weekly* (starred review)

"Funny, smart, and a fantastic read! *Bringing Down the Duke* was absolutely brilliant!"

—Corinne Michaels, *New York Times* bestselling author

"Full of witty banter and swoonworthy moments . . . a deliciously delightful romance."

—*Woman's World*

"Dunmore's beautifully written debut perfectly balances history, sexual tension, romantic yearning, and the constant struggle smart women have in finding and maintaining their places and voices in life and love, with the added message that finding the right person brings true happiness and being with them is worth any price. A brilliant debut."
                                        —*Kirkus Reviews* (starred review)

"Chock-full of verve, history, and passion."
                                        —*Library Journal* (starred review)

"Full of witty banter, rich historical detail, and a fantastic group of female friends, the first installment in Dunmore's League of Extraordinary Women series starts with fireworks as Annabelle and Montgomery try to find a path to happiness despite past mistakes and their vastly different places in society. Dunmore's strong debut is sure to earn her legions of fans."   —*Booklist* (starred review)

"What an absolutely stunning, riveting, painfully gorgeous book! It's not only the best historical romance I've read in a long, long time, it's one of the best books I've ever read! I adored it!"
  —Megan Crane, *USA Today* bestselling author of *Special Ops Seduction*

"With just the right blend of history and romance (and a healthy dash of pride from the British suffragists that would make Jane Austen proud), I was hooked on Annabelle and Sebastian's story from the very first page. I can't wait for the rest of the League of Extraordinary Women novels!"
  —Stephanie Thornton, *USA Today* bestselling author of *American Princess*

"Evie Dunmore's *Bringing Down the Duke* delivers the best of two worlds—a steamy romance coupled with the heft of a meticulously researched historical novel. . . . Readers will be entranced watching Annabelle, a woman ahead of her time, bring the sexy Duke to his knees."   —Renée Rosen, author of *Park Avenue Summer*

"Evie Dunmore has written a story we need right now—strong, smart, and passionate, featuring a heroine who won't settle for less than what she deserves and a swoony hero who learns to fight for what really matters. With her debut novel, Dunmore has instantly become a must-read for me."

—Lyssa Kay Adams, author of *The Bromance Book Club*

"A deliciously original debut featuring a fiercely passionate suffragette who melts an icy duke's heart. Set against the backdrop of the fight for women's rights, *Bringing Down the Duke* is the perfect blend of romance and history."

—Diana Quincy, author of The Rebellious Brides series

"Dunmore creates pure magic with this charming, romantic novel featuring a strong, stubborn heroine and a sexy, slightly broken hero. Full of romance, humor, and heart, all revolving around the fascinating dynamics of the suffragist movement, it's one of my favorite novels of 2020!"   —Jennifer Probst, *New York Times* bestselling author

"A truly delightful historical romance, with oodles of period detail and lots of laugh-out-loud moments. Evie Dunmore is an author to watch, and this book will delight fans of Tessa Dare, Eva Leigh, and Julia Quinn."   —Historical Novel Society

"Evie Dunmore is a phenomenon! . . . Breathtaking, high stakes romance, with one of the loveliest endings I've read in years."

—Anna Campbell, author of the bestselling Dashing Widows series

"The perfect intersection of fierce feminism and swoon-worthy romance."   —Eva Leigh, author of *My Fake Rake*

"A modern romance in a Victorian dress, sans the corset."

—Amy E. Reichert, author of *The Coincidence of Coconut Cake*

Portrait of a Scotsman

The League of Extraordinary Women Series

EVIE DUNMORE

JOVE
New York

A JOVE BOOK
Published by Berkley
An imprint of Penguin Random House LLC
penguinrandomhouse.com

Library of Congress Cataloging-in-Publication Data

Names: Dunmore, Evie, author.
Title: Portrait of a Scotsman : the league of extraordinary women series / Evie Dunmore.
Description: First Edition. | New York: Jove, 2021. | Series: A league of extraordinary women ; 3 | "A Jove book"—Title page verso.
Identifiers: LCCN 2021027600 (print) | LCCN 2021027601 (ebook) | ISBN 9781984805720 (trade paperback) | ISBN 9781984805737 (ebook)
Subjects: GSAFD: Love stories.
Classification: LCC PR9110.9.D86 P67 2021 (print) | LCC PR9110.9.D86 (ebook) | DDC 823/.92—dc23
LC record available at https://lccn.loc.gov/2021027600
LC ebook record available at https://lccn.loc.gov/2021027601

Printed in the United States of America
1st Printing

Book design by Laura K. Corless

For Mama and Oma

Chapter 1

London, August 1880

As she hovered on the rain-soaked pavement in front of the Chelsea town house she was about to infiltrate, feeling hot beneath her woolen cloak, Hattie Greenfield couldn't help but think back to the last time she had run from her protection officer. It had resulted in an altercation with a toad of a policeman and a dear friend being held at Millbank prison. She supposed all the most perilous adventures began with escaping dour Mr. Graves. All the best ones, too.

She eyed the lacquered front door atop the steps. The iron-cast lion's maw holding the door knocker had absurdly long, pointy teeth. The warning that she was about to enter the lion's den was almost too shrill to ignore for someone selectively superstitious. But this time, her adventure wasn't an inherently risky women's rights march on Parliament Square; it was a private art gallery tour. Perfectly harmless.

She lifted her skirts in one hand and began the ascent.

Her friends would point out that the gallery was owned by Mr. Blackstone, a man society had nicknamed Beelzebub, and that he also happened to be her father's business rival, and no, she shouldn't be found admiring his Pre-Raphaelites unchaperoned.

However, it was safe to assume that Mr. Beelzebub wasn't present; in fact, very few people had ever seen him in the flesh. Second, she had registered for the tour as Miss Jones, classics student at Cambridge, not as Harriet Greenfield, Oxford art student and banking heiress. Third, the full tour through his gallery of arts and antiques comprised a handful of other young art connoisseurs and likely *their* chaperones, and the invitation in her reticule said she was keeping them waiting. The tour had begun at two o'clock sharp and her small pocket watch was all but burning a hole through her bodice.

The thuds of the door knocker appeared to fade away unnoticed into the entrance hall beyond. She rang the bell.

Silence.

Beneath the hem of her plain cloak, her wet foot began to tap. They must have started the tour without her. She had climbed from the cab, which had become hopelessly stuck in rain and traffic soon after leaving Victoria Station, and had braved the remaining quarter of a mile on foot—for nothing? The pounding of iron on oak became insistent.

Or perhaps she had done it again. She fumbled for her reticule between the folds of her cloak and pulled out the invitation. She squinted at the address, then back at the house number with full attention. It was still number twelve Carlyle Square. The square was small; she doubted there was a house number one-and-twenty. She knocked again, and again.

The heavy door swung back unexpectedly.

The man facing her was not a butler. His thinning gray hair was disheveled, he wore a paint-stained apron, and he smelled pungently of . . . antique wax polish? She tried to assess without staring whether his long, lined face was familiar to her from the artistic circles. His assessment of her person wasn't subtle: his gaze searched the empty space where a female companion should have been, then roamed from her sodden hem up to her undoubtedly frizzy red hair.

"And you'll be?" he drawled.

She cleared her throat. "I'm here for the tour."

"The tour?" Comprehension dawned in the man's eyes. "The tour." "Yes."

His thin lips curled with derision. "I see."

She shifted from one foot to the other. "I'm afraid I was delayed on my journey. I have come all the way from outside London, you see, then my companion was . . . unwell, and then there was such dreadful traffic on Lyall Street because of the heavy rain; the roads are—"

"Come on, then," he said, and abruptly stepped aside with a wave of his hand.

He was cross; male artists had this prerogative, to let it be known that they were cross when one interrupted their work.

No maid was in sight to take her cloak; in fact, the place felt yawningly empty. A nervous sensation fluttered in her belly. But the wax-polish man was already several paces ahead, his hasty footsteps echoing on the black-and-white tiles of the entrance hall.

"Sir." She hurried after him, water squelching between her toes.

They turned into a shadowed corridor. To her left, intriguingly elegant lines of statues and vases beckoned, but not slipping on the floor in wet heels demanded her full attention. Ahead, the man had stopped and opened a door. He motioned for her to enter, but she hesitated on the doorstep, for while the room was brightly lit, there was no trace of the group. There was no one here at all. The painter flicked his fingers impatiently at the nearest settee. "Go on, take a seat."

Even from here she could tell the settee was from the days of Louis XIV, and sitting on the butter-yellow silk in her damp cloak would damage it.

"Will you send someone to take my coat, please, Mr. . . . ?"

The man inclined his head in a mock bow. "You shall be seen to shortly."

"Sir, I must ask you to—"

The door was firmly closed in her face, and she stood blinking at white wood paneling.

"Right." She blew out a breath.

In the silence, her heartbeat was loud in her ears. Warm sweat trickled down her back. *Dangerous*, said her instincts. *Underworld lord.* Those were her friend Lucie's words after finding out her fiancé, Lord Ballentine, had borrowed money from Mr. Blackstone to purchase a publishing house quite recently . . .

She tried a smile. "Adventurous," she said. "This is fabulous, and adventurous."

She turned back to the room. This was a pirate's lair. And the treasures were piled up high. Every shelf and table surface coming into focus was crowded with splendor: glossy porcelain couples—Meissen, at a second glance—filigree ivory-and-gold statuettes, ornately carved boxes with softly rounded edges in all shades of jade green. Select pieces were illuminated by small table lamps with ceramic shades so fine the gaslight shone through them as if they were made of silk. The wall opposite was papered in a riotously floral Morris wallpaper—a waste, because it was covered from floor to ceiling in paintings, their gilded frames nearly touching.

"Oh my." She laughed softly. A Cranach the Elder was on display next to a picnic scene that looked like a Monet. Objectively, more intriguing than the Pre-Raphaelites. Shockingly, the glowing embers in the fireplace to her right held the greatest appeal today. As she carefully picked her way through the array of decorated side tables, her cloak jostled one of them and sent a porcelain ballerina swaying precariously on her pointy toes. Goodness. What had possessed Mr. Blackstone or his curator to jumble these precious pieces together like guests of a carelessly composed dinner party, and in a room open to the public no less?

The heat coming from the fireplace was feeble. Her reflection in the wide mirror above the mantelshelf was equally disappointing: the purple feather on her hat was thin as a rat's tail, her usually silky curls were a riot, her upturned nose glowed pink. If this was what her brief walk had done to her face, what havoc had it wreaked upon her slippers? She stuck out a foot from beneath her hem. Dainty heels, white silk, embroidered with the tiniest pearls. A wholly inappropriate choice for an outing, but one of her favorite pairs. Clearly damaged beyond repair. Her stomach dipped.

It was Professor Ruskin's fault. Had he not called her *Abduction of Persephone* "lovely" the other week, she wouldn't have boarded the train this morning. It had been one such *lovely* too many since she had enrolled at Oxford last year. He had said it in passing, with a friendly nod, then he had lingered next to Lord Skeffington's easel and had critiqued his work in depth, and she had stood with her ears straining to catch his advice on how to strengthen the Gothicness in a painting. Somehow, the idea of taking a good long look at Millais's *Ophelia*, which Mr. Blackstone had secured for his private collection, had taken root during that class. And yes, there might have been a tiny, tantalizing temptation in the prospect of setting foot on property owned by Mr. Blackstone—the one man in Britain who dared to let her father's lunch invitations pass unanswered.

Her attention, of its own volition, shifted to the pair of green-glazed, round-bellied vases flanking the mantelshelf clock. They were easily overlooked at first glance, unremarkable in their earthy simplicity, like the poor relation in an opulent ballroom. And yet . . . her eyes narrowed at the relief on the nearer vase. A keen sensation prickled down her neck—she was looking at something extraordinarily indeed. Still, she shouldn't touch it. She really should not. She tugged the glove off her left hand, stuffed it into her cloak pocket, and skimmed her index finger over the pattern on the vase's rim. With some luck, there was a mark to confirm her suspicions—if she dared to check for it.

Her deliberation was brief.

She took the vase in both hands, handling it with the anxious care she would afford a raw egg, and turned it bottom up. There was a mark. All the fine hairs on her arms stood erect. This unassuming piece was almost certainly a Han vase. If it was authentic, it was near two thousand years old. Her palms turned hot and damp.

"I'd rather you not touch that," came a gravelly male voice.

She jumped and shrieked, pressing the vase to her breast.

What she saw in the mirror made her freeze.

The pirate had returned to his cave.

She had seen and heard nothing while engrossed. He must have been watching her awhile, with one shoulder against the doorjamb of the side-chamber door and his arms folded across his broad chest. She turned slowly, her stomach hollowing. Of course he wasn't a pirate, but he wasn't decent: he wore no jacket, no cravat, and his sleeves were rolled up to expose muscular forearms. His unruly coalblack hair was too long, and his strong jawline was shadowed with stubble. But the most uncivilized part of him was his eyes—they were trained on her with a singular intensity that curled her toes in her wet stockings.

"I just . . ." Her voice faltered.

He closed the door. Her grip on the vase tightened. Obviously, he had been sent to fetch her, but her nerves shrilled, urging her to retreat. He moved in on her smoothly, too smoothly, rattling precisely nothing during his prowl through the delicate artifacts. She was motionless like a stunned rabbit until he was right in front of her.

He *was* arresting. His contrasts in coloring drew all attention to his eyes: hard and gray like slate, with inky brows and lashes, set in a pale face. His features were decidedly masculine, their well-done symmetry vaguely disturbed by a once-broken nose. He had the ageless look of a man who had lived too much, too soon.

He held her in his gaze while he slid two fingers of his right hand into the mouth of the vase. Which she was still clutching like a thief caught in the act.

"Why don't you give this to me," he said.

Her skin pulsed red-hot with embarrassment as she released the precious ceramic. She had brothers and she studied alongside men, and she was never tongue-tied in their presence—she was never *tongue-tied*. But as the man placed the vase back onto the mantelshelf, she breathed in his scent, an attractive blend of pine soap and starch—incongruently clean with his piratical appearance—and she didn't know where to look. She was altogether too aware of this man being a man. He stood just above average height, but his soft cotton sleeves clung snugly to the balls of his shoulders, hinting at swells and ridges of muscle no gentleman would possess. She glanced back up at his face just as he inclined his head, and their eyes met in another mutual inspection. A thin scar bisected the left side of his upper lip. Her mouth turned dry. It was a trick of the light, but his irises had darkened by a shade or two.

"I had not meant to touch it," she said primly.

A faintly ironic expression passed over his face. It failed to soften the hard set of his mouth. "And with whom do I have the pleasure, Mrs. . . . ?"

"Miss. My name is Miss Jones." It came out in an unnatural pitch.

His eyes flashed as he registered the lie. "What's the purpose of your visit, Miss Jones?"

He was a Scotsman. His *r*'s were emerging as softly rolling growls. It explained the fair skin and Celtic-dark locks. . . . More interestingly, the heat emanating from his body was warmer than the embers on the grate. She knew because he stood too close. His right hand was still braced on the mantelshelf near her shoulder, his arm cutting off any escape route to the left.

She licked her lips nervously. The purpose of her visit? "The full tour?"

A subtle tension tightened his shoulders. "And are you certain of that?"

"Of course, and I would be much obliged if you could—"

He raised a hand to her face and his fingertip lightly touched her cheekbone.

The man was touching her. *A man* was touching her.

The world slowed to a halt. She should scream. Slap him. Her body did not obey; it stood immobile while the air between them crackled with a premonition that she was on the cusp of something vast.

The gray of his eyes was as soft and menacing as smoke. "Aye," he murmured. "Then I'll give you the tour, Miss Jones."

His fingers curved around her nape, and then his mouth was on hers.

Chapter 2

His lips are soft. The alien pressure of a soft, warm mouth against her own was all she registered in her frozen stupor. Bristle abrading her chin. The slick touch of a . . . tongue against her lips, demanding entry. . . . Her head jerked back as her hand flew up, and the *crack* of her bare palm hitting his cheek was sharp like a gunshot. She screamed, belatedly, because she had just slapped a man forcefully enough to turn his head to the side.

He gave a little shake, his expression incredulous for a beat, then his gaze narrowed at her. "Madam isn't here for that type of tour, I gather," he said darkly.

She scurried backward out of his reach, her heart hammering. "Don't touch me."

Her skirt met an obstacle; something scraped across parquet and something crashed. Her left heel slipped, and bright, hot pain seared through her ankle as it turned, making her cry out.

The man muttered a profanity and came after her.

"Stay away from me!"

He approached, his brawny shoulders looming. A hasty glance said she was halfway to the door. *Help*—would there be anyone to help her in this vast, empty house?

Another crash.

"Miss—"

She blindly grabbed something off a table and pointed it like a foil.

"Stay where you are, or I shall stick you with this."

Now he heard her. His eyes fixing upon her makeshift weapon, he came to a halt and slowly raised his hands, palms forward as if attempting to soothe a spooked horse—as though *she* were the unhinged person in the room!

"Very well," he said. "But put that down."

She realized she was holding the tiptoed dancer she had nearly toppled earlier.

"It's a unique piece," the man added.

"I'm aware," she snapped. "Meissen, and a limited edition from 1714."

Surprise sparked in his eyes, there and gone in the split of a second.

"So you agree it shouldn't be destroyed in the wake of needless theatrics," he said.

"Theatrics?" Outrage made her squeak. "You, sir, just forced yourself on me."

"A regrettable misunderstanding," he said, not sounding particularly regretful.

She shook the dancer at him. "Mr. Blackstone will hear about your wicked behavior."

His lips quirked. "Without doubt. Miss Jones, why don't you take a seat"—he gestured at her skirt hem—"you appear to have done yourself some damage."

He had no business thinking of or alluding to any one part of her anatomy, but of course, he had to add insult to injury by mentioning her twisted ankle. He was also watching her with deepening annoyance, like a predator wondering why he was being ordered around by his prey.

Pain throbbed in her left foot as she inched toward the door, sideways like a crab, because she was not letting him out of her sight. Her heart thumped with relief when she burst into the corridor: the disgruntled painter and a slim young gentleman with a respectable blond mustache were hovering just a few paces away in the hallway, their expressions alert.

"Thank goodness." She hobbled toward them. "I require your assistance. There is a man"—she pointed over her shoulder with her thumb—"and I'm afraid he is not acting like a gentleman."

The men exchanged a wary glance. It occurred to her then that they must have heard her scream—why else were they here in front of the door? And yet neither had come to investigate. Her stomach fell, and she felt dizzy, as if taking ill. Of course. She looked a fright. She was here without a guardian. Her incognito cloak was a theater prop from the old trunk in the nursery playroom. Right now, she was not Hattie Greenfield; she was not even a properly chaperoned young woman. The absence of her father's name slapped with cold force, as though an invisible shield had been taken from her, as though she had suddenly been stripped bare in front of a crowd. Right now, she was . . . no one.

She turned to the blond one, who, though timid, still looked vastly more likely to help a damsel in distress than the painter. "Please, good sir, I might need an arm to lean on . . ."

The men's attention shifted to something beyond her shoulder, and she knew the barbarian was in the hallway. She could *feel* the dark energy swirling around him.

"And if you could hail a cab for me, that would be awfully kind," she added quickly.

"Not so hasty," came the mean voice.

"You also must inform Mr. Blackstone that he has a ruffian in his employ who accosts the female guests under his roof."

The blond man's eyes widened with alarm. "Erm," he said, his throat moving convulsively. "Miss . . ."

A pathetic gasp burst out of her as realization struck. She closed her eyes. "He is standing right behind me, is he not?" she said. "Mr. Blackstone."

"He is, yes," the young man replied, his tone apologetic.

She really was silly sometimes. The Scotsman's identity should have been plain to her the moment he had stalked across the reception room as though he owned it; at the very latest, when he had tried to ravish her next to a Han vase as a matter of course. Everything horrible she had heard about him was evidently true.

A tug on the figurine reminded her she was still holding on to the thing.

It was of no use now, anyway.

Mr. Blackstone's brutish countenance was right in front of her, his regard intent. In his right hand was the dancer, his broad fist nearly swallowing the dainty woman. *Beelzebub*. One of the wealthiest, most ruthless, ill-reputed businessmen in England, and if rumor could be trusted, he had driven several peers into financial ruin. He looked the part, from his eyes, which seemed to know no joy, to his broken nose, to his bull-like build, which made her think he enjoyed throwing anvils for sport. Few people knew what he looked like; he was as elusive as a phantom. And she had kissed him. Heat crept up her neck. Her father was going to send her to a convent.

Recognition passed behind Mr. Blackstone's eyes then, and the furrow between his dark brows eased. He took a step back and inclined his head. "Blackstone, at your service. My assistant, Mr. Richard Matthews." He thrust the figurine at the blond man while keeping his eyes on her. He didn't introduce the disgruntled painter.

"Miss Jones," she replied stiffly.

"So you said."

His Celtic lilt had vanished, but his sarcasm was loud and clear. She had made his acquaintance mere minutes ago and she already knew that he was one of the least refined people to have ever crossed her path. And he knew that she was lying. She had to leave before he came to the bottom of her identity, because then her ill-advised excursion would definitely reach her father's ears.

"Now," he said. "What's this tour you claim you've come for, Miss Jones?"

She shook her head. "I just wish to take my leave."

His gaze narrowed.

"I'd rather trouble you no longer," she tried. If it weren't for her ankle, and her narrow skirts and damaged shoes, she'd make a dash for it.

Mr. Richard Matthews made a faint sound of dismay. "I'm afraid the tour you are referring to was canceled."

Blackstone's head had swung around toward his assistant as if he were surprised, and Mr. Matthews was squirming on the spot, but her chest lightened with sudden relief. "So there was a tour? I had begun to think it was a figment of my imagination."

Matthews was avoiding his employer's eyes. "There was. I had all the cancellation notices sent out yesterday. The continuous rain has caused a leak in the main gallery roof and some of the artwork exhibited there was affected."

"Not the *Ophelia*, I hope?"

All three men were looking at her blankly.

"I came to see the Pre-Raphaelites," she told Mr. Matthews. "The *Ophelia* in particular."

"No, the *Ophelia* is in perfect condition," he was quick to reassure her.

Damaged artwork might explain the painter who lingered behind Mr. Blackstone with a bored expression—he was probably the restorer. It did not explain why she had been mauled. The only way to explain *that* was if they had all taken her for one of Mr. Blackstone's fancy women. . . . She felt herself pale.

Mr. Matthews tugged at the knot of his cravat. "My profound apologies, Miss Jones. Perhaps there was a confusion at the post office."

"Please, don't trouble yourself." She forced a smile to put him at ease. The Royal Mail service was in perfect working order for all she knew. But her cancellation letter would have gone to her collaborator in Cambridge, and for some reason, Miss Jones hadn't notified her of the change in schedule on time. Also, she, Hattie, had failed to stop by her pigeonhole at Oxford to collect her mail this morning, pre-occupied with mentally practicing the steps for her escape from Mr. Graves in Oxford's University Galleries.

"Matthews," Mr. Blackstone said abruptly. "Tell Nicolas to take Miss Jones home."

She took a step back. "Thank you, but that is hardly necessary."

He cut her a dark look. "It is."

Mr. Matthews was already hurrying down the hallway on lanky legs.

"How kind of you to insist," she said to Mr. Blackstone. "But I merely require assistance with hailing a cab."

"My coach is faster, more comfortable, and is waiting out the back."

She shook her head, her heart pounding unpleasantly fast again. "I don't wish to inconvenience you, sir."

"I'll be blunt, then, Miss Jones," he drawled. "It may have by-passed your delicate ears, but I have a reputation." He nodded at her bedraggled, lopsided appearance. "And if you care to keep yours, you'd better not be seen limping out of my front door unchaperoned."

She hadn't thought her cheeks could burn any hotter, but they did. A lecture on propriety from such an ill-bred man, well deserved no less, had to be a peak of humiliation in a young woman's life. She raised her nose. "Fine."

Mr. Blackstone bared surprisingly strong, white teeth in a smile. His left canine tooth was badly chipped, a continuation of the scar splitting his upper lip. His gaze holding hers, he rolled down his sleeves in a hopelessly belated attempt at decency. The sight of rumpled cotton and cuffless hems grazing his wrists worked to the contrary, as a man would probably look just like this when he hastily dressed after an illicit encounter. She glanced away, her throat strangely tight. Her lips were still tingling from his kiss; her left palm still stung from the collision with his cheek. Her ankle was on fire. The truth was, had it been the fastest available means of transportation, she would have ridden out of the gallery on a donkey.

Chapter 3

A distinct sense of foreboding crawled down his spine as he watched his carriage containing the red-haired baggage join the London traffic. Odd, because Lucian Blackstone had long ceased to believe in fate and preferred to forge his destiny by way of his own machinations.

"She was one of Greenfield's daughters, wasn't she?" he said.

It had dawned on him when he had studied her face in the corridor, when she had finally stopped flailing, screeching, and smashing antiques. It would explain the visceral pull in his gut when first clapping eyes on her, a sensation every seasoned thief knew when he had spotted something precious.

"I believe so, sir." Matthews sounded more nervous than usual. "The red hair, the short, plump stature—"

"I have eyes, Matthews. You—" He turned to Renwick, who had come to lurk on the backdoor steps with him and Matthews instead of resuming his work. "Why had you thought she had come here to fuck?"

Renwick scratched the back of his head. "She was unchaperoned?"

"A necessary but not sufficient condition, you fool."

"And I understand ladies are seeking you out for a tumble now and again—"

"In bright daylight?" snarled Lucian. "And coming through the front door? Here it is, Renwick: even if the great big whore of Baby-lon comes a-knocking, you don't let her into my house."

He rarely slipped into the Scottish vowels of his youth; today, it kept happening—*whore* had just come out as *hoore*. Next to him, Matthews shifted uneasily.

"She was raising a racket," Renwick said stubbornly. "Banging away at the door as though a rampaging regiment was at her heels." A shudder ran through his long body—he loathed noise.

Lucian's eyes narrowed.

This caught Renwick's attention. "All right," he muttered. "No visitors."

"Good," said Lucian, and he left it at that, for while Renwick was the type who would inadvertently let spies into Lucian's home, his talent as a painter still made him the best man in London to dis-creetly restore a five-hundred-year-old canvas.

When the door had fallen shut behind the sulking artist, he turned back to Matthews. "Now. When exactly did I approve gallery tours for the public?"

His assistant looked ready to bolt. "Approximately two months ago, sir," he said. "Part of the measures you approved to, erm, bolster your reputation."

"Two months?" The memory flashed, and lo, he recalled a list. Vaguely. Matthews had presented it to him the moment he had emerged from his annual week of drunken stupor, his week of dis-grace, nursing a black mood and a heavy head.

"Matthews."

The man's eyes widened with alarm. "Yes?"

"I've trouble comprehending how having toffs stroll around my collections would endear me to the House of Commons."

Matthews ran his fingers over his mustache. "Philanthropy is a winding path," he said between mustache strokes. "It is a gradual strategy, and it includes a variety of activities such as inviting the public into your collections, being a patron of the arts—"

"I know what philanthropy is. Remove everything from your list that invites people onto my properties. Now, hail us a cab to Belgravia. And think. I want to know all you know about the Greenfield girl."

The two miles to his town house were slow—the roads were wet and cluttered with debris left behind from the gushing rain pipes and overflowing gutters, and carts and carriages formed haphazard clusters rather than move along in manageable queues. The cab windows were foggy and the smell of damp fabrics cloyed the interior. Pity his clean, competently driven two-in-hand was presently occupied with delivering wayward heiresses.

Matthews sat across from him, his brows pulled together in concentration. "If she was his middle daughter, she should be around twenty years old—in any case, not yet of age."

"Is she betrothed? I know the eldest is married."

Matthews shook his head. "To my knowledge, she is not formally promised to anyone. Presumably, she's the one Greenfield allowed to go up to Oxford—one of his daughters studies under Ruskin."

A *new woman*, then. A woman with opinions. A bluestocking. Her traipsing around unchaperoned and her loony tale about wanting to attend a gallery tour—rather than spy on him—might well be true, then. Her strange old cloak remained incomprehensible. He realized he was running his index finger over his bottom lip, back and forth, as though he were chasing any traces her soft mouth might have left behind. A very soft mouth. She had tasted sweet, a hint of sugared tea mixed into the flavor of the rain on her skin. Her scent still clung to him; he thought he could smell roses whenever he moved. He should've known the moment he'd seen her that Renwick had been wrong about her—her round brown eyes had held no knowledge or guile. Or he had known, and she had tempted him anyway—after all these years, precious things still exerted a magnetic pull.

"Greenfield is a fool to leave her reins so loose," he said, more to himself than to Matthews, but his assistant nodded, as always officious.

He supposed Julien Greenfield, patriarch of Britain's largest family-owned bank, currently had other worries than keeping an eye on his brood. The man was struggling with his private investment portfolio in Spain, thanks to Madrid's recently re-empowered monarch launching a new banking reform policy. And he had almost been strong-armed out of the Spanish railway sector by the Pereire brothers' bank a few years ago. It was why the banker had sent two private lunch invitations in as many months, Lucian suspected, when they had never met to date. Lucian, for his part, had long reduced his operations in the Spanish market—except for a few investments in railway companies. He still owned a thirty percent stake in railway conglomerate Plasencia-Astorga, and Greenfield must have ferreted this out. *Now, that would be a* measure *to advance my mission*, he thought—trading his last substantial investment in Spain.

"This do-gooder list of yours," he said to Matthews, "remind me, what else is on it?"

His assistant tensed, like a lad who had been called to the blackboard unprepared. Sometimes, Lucian forgot that at age thirty, Matthews was one year his senior. He felt decades older than the man on a good day.

"I recommended you reveal your name behind your charitable activities," Matthews said. "The hospital in York, for example, would cease to exist without your financial support—we should make it known you are the benefactor before the season is over."

Lucian grunted. "Charity fares better without my name blackening it."

"Precisely why I carefully selected appropriate causes—since the hospital is frequented by only the destitute, how could anyone of consequence object?"

They wouldn't, because no one of consequence cared about a hospital treating the dregs of society.

"All right," he said. "Reveal my name."

Matthews looked pleased; his list must have been much reduced in length after taking off gallery visits and such. He'd probably withdraw to his quarters as soon as they arrived in Belgravia and play the same song on his traverse flute over and over as he always did to soothe his nerves.

It wasn't that Matthews's approach was foolish—not entirely—but Lucian suspected it was ineffective and, as such, not worth the trouble. He had already changed his ways during the past months: he had sold a few debts into hands less villainous than his and forgiven one debt entirely—unprecedented behavior on his part. Thus far, it had failed to yield results—such as, say, an invitation to the back rooms of the exchequer.

"Sir, there is one thing you could do that would have an immediate and advantageous effect on your reputation," Matthews said.

"I'm all ears."

His assistant was looking at a spot next to his shoulder rather than into his eyes. "You could stop tormenting the Earl of Rutland."

Ice coated his chest at the sound of the infernal name. "Never," he said, his voice soft.

Matthews's lips paled, and Lucian looked back out the dirty window. Milksoppery grated on his nerves. But he wagered Matthews disliked him, too. The man was the fourth son of a baron—low in the hierarchy of the peerage and afflicted by genteel poverty—but he'd still consider himself a better breed of man. He doggedly upheld his upper-class ways and wore his waistcoat, jacket, and trousers all in different colors, with his coat of arms prominently on display on his scarves. He made comments in softly murmured Latin, and his fingers were long and white and had never exerted themselves much beyond playing the bloody flute or holding a deck of losing cards. Yes, he'd loathe taking orders from a man like Lucian. Even if that man had lifted him from a stinking cell in the debtors' prison.

With much delay, they arrived at his Belgravia residence. His house welcomed him with cool quiet, a side effect of having every window bricked shut. The gas lamps along the walls guttered to life and bathed the cavernous room in sooty yellow light. It leached the colors from the Persian rugs on the floor and the various stacks of science and trade journals that were gradually growing toward the ceiling. Gaslight was bad light, dim and sooty. He had to stand close to the large business map covering the east wall in this light just to discern the different colors of the threads that visualized financial flows in Europe and to the American East Coast. And he was ruining his eyesight studying his tightly written notes and clippings on British fiscal policies, which he had pinned to the wall behind his desk. As soon as Edison's new bulbs and electric wiring had proven themselves safe for indoor use, he'd retire the gas pipes in his houses.

For now, his most pressing issue was Greenfield's daughter.

He leaned back against the edge of his desk. On the business map across from him, dozens of threads representing loans, equity, and revenue flows fanned out from a pin with the Greenfield name to various countries, institutions, and industries. The picture confirmed that Greenfield was on shaky ground in Spain. Without a majority share in one of the railway companies, he stood to be delegated to the back bench in that market. And men like Greenfield didn't care for second place.

Save the soft howl of stale air coming through the ventilation shaft, a heavy silence filled the room. He could sell Greenfield his shares. But the moment the transaction was completed, the banker would lose interest in him. Business relations were fickle bonds: reliable only as long as one could expect return favors in the foreseeable future. It was why he had ignored the lunch invites—they were, potentially, rare tickets for a place at the table, but he wasn't yet certain how to leverage them. And he wanted that place at the table. It had taken him long enough to understand that his wealth wouldn't buy him the changes he wanted to effect. Money, he had learned, was a wholly different beast from power. *Power* was held by polite society within the hermetically sealed fortress of shared experiences at Eton, Oxford, and Cambridge, strategic marriages, and inheritance laws. Politics was made in private back rooms, after dinners, during grand tours. Their crumbling castles and unproductive estates notwithstanding, these inbred circles still ranked money below name and connections. But Julien Greenfield had a foot in the door. A century after his family had settled in Britain, their money wasn't quite new money anymore and his landholdings didn't count as flash gentry.

He returned to his desk and took up his pen, because an altogether different avenue into these hallowed circles existed. The specifics of his plan were unclear, but his muscles were tense with the purposeful impatience he knew from spotting a winning investment. He would put his money on *Miss Jones*.

Chapter 4

Ruskin was right: Persephone looked lovely.

The realization struck Hattie not two minutes into her class, and she backed away, her gaze flitting erratically across the painting. The soft scratch of chalk and brushes on canvas and Ruskin's footsteps among the easels faded into a white roar. How had she not seen it before? Here was Persephone, in the process of being dragged from her flower field into the underworld by a muscular arm around her waist, and while her expression was horrified, it was . . . politely horrified. The dynamic of her body as she twisted away from Hades, god of the underworld, was, at second glance, restrained. This was probably not how one would resist an abduction.

She wiped her damp palms on her apron. Disaster. Without intending to do so, she must have focused on preserving Persephone's poise throughout her ordeal; now her heroine looked as though she was conscious of her coiffure while fighting her attacker. Where was the passion, the fury, the truth? An Artemisia Gentileschi she was not. In fact, this had to be the most tepid interpretation of the abduction since Walter Crane. . . . At her plaintive whimper, the collective attention of the all male students in the University Galleries shifted onto her with an audible *whoosh*, and she quickly shrank back behind her canvas. To her right, Lord Skeffington had ceased sketching and was watching her curiously. "Is anything the matter, Miss Green-field?" he murmured.

Where to begin? The warmth in her cheeks said her face was red as a beetroot. She pasted on a smile. "No. Not at all."

She dabbed her dry paintbrush aimlessly at a bit of sky, pretending to be immersed. Soon, the attention was drifting away from her. Her distress lingered. Her work, five weeks in the making, was soulless, dead.

It was the kiss's fault. The kiss.

Three days after the fact, the memory of Mr. Blackstone's mouth on hers had not faded. On the contrary: during her daydreams and when in bed, she had shamelessly revisited the fleeting contact over and over, and by now it was so thoroughly embellished, it had become a vivid, drawn-out, and voluptuous—rather than shocking—affair. She didn't really *wish* to forget it. Several white spots on the topography of her daily life had now been colored in: she could insert the warm pressure of Blackstone's mouth into all the countless romantic novels she devoured, when before, her understanding of what kissing felt like had been limited to feeling her own lips on the back of her hand. She finally understood what her friends Annabelle and Lucie enjoyed behind closed doors ever since they had paired off with their betrotheds. But she also knew now that being grabbed by an underworld lord elicited shock, disbelief, heat, confusion. She had slapped Blackstone before she could think. None of these base emotions were present in her Persephone. Her painting was *ignorant*. Now she knew. Blackstone's kiss had made her see.

She turned to Lord Skeffington. "My lord," she croaked.

"Miss Greenfield." He lowered his brush, his expression inquisitive.

"Do you think it is possible to make good art without experience?"

His high brow furrowed with surprise. "Hmm. Are you having trouble with your painting?"

"No, no, it is a general question I ponder."

"Ah. A matter of philosophy."

"Of sorts. I wonder: must an artist have personal knowledge about the subject of her art for it to be . . . art?"

Lord Skeffington chuckled. "Thinking grand thoughts before lunch—oh dear."

His smile briefly edged out her troubles. He was so charming. In the brightly lit room, his fluffy golden hair glowed like a halo around his face. His lips were rosy and delicately drawn—if he were a girl, such a mouth would be described as a rosebud. He was very much how she imagined her favorite Austen character, Mr. Bingley, and it wasn't a coincidence that she had chosen to work next to him during class.

"Let's see." He was tapping his index finger against his chin as he feigned contemplation. "Well, I know that not one painter of classical paintings has ever seen a Greek god in the flesh. Hence, I declare that no, no personal experience is required to create something delightful."

She hesitated. Did he truly believe the purpose of art was to be *delightful*? But he looked so pleased with his answer . . . and she could feel the attention of the other students shifting their way again, like ants scurrying toward a fresh carcass. Today, it irritated her. It had taken the young men months to not murmur and stare when she showed up during the lectures. Ruskin's general drawing class was open to the public and welcomed both men and women without further ado, but a woman properly enrolled in his actual art history lectures? Scandalous. Next she'd want the vote. She did, actually. And a woman with permission to attend the academic drawing courses in the galleries? Shocking, even with her chaperoning aunt stitched to her side. Aunty was presently taking a nap in a specially provided wicker chair, cozy in a shaft of sunlight by the nearest window, and in no position to dole out withering glances.

Hattie caught a glimpse of her Persephone, looking so boring and bored, and her stomach squirmed.

"You see," she whispered to Lord Skeffington, ignoring the ears straining toward them, "I read an essay by John Dewey a little while ago. He argues that art is *art* only when it succeeds at creating a shared human experience—a communication, if you will—between the work and the audience. If it doesn't, it's just an object."

His lordship was blinking rapidly; she must have spoken too fast.

"There is a sense of recognition," she tried again, "between the artist, whose art embodies a universal experience, and the personal experiences of the observer. A moment of strangers' minds meeting?"

"Dewey, Dewey," Lord Skeffington said, his expression polite. "The name is familiar—isn't he American?"

"He is."

"Ah." The corners of his mouth turned up. "They usually have funny ideas."

Funny? To her ears, it had rung true. And with her limited experiences, she might well create something *delightful*, but how could she create something that was also moving and true? If one's spirit happened to be born into a female body in the upper classes, the leash was short. The nosy men in this room could draw directly from the rawness of the world if they wished, from ill-reputed or far-flung places she could never go. Acclaimed contemporary female painters existed—Evelyn De Morgan and Marie Stillman came to mind—but they hailed from artistic families or had been allowed to study in Paris. Besides, there was an expectation that women depicted quaint motifs. And while she liked her dresses frilly and her novels swoony, Hattie wanted something different for her art. . . . She wanted. . . . She supposed she foremost *wanted*.

Lord Skeffington stepped in front of her painting. "Why, it's fine work. Nice bit of scumbling technique here. Weren't you planning to exhibit it at a family function?"

She groaned inwardly. "Yes. Next week. At a matinée."

A dozen men of influence and their wives would attend the event in her parents' St. James's residence and stay for luncheon. She already knew she would rather exhibit nothing than this.

"It shall do nicely for a matinée," said Lord Skeffington. "Though again you chose quite the grim subject matter."

She smiled cautiously. "Grim?" *Again?*

"You seem to have a penchant for, how to put it, violent scenarios, Miss Greenfield."

"I . . . wouldn't say that I do."

"I recall your Apollo hunting an unwilling Callisto."

"Oh. That."

"Then at the beginning of last term, there was your ravishment of the Cassandra."

"Which is one of the most popular depictions in Greek art."

"I was merely observing a theme," Lord Skeffington said mildly.

She supposed there was a theme. She had painted Helen of Troy last term, her best work yet, but then again, in her interpretation, Helen had been the only one left standing against the smoking ruins of a ransacked city with both Paris and Menelaus broken at her feet.

"Well," she said, "is there a subject in the classics that is not at least a little . . . violent?"

"Dancing nymphs?" Lord Skeffington suggested. "Demeter and her cornucopia, tending to the fields? Penelope weaving cloth? All perfectly wholesome, suitable subject matters."

Suitable for a *female artist* were the unspoken words. Her mood turned mulish.

"I believe Hades was desperate when he snatched Persephone," she said demurely, because she mustn't repel the embodiment of Mr. Bingley in a fit of temper. "Being surrounded by darkness and death every day gave him the morbs. He needed company, someone who was . . . alive."

Lord Skeffington tutted. "Making excuses for the villain, Miss Greenfield? Shocking. Though I suppose the tender female heart cannot help but hope for good in even the lowliest man, and that includes"—he raised his fine hands dramatically—"the king of the dead." He chuckled again, and so she kept smiling, and her cheeks ached a little from the effort.

Aunty was wide awake and opinionated during the brief walk from the galleries' side entrance to the Randolph, where they had rented rooms during term time.

"Young Lord Skeffington is rather forward," she said loudly enough to make Hattie wince. "I saw him distract you from your work with chitchat."

She slowed their pace by hooking her thin arm through Hattie's and dizzied her with the heavy scent of her French perfume. Now they made a formidable obstacle for other passersby on the narrow pavement.

"He was just making conversation about the painting, Aunt."

Aunty cupped her ear with her hand. "Your pardon?"

"He was just making conversation," Hattie bellowed. Mr. Graves, her spurned protection officer, trailing behind with his bland face and gray coat, was overhearing every word whether he wanted to or not. Aunty's hearing was mysterious, it seemed to wax and wane depending on whether she actually wanted to hear something, and Hattie had caught her speaking in perfectly hushed tones with her lady friends.

"Ah," said Aunty, and forced a gentleman who tried to stride past onto the road with a wave of her cane. "They always started with just a conversation, in my day they did. Next, they demand to accompany you for a walk."

"Mama would be delighted if he started something."

"What?"

"I said: Mother would be delighted!"

"Ah. Would she now? He's a bit reedy, isn't he?"

Reedy? Lord Skeffington had the perfectly pleasant, nonthreatening build of a young gentleman who enjoyed the fine arts. Besides, his looks would hardly matter—ever since Papa had married Flossie to a ham-fisted Dutch textile tycoon, her mother had her eye on someone *titled* for her remaining daughters. And since Mina was expecting a proposal from a mere knight before the end of the summer, the task of securing a blue-blooded match fell onto Hattie's shoulders. On a normal day, she absolutely fancied a nobleman for herself. *She* found Lord Skeffington's appearance ideal: golden, noble, and only a little older than herself. They would have many years left for him to sit for her paintings as Knight in Shining Armor. . . .

"Watch out." Her aunt tugged at her arm with enough strength to stop her in her tracks.

They had reached the crossing to the Randolph, but the next approaching carriage was still a long way away.

"This head of yours," Aunty muttered. "Always away with the fairies. It will get you into trouble one day."

Hattie patted the frail hand clutching her arm. "You're watching me, so I shall be fine."

"Hmph. Then why have you been limping?"

Because her turned ankle continued to be a painful reminder of her foolish bid for an hour of experiences in London.

"I took the stairs too hastily." Having to yell the lie made it much worse.

"That should teach you not to hurry," Aunty said. "I suppose his lordship should be invited to dinner, then. Tomorrow!"

"Tomorrow is terribly short notice, Aunt—and it's the family dinner."

"Very well. Then we shall prevail on your mother tomorrow night to extend an invitation to Lord Skeffington for a more formal occasion, and soon."

Aunty waited until they had crossed the street and entered the cool, resounding lobby of the Randolph to ask, "You do know his Christian name is Clotworthy?"

She had known. Now the hotel staff manning the reception

desks, Mr. Graves, and some wide-eyed guests who had been in conversation on the settees near the fireplace knew it, too.

"Yes," Aunty boomed as she took course toward the lift, "Clotworthy, like his late father—come to think of it, his grandfather was a Clotworthy, too."

"Right—"

"I thought you should know before we extend an invite. A woman must give it due consideration whether she should like to be eternalized in the annals in a long line of Clotworthy Skeffingtons. They would name *your* son Clotworthy, too—a mouthful for a small child. I suggest you could call him Clotty."

Hattie cringed and cast a covert look around. This—this was how rumors began. Such rumors could get a young woman into terrible trouble, and she liked to think that she wasn't skirting trouble for the sake of it. In fact, after her latest excursion had ended with her mouth glued to that of a scoundrel, she had decided to behave impeccably for the foreseeable future. Mr. Graves would appreciate this, too, she thought as her protection officer brushed past her into the apartment to do his usual round of checking whether any potential kidnappers had stolen inside during their absence. For now, Graves chose to keep his employ with the Greenfields rather than report her absence three days ago, but he would not do so forever.

In the drawing room, she dropped her heavy satchel onto one of the divans surrounding the fireplace and stretched with a sigh. Aunty disappeared to the side chamber, and so she moved to the nearest window for some respite. Her apartment faced busy Magdalen Street, and from the lofty height of the second floor she could indulge in watching snippets of strangers' lives drift by without being caught staring. Today, her gaze meandered restlessly over the pavement below. She still felt subdued from her Persephone fiasco. Painting was the discipline where she had set her sights on "outstanding" rather than "passable," a dream born from ambition as much as necessity. Painting required none of the usual skills required for excellence, such as writing or arithmetic. She couldn't write a line without making spelling mistakes and she couldn't copy a row of numbers without switching figures around. Today had been a harsh reminder of the fact. *It is not the eyes, but one could call it a word blindness of sorts*, the last of many doctors had concluded years ago, when she had failed to improve despite rigorous schooling. Her father had been aghast. *If it's not her eyes, is it . . . her brain? Something wrong with her brain?* A stupid Greenfield, hopeless at investments, and from his loins! His disappointment had cut deeper than her tutor's ruler, which used to crack across her palms over and over, punishing her for writing with her left hand and for writing wrongly with whichever hand. A life of sore fingers and bruised spirits, until she had found her talent in a colorful paint palette. Still, she had heard her father's words loud and clear in the gallery earlier.

"Harriet," came her aunt's voice from the adjacent room. "I'd like to play bridge."

Bridge. Please, no, not again. "I'll be a moment, Aunt," she said without turning.

Across the street, the sun-kissed sandstone wall of Balliol College radiated stoic, golden tranquility. If walls could look wise, the walls of Oxford would win first prize.

She pulled back her shoulders and took a deep breath. She had come so far. Her place at Oxford was the culmination of hard work, and this held special weight for someone who was usually given things before she even knew she needed them. Her paintbrush used to be awkward and slick with her fear in her right hand; she had practiced for a thousand hours with gritted teeth until she had wielded her tools as competently with her right as with her left. She had battled through all of Ruskin's wordy books, including *The Laws of Fésole*. Word blind or not, she was currently learning from the best. Fine, Oxford was not Paris, where she, like any artistically inclined, fashionable young woman would have preferred to go—but it was as far as they had let her go, and she would not give it up because of a crisis over a kiss. . . .

"Harriet!"

A small sigh escaped her. Perhaps it was also time to escape from under her family's thumb. Inviting a potential husband to dinner was the first step.

The memory of a cool gray gaze brushed her mind then, and a tiny, indeterminable shiver prickled down her spine.

⁂

The Friday family dinner in St. James's quickly verged on riotous. Flossie was visiting from Amsterdam with her baby son because she had fallen out with her husband, and Zachary had returned from Frankfurt. Debates were heated before the main course was served. Flossie sat across from Hattie between Benjamin and Aunty, the color in her round cheeks high with chagrin. "I hadn't expected such a laissez-faire attitude on the matter of starvation, not from you, Mama," she said as she stabbed her fork at the steaming mushrooms on her plate.

Their mother's displeasure washed over the table with the cool force of a wave.

"Quarrelling so severely with one's husband is excessive and in poor taste."

Flossie's red curls bristled. "Not when he is defending grain-price speculation."

"Your tone has a strangely proselytizing quality to it, which I find tiring."

"Hardly as tiring as hungry children! Have we learned nothing from the latest Indian famine?"

"Or the Irish one," Hattie murmured.

"As for that, Lord Lytton hasn't learned a thing," Zachary remarked between bites. "I hear he's still objecting to the Famine Codes for India. Deranged creature."

Flossie raised her brows at her mother, as if to say, See?

"Famines, dreadful as they are, are a natural occurrence," Adele said. "As inevitable as snow falling from the skies in winter."

"However, financing the British infantry in Afghanistan with famine relief money is not a natural occurrence," Flossie said, "which is what Lytton did last year. This famine was greatly exacerbated if not caused by the British government by transporting all the wheat of Bengal straight to London, and then *certain men* compounded the issue by deliberately withholding the distribution *and* speculating on grain prices."

"According to whom?" Adele demanded.

"According to Florence Nightingale," Mina said calmly. "I read her reports."

"I say."

"She concludes that the famines are a result of gross failures on the part of the British government," Mina added. "This includes the diversion of famine relief funds to finance the infantry in Afghanistan."

Adele's lips flattened. They all knew she admired Florence Nightingale's contribution to the nursing profession and occasionally turned to her for advice on her own charitable efforts. From politics, she respectably stayed away.

"My dear, these mushrooms are excellent," said Julien Greenfield. "A new recipe?"

Hattie eyed him with suspicion. Her father rarely intervened in dinner quarrels, but he had been radiating quiet satisfaction all evening, and with the white beard framing his mouth down to his chin, it gave him the look of a contented walrus. Probably because Flossie was home. Flossie was a credit to him. She knew about shorting stock, how to hedge a long position, and which industry would boom next. She and Zachary would be debating the best strategy for this or that in Uncle Jakob's German portfolio by the time the main course arrived. Mina would join them—she was already following every word, occasionally making a blind pick at the food on her plate. Benjamin, at fourteen years of age, in the awkward place between boy and man, would just fervently support anything Zach had to say. Mina would ridicule him for it. She had already poked fun at him for wearing his chestnut hair the same way Zach wore his: short at the sides, wavy on top. Inevitably, when matters became too rowdy, someone, probably Zachary, would turn to Hattie and say, *How is your art, Pom Pom?* Her art was neutral territory in that it roused no strong emotions in anyone present. It was the palate cleanser in between the meaty courses.

She sipped her wine, overly aware of her position in the dining table hierarchy tonight. She had been relegated to the *lovely* spot when it had become clear that her brain was odd and that her interest in banking was limited. And whenever she entered her parents' home in St. James's, she inevitably left the *new woman*, the one who had her own studio at Oxford and ran with the suffragists, at the door. A husk of her younger self would be waiting for her in the entrance hall every time, to be slipped on like a badly fitted gown. The feeling of wearing her old skin was particularly strong tonight; she felt itchy. But this was how they all knew her, and they would not see her otherwise.

". . . I would go as far as calling speculation of any kind immoral," Flossie said, "since it caused most of the panics and depression of the past decades—"

Her father put down his wineglass. "Now, Florence, be a dear, take a breath, and stop provoking your mother. Do you think your dowry consisted of charitable donations?"

Flossie sputtered. The signal for Zach to turn to Hattie with a twinkle in his brown eyes. No, she had no desire to be their light interlude tonight. She looked past her brother, at her father. "Papa," she said. "I have been wondering about some rumors."

Her father's bushy brows pulled together. "Rumors? Do I look like an edition of *The Tatler* to you?"

"The rumors are about Mr. Blackstone."

It had been inevitable that his name would slip out; it had been teetering on the tip of her tongue all week. A confounded silence promptly filled the dining room, and her heart drummed faster. Her father's eyes kindled with alertness, and for a terrible second, she worried that he knew.

"Blackstone, you say," he said. "The man of business?"

She nodded. "They say he ruins peers. I was wondering what exactly he has done."

"Whatever made you wonder about him?"

What indeed. She should have just quietly finished her roll; now all eyes were on her.

"Well, Julien, you hardly hide your vexation every time the man ignores your lunch invites," her mother said.

"Which happened all of twice," her father said mildly.

"You invited him?" Flossie asked. "Was it about Spain?"

He squinted at her. "I don't recall discussing Spain with you."

"You sent Zachary to negotiate with Uncle Jakob on the matter," Flossie said. "Then we have the banking reform, the railroad speculation bubble, the Pereire brothers—"

"Yes, yes, for Spain," he said, and grabbed his glass again.

"If I may, Father," said Zach, and he turned to Hattie. "To answer your question: Blackstone has *ruined peers* by calling in their debts at precisely those times when they lacked the funds to cover them. One can speculate how he knew when exactly to strike. Either way, with nary an exception they had to sell the family silver or an estate to pay up."

Flossie looked appalled. "What gentleman in his right mind would inflict such horror?"

"Blackstone isn't a gentleman," Zachary said dryly.

"Is he a client with us?" Hattie asked.

"Lord, no. I suspect he is with one or two small, private banks like Hoare and Company. And they keep silent because if he were to withdraw his deposits, it would close their entire house."

"Is he as rich as they say, then?"

"Indecently rich, from what we can see."

The tension left her shoulders. No one seemed to suspect a thing about her excursion. "Why would he do it?" she murmured. "Humiliate those peers—it's awfully spiteful of him."

Flossie made a face. "More interestingly, why would gentlemen in their right mind continue to become indebted to him?"

She thought of Lucie's fiancé, Lord Ballentine, who had taken money from Blackstone in order to purchase his half of London Print. Admittedly, he was the devious sort.

"Men are a bit silly sometimes," Mina said. "They enjoy gambling at either the stock market or the roulette table but frequently overestimate both their luck and their prowess."

"Mina," said Adele. "You are not to talk like this."

"Apologies, Mama."

"Cynicism in a young woman is never endearing. Neither is political fervor."

"I shan't say it again, Mama."

"See that you don't. Your betrothal is not official yet, and Sir Bradleigh may well still abscond." While admonishing Mina, she skewered Hattie with one well-aimed glare as Hattie was angling for another bread roll. Twenty-some years after the fact, Adele Greenfield was still put out that she had passed on her red hair to each of her three daughters but not her lithe frame, which she considered most elegant, and she never let any one of them forget it. With a sigh, Hattie put down the tongs for the bread basket.

"Gentlemen rarely have direct dealings with Blackstone," Zach told Flossie as he took the roll for himself. "He is notoriously private and very mean. I understand he bought some of the ruinous debts from other gentlemen—and at a hefty surcharge."

Flossie's eyes rounded. "How calculating—why, it's as though he had a bone to pick."

Mina nodded. "He sounds like a cartoon villain—apologies, Mama."

"One wonders how such an unsavory man was able to forge a fortune from nothing," Flossie said, reluctantly impressed.

"It started by him trading bills of exchange ten years ago," Papa said. "And cleverly so."

"He also appears to have a habit of investing in industries that turn a greater profit as soon as they employ new technologies, into which he also invests," Zach said. "It seems his only duds are mines. He can't make much profit off the ones we know he acquired here in Britain."

Her father split a roasted potato. "He does set his cap for the ailing ones, though there might be method to the madness."

"I'd wager on it," Zachary said with grudging respect in his voice. Hattie adored him for it. Zach was a skilled banker at only four-and-twenty, but she loved him most for his fairness.

"Trading requires capital in the first place," Flossie insisted. "Who gave him the funds?"

Beneath the table, Zach nudged Hattie's skirt with his foot. A moment later, he placed something onto her lap. She peered down most discreetly. There was the roll Mama had denied her. Oh, she loved him the very most for his protectiveness. She stuffed the roll into her skirt pocket while her mother began enumerating the many misdeeds of Mr. Blackstone, which were chiefly his murky origins and his horrid treatment of a Lord Rutland.

"He has changed tactics, lately," her father said. "Has sold and forgone a few debts. The chaps at the club are taking note."

Benjamin inclined his head. "Is that why you invited him?"

"Well spotted." Her father sounded pleased, as though Benny had said something astute.

"Why is this a reason?" Hattie asked, feeling sullen because she failed to see a connection.

"The reason," her father said, "is that Blackstone might be no longer content with a position in the shadows. He might feel that he has exhausted its potential—which is the point when men become hungry for more."

"Father thinks he might consider selling some shares that are of great interest to us," Zach added. "We are keen to exploit the man's potential desire for some social elevation."

"Sometimes, a man's own lips become a strong snare to him," Adele remarked.

"We shall find out soon enough," Papa said, and the purr in his tone raised the hair on Hattie's nape. "Blackstone has sent word," he continued. "And I invited him to the matinée next week. He has accepted."

She gasped. It went unnoticed; everyone was preoccupied with their own surprise.

"Have you now?" came her mother's cool voice. "For the matinée, you say?"

It is because of me. Ice-cold heat poured over her. Was he coming to tattle on her?

"Yes, the matinée," her father said. "And I'm expecting each of you to act perfectly natural around him. The fish may be hooked, but has not yet been reeled in."

Blackstone. Blackstone was to prowl around in the sanctity of their home.

"Mr. Greenfield, this is ridiculous," said her mother. "Whether he has changed his ways or not, he isn't Good Society. If he attends the matinée, I shall have to introduce him to respectable people, and how can I possibly do so when we know nothing about him?"

"My dear, where is your charity?"

"Well, it certainly ends where our reputation begins!"

"The matinée!" Across the table, Aunty's head had jerked up as though she had napped with her eyes wide open until now. She picked up her ear trumpet, a bejeweled accessory, which she kept on her lap, raised it to her right ear, and turned to the foot of the table. "Adele, we must extend an invite for another guest: the young viscount Lord Skeffington."

"No." The word was out of Hattie's mouth before she could stop it.

"No?" Aunty's wizened face was bewildered. "Why, you were adamant that he join us."

Mina, Benny, and Flossie were smirking, intrigued.

"Adamant, was she?" her father said. "Do we know the young man? Skeffington—Lord Clotworthy Skeffington?"

The walls of the dining room were not quite steady. "We must invite Lord Skeffington some other time, Mama," she said, her voice tinny like cheap brass. "I shan't be in attendance during the matinée."

Her mother's expression was at once alarmed. "Whyever not?"

"I . . . shall be indisposed."

"How do you know? Are you not well?"

She wasn't. And it would likely get worse.

Chapter 5

There seemed to be no suitable moment to speak to her friends after Harriet returned to Oxford on Sunday. On Monday, they all gathered in Lucie's drawing room in Norham Gardens for the weekly Oxford suffrage chapter meeting. But Lucie greeted her at the door with her blond hair flying around her pointy face and sparks shooting from her eyes—apparently, the *Manchester Guardian* was in trouble for publishing their latest suffrage report. This had been expected, for few things were more outrageous than women loudly demanding to be treated as people before the law. Naturally, the entire meeting revolved around how the suffrage chapters across Britain should proceed amid the public outcry, and it seemed inappropriate to raise her hand and say: "I ran from my protection officer—again—and kissed Mr. Blackstone, and now he is coming to visit my parents' house."

She spent Tuesday in a panic over which painting to pick in place of Dull Persephone, because of course Mama had insisted she be present on Saturday since she had already *told all her friends* that Hattie would exhibit a piece. She finally settled on an old watercolor still life depicting fruit and vegetables in a wooden bowl, an exceedingly safe and boring choice.

On Wednesday, she had a headache and stayed in.

On Thursday, Lucie announced that Lord Ballentine had offered to take her to Italy because it would be more amusing to weather the storm raging around the suffrage report on a southerly beach, and quite unlike herself, Lucie had agreed. As Hattie counseled her on which hats and dresses to pack and where to best purchase fabrics in Naples, her confession kept surging up her throat like heartburn, but she couldn't seem to form the words.

On Friday, she broke. She convinced Aunty to write a pretty invitation, then she went to the residential wing of St. John's College to call on Catriona.

Her friend sat at her father's desk, as usual wrapped in her battered Clan Campbell tartan shawl, her glossy black hair tied in a loose bun. She was studying an old tome through a magnifying glass.

The weight of a boulder rolled off Hattie's chest. "Thank goodness you are home."

Catriona turned to her and blinked, confused like an owl rudely woken from a snooze. "Hattie." Her voice was scratchy, as though she hadn't yet spoken to anyone today. "Apologies. I forgot you were coming to call." She rose and put on her glasses. "Is your officer being attended to?"

"Your housekeeper took him to the kitchen, so I assume he is currently drinking tea. And you haven't forgotten a thing—I'm calling unannounced." She opened her reticule and fished for the small envelope as Catriona approached. "I'm delivering an invitation to a matinée tomorrow. In our residence in St. James's. It's a little short notice, but they are playing Chopin—you adore Chopin, don't you?"

Catriona was still holding the magnifying glass, which she appeared to notice only now. She looked at it blankly for a moment, then she returned her attentions to the envelope Hattie was holding under her nose. "Thank you? But I'm afraid tomorrow—"

"And you must tell me all about your research on Tunis," Hattie said. "I'm so intrigued."

Catriona dipped her chin and stared at her over the metal frame of her glasses. "The research is on Tyrus. A city in the Levant." Her Scottish lilt was a little stern.

"Even more intriguing," Hattie said quickly.

The stare did not waver. "What is it, Hattie?"

Hattie made a pout. "Whyever would you sound so suspicious?"

Catriona's eyes were a stunning cerulean blue, a formidable contrast to her straight black lashes. She usually hid their charm behind her spectacles or a faraway look that said she was sifting through an old parchment on Tunis or Tyrus rather than seeing the person in front of her. Now her gaze was alert with intimidatingly sharp intelligence. "You're in trouble, and you think I can help," she said. She nodded at the Chesterfield wing chairs to either side of the cold fireplace. "Have a seat. I shall fetch us some tea."

She left for the kitchen rather than use the bell pull, and Hattie settled in the creaking leather chair and arranged her skirts. Her pulse gradually slowed to a normal pace for the first time in a week. The quiet in Professor Campbell's study was absolute, not even disturbed by the tick of a clock, and the low ceiling and thick old walls shielded against all outside sound. Only the scent of inked paper and Catriona's lavender soap permeated the air. The stained-glass windows faced a walled garden, and the sun streaming in painted red and blue vignettes onto worn floorboards. This was a room of timeless calm, promising that one could safely weather a storm here. It wasn't an abode befitting a Scottish earl and his heiress, but it suited their scholarly minds: one could picture them in these armchairs when the fire crackled, immersed in their reading, occasionally adjusting their glasses or glancing up to say something clever. Catriona was to Professor Campbell what Flossie was to Julien Greenfield, Hattie supposed: an admirer of her father's interests from the cradle. She would find Hattie's current woes frivolous at best. By the time Catriona returned, carefully balancing a small tray, she had steeled herself.

"You are right," she said once her friend had poured the tea and taken a seat. "I'm in trouble, and I need your help. I need you to be at the matinée because Mr. Blackstone shall be there, and I cannot face him alone and Mother forbids me to be indisposed."

"Blackstone?" Catriona lowered her cup again, intrigued. "The industrialist who loaned Lord Ballentine money for London Print?"

"The very same."

"Why would you rather not face him alone?"

She stared at her tightly laced fingers in her lap. "We kissed," she said. "Each other."

A soft intake of breath came from the direction of the other armchair. "Perhaps," Catriona then said, "you can explain."

So she did. She explained about shaking off Mr. Graves, her hope to see the *Ophelia*, and the kiss. Then the shock of learning he was coming to the matinée.

Catriona was silent for a rather endless minute. "Och aye," she finally said. "That is a situation."

Luckily, Catriona had the rare habit of studying a *situation*, any situation, free from the distorting influence of sensibilities or judgment, quite as though she were looking at an archaeological artifact. Hattie should have spoken to her much sooner.

"Where was your aunt throughout this excursion?" Catriona asked.

Hmm. She glanced away. "I left her under the impression that I was painting in my studio with Mr. Graves manning the door so she could attend a tea-and-bridge session. She usually naps afterward. I had planned to return before long."

Catriona's expression was equal parts disapproval and disappointment. "You might get yourself into terrible trouble one day."

"Yes—in fact, that day is tomorrow." She unleashed her most pleading look. "Please say you shall come. I should feel less nervous with a dear friend by my side."

"Mr. Blackstone will hardly try to ravish you in your parents' drawing room," Catriona said. "Especially since the first time appears to have been a misunderstanding."

The thought of being ravished by Mr. Blackstone in any one location made heat rise to the surface of her skin. She was thinking about his kiss far too often as it was.

"I cannot rationally explain it," she said. "I'm aware I'm being silly, but I feel my stomach flutter and my hands tremble when I think of seeing him again, and I know my nerves should be much calmer if you were there."

Catriona gave her a long, unreadable look. "I suppose it would be better if one of us were there," she finally said. "However, as I meant to explain earlier, I have an appointment at the Royal Society with my father tomorrow. Have you considered asking Annabelle?"

"She is preparing to leave for France for the summer. Besides, Mama would never allow me to invite a duchess to the event—it's a luncheon, quite informal."

"Hmm." Catriona made to bite her thumbnail before sheepishly lowering her hand again. "Burlington House is perhaps half a mile from your parents' residence—"

"It is," Hattie said quickly.

"—so it should be possible for me to be there on time for my appointment if I left promptly after the concert."

"Yes!"

"For the luncheon, I'm afraid you are on your own."

❧

He had not shown before or during the concert. She had sat tense and perspiring through forty dramatic minutes of Chopin and Brahms, and Mr. Blackstone was glaringly absent.

"I don't understand," she said to Catriona as they followed the throng of guests down the corridor toward the lunchroom. "Why would he snub my mother on the day of the event after first accepting the invitation?"

"Perhaps he has fallen ill," Catriona murmured.

"He looked in perfectly robust health to me."

"Why not ask your mother? She would know any excuse he gave."

"And risk looking interested in the subject?"

She was certainly glad he hadn't come. Her mother had selected the linden-green gown for her to wear, and while for once the color suited, the style was dreadful: the sleeves were too wide on top, the hem was heavy with not one but two rows of pleats, and there was a startling excess of lace foaming at the front of her bodice—each feature on its own, very well; their combination: an atrocity. And of course, it was too tight. Sometimes, she wondered whether her mother was simply oblivious or consciously intending for her to look like a frump. Even Catriona was more elegant in plain navy-blue velvet, and Catriona lacked all fashion sense.

A light melody of string instruments filtered into the room from the side chamber, and the guests had formed groups and were selecting beverages from the trays carried by quietly circling waiters. Since the luncheon was informal, no escorts for the women were required. Her mother, flanked by Aunty, was making conversation with young Mrs. Astorp and Mrs. Hewitt-Cook, an American. Right next to the easel that hosted Hattie's very large, very unimpressive still life of fruit and vegetables in a bowl.

She cringed and took Catriona's hand. "Have you time for a refreshment? A glass of cider or champagne? And let's look at the food."

Catriona's gaze went across the room to the pendulum clock between the sideboards that presently served as tables for the buffet. "One glass of cider," she said.

Hattie's cheeks slowly cooled as she sipped the cold, tart drink from the long-stemmed glass. The savory scent wafting from the nearest sideboard should have made her stomach growl, and the food did look tempting: the steaming silver tureens and plates with cold cuts of meat and golden-brown pies were set handsomely between hothouse flower arrangements. Mina must have had a hand in the décor. Even more intriguing were the tiered platters on the other table: filled with small pots containing boiled fruit, buttery pastries, and glazed chocolates . . .

She froze. A dark figure had entered her peripheral vision.

A thrill of panic ran down her back. It was him, standing in the wing doors. Her skin prickled from top to toe as his presence rippled like a disturbance through the ether.

"I think he's here," she whispered without moving her lips. "Do not look."

Catriona's gaze slid sideways as she raised her glass to feign a sip. "Oh my."

They angled their backs to the main door as one and pretended to study the buffet.

Hattie wasn't seeing a thing. "Do you see? Do you see why I first thought he was a pirate?"

"I don't, to be truthful," Catriona murmured after a small pause.

"You don't?"

"He's hardly a gibface, Hattie."

"He isn't," she conceded. "But he is no gentleman."

"You said he's a Scotsman. Perhaps from the Highlands? He would look braw in a kilt."

Hattie blinked. Would he? And why was Catriona picturing men in kilts?

"Why do you think he's a Highlander?"

Catriona's smile was a little crooked. "They have a certain look about them when they enter a room full of Englishmen. A sharp glance in their eyes, like a broadsword at the ready to be drawn—*You beat us at Culloden*, it says, *but our spirit remains unbroken*."

Hattie's mouth fell open. "Is that what *you* think when you enter a room full of Englishmen?"

"Oh, worry not," Catriona said. "My mother was from Sussex.

And I spent more time in Oxford than in Applecross." She glanced back over her shoulder. "You can look now—he is engaged in conversation with your mother."

Her fingers tightened around the stem of her glass. "Oh golly."

"It means nothing—he must address the hostess."

She saw it, the furtive glance Catriona cast at the clock. "No—please stay."

"I'm sorry," Catriona said reluctantly. "I truly am, but I must be on my way." She put her empty glass onto a tray floating past. "Could you not accompany me to the door, then go and hide in your room?"

"Yes," Hattie murmured, feeling ill. "Excellent plan."

She avoided looking at him while she approached. She avoided looking at him while Catriona said her good-byes to the hostess. Through her light-headed state, she still heard her mother instruct a footman to escort Catriona to the door. A last, helpless exchange of glances with her friend, and the inevitable was upon her.

"Harriet, I would like you to meet Mr. Blackstone," her mother said. "Mr. Blackstone is a man of business here in London. Mr. Blackstone, allow me to present Miss Harriet Greenfield, our second-eldest daughter."

His cool gray gaze locked with hers and her heart began to race. He was as striking as she remembered him: pale, dark brows, broad cheekbones. His lips were well drawn but not full. How had his mouth felt so soft? A mistake to even think of it. His eyes brightened knowingly, and the memory of their kiss flared between them like embers leaping back to life, the heat so palpable, everyone in the circle would have to feel the warmth, too.

She tilted her flaming face. "Sir."

"Miss Greenfield." His voice was deeper than she recalled. She cast him a nervous glance from beneath her lashes. He was properly attired today in a navy jacket, oxblood cravat, gray waistcoat, and fawn-colored trousers, and he had rigorously slicked back his hair.

He still could not suggest good breeding. He had an untamable quality to him that radiated from his very core, and clothing would not conceal it. Catriona was right; a kilt and a broadsword would suit him better, enhancing rather than poorly disguising him. . . .

"Miss Greenfield," Mrs. Astorp said, making her snap to attention. "Mrs. Greenfield mentioned you are still up at Oxford?" Genuine curiosity shone in Mrs. Astorp's hazel eyes. The young woman had been married to an industrialist twice her age for a few years now, though she was scarcely older than Hattie. Acquiring a university degree had to strike her as an alien form of life.

"I am," Hattie said. "I'm at Lady Margaret Hall. Trinity term finished last week."

"How neat," said Mrs. Hewitt-Cook, the American. "How many female students are enrolled at present?" Mrs. Hewitt-Cook was a handsome brunette and older, closer to Hattie's mother's age. Her burgundy ensemble was very fashionable, and if it was a little tight, it was probably a deliberate choice. Hattie fixed her gaze on the oval brooch at the woman's throat to avoid Mr. Blackstone. "There are five-and-twenty women enrolled between Somerville Hall and Lady Margaret Hall," she said.

"What a jolly bunch," Mrs. Hewitt-Cook said brightly. "You must have a famously good time, being a *new woman*—tell us, what is it like?"

Too many answers at once rushed at her, none of them appropriate. The pet rat she had contemplated keeping in order to appear sufficiently eccentric in her new student role came to mind, and how just before the term began, she had learned that another female student already kept a rat, a white one that sat on her shoulder. . . . She felt the weight of Mr. Blackstone's gaze on her profile. Her reply came out in a mumble: "It's very diverting," she said, and touched her hair. "Being a new woman, it's diverting."

"I imagine," said Mrs. Hewitt-Cook. "Such terribly colorful characters among the bluestockings, surely."

Hattie saw her mother's back stiffen at the veiled barb. "Perhaps one or two," she said. "Most of us, however, are still perfectly monochrome."

Mrs. Hewitt-Cook laughed softly. "Why, she's charming, Mrs. Greenfield."

"A lot of excitement surrounds the matter of women in higher education," Adele said with a cool undertone. "The truth is the young women are more rigorously supervised at university than they would be in any other place. Harriet, for example, is never without Mrs. Greenfield-Carruther"—and here she nodded at Aunty—"and of course she is always under the watchful eye of her protection officer."

At this, Mr. Blackstone's left brow rose very slightly. *Help.*

"It's lovely to see female talent fostered," young Mrs. Astorp said. "We were admiring your painting earlier, you see."

Worse and worse. Everyone turned to look at the practice piece she had so haphazardly chosen during her crisis over Persephone. There was the bowl, the wood-grain texture of it poorly done. Therein followed the uninspiring assortment of fruit and some vegetables.

Mr. Blackstone looked her in the eye. "You painted this?"

She thought of how his reception room alone was overflowing with artistic masterpieces.

"I did, yes." *And I can do so much better.*

"Remarkable," Mrs. Hewitt-Cook said politely.

It wasn't remarkable and she was well aware of the fact, but of course she must not say so, and so she smiled and said, "Thank you, ma'am."

"What is the symbolism behind it?" Mrs. Hewitt-Cook asked. "I was wondering about it."

She gave the woman a baffled glance. "I had no particular symbolism in mind."

"But the gourd." Mrs. Hewitt-Cook was pointing at it with a thin finger. "It doesn't share the season with any of the other vegetables, nor the fruit. Why did you include it?"

Now they were all studying the gourd, which looked more obscenely bulbous and flesh-colored by the moment.

"I suppose it provided the best complementary shape for the composition?" Hattie's voice was a little shrill.

"Ah," Mrs. Hewitt-Cook said. "Such a creative solution."

"Our Harriet is very talented," Aunty said loudly. "I tell Mr. Greenfield that not everyone is required to excel at mastering figures and investments—I know I had no talents lying that way, either, when I was Harriet's age, and yet I thrived. Some of us are meant to beautify the world with a brush or needle, not make it more profitable by way of a rational brain."

She stood in silence, feeling her head glow a beaming red. Her mother was speechless, too. Mrs. Hewitt-Cook appeared to take pity. "Mr. Blackstone," she said, turning to the man. "I understand you do have a head for profitable investments."

Mr. Blackstone countered Mrs. Hewitt-Cook's inviting smile with a bland expression. "Often enough, yes."

"Then you must share some of your insights," Mrs. Hewitt-Cook said. "I should like nothing more than to surprise Mr. Hewitt-Cook with an accurate market prediction."

His lip curled with faint derision. "I don't want to bore you with business talk, ma'am."

"How about an invention or two that shall unleash the next industrial revolution?" With true American tenacity, Mrs. Hewitt-Cook refused to be deterred by his rudeness. "At least give us hapless females some clues about exciting new technologies—wouldn't that be amusing?" She cast a glance around the small group that demanded approval.

"Very amusing," Mrs. Astorp murmured.

"Hear, hear," Adele said with faint reluctance.

Mr. Blackstone's expression softened only when Hattie gave a tiny nod.

"Electricity," he said.

A pause ensued while all eyes were on him. Mr. Blackstone's gaze furtively flickered across the room, perhaps in search of staff bearing stiff drinks, perhaps attempting to locate the quickest exit route.

"Electricity," Mrs. Hewitt-Cook said, and waved at a waiter to pick up a glass with pink champagne. "We should invest in electric lightbulb stock is what you say?"

Mr. Blackstone chose a tumbler with an amber liquid from the tray. In profile, one could see his brushed-back hair curl at his nape, winning the rebellion against the pomade.

"Invest in stock," he said. "Also, invest in a company that has patented the process for the serial production of high-temperature-enduring boiler feed pumps."

Mrs. Astorp blinked. Hattie wagered her own face looked just as perplexed.

"Boiler feed pumps," Mrs. Hewitt-Cook enunciated. "I'm so intrigued because I don't understand a word."

Any normal man would have smiled and retorted a few bons mots, but Mr. Blackstone was unable or unwilling to follow procedure. "Boiler feed pumps are an essential part of electric generators," he said, "necessary for converting steam into electricity. In ten years' time, we'll have hundreds of power plants working across Britain and the continent—the moment we can safely use electricity to light a home, it will be used for other things, too," and, noting Mrs. Hewitt-Cook's eager expression, he added, "A byproduct of electricity is heat, so electricity should replace current ways of heating household devices—stoves and the like."

His aloofness was rare in a man of business—Hattie knew many, and they inevitably used the topic at hand to relate messages about their own cleverness rather than the subject matter, and they more or less subtly imparted the expectation that their female audience nod along with large, impressed eyes. Mr. Blackstone, however, appeared wholly self-contained and kept his gravelly voice low; he wasn't desiring their admiration in the slightest. Alarming. A man immune to female charm was a dangerous creature when charm was one's chief line of defense. It certainly intrigued Mrs. Hewitt-Cook; she was observing Mr. Blackstone as though he were some exotic specimen requiring urgent classification. "Riveting," she murmured. "The feed pumps have been noted. But I'm afraid my appetite's been whetted— tell us more?"

Again, Hattie had the unnerving feeling that Mr. Blackstone was waiting for her acquiescence. When she nodded, he emptied his drink and said, "Two-way mirrors."

"What's that?" Aunty demanded. "Two-ways?"

"It's a mirror you can see through as though it were a window."

"What good is a mirror one sees straight through?"

"Because one can see through it, but only from one side, and in bright light," Mr. Blackstone said. "The other side shows a reflection."

Mrs. Hewitt-Cook gasped. "Ingenious—where can I find such a thing?"

"Difficult. The developments are in the early stages."

"But what on earth is it good for?" Aunty wondered.

Mr. Blackstone leaned slightly toward her. "I'm expecting them to be used in police offices and department stores for surveillance purposes, ma'am."

"Department stores," her mother said sharply. "You mean it will be employed to spy on innocent women customers?"

"They'd call it studying their customers," Mr. Blackstone said. "Department stores are becoming a rather competitive industry, and studying customers' natural shopping habits when they feel unobserved will help a store optimize sales potential."

Mrs. Hewitt-Cook shook her head. "How clever," she murmured. "How does one come by such clever ways of thinking?"

Mr. Blackstone gave her a thin smile. "It's simple. Just assume people are chiefly motivated by convenience, vanity, or greed. Any product serving those will be a commercial success."

An uncomfortable pause ensued.

"I daresay that is a rather godless view of the world," Adele said, her eyes cold.

Mr. Blackstone gave a nod. "They do say capitalism worships only itself."

Aunty cackled. "Mr. Blackstone should meet our Florence," she said to Adele. "They would have much to discuss."

"First I should like to introduce Mr. Blackstone to Mr. Greenfield," Adele said tersely, her gaze moving toward the door to the side chamber, where her husband had made an entrance. "Do excuse us."

Hattie's anxiety buzzed like startled bees as Mr. Blackstone approached her father.

Mrs. Hewitt-Cook snapped her ivory-plated fan open with a *snick*. "Good grief but he is beastly," she murmured as she peered at Mr. Blackstone's broad back. "Every inch as bad as they say he is." The predatory delight in her voice grated on Hattie's tightly wound nerves.

"Poor Lord and Lady Rutland," Mrs. Astorp said. "I doubt they have a moment of peace."

Rutland. The man's face appeared before Hattie's mind's eye, vaguely, as seen once at a ball: the regular, impassive, long face of an older English aristocrat with cold eyes and iron-gray hair. "What is he doing to Rutland?" she asked.

"Killing him slowly," Mrs. Hewitt-Cook said, her gaze still glued to the introduction scene across the room. "Rutland is in a pecuniary pickle. Rumor has it that over the years, Mr. Blackstone here has bought up most of his debts, and Rutland currently has no solid financial leg to stand on. Mr. Blackstone is holding his debts like the sword of Damocles over his head."

Mrs. Altorp shuddered. "Ghastly. I understand Lady Rutland is not in good health."

Hattie wished she hadn't asked. Such villainy on Mr. Blackstone's part made her question her father's ethics; worse, it felt surprisingly disappointing, quite as though she had harbored personal hopes for Mr. Blackstone's moral character.

"Men can be so bloodthirsty," purred Mrs. Hewitt-Cook. "Now, what is your opinion on his nose—how do you think he broke it?" At their startled silence, she raised her fan higher as if to share its protection. "Mrs. Altorp—I'm sure you have thoughts."

A nervous giggle burst from Mrs. Altorp. "Very well." She leaned in. "He broke his nose when . . . when he was brawling over a lady."

"Hmm, intriguing. No doubt he won and vigorously claimed his spoils. Personally, I like to imagine it happened during a boxing match, in Elephant and Castle or some such place . . . but, Miss Greenfield, are we shocking you?" Her gaze slid over Hattie with faux concern.

Some married women had a habit of reminding the unmarried ones of their undesirable status by pretending consideration for their innocent sensibilities. It drew a line in the sand, separating the knowing from the ignorant, a subtle demonstration of power that always puzzled Hattie, for she thought of herself as perfectly unthreatening. But looking into Mrs. Hewitt-Cook's amused face, she was for a moment tempted to say that she knew things about Mr. Blackstone. She knew his clean scent and the taste of his lips. She knew his kiss was commanding and that his chest felt solid as a wall against her breasts. A sordid corner of her mind was aglow with triumph to know these things, knowledge that lay beyond the men who wanted his money, beyond even the worldly Mrs. Hewitt-Cook. Of course, it meant Mr. Blackstone knew all these things about her, too. Color rose all the way to her hairline. Mrs. Hewitt-Cook would undoubtedly, happily, attribute this to maidenly discomfiture.

"No," she said lamely. "I have no idea how he broke his nose."

Mrs. Astorp gave her a kind smile. "Mr. Astorp is more interested in how he acquired his money in any case—now, that would be interesting to know."

"Money, how dull," Mrs. Hewitt-Cook mocked. "But I reckon by some criminal activity. Smuggling, perhaps? There is something decidedly piratical about him . . ."

Hattie decided she would rather endure her mother's irate lecture than this. Yes, she would take a glass of pink champagne, sneak to the dessert table to scoop up some of the chocolates, and then take to her room. She would not steal another glance at Mr. Blackstone, not at how the fabric of his jacket pulled just a little across his back whenever he took a sip from his glass, nor at the way his hair curled at his nape.

Chapter 6

Greenfield's daughter hadn't fled the room at her first opportunity. She eventually moved out of his field of vision, but he felt her presence all throughout his first personal encounter with Julien Greenfield.

"I hear you recently nabbed a coal mine up in Fife," the banker said as he shook Lucian's hand in a practiced grip.

"I have. Drummuir."

"I assume you know things about it that we don't," Greenfield said, "because it certainly looks like a lousy investment from where I stand."

"I suppose we all have our pet projects," Lucian replied. "Some in the North, some in the South."

Greenfield's eyes squinted when he chuckled. One of those deceptively jolly men. If one were to clothe him in plain brown tweed and remove his golden pocket watch and the heavy signet ring on his stubby little finger, nothing about him would suggest a man of both power and old money. He stood with a slight hunch and was short, rotund, and florid, as though he enjoyed wine overly much. His gaze was diffuse, though doubtlessly this could change in a quick second. He'd mastered the subtle art of having delivered the fatal blow long before the opponent realized it had been inflicted.

They kept the conversation brief—Lucian tactically mentioned his philanthropic plans for the arts and extended an invitation to a gallery tour for next Saturday, which elicited a frown from Greenfield's wife. The banker, however, invited him to his smoking chamber in return. Usually, Lucian declined to enter smoke-filled rooms, but today he accepted. The moment the Greenfields' attention was engaged by the next guest, he turned back to the room.

The daughter was still at the buffet, alone, pondering the sweetmeats.

He kept to her blind spot as he approached. With her champagne glass tilting at a precarious angle, she was awkwardly bending over a pastry platter to reach the farthermost chocolates. The position stretched her gown snugly across the generous flare of her hips, hips only a dead man would fail to notice. Heat filtered through Lucian. He had expected to find her changed from the urchin in his reception room, but he had still been taken by surprise when first seeing her here. Harriet Greenfield stood a little below average height, and with her gleaming red curls piled high and her luscious figure wrapped tightly in ruffles and green taffeta, a bonbon had sprung to mind, a fancy piece of French confectionary. If he were to step closer now and graze his teeth against the exposed curve of her neck, he'd probably find her tasting like cream candy.

He halted next to her, close enough to smell roses, and reached for a plate. "Why the *Ophelia*?" he asked, his voice low.

Pink champagne splashed onto the tablecloth. She spooked easily and like a cat, all four paws in the air.

"Your pardon?" She was keeping her body angled away from him.

"When you were at—"

"Hush," she hissed, then cringed, presumably for shushing him. He randomly selected a pastry while she composed herself.

"Why the *Ophelia*?" she then said under her breath. "Because she is a marvel."

"You've seen it before?"

Her gaze was darting around the room, he could tell from the corner of his eye. She was engaging him only to keep him from attracting attention. Undoubtedly, all attention was on them already. It was true that ladies appeared at his doorstep once in a while, and though they wanted what he offered in the bedchamber, at a social function such as this the same women would herd their precious daughters and nieces out of his reach at all speed. His little chat with Miss Greenfield was on borrowed time.

He turned to her just as she reluctantly turned to him. Her face was already familiar; he knew the smattering of freckles across her nose and that her plush bottom lip could taste like sugar. Her eyes were dark and shiny like the chocolates piling high on her plate. He knew the wholesome impishness was a decoy—he'd never forget the impressive slap she had dealt him. She was a southpaw, the only reason why she had managed to catch him, he had reflected later on—he hadn't expected a blow from the left. He hadn't expected a blow at all; no one dared raise a hand to him outside the boxing ring. Aoife Byrne would like her for that slap. . . .

"I have seen prints of the painting," she said. "In its original color and size, it should be utterly enchanting."

"Enchanting," he echoed.

Her chin tipped up. "Dreamlike, of a yearning quality . . . Pre-Raphaelite. I understand the *Ophelia* embodies all their best principles. I thought if I looked at her long enough, perhaps I could decipher the brotherhood's secret."

"They have a secret?"

She nodded. "Something in their technique that renders a scene lush and romantic but not mawkish; whimsical but not saccharine."

She talked fast and said things he hadn't thought real people would say. He imagined characters in a novel spoke like her. "And it doesn't offend you that Ophelia is about to take her own life?" he asked, far too sarcastic in tone. He meant to lull the girl, not shock her. Her wee perky nose and her naïve enthusiasm about death by drowning were grating on him.

Unexpectedly, her stance eased, as though they were falling into a regular conversation. "I prefer to think of her dying from unrequited love," she said, "which I find tragic rather than deserving of spite."

He looked her straight in the eye. "Then you think tragedy enchanting?"

She returned his stare with a small pucker between her brows. "I think everyone should have at least one person they love well enough to die for."

He gave a soft grunt of surprise. "Ophelia didn't die *for* Hamlet," he said. "She died *because of* him." He knew this because he had been dragged along to Shakespeare's plays by old Graham, who had occasionally felt called to civilize the adolescent Lucian.

Miss Greenfield's frown had deepened. "I gather you have strong feelings about the difference."

"It matters not to me either way—no one person is worth dying for."

She looked at him very earnestly. "I'm terribly sorry this is the case for you, sir."

He felt winded then, as though he'd abruptly run out of breath. His gaze dropped to his plate, now filled with costly delicacies that he'd never planned on eating.

"Why did you purchase her?" came her soft voice.

He looked up. "Because she will fetch a high price one day."

Her face fell. The very concept of profitability seemed to displease her, naturally, since she would've never known a day without all the comforts money so conveniently provided. Her skin was proof of it: it had the muted glow and smooth texture of milk glass. Such skin had never seen the sun or strain.

"If profit is your only motivation," she said, "I'm surprised you aren't protecting the Han vases on your mantelshelf with greater care."

He stilled. "Why do you think they're Han vases?"

"I know they are; I studied art history books long before I went up to Oxford," she said with a small shrug. "One could argue they belong in the British Museum. Or that the Chinese Legation in Portland Place would be pleased to receive them." She sipped champagne and absently licked her lips.

He dragged his gaze away from her damp mouth. "There's nothing unusual about keeping one's Han vases instead of letting them gather dust in a museum."

"Even if they are part of the long-lost Empress Lingsi Collection?" she chirped.

This unnerved him again, and he couldn't remember the last time another person had had this effect on him, which unnerved him more. He supposed she had the advantage of being underestimated in her fluffy, glossy, chirpy disguise.

"I had a feeling I had seen the pattern of the relief in the context of Han vases before," she continued. "I confirmed my suspicions in the Bodleian with a textbook, a fifteenth-century book on ceramics containing copies of old relief patterns. Of course, I could be wrong."

"You know you're not wrong," he said quietly. He had consulted the same book a few years ago and she was correct on all counts. "You are remarkably observant. Contrary to what your aunt thinks, you might well be one of the cleverest people in this room, certainly the one with the best visual memory." He leaned a little closer. "But what you might find impossible to fathom is that, sometimes, a man will hoard priceless things and yet treat them with no more care than cheap trinkets, simply because it gives him pleasure that he *can*."

He knew his words were shocking; more shocking was that she had drawn them out of him.

Her eyes were wide, and very near. "If this is true," she breathed, "it would be terribly decadent."

"I can be decadent, Miss Greenfield."

The warmth of her fine skin touched his cheek, for the distance between them had shrunk to nothing. If he were to lean down, he'd be close enough to taste the corner of her mouth. He wanted to. The room dimmed and blurred as the urge took him, while her face remained precisely etched, down to the last golden freckle.

"Harriet."

He straightened and stepped back.

Greenfield's son was next to his shoulder and he hadn't sensed him coming. The young man put his body between him and the girl, his eyes cold with distrust. At last, here was the vigilant Lucian had been expecting from the moment he had gone to the dessert table. He nearly asked, *What took you so long, fool?*

"Mr. Blackstone was explaining things to me about art," Harriet told her brother, her voice a little shaky.

"It was the other way around," Lucian said.

The hostility in Zachary Greenfield's gaze only intensified.

Lucian looked past him at the girl. "I recently opened my collections in Chelsea to visitors," he said, and she promptly turned white as chalk.

"How interesting," young Zach said coolly.

"I'd like to extend an invitation to the tour next Saturday," Lucian continued. "And if you like what you see, Miss Greenfield, perhaps I could interest you in supporting my new charity for aspiring artists."

"Charming, but whether she attends your tours is not for Harriet to decide," Zachary Greenfield snapped, and clasped a possessive hand around his sister's elbow. "Harriet, Mother wishes to speak to you before she opens the buffet."

"Zachary," Harriet muttered. She was redder in the face than when her aunt had insulted her brains earlier. Seemed like she wasn't used to being treated like chattel in front of strangers, and she made her displeasure known. Her cheeks were still flushed when she permitted her brother to lead her away.

Lucian ate his luncheon thinking that his one true mission today was to convince Harriet Greenfield's father to send her back to his house in Chelsea.

An hour later, his mission had been successfully completed in the smoking room, and he was again in a muggy carriage en route to Belgravia. He sifted through the gossip Matthews was reporting from his time downstairs at the Greenfield house and found there was nothing of interest except talk of an imminent betrothal of the youngest Greenfield daughter to a knight.

"As for the public visits to my gallery," Lucian said.

"Yes?" Matthews was scrabbling for the little notebook and pencil he always carried in his breast pocket.

"Put them back on the list."

Matthews's face brightened in the shadows. "Gladly."

"We'll have the first tour next Saturday. Also, have a charity set up by then, one that supports aspiring artists."

His assistant glanced up from the page. "A tour is possible, but a charity—I'm afraid it, erm, will be a challenge to find patronesses of quality on time."

"Make it known, discreetly, that Greenfield's daughter will support the charity, and they'll come flocking."

Matthews had gone still. His gaze was on the floor.

"Sir," he eventually said. "Greenfield's daughter . . ."

"Yes?"

"Will . . . will any harm come to her?"

Lucian contemplated him. "If the answer were yes, what would you do?"

The man's shoulders sagged. "I'm much obliged to you, sir," he murmured. "But it pains my conscience to abet the demise of an innocent girl."

"Demise," Lucian repeated, contempt lacing his voice. He wondered what it would take before Matthews legged it. Murder, he guessed. Matthews couldn't afford to bite the hand that fed him.

He drew back the carriage curtain and squinted against the glistening brightness outside. A row of identical white Belgravian terrace houses blindingly reflected the sun like fresh snow, and the contours of the street continued to glow behind his eyelids. Belgravia. One of London's wealthiest districts, now his home. Even these middle-class houses here on the fringes had looked palatial to his eyes when he had first explored the area years ago. The air had smelled of lilac, and the calm and neatness of the place had made his body tense with diffuse alertness. He had stood on the pavement in his fine attire and top hat, feeling strangely outside his own skin, and had half expected any of the gents walking past to see him for what he was and chase him off these streets. His wealth, his new life, had felt brittle, like a soap bubble, ready to burst into oily speckles at the tap of a fingertip. Surrounded by clean white splendor, he had had memories of hunger pangs and a cold that bit to the bone. When passing by this particular row, he still sometimes wondered what his grandmother would have said had he given her one of those pristine homes with two columns holding up a portico. He could've set her up in a mansion, but she would've refused anything more flash; Nanny MacKenzie had taken pride in making do.

I think everyone should have at least one person they love well enough to die for. The scarred corner of his mouth twisted. What if one's persons were long dead and gone to dust, Miss Posh Tottie, what then?

He let the curtain go and leaned back into the plush seat. He'd never know what his grandmother would have said to a new home; he had been too late to fetch her. But it wasn't too late to make good on his other promises: Justice for his mother. Justice for Sorcha. A future for the faceless mass of men whose lives were but cogs in a machine, deemed worth less than one of Greenfield's stinking cigars. Ironic, that it required him to make yet another vow to another woman.

He glanced at his assistant. "Don't worry about the Greenfield girl, Matthews. My intentions are entirely honorable."

Matthews's eyes widened in shocked comprehension. "Oh dear," he finally stammered, looking more despondent than before.

Chapter 7

⁂

"I'm terribly tempted to obey my father and attend the gallery tour," Hattie told Catriona a few days later in her drawing room at the Randolph.

It earned her a wry glance over a gilded teacup rim. "Are you tempted by the tour or by another scandalous encounter?"

"Ha ha," Hattie murmured. "Would you be shocked if I told you I wish to support his charitable efforts for the arts, too?"

"Whose charity?"

"Mr. Blackstone's."

Catriona put cup and saucer down on the low-legged table between them. "Would that be wise?"

With a sigh, Hattie abandoned her dramatic sprawl across her fainting couch to select a cream-filled éclair from the pastry platter.

"Probably not," she conceded. "But the truth is, normally when I receive a request for my work or my patronage, I can never shake the suspicion that I'm asked because of who my father is."

"Why?" Catriona looked puzzled. "Your work is fine in its own right."

"Do you remember the grand birds-and-flowers exhibition sponsored by the Royal Horticultural Society?"

"I don't, no."

"Well, my painting was the only one that had not a single bird in it."

"Oh."

"Now, Mr. Blackstone's invitation can't be an attempt to curry favor with the Greenfields, since my father was the one repeatedly approaching him."

"Then the question is, what *is* his motivation?" Catriona muttered.

It was a justified question. She doubted it was Mr. Blackstone's admiration for her talent since the only example of her work he had seen thus far was *The Gourd*. . . . But it was such a pretty idea, to be chosen for herself. . . . She wished their usual quartet of friends was complete, so she could have opinions other than just Catriona's mercilessly rational ones to consider. But Annabelle and her duke had retreated to their castle in Brittany last week, and Lucie's usual place on the yellow settee was empty, too, as she was en route to Italy. She herself was expected in London tonight, since the term had concluded and the additional week her parents had granted her in Oxford was over.

She nibbled on her pastry with little enthusiasm. "I should like to join both the gallery tour and Mr. Blackstone's charity, because I shall be dreadfully bored a fortnight from now. I don't care for summer in London and I already miss you."

Catriona's brows rose with surprise. "You're staying in London?" Catriona would be on her way to a windswept glen in Applecross soon, fleeing London's sooty summer heat like a regular person.

"My father requires fast access to Frankfurt and Paris because of the Spain crisis," Hattie explained. "Mama is staying to give Sir Bradleigh and Mina some more time to court in public."

Repetitive weeks in town stretched before her, muggy and treacherous like a narrow path across a swampland under her mother's scrutinizing eye. Meanwhile, Mina would enjoy outings with her knight.

She couldn't even make herself useful by helping Lucie with suffrage work, since her parents had no knowledge of her political activism. She'd have to occupy herself in other ways. Drawing sketches of hands and feet. Envisioning provocative ballgowns she'd never be allowed to wear. Accompanying Mother to her respectable charitable activities, which consisted mainly of drinking tea.

"Let's hope Sir Bradleigh's proposal is imminent," she said. "It would at least focus all my mother's attentions on planning a wedding."

A shudder ran down Catriona's back. "Aren't you worried she will then turn her marriage designs on you? You're older than Mina, after all."

"I'm not worried," said Hattie. "In fact, it's time someone offered for me, because Mina will shamelessly lord her elevated position over me at every opportunity." This had been troubling her more than she cared to admit.

"Are you certain this is what you want?" Catriona looked skeptical.

"It's hardly a secret that I look forward to finding my knight in shining armor."

"No, but I hadn't realized you were in a hurry," Catriona said, "and you had two risky adventures recently, which, if exposed, would have made the marriage mart look quite grim for you."

Laid out like this, her behavior was indeed contradictory. She shifted on the upholstery, discomfited. "I intended no self-sabotage, not knowingly," she said. "I even decided on a suitable candidate last week."

"That's . . . news?"

"It's Lord Skeffington."

Catriona's brows arched high. "Lord Clotworthy Skeffington?"

"Yes. He's titled, young, mild-mannered, handsome, and he's an artist," she enumerated. "He would understand my need to paint."

Catriona was shaking her head, slowly, as if dazed. "He would own the rights to your work. He could forbid you to paint. His name is Clotworthy."

"Annabelle is married," Hattie said. "She still studies at Oxford."

"Annabelle agreed to the match after the duke had publicly declared his support for women's suffrage," Catriona pointed out. "Do you know Skeffington's politics?"

"He's a peer," Hattie said, avoiding her eyes, "so he's a Tory."

Catriona was quiet, in the way her whole body went quiet when she had opinions. Annoyingly, it gave her point more gravity than had she been lecturing out loud. There was no need for words in any case—Hattie could recite their suffrage chapter's litany on the matter of marriage in her sleep: marrying was risky business. Coverture, an English common-law doctrine, demanded that a wife was subsumed in her husband's legal persona. On paper, she ceased to exist as a person. Save for a few narrowly defined exceptions, she lost her right to own property, too. As a result, the right to vote, which was tied to property and rent qualifications, would elude a married woman unless the toothless Married Women's Property Act was properly amended. *Amend the Married Women's Property Act* had long been their battle cry, and she was currently contemplating treason.

She finished her éclair and washed it down with tepid tea. Sometimes, there were disadvantages to counting only suffragists and hermity scholars among her closest friends. Sometimes, she missed having a confidante who unreservedly shared her excitement for fabrics and fashion and art and who enjoyed chattering about attractive eligible bachelors. She used to have such friends, but they lived in London and Europe and were married now, and they found her a bit odd.

She glanced at her brooding friend, who sat wrapped in a tartan shawl despite summery temperatures. "Did I ever tell you that one of my first conscious memories is watching a cousin say her wedding vows in St. Paul's?"

Catriona shook her head. "You didn't."

"Now I have forgotten which cousin, but I still remember the gown." She closed her eyes. "A diamond-sprinkled ethereal cloud of lace and white taffeta silk," she said. "It was otherworldly: the gown, the choral singing, the sky-high rib vaults of the old cathedral. And there was the victorious elation radiating from my mother and my aunts because the bride 'had made a grand match.' I was perhaps six years old, but I recall reveling in the women's levity. It was as though their muscles had been tensed for years, and now they were finally at ease. This was the true beginning of my cousin's life, and the time before was merely diligent, hopeful preparation. Oh, don't look so alarmed—I was a girl, a young child. I know better now; I attend the same suffrage meetings as you, don't I? I read the same letters from maltreated, unhappy wives; I understand the curse of coverture."

Catriona raised a soothing hand. "All right."

"It just occurs to me that my notions about marriage have been nurtured over a dozen years, and undoing such beliefs with factual evidence is impressively ineffective."

Worse, the things one had learned early often felt instinctual, as unquestionable as the act of breathing, and the familiarity of them mattered rather than whether they were good or harmful.

"Most of the leaders of our movement are married," she tried. "And I *like* the idea of being a wife, and of doing wifely things, such as embroidering his socks and braces. I wish to spend my life with a best friend. I can't explain my feelings; I can only ask you to not think me feebleminded."

Catriona looked taken aback. "I would never think you feebleminded. But a husband could stop my research—the expectations are that I serve him how he sees fit."

"Expectations are also that he protect you with his life," Hattie said with a frivolous little wave. "At least there's no grand expectation that you die for him if required."

"Death is but an instant," Catriona said softly. "You, however, would be asked to live your one life for him."

"Well, drat," Hattie said. "And here I thought a little silliness would lighten the mood."

"Oh. Of course." Catriona's cheeks flushed—sometimes sarcasm eluded her. It was probably why her own words rarely had a double meaning. *This is where we differ greatly*, Hattie thought. *I blurt out words and half the time I still don't mean them.* Her medium for truth was supposed to be paint. Her words, they came from a place desiring to please or appease, to appear normal or silly, which were usually considered the same in a girl. It was a malaise afflicting most women in Britain, this compulsion to say one thing while thinking another, to agree to things one disliked, to laugh about jokes that were dull—most women, but not Catriona. When Catriona wished to conceal her thoughts, she was silent. Quite sensible, actually, but when all suffered the same ill, the healthy ones appeared abnormal.

Hattie slumped back into the pillows. "Never mind, my dear. I cannot fault your reasoning. But what life have I now? Look at me. Under my parents' roof, I can't even choose my gown or the style of my hair in the morning, nor how much I eat at dinner or whose company I keep. Why do you think I so often try to dress vicariously through you with fashion advice? As a wife, I would at least reign over my own household."

Catriona nodded. "But do you wish for independence from your parents, or for marriage?"

"Is there a difference, for a woman in my position?" she snipped. "I'm not in possession of a trust fund like Lucie. I don't have a father like yours, who is content to remain a bachelor and to employ you as his assistant. I do know that I'm not suited for living as a spinster."

"I shouldn't have brought my own worries to this conversation," Catriona murmured, already shrinking back into her shawl quite as though she had only now become aware how far she had ventured from her shell.

A pang of remorse went through Hattie like an electric jolt. "I adore our conversations," she said quickly. "And I will miss them badly. It's why I'm irritable today. What are you worrying about, will you tell me?"

Catriona smoothed her shawl with ink-stained fingers. "It's nothing."

"I'm chatty," Hattie said, "but I can keep secrets."

"I know," Catriona replied, smiling now. "Why don't you tell me the first thing you should do if you ruled your own household?"

Clearly, Catriona wished to keep her own counsel, so she said, "First I'd give my entire wardrobe to charity. Then I shall live my dream: I shall travel across France with only my watercolors and my dearest friends—you must come. Paris has the best bars and the most scandalous literary salons, and in the South, you can look across a sapphire-blue sea."

"Have you ever been to a bar?" Catriona asked curiously.

"No. But I hear the best ones are in Paris, and all of them are frequented by renowned artists."

"I should join you," Catriona agreed, "but wouldn't you want to travel alone?"

"Alone?" Hattie made a face. "What would I do on the Montmartre or in Marseille by myself? I would feel lonely and then I would get myself into trouble when accepting unsuitable company. Also, I loathe being in charge of the logistics. Loathe it."

"Well, we are taking Lucie along," Catriona said. "She excels at logistics."

Their sisterly conversation ended when Aunty emerged from her chambers, well rested after a nap and adamant that it was time to oversee the packing for London.

Hattie put her cheek next to Catriona's during the good-bye. "Would there be any harm in joining the gallery tour, you think?" she whispered.

"Not if you stay by your mother's side," Catriona whispered back.

"Why am I not surprised?" her mother muttered when they spotted Mrs. Hewitt-Cook at the center of the small crowd that had gathered in Mr. Blackstone's entrance hall. "However, I had not expected to see Oaksey here."

Lord Oaksey was the only aristocrat in attendance, but the group was comprised of several members of the middle upper class: wives and sons of wealthy industrialists. Glaringly absent, however, were other single young women of her station.

"Oaksey owns one of the largest private collections of Renaissance paintings in England," Hattie said softly. "He must have been very curious." Curious enough to risk the potential etiquette breach of acknowledging Mr. Blackstone. Her own nerves were dancing and her mouth was dry, back here at the scene of her latest transgression.

"Mr. Greenfield and his business politics," her mother said in a low, disapproving voice. "Sometimes I wonder whether age is already addling his brain."

Silently, Hattie agreed. It seemed Julien Greenfield, too, had tired of his current position and was hungry for more, but when a man had already reached the pinnacle of essentially everything, his idea of *more* veered toward the eccentric, such as racing to monopolize a beastly investor as a point of principle.

While they exchanged greetings with the other attendees, Mr. Richard Matthews fluttered toward them, and Hattie's stomach dropped. But Mr. Blackstone's assistant, dressed in a highly fashionable burgundy jacket, gave no indication of recognizing her during his introductions; his eyes were darting over her impersonally, then he announced that the group should please follow him to the refreshments in the reception room.

Hattie's pace slowed when relief gave way to a treacherous disappointment. There was a distinct possibility that Mr. Blackstone wouldn't show. She had been well prepared to face him for once, in her favorite dress of pale lilac damask with three rows of white tassels across the skirt. *Are you tempted by the exhibition or by another scandalous encounter?* It seemed it was the latter. The truth was, despite hot mortification, she had enjoyed debating Mr. Blackstone by the buffet a week ago. She had spouted words unthinking, like a fountain, under his steady gaze, as she did when she was nervous, but the colors of the lunchroom had burned brighter, the scent of the food had been spicier. Her whole being had felt . . . keen. Exhilarated. Alive. The sensation after escaping Mr. Graves magnified tenfold. She wanted to feel it again.

Ahead of her in the corridor, the group slowed when passing an open door. Her mother was right up at the front, having unwittingly abandoned her while engaging Lord Oaksey in conversation. "Look, a Degas," came Lord Oaksey's voice. "Freshly imported from Montmartre, I reckon."

Impulsively, Hattie took a step back against the wall, into the shadow of a statue. When the group had vanished around the corner at the end of the corridor and their chatter faded, she hurried to the door on light feet. As suspected: it was the side entrance to the gallery. The room stretched deep and wide under a vaulted glass ceiling like an inner courtyard. It was noon, with the sun high in the sky and the vast space filled with bright white light. The odor of beeswax polish lingered in the air.

She advanced on tiptoes. The main entrance was to the right. On the left wall and ahead, paintings hung evenly spaced. Lord Oaksey was correct: there was a Degas, the motif of ballerinas in white dance costumes unmistakable. Her own reflection was creeping along in the square-shaped mirrors set into the right-hand wall; presumably they helped illuminate the room on cloudy days by reflecting the natural light. Mr. Blackstone should have the roof covered—while gas lamps weren't ideal, the sun would damage the artifacts over time. Then again, it was the perfect light for keeping the white oil colors from yellowing too quickly . . .

She found the *Ophelia* at the center of the left-hand row, and her mind went quiet. The young woman was floating beneath the arching branches of a weeping willow, half-shrouded in the billowing fabric of a gown embroidered with stars. For a breath, Hattie was there by the riverbank, inhaling cool, damp air and the earthy smell of decay. Subtle shades of green surrounded her, dotted with the deep blues and reds of wildflowers. Ophelia's face was bathed in a dreamy glow that placed her right in the liminal space between the living and the dead.

She knew Millais had painted the landscape part at Hogsmill River, near Surrey, rather than take a sketch and then finish the painting in his studio. His model for Ophelia, then Miss Siddal, a paintress in her own right, had caught a terrible cold while lying in an unheated bathtub. Yet none of the factual knowledge diminished the magic emanating from the scene before her. She knew other interpretations, by Alexandre Cabanel, for example, and they were jarring and barely hid the usual moralizing lesson that mad, beautiful women inevitably faced demise. But Millais, he had given Ophelia serenity. Her pale hands lay quietly on the surface of the stream, the palms open toward a sky outside the frame. Her half-lidded gaze was calm, her lips slightly parted. There was a suggestion of bliss in her surrender.

Mr. Blackstone had accused her of finding tragedy enchanting. But perhaps every woman had known a moment when she felt as though she were drowning, and the only comfort was that there could be some beauty, some dignity, in that, too.

How had Millais captured such sentiments? *He* was a man, and older now, but his brush clearly transcended such limitations, had dipped right into the essential experiences shared by humanity. Oh, to bridge that obscure gap that forever separated an artist's intentions from such flawless execution. . . . Her neck tingled, pulling her from entrancement.

Mr. Blackstone. Standing quietly on the threshold of the side entrance.

She wasn't half as shocked as she should have been. Her heart still began a wild drumroll against her ribs. His face revealed no clear emotion when their eyes met; he must have expected her. She turned her attention back to the *Ophelia*. Blackstone's approaching footsteps echoed in the emptiness of the room, and her mouth was dry as dust. By the time he stood by her side, her mind was a blank.

"Is it what you expected it to be?" he asked.

She gave a small shake. "She is better."

His voice always sounded as though he rarely used it. It would go well with work-hardened hands, which some would find appealing. The awareness that she must not converse with him, alone, in a room where their voices echoed, pressed acutely on her mind.

"Must be interesting," Blackstone said, "to see something other than just flecks of paint."

She glanced at him. "Is that truly all you see?"

"That, and what it could be worth twenty years from now."

He wore black, save the muted gray of his waistcoat. He had again brushed back his hair, perhaps in anticipation of respectable visitors, and again his dark locks curled at his nape. Like the whorls on a mallard's tail. The touch of vulnerability emboldened her, as did the possibility that he should care enough to try to provoke her.

"I believe that flecks of paint, when arranged by an artist like Millais, are proof that your thesis is wrong," she said.

Now he faced her, and her breath hitched. "My thesis?" he said.

"Yes," she managed. "That people are primarily guided by convenience, vanity, or greed."

He inclined his head. "You remembered."

She remembered their kiss, too; it was a memory she carried in her body and it surged hotly through her veins and other, nameless places when she looked into his eyes. It couldn't be attraction. The most severe judgment was reserved for society women who blushed over lower-born men—they were considered deranged and, if caught, were sometimes sent to special clinics.

She cleared her throat. "People travel dozens of miles to look at the Pre-Raphaelites for the sole reason that they are beautiful," she said. "Where is the vanity and greed when enjoying a painting?"

"Touché, Miss Greenfield."

A series of tiny sidesteps had melted the space between them. Definitely deranged, because she discreetly tried to smell him rather than flee.

"It'll be over soon enough," he said, "realistic painting, that is. Even blurry styles such as this. Impressionism was the beginning of the end."

She frowned. "How so?"

"Because one can capture realistic images more effectively these days. You won't have artists trying to replicate what a machine can do better and faster for much longer."

"What can you mean?"

He cut her look that implied she should know. "Photography."

She recoiled. "I disagree."

"Why?"

"No camera can capture emotion in the same manner as a brush."

He shrugged. "If done right, who knows, eh?"

The interchangeably stolid, lifeless expressions of portrait photographs chased past her mind's eye. Of course he would think it would do—he was a self-made man who had ascended to his position based not on bravery in battle, or on the organic yields of an estate, but on iron tracks and factory smoke.

"A camera has no soul," she said, a bit too loudly. "It's a piece of technology."

"So is a brush," he said, "just a much more primitive one." The supercilious look in his gray eyes said: *Parry that!* He had angled his body toward hers and stood too close, and her breathing had turned shallow. None of this was amusing to her.

"I gather you place your trust in machines," she said. "I, however, trust in humans."

His mouth softened. "I don't trust in anything, Miss Greenfield," he murmured. "But if I did, I'd put my faith in the future, not the past."

Was that what she was doing, then—looking backward? Replicating long-gone glories? Deep down, she had suspected it. She was never the avant-garde. Her thoughts were swimming. The sun was painting reddish streaks into his black hair.

"Rossetti and Millais show that romantic beauty isn't mutually exclusive with grave truths," she said hoarsely. "Why does the world insist that substance worthy of acclaim always comes in the shape of machinery or old men?"

"In other words," Blackstone said, "why is no one taking you seriously?"

His words went through her like a knife through butter and sliced open a sensitive place inside her chest. He either had a much, much more astute eye than expected, or she was hopelessly transparent. She felt gauche and exposed, that a man like him should tell her things about herself or that she had underestimated him. She resented him, him and the thick tension pulsing between them and his intent gaze and how his body heat was seeping through lilac damask into her skin like the glow of a fire. She noticed her breasts were near touching his waistcoat. She noticed his gaze dropping to her lips.

It was going to happen again.

The kiss was already hovering mere inches away. Her heartbeat came in hard, erratic thuds. But Blackstone stood quietly, dark and solid amid the white haze burning up the rest of the world.

She leaned in.

His face was close, then mouth brushed against mouth, light like a breath. She soared and swayed at the delicate contact, and his arm slid around her waist in support. When her lashes lifted, her left hand was flat against the lapel of his jacket. She stared at it, amazed at how small it looked there and that she was touching him.

This was how they stood when the main entrance door to the gallery opened and revealed her mother, frozen into a column. And Lord Oaksey. And Mrs. Hewitt-Cook. The whole group, a wall of wide eyes and hands clasped over mouths. She registered that Mr. Blackstone released her and turned to face them, his movement slow and controlled.

A creative mind had the ability to spiral deep into dark places, and sometimes she had tried to picture the moment when a great catastrophe befell her. What it would be like when she first knew her world had been upended. She had never envisioned that it would be a deathly silence, powerful enough to suffocate a whole gallery.

⁂

Two hours after the incident in his house in Chelsea, Lucian called on Julien Greenfield to begin the haggling over the daughter. A butler who greeted him with cold hostility led him directly to the patriarch's study. Greenfield sat behind his desk, and he had company: his heir stood next to him and regarded Lucian with murder in his eyes.

"I should have you taken out the back and shot," the banker greeted him. "Give me one reason why not."

"How about thirty?" said Lucian. "My percentage of shares in Plasencia-Astorga. I understand you would need them to consolidate your railway portfolio in Spain."

Greenfield leaned back in his chair. His gaze betrayed his rapid weighing of options: a deal to soften the scandal. A substantial peace offering after having had his hand forced. Worthy reasons for which to barter one of several daughters. "If you think I'll pay a penny for them," he then said, "you are deluded."

"I was thinking half price," Lucian replied.

Greenfield's teeth ground into the tense silence. "Sit." He gestured at the chair in front of his desk.

Zachary Greenfield made a sound of angry surprise. Greenfield turned to the young man. "Leave us, son."

Father and son were staring at each other, locked in a wordless battle. Lucian found he was respecting the son's righteous but futile outrage more than the father's rational calculation. When his own stepfather had sold him for a pittance years ago, he would've appreciated some support in his corner.

Young Greenfield left, his shoulders stiff with suppressed emotions. Lucian took his seat and brushed an invisible fleck of smut off his sleeve, and Julien Greenfield's gaze sharpened on him. "Not a penny," he repeated.

Odd, how this ruddy, hard-nosed man with questionable taste in facial hair had sired a bonnie lass like Harriet. As he countered Greenfield's propositions, Lucian's thoughts kept straying to the young woman. She had given him one of the greatest surprises of his life when she had leaned in; it had been barely half an inch, an upward tilt of her head with her full lips slightly parted. But that moment, her face had been the only thing in existence and he had registered nothing but the petal-soft brush of her kiss. There were other upper-class daughters who would serve his plans, but he found he wanted this one. This wasn't as much a conscious thought as the bewildering feeling that he'd give Greenfield whatever he demanded if it came to it. Though should Harriet ever find out about the details preceding their betrothal, he suspected she wouldn't like it, not at all.

Chapter 8

─❦─

H arriet. Tell your father that you were forced."

Hours after the sun had set, her parents summoned her to the library and she had entered feeling sick and light-headed with nerves. Her father stood next to the fireplace and was staring into the flames with his hands shoved into his trouser pockets. Her mother hovered near a chair against the wall, her face so pale and shiny she looked embalmed rather than alive. She still pinned Hattie with an imperious look.

Hattie stood in the cold draft, stupefied. Her mother had been there; she had seen it. The mirrors on the right-hand gallery wall had turned out to be two-way mirrors. In the bright light of noon, the room had been a fishbowl; everyone standing in the dim corridor running behind these treacherous windows had seen them, and had seen them kiss—willingly. Was it true that all she had to do now to make this nightmare disappear was to tell an enormous lie? A shy glance at her father said he was ignoring her. *Yes.* The small syllable was just a breath away. Her mother clearly, desperately, wanted her to say yes. But what difference would it make? Forced or not, they would send her away. Besides, lying about such a matter was a wretched thing to do. She looked at the floor. "No." Her life as she knew it was over.

"What was that?"

It was impossible to face her mother. "He wasn't forcing me."

"How, then! How could this happen?"

If only she knew. One minute, Mr. Blackstone and she had been sharing an impassioned discussion about art, and the next she had wanted to cling to him. It had felt as impossible to stop herself from kissing him as turning around mid-fall off a cliff. *She had leaned in.* And then, the shock. The frozen faces and the stares. A shudder ran through her; she wanted to crawl out of her skin to escape the pain of shame raking its claws against her gut.

She closed her eyes. "I'm so terribly sorry," she whispered.

"None of that matters, as you well know," her father replied.

Her studies at Oxford were done, she knew it confirmed then. She was to never take a single step alone again without a chaperone. People would whisper behind her back at every dinner, every dance, picking apart her loose morals. No decent young woman put herself into a position that enabled an unsuitable man to kiss her—actually, she wouldn't receive any invitations at all. Her friends might turn away from her. . . . She pressed her hands over her stomach as nausea threatened to climb up her throat.

Her mother rounded on her father. "My daughter is innocent," she said. "She was mauled by this man—it was plain for everyone to see."

"Oh, there definitely was something to see," her father said, his gaze still fixed at the fire hissing on the grate. "Though I hear it wasn't clear who was mauling whom—apparently, she *leaned in.*"

"Mr. Greenfield—we know nothing about that man. . . ."

Now he faced them. "I told you, I have learned a few things," he said. "He is at least as wealthy as the Astorp-Venables, and that is only to what he admits. He is nine-and-twenty years old. He is the illegitimate son . . ." He paused. *Illegitimate.* The word jarred like the sound of something precious smashing on the tiles. "The illegitimate son of a late Sir Murray," he continued, "an estate owner in Argyll, though his stepfather gave him his name upon marrying the mother—

as such, I'm uncertain why he felt the need to disclose his bastardy, but I assume he takes pleasure in adding insult to injury. His mother, also deceased, was in Sir Murray's employ, I understand as a kitchen maid."

"Illegitimate." Her mother sat down hard on the chair. "Mr. Greenfield, how can you even contemplate such an absurdity?"

"Well, you announced to everyone that they were engaged all along."

Engaged. Hattie saw that her parents' lips and hands were moving, but not a sound reached her ears. She had missed that announcement in the aftermath, but now it was clear: they weren't going to send her away. They were marrying her to Blackstone.

Her mother shot back to her feet. "I had to do something—everyone had seen it! These mirrors—they were like windows."

"And you did the right thing, Adele."

"I can't abide it," her mother said. "Harriet was to marry a peer—"

Her father threw up his hands. "Then she should have dallied with one—preferably in plain sight of the biggest gossipmongers of society."

"He looks coarse and has a disagreeable disposition," Adele cried, red in the face. "He will give her coarse-looking, disagreeable children!"

"He's not my choice of son, either! If handsome grandchildren matter to you, support this match—as things are, it is the only chance for Wilhelmina to still receive an offer from fair Sir Bradleigh."

"Mr. Greenfield—"

"We can now disown Harriet and magnify the scandal," he cut her off, "or we can send her away and become an object of gossip for decades anyway. Or we could try our damnedest to elevate Blackstone's position, manufacture a respectable family tree for him, and stand by this match." He was looking directly at Hattie with bloodshot eyes as he kept speaking to his wife. "Make no mistake, I was of a mind to let her fall, for someone so foolish doesn't deserve to call herself my daughter. But the Greenfields never leave a Greenfield behind, no matter their failings, and if you believe for one moment that I'd break with that tradition, you are mistaken. We don't abandon our own, and I shan't dishonor my father's legacy just because Harriet acted like a strumpet."

The floor threatened to slide from beneath Hattie's feet. "No." She had shouted it, or perhaps she had whispered. "You can't mean it."

Her father's eyes narrowed. "Can't mean it?" he repeated. "What did you *think* was the conclusion to this spectacle, hmm?"

"Papa, you cannot mean for me to *marry* him."

"I do. He called on me today to offer for you, and in my capacity as head of this house, I said yes."

"Julien." Her mother raised her hands. "Look at her. She doesn't have the constitution to be a wife to such a man. Julien, she is stubborn but she is a sweet girl—"

"Ah, but she's not as sweet as you think," he said. "This one"—he jabbed his index finger at Hattie—"ran from her protection officer at least twice this year to hobnob around London unchaperoned, which is how she first came to Blackstone's attention. The wanton display in the gallery wasn't their first private encounter. Graves is out on the street now, by the way."

Hattie's stomach lifted as though she were falling into a pit. Poor, poor Mr. Graves. What a mess she had made.

Her mother's expression was utterly horrified. "You ran away?" she said. "You were alone? Unprotected?"

"Please, Papa," she said. "You are one of the most powerful men in England—"

"Most powerful?" He suddenly seemed twice as tall. "Most powerful, you say?" She flinched when he thumped his chest with his fist. "How *powerful* do you think I look," he roared, "when I cannot even control the females in my own household?"

The raw aggression exploding from him edged the air from the room. There was one thing Julien Greenfield could not abide: appearing weak. The viscous slowness of a nightmare engulfed Hattie, except there was no assurance at the back of her mind that she would eventually wake from this. This was real. And she would have to live through every single dreadful consequence.

Her life might be over, but a new morning dawned nonetheless. She lay flat on her back and stared up at the bed canopy with the desperately tired eyes of a sleepless night. Outside her curtains, London was waking with a rosy glow; the first hackneys were clattering past the house and the unintelligible cries of a newspaper boy carried across the street. Her escapade with Mr. Blackstone was likely one of the headlines. . . . Mr. Blackstone, her future husband. Mrs. Whichever Blackstone. She didn't know his Christian name. Her eyes remained dry; she had cried all her tears before midnight. Had exhausted all her options, too, for there were few:

One—running away. However, a scandalous young woman had nowhere safe to go, and her face went hot with embarrassment at the mere thought of implicating her friends. Besides, she wouldn't reach the age of majority for another three months. She was the property of Julien Greenfield, and no one would dare steal from a man like him.

Two—eloping with another lover. Alas, there were none available at such short notice.

Perhaps this was her punishment, not just for stupid conduct, but for challenging fate by making rather too specific requirement lists about her husband. She might have fantasized about masked highwaymen and brazen privateers since borrowing her first romantic penny novel from Aunty's embroidery basket—had secretly delighted in ruthless men who knew no fear and simply took. But visions of her real groom had been the opposite: a Skeffington, a Bingley. Kind, titled, young, and yes, lovely. Men with a dangerous glint in their eyes and a good sword arm were best left between book covers. Now her orders had been switched clean around.

The door to her chamber opened without a knock, and Mina marched in carrying a tray. Her puffy eyes and pink nose were well noticeable from across the room. Nausea spread through Hattie's stomach, and she turned her face away.

Mina put the tray down on her night table abruptly enough to make the china rattle, then she tossed something onto the bed.

A newspaper.

Hattie peered at it gingerly from the corner of her eye.

BLACKSTONE ART GALLERY EXHIBITS MORE THAN MISS G BARGAINED FOR!

The headline was screaming at her in bold black letters that took up half the page. White dots danced across her vision. "This happened last evening," she croaked. "How is it in the papers today?"

Mina didn't grant her a glance; she was on her way to the door, her back stiff as a board.

"Mina."

Her sister whirled back round like a cat whose tail had been grabbed. "Are you truly surprised?" she hissed. "Blackstone, in a compromising position with a Greenfield? It is remarkable that no special editions fed out last night!"

She closed her eyes. "Yes. You are right, of course."

Mina was breathing heavily. "How could you?" she said, her voice low and shaky.

"I didn't mean to."

"Mama and Papa have been quarreling half the night, blaming each other for your waywardness. Aunty hasn't slept a wink—she looks ill."

She swallowed hard. "Aunty hates me, too?"

"Not entirely," Mina conceded. "She blames much of it on our ancestors for moving to London and converting the Greenfields to the Anglican Church."

"Lord." And Zachary . . . the thought of her favorite brother knowing about her depravity made her shudder.

"If Sir Bradleigh doesn't offer for me now, I shall hate you forever," Mina said, her eyes glittering with barely checked tears.

She sat up straight. "Mina, he must; he adores you—"

Mina's small hands sliced through the air. "Of course he does. And if it were my decision alone, I should just elope with him—but he is an honorable man with a reputation to heed, so we can't; and currently I'm an inch from acquiring a reputation as damaged goods by association. Good heavens, just what possessed you to tryst with that man, and in public?"

"I—"

"Why not with Lord Skeffington—I thought you had a tendresse for him!"

She looked down at her hands. "I had," she said miserably.

Mina was glaring at her. "I knew you were eccentric, but not that your tastes were so . . . base."

"They're not," Hattie said, but she sounded small. *Strumpet.* She shook her head.

Mina crossed her arms over her chest. Her red hair moved around her angry face like flames. "You have lost the opportunity for a good match," she said. "However, you can still make it right for me. Pray, make it right." She swept out of the room with her snub nose high in the air. Undoubtedly, she would have made a magnificent wife for a knight.

But marry Mr. Blackstone? She fell back into her pillows, feeling faint again. If she didn't marry him, these headlines were only the beginning. She would suffer a death by a thousand cuts if she refused his hand. *Look, it is Harriet Greenfield, who committed carnal indecencies in public, oh, in a gallery you say, my word.* She couldn't even blame the gossips—granted, some took mean-spirited pleasure in eviscerating a scandalous woman, but most people were genuinely at a loss as to what to do with one. Few could afford to be seen conversing with her; once the good and righteous had formed a mob to uphold proper conduct, snubbing the downtrodden was the only safe way to avoid having one's own moral character called into question, too.

She pulled the covers over her head. Her mind sluggishly circled over the same arguments only to reach the same conclusions: if she married him, scandal would be kept at bay. Cross-class marriages had become more common ever since Jennie Jerome had brazenly nabbed Lord Churchill off the marriage mart several years ago, thus opening the floodgates for other American dollar princesses eager to trade dowries for aristocratic titles. However, there was nothing to be gained for her family from the Blackstone match other than the avoidance of scandal; they required no funds, and Blackstone's social rank was beneath theirs thanks to his murky origins. And all of this paled against her own personal cost: if she married the man, all hope for a future love match would be lost. In her nightmares, she was bound to a husband only to unexpectedly meet her soulmate, to lock eyes with him across a room and just know what she had lost by marrying the wrong person. Tragedy! Then again, that opportunity was lost now anyway. No gentleman with options courted damaged goods.

A knock sounded on the door. She remained hidden and silent. Someone was in her room and softly cleared their throat. Couldn't be her furious sister, then. She peered over the blanket and found Bailey, her lady's maid, at the foot of the bed, with her slim hands clutching nervously at her apron.

"I'm sent to inform you that Mr. Blackstone shall be here in an hour," Bailey said in her gentle voice. "You are to meet him and Mrs. Greenfield in the Blue Parlor."

She wasn't ready; not now, not in an hour, not in a year.

"Bailey," she said. "Bring me a sherry, please. No, make it two."

The two sherries had been a poor idea. The liquid burned like acid in her empty stomach on her way to the Blue Parlor. It threatened to surge straight up her throat when she entered and spotted Mr. Blackstone's forbidding figure next to the fireplace. Her mother looked pale and pinched and had recruited Flossie for reinforcement.

This would not do.

She tried to stand tall. "Mama. I wish to speak to Mr. Blackstone alone."

Her mother drew back, a hand on her chest. "Now, Harriet—"

"Alone, Mama."

Something in her voice made her mother fall quiet. She wasn't certain what precisely she would to do if they refused to give her some privacy, but it would be sherry-fueled and wildly embarrassing in any case, and her mother realized it. "Very well," she said. "Florence." She nodded sharply at Mr. Blackstone as she swept past. "You have fifteen minutes—we shall be right outside."

Hattie stiffly lowered herself onto a chair. The stale smell of cold ash came from the nearby fireplace, and she clasped a hand over her unsettled stomach. Mr. Blackstone remained standing since she had not invited him to sit. He looked offensively well rested and was dressed somberly in black and gray again. His jacket, however, was made of velvet, an oddly soft choice for a hard man.

"Mr. Blackstone."

He inclined his head. "Miss Greenfield."

"Do you wish to marry me?"

"Yes." He said it calmly and without hesitation.

Her heart sank. "You aren't known for heeding convention," she said. "You could shirk your responsibilities and throw me to the proverbial wolves without much consequence to your routine."

He paused. "Is that what you want?"

"Well, I'd rather we not both suffer needlessly when it could be only me."

"You seem to greatly underestimate your father's reach," Mr. Blackstone said dryly. "As it is, I'm in need of a wife. And I'd rather not throw you to the wolves."

No—he'd rather devour her himself. Her fingers skated nervously over the trimming on her pale green skirt. His posture was relaxed, but his eyes missed nothing. She felt him studying her face and noticing every embarrassing detail: the shadows beneath her eyes, her swollen nose, the entire sleepless night. She'd rather not be here, exposed to him, but she had questions. Of course, asking him whether he indulged in excessive gambling or debauchery—common husbandly vices that normally blighted a wife's life—seemed ridiculous.

Are you cruel?

Have you killed anyone?

Tell me how you came by all your ill-gotten gains.

"Do you recall my aunt mentioning how I beautify the world with a brush rather than my rational brain?"

He nodded.

"She said it because my head is not quite right."

"Is that so?"

"Yes," she said quickly. "I cannot spell properly. I have difficulty copying a row of numbers in the correct order." He gave no reply, was just watching her calmly, so she added, "My father spared no effort: tutors, doctors, exercises—I'm a hopeless case. You can't rely on me for your social correspondence, nor for controlling the household accounts."

He contemplated that for perhaps two seconds. "It matters not," he then said, "not to me."

She blinked. "You don't mind whether your wife is slow in the head?"

"You seem bright enough to me."

"Sometimes I go to the wrong address because I misread the house number."

He arched a brow and said nothing. He knew what she was attempting.

"Then there's the matter of my attention," she tried. "It is either scattered or directed with an unnatural focus. I lose track of time when I paint, for example."

"And yet you study at Oxford," he said. "You correctly identified a rare Han vase on the spot—few people in Britain can. I've no worries about your brain. Besides, I'm taking you as my wife, not as my accountant."

Worse and worse. Apparently, he was one of those men who were content with their wives quietly doing doily work and breeding rather than making clever conversation.

"What of children?" She couldn't keep the agitation from her voice. "What if my defect runs in the family—imagine your heir, unable to write."

He shrugged. "My heir will be wealthy."

This, apparently, settled the matter to his satisfaction. Frustration crackled through her like an electric current and launched her to her feet. "We have scarcely spent an hour in each other's company," she said, "nor exchanged a single letter. We know nothing about one another."

He clasped his hands behind his back. "What is it you need to know?"

"I cannot see how you would possibly suit me."

A sardonic gleam lit his eyes. "I suffer no misplaced vanities, Miss Greenfield—I know you wouldn't have chosen me for a suitor. But be assured that I'll keep you in the comforts to which you are accustomed as well as any man in your circles."

She raised her fingertips to her temples. "I'm aware you are a wealthy man," she said. "But I had very much hoped to marry a friend."

"A friend," he said, slowly, as if it were a foreign word eluding a confident pronunciation. His Scottish brogue was showing, too.

She half turned away to look out over the rooftops of London.

"Yes, a friend," she said thickly. "I wished for a husband who shares his time with me, who would enjoy inhabiting our own small world, which we alone created. And he would be kind."

Would a man like Blackstone know how to be kind? These were not the questions she should ask him, nor the things she should hope to expect. She had been taught the tenets of a good marriage and a good wife since girlhood and understood very well that a woman should desire marriage only insofar as it finally allowed her to fulfill her highest purpose: becoming a mother. Only a selfish girl would dream of romance and companionship with a man before she thought of all the lovely children she could nurture. She was selfish, then. She also understood a marriage was best when much of it was spent apart, giving a wife free rein over the domestic sphere, and in turn, she'd never prevail upon her busy husband's time for attention. Unfortunately, she had a feeling she would desire a lot of attention from her husband. In her wildest dreams, she loved and was loved all-consumingly and beyond reason. The heated emotion in her chest boiled higher.

"I wished for someone who has fine hands," she heard herself say. "Someone who is content to spend his Sunday afternoons reading to me, someone who takes me to Italy when the weather turns dreary in London so we can study the old masters and discuss them while drinking hot chocolate in the shadow of the Duomo." She glanced at him. "Have you been to Florence, Mr. Blackstone?"

"Yes," he said coolly. "I've been to Florence."

"And do you read?"

"Aye, I know how to read," he said, his voice colder still.

"I'm referring to novels. Do you have any favorite novels?"

His dark brows pulled together. "No," he then said. "I read Trollope's *The Way We Live Now*, if you'd count that. But no other novels, no."

So he had read one novel in his life, one about a murky financier and banking scandals. She swayed on her feet. "I'm afraid we shall never suit."

Mr. Blackstone bared his chipped tooth in what she supposed was a smile. "Courage," he said. "We've ten minutes—you may find something to please you yet."

Unlikely. And they both knew she would have to accept him regardless, unless perhaps he confessed to something truly outrageous, something of the magnitude of regicide. He wouldn't confess to any such thing, and the purpose of this conversation had been to find something, anything, that would make the days leading to the wedding more pleasant. There *had* to be something good in the strange turn her life had taken. Thus far, his answers only filled her with more dread. She looked at him thinking that she had kissed him; she had kissed this snarling, taciturn mouth—twice. It had excited her. What had possessed her?

She slumped back down into the chair and gestured at the chaise lounge across. "Have a seat, if you please."

He sat, unnervingly shrinking the dainty piece of furniture with his frame.

She decided to continue with something simple. "What is your given name?"

Apparently, it wasn't so simple—he had stiffened infinitesimally at the question, and for a moment, his gaze went straight through her as though he were not seeing her at all. "My name is Lucian," he finally said.

Lucian. The name meant *light*. His mother must have had a penchant for irony. Or remarkable foresight . . . Lucian—Lucifer—Beelzebub. She shivered.

"And how did you damage your tooth, Lucian?"

He absently ran the tip of his tongue over the tooth in question. "There's no delicate way of putting that."

"I presently feel rather unshockable."

"It happened when I took a fist to my face," he said. "And there was a ring on one of the fingers. A heavy ring."

She cringed. The scar on his lip would have been a gaping gash. "Are you a violent man, then?"

He considered this a moment. "No," he then said. "Sometimes the violence finds you."

"Plenty of gentlemen never find themselves inconvenienced by a fist in their face."

His features hardened. "I've never hurt a woman, nor a bairn," he said. "And I'd never raise my fists to you—and that's what you are asking, isn't it?"

Indeed. "I'd rather my husband not hurt anyone at all," she told him. "They say you have purposely ruined upstanding gentlemen."

"Have I?" he said blandly.

"Well," she said. "How would you phrase it?"

"Perhaps they just lived beyond their means?" he suggested.

"Most gentlemen do," she said. "It is an unwritten rule to keep granting them credit."

A tension radiated from his body, and for a beat, it hummed in the silence between them. "I've changed my ways in that regard," he then said.

Her father had said as much at the dinner only a fortnight ago. "And have you any regrets about what you have done?"

The brief flash of contempt in his eyes was icy cold. "No."

Best not to pursue this particular topic, then. He had probably decided how much he would reveal about himself before entering the Blue Parlor in any case. She was ill-equipped for debating such a man. She was ill-equipped to be anything to this man.

"People say you created your fortune from thin air," she tried instead. "Is it true?"

"Thin air," he mocked. "That would be nice. But no. I became wealthy after trading bills of exchange and have become exponentially wealthier since. I had the capital for trading from selling company shares that had done well," he added. "The funds to purchase those shares I had from renting out and selling property."

"And who gave you the starting capital?" Her strength was fading. Her palms felt sticky. The sherry was roiling in her stomach. She was kept upright only thanks to the comfortingly snug lacing of her corset, and Blackstone seemed to notice. Perhaps that was why he decided to indulge her. "When I was thirteen years old, an antiques dealer near Leicester Square took me as his apprentice," he said. "He died several years later and left me the shop. I sold it and invested the money in property with better-value growth potential."

She had an idea of the sums required for investments her father would call worthwhile, and a shop—even if near Leicester Square—hardly had the potential to enable a man's ascent to the upper echelons of the financial elite.

"My work with antiques gave me a taste of how the monied lived," Blackstone said, his tone laced with faint derision. "Must've given me grand ambitions above my station early on."

His ambitions had brought him far, she had to grant him that. Was she to be the jewel in his ruthlessly acquired crown?

She avoided his eyes when she asked her last question: "What of your wedding vows?"

He paused. "What about them?"

"Do you intend to keep them?" *Or do you plan to take lovers and risk exposing me to scandal and diseases?*

He was silent until she reluctantly met his gaze. Surprisingly, he looked serious. "I always keep my vows, Miss Greenfield," he said. "I'll keep my vows to you."

Regrettable. It left her with no acceptable reason to refuse him. She folded and unfolded her hands, her movements slow and shaky.

"I have conditions," she muttered.

He tilted his head. "Then, let's hear them."

"I wish to finish my studies at Oxford."

"That would be highly unusual."

"So are the circumstances of our match."

He considered it for what seemed an eternity. "All right," he finally said. "But not five days a week, surely."

She had expected this; he didn't strike her as a man who contented himself with less than half. "Four days, then. It's only eight weeks per term, after all." She was prepared to go down to three days. Three days was what Annabelle had negotiated with Montgomery, and Blackstone could hardly be more demanding than a duke.

"Four days," he agreed, unexpectedly. "What else?"

"I require my own studio at your house, and your word that I may continue painting."

"Done."

"And I shall ask my father to put a trust fund in my name."

He looked bemused rather than offended. "You won't find me tightfisted, if that's your worry," he said. "And your father and I agreed on two thousand a year in pin money."

Two thousand! Admittedly, a hefty sum for her incidental expenses.

"I shall ask him regardless," she resolved when she had recovered her voice.

The scarred corner of Blackstone's mouth quirked. "Very well."

He could of course hinder her from accessing the money, but she had been interested in his reaction. It was satisfactory enough, she supposed. She rose, so he rose, too.

"I should like to shake hands on the conditions," she said, expecting him to finally lose his patience, but he didn't—he offered his hand. A trap—his palm engulfed hers, and the warm confidence of his grip made her weak in the knees. She glanced up at him shyly. "Is there nothing you should like to know about me?"

He retained his businesslike expression. "I know all I need to know," he said.

He didn't care to know about her, then. Meanwhile, she had asked all the questions and still felt she knew nothing.

On impulse, she leaned in. "Tell me something no one else knows about you."

The cold depths of his eyes went very still. "I already have," he then said.

"You have?"

He nodded. "My name."

"Lucian?"

"Yes."

Disturbing. Her gaze dropped to the floor, defeated at last. Then Blackstone shocked her again by raising his hand to her face and tipping up her chin with his thumb. A nervous sensation fluttered in her belly when their gazes locked. He looked as though he meant to say something, but instead, he was watching her closely while he brushed the backs of his knuckles over the curve of her jaw, then over the softness of her throat beneath. It was a liberty a lover or a husband would take, the kind of caress that left confusing heat in its wake, and her breathing quickened. He had to feel her treacherously galloping pulse against his fingers.

He dropped his hand. "Harriet," he murmured. "I think we'll suit just fine."

She hadn't a fraction of his optimism, and when the doors opened and her mother and Flossie marched back in, she couldn't help but think that this was how Persephone would be dragged into the underworld in 1880s London: not screaming, not twisting wildly, but painfully composed while Hades wore a velvet jacket.

Chapter 9

A line by Trollope crossed Lucian's mind while he walked away from Greenfield's fine town house: "There seems to be reason for fearing that men and women will be taught to feel that dishonesty, if it can become splendid, will cease to be abominable." Since the early seventies, a growing number of common men had been accruing wealth beyond measure with well-placed investments and a lucky hand at trading. It provoked envy and suspicion from the peerage and the working classes alike since the brutal financial crisis of '57 was still on people's minds, and enough crooks continued to build investment schemes that left them either rich or, more likely, ruined alongside the countless poor sods whose savings they had lost. The few who successfully secured their fortunes planted their flags in the hearts of old-money strongholds: Belgravia, St. James's, the Cotswolds. Such injuries to the rigid British social hierarchy inspired authors to churn out novels featuring newly monied men as The Villain. Wealth, it seemed, was morally above reproach only when it was made on the backs of other people tilling one's long-inherited lands. Being a reprehensible self-made man himself, Lucian knew there was some truth to the moralizing—when he strode through any of his *splendid* houses, where Bohemian crystal sparkled alongside gilded fittings and polished ebony wood, he felt no shame. Whenever he stretched out on a clean, soft mattress after a good meal, he regretted none of the things he had done to become filthy rich. But contrary to Trollope's concerns, Lucian had never reframed his misdeeds. He remembered all the violence and theft, blackmail and fraud, he had committed during the early years and knew it exactly for what it was. He simply couldn't find it in him to care, not when so many pigs stood there lazily feasting at the trough thanks to a simple accident of birth.

He had never, however, stolen a woman. *That* was wholly of the old world. His ancestors might have secured a bride that way when the clans had still gleefully raided one another's cattle herds. Of course, they would have taken their equals for a spouse. He had snared himself a Sassenach princess. He should be reveling in cold satisfaction, he realized as he passed the weathered redbrick façade of old St. James's Palace, but he wasn't. At the back of his mind buzzed the fact that he was soon to be a married man. He would have a wife to provide for. Judging by her wan face and requirements list—pretty hands! hot chocolate!—his intended felt rotten about the prospect of becoming that wife. Shouldn't have played with fire, then, if she didn't want to get burned.

Back in his own residence, he called for Matthews and informed him that he would marry Greenfield's daughter and that he needed the rooms adjacent to his private chambers prepared. Since his usual perceptiveness was blunted by his preoccupation, he missed the expression of keen disapproval flashing across Matthews's face.

She now knows the name your mother gave you, he thought as he made his way to his study. Even Aoife only knew him as Luke. Apparently, the dirty, ignorant boy from several lives ago wanted to be a part of their union.

⁓∂⁓

He collected his special marriage license on Wednesday. On Friday, the *Times* announced the date and venue: the Saturday after next in a chapel in St. James's. It wasn't St. George's at Hanover Square, but it would do, and Saturday after next meant he had four days to settle Harriet in his Belgravia house before traveling up to Drummuir.

He was at his desk analyzing last week's movements of the New York Stock Exchange when Matthews delivered the weekend mail. A letter plastered in Scottish stamps from Mr. Stewart, the man he intended as the new mine manager for Drummuir.

"What's this?" he asked, nodding at the slip of paper remaining on the silver tray as he sliced open the envelope.

"A telegram from Italy," said Matthews. His voice was bright, his complexion glowing. His eyes, however, were rimmed red. He must have drunk and gambled deep last night in his chosen den of iniquity, and won. He'd have a new pocket watch soon, or a new suit, or be off to the racecourses to bet on a losing horse. Or perhaps he'd install a new woman in his personal flat in Camden. The women never stayed long.

"Italy," Lucian said. He had no active contacts in Italy, so he set the telegram aside and told Matthews to go and supervise the airing and refurbishment of Harriet's rooms.

Stewart's letter was to the point: all required rooms at the Drover's Inn had been successfully booked for the dates Lucian had requested; the conditions in Drummuir's collieries were dire; the spirit in the mining community was low. One could expect no less from a mine that had been in the Earl of Rutland's neglectful hands. Resentment washed over Lucian; he had to physically shake it off before he could continue reading.

He picked up the telegram, which had been sent from Naples.

Blackstone old boy STOP Heard you are to marry Miss Harriet Greenfield STOP Congratulations STOP May I humbly recommend "The Art of Begetting Handsome Children" to ensure connubial bliss STOP In emergencies and I cannot stress this enough say it through flowers STOP Yrs Ballentine

He gave a grunt of disbelief. The arrogance. He read the lines again just to be certain. No, it still sounded as though his lordship was trying to instruct him in how to fuck. Lucian crumpled the telegram in his fist. Ballentine had effortlessly seduced men and women by the dozen before he had settled down with a fiancée last month; he was good counsel for any man in need of carnal performance advice. But the viscount knew that Lucian wasn't an untried lad. No, this message implied he needed help with approaching his bride because Harriet Greenfield was a gently bred virgin, while Lucian was anything but.

He loosened his cravat and tugged his shirt collar away from his throat. He had thought about it yesterday when they had delivered her new bed. Yes, he was aware that he had never shagged a virgin before. He knew that she and her ilk wouldn't deem his bastardly hands fit to touch one silky inch of her. She was still a woman, and he a man, and the mechanics would be the same as always. Ballentine's telegram didn't merit so much as a *vaffanculo*, and he returned to his stock exchange data table. For all of two minutes. Visions of Harriet Greenfield's naked, softly rounded body made the figures swim before his eyes.

He leaned back in his chair, uncomfortably aroused and distracted. First impressions mattered, and he wanted her to like it. *Needed* her to like it, for he had been serious about honoring his wedding vows. It was common for upper-class husbands and wives to romp around outside the marriage bed, but he wasn't in the habit of whoring, and he'd grown up thinking of men who strayed as weak. He'd seen the troubles it caused in small communities and the bastard babies it inevitably left scattered around. Now, a saintly husband would probably resign himself to a life of tepid couplings, while a polite one went to a brothel for his pleasure. He was neither saintly nor polite. He wouldn't approach her with his more deviant preferences, but he sure as hell wouldn't spend the rest of his life joylessly rutting over an appropriately martyred woman in the dark. He'd find a way, as always.

The next morning, he undertook the four-mile journey to Aoife's town house in Shoreditch for their fortnightly appointment. When he entered her reception room, his informant rose from her divan with the lazy grace of a cat, her blue eyes sparkling. The actual cat, a floofy, flat-faced thing, lounged on the divan's whorled armrest and dismissed him with a swish of its thick tail.

"A Greenfield daughter?" Aoife's throaty laugh said she was highly amused. Her cropped curls were positively bouncing round her ears. "By what dark sorcery did you accomplish that!"

"The usual," he said. "Luck meeting preparation."

"I hadn't known you were in the market for a wife. Not for a Sassenach, in any case."

He settled in the Chesterfield armchair across from her divan while she went to the drinks cabinet to pour him a Scotch. She wore skirts today, made of soft blue cotton that moved fluidly with her slender figure as only an exquisitely well-tailored garment would. Her face had the hard features inflicted by life in the gutter, and she spoke a soothing blend of monotone Limerick inflection mixed with Cockney, but her taste was distinctly toff.

She handed him the tumbler. "What's she look like—is she pretty?"

"I don't know."

Her brows rose. "You don't know? You must've seen her—the papers say you were caught in the act."

Aoife was acting strange, and he didn't know what to say. He found himself respecting Harriet Greenfield's quick wit and her grit—that she had tried to negotiate with him, unexpected in a woman so spoiled and young. He liked the generous curve of her hips and that she looked sturdy enough to take him.

He crossed his legs. "Her looks are of no consequence," he said.

"How boring you are." Aoife sprawled back down onto the divan.

"I'll just have to find out for myself, then. I did sometimes wonder what sort of woman would suit you, you know, and I couldn't fathom a good fit—a hard-nosed one who favors coin and doesn't give a damn about tender feelings would thrive best by your side. But you'd probably prefer someone soft and sweet for your bed—sadly, such a sweetheart will wilt away."

He shook his head. "What is the news on Rutland?" he said, pretending he hadn't heard the inanity.

"There's some news on your sniveling assistant," she replied.

"Matthews?" He recalled his assistant's blood-rimmed eyes earlier. "What's he done?"

"He needs to watch himself," Aoife said. "I saw him with my own eyes in Ritchie's den in Covent Garden the other night, losing money he doesn't have. And Ritchie's people—you don't mess with them. They take an ear as a warning, rather than giving a warning before taking an ear."

That was a nuisance—he wouldn't tolerate having his staff maimed by gambling kingpins. "I'll settle his accounts in time," he said.

"Wish you'd just cut him loose," Aoife muttered.

"He owes me. Owning people helps them to be loyal."

She gave him a mean look. "I'm loyal to you and I don't owe you a bloody thing."

His glanced at the room, the lush drapes and costly paintings and the cabinet with gilded inlays that had almost certainly been imported from France. "I'm paying for this house," he said.

Aoife's smile showed crooked teeth. "Because I give you permission to do so," she said. "So you don't feel *you* owe *me*—for the intelligence you get off me so cheaply. Or for when I kept you alive and unmolested on the streets."

"Fair enough," he allowed. "What news of Rutland?"

Her expression darkened. "I don't like that my Susan has to bamboozle his chinless wonder of a son. Lord Percy is a spineless brute." Her gaze lingered on the scar on his lip. "When will you feed the son to the fish? I hear the Thames crying his name lately, *Lord Percy, Lord Percy*."

He tasted his drink. Very smoky, a good-vintage Talisker he guessed. "It's the father I want," he said. "To the son, I owe a debt of sorts. You know that."

She grimaced. He didn't expect her to agree. She didn't understand vengeance the way he did, for she was quite content and settled now, at leisure to pose for painters and trade in information instead of being in the thick of a smuggling ring to make coin. It was more complicated for him, perhaps because his revenge wasn't just for him but for other people. He couldn't just say, *Enough is enough now*. It wasn't for him to decide. As for Rutland's son, Percy, he hadn't crossed paths with his lordship since he had been thirteen and stupid, creeping around the grounds of Rutland's vast Norfolk estate. That day, a late, wet afternoon in autumn, was still as fresh in his memory as though it had happened last week. He had learned the address from Master Graham by way of an innocent conversation. He hadn't meant to murder the earl just yet, but he had been keen on information about the man who had killed his family, had wanted to see how he lived. His *sgian dubh* had been tucked into the elastic of his right sock, but such a small knife could have been there for any purpose. He had felt breathless upon seeing the manor house rise from the evening mist, hating that he found the sprawling, indomitable splendor both threatening and alluring. The gamekeeper had discovered him near the rose garden and had promptly dragged him to the kitchen by the scruff of his neck. Rutland had been in London for the season—he hadn't known about seasons then—but his son had been in residence. Young Lord Percy had swiftly been summoned down to the kitchen.

"Poaching?" his lordship had asked the gamekeeper.

"He had nothing on him, my lord, no snares or slings, no bounty."

"I just got lost," Lucian had said.

The lordling had looked at him, astonished. "It speaks." He had leaned closer. "Say, should I report you for poaching, and have you sent to the jail?"

"No, sir."

"That would be *no, my lord* to you."

Lucian had said nothing.

"Hold him."

The gamekeeper, with some reluctance, had shoved his arms up behind his back and gripped him tight. Lucian hadn't struggled; he had known what was coming but he hadn't wanted to go to the jail. Rutland's son had punched him in the mouth so hard he had heard the crack of his tooth inside his skull. He hadn't felt the blows to his gut until he had come to, curled up and wheezing on the kitchen floor. The gamekeeper had given him a tea towel to mop up the blood, then he had marched him all the way to the gatehouse and told him not to lurk on his betters' property. Back in London, Master Graham had been very disappointed in him for brawling and ruining his shirt and had told him to work at the back of the shop until he didn't look a fright anymore. The cut on his lip hadn't stayed closed, so the payment for the stitches had been taken out of his meager wages. Nothing could fix the broken tooth.

In the days after the beating, while he had swept the shop floors and carried antiques in and out the back entrance, his daydreams of revenge had morphed from a boy's naïve idea of justice to something more systemic and vast. He wouldn't just kill Rutland—he would wound him in the only place that truly hurt a man: his coffers. It required him to become wealthy and powerful, too.

"How does a man become rich?" he had asked Graham when his mouth had healed.

"Well, he must be born rich," Graham had replied, visibly puzzled by the question.

"And what if he isn't?"

"Then he must employ other men and have them earn money for him, while he's working on another enterprise, and so on," Graham had explained.

Lucian had watched him suspiciously. "If you know all that, why are you doing this?" He had waved at the menagerie of frivolous, broken things crowding the room. Graham had shaken his head as though Lucian had said something stupid. He had run his age-speckled hand over the winged back of a French divan, as if to soothe the piece. "Why would I make money for the sake of money, if I can spend my life working with beauty? History? Things that require care?"

Lucian had thought Graham stupid then, at least on the matter of money. The next time he had been sent to fetch a damaged side table from a fancy house, he had stolen his first valuable. Then he had enrolled in evening and Sunday classes to improve his writing, arithmetic, and rhetoric. He began reading trade journals and the finance section in Graham's newspaper, and Graham, delighted by his apprentice's effort to *better himself*, had offered him the spare room above the shop for a shilling a week. This had saved Lucian time, and he soon learnt that time was money, too. Had Lord Percy not split his lip with his signet ring, he might've done something brash and ineffective instead of using his brains. No, he wouldn't feed Lord Percy to the Thames. Yet.

"Lord Percy intends to bid for a majority share in that textile company that fell apart last month and is being set up anew, together with Rutland," Aoife said. "Bragged about it to Susan when he was in his cups—an opportunity for easy profits. God knows he needs those."

"Mill and Cloth, down in Bristol," he said absently. "I believe their securities are traded through the Bristol stock market."

Aoife shrugged. She only delivered the intelligence. "That a good thing?"

He smiled. "I know the secretary who gatekeeps the trading."

She was smiling, too. "I s'pose Rutland and ol' Percy won't get their profitable shares, then. May I call my Susan back now?"

"By all means."

"Good. Where are you taking her for the honeymoon?"

He blinked. "What?"

"Your wife."

He finished his drink. "I won't. I'll be in Fife right after the wedding."

"At the mine? Drummuir?"

"Aye."

"What a rotten groom you are to not give her a honeymoon."

He gave a shake. "She'll be glad enough to be shot of me. She doesn't favor my type, judging by her wish list."

"All right," Aoife relented. "Must be bad in the mine, if you go to see for yourself."

"The reports weren't good."

"But you don't like going up North and beyond."

"I don't, no."

Her face softened. "Still trying to change the ways of the world, are you?"

"I've just made headway," he said curtly.

She gasped when understanding dawned. "Your new father-in-law?" She barked a laugh, startling the dozing cat on the armrest. "Luke, no single man can turn politics. It's a cesspool and they're all drowning in it, Greenfield, too." She ran her hand over the cat, and the animal stretched and kneaded air with clawed paws.

"Enough influential peers are Greenfield's clients," Lucian said. "He could enforce private loan contracts, but for a select few, he doesn't. If he did, the card houses would come tumbling down. At the very least, he'll get me the right dinner invitations."

"You think he'd do all that for a daughter?" Aoife mocked. "He's got several, hasn't he? He can well spare one."

"From what I can tell, her family sticks together like lemmings."

"They can't love her too much if they gave her to you, that's for certain."

Her impertinence was habitual, so he ignored it. "He'll want his grandsons," he said.

Aoife's mouth formed a perfect O. "So it's not even her you're after but the children," she said. "Bloody hell. When's the wedding, you said?"

"Next Saturday."

She cackled. "You have less than a week to become charming, then," and, at his blank expression, "To woo your wide-eyed bride, of course. Babes don't grow on trees."

"Not you, too," he muttered, thinking of Ballentine's bloody telegram.

"What?"

"Never mind," he said. "In any case, I always begin as I mean to go on."

"Not counting your staff, you haven't even shared lodgings with anyone in over a decade," she said. "Will be a change."

"My houses are big."

"You should've taken my advice to get a dog."

His brows rose with acute displeasure. "Are you likening *pets* to my wife now?"

"No," she said with a faint smile, "I'm saying you've never cared for another creature."

He shook his head. "There's no point in keeping a dog."

"Why not?"

"Their lives are short. They die."

Aoife made to reply something cynical, but then an understanding passed behind her eyes and she resumed stroking the cat. "I hope you know that if you ride the likes of her too hard, they break before you get much use out of them."

Back in Belgravia, Matthews had refilled all the vases with fresh hothouse flowers, and the scent of roses followed Lucian down the corridor all the way to the study. His work progressed unusually slowly, and he finally closed his folder. Perhaps he should have informed Harriet that there'd be no honeymoon. It hadn't been relevant to him, so he hadn't thought of it. But he never left his business commitments unattended for more than a day; besides, where would he take her? Italy? Then what? He hadn't time, not for the trip nor the planning. He needed to prepare his stock portfolio and thoroughly instruct his men of business so that his affairs remained in sound condition during his week in Fife.

Ride the likes of her too hard, and they break . . .

He cursed softly and rang for Matthews.

"Matthews. I need you to find me a book about flower language." His assistant looked puzzled but began taking notes. "And a book, or perhaps it's just a pamphlet, called *The Art of Begetting Handsome Children*."

Matthews's brows flew up.

"I need it on my desk within the next three days," Lucian said stonily.

"Of course," Matthews said. "I shall try my best. Sir."

He nearly added a current etiquette guide for gentlemen to the list, but he could probably procure that himself quickly enough. His mood darkened. He hadn't touched an etiquette manual in years.

Matthews delivered the requested reading material the evening before the wedding. By then, Lucian's suit and hat were brushed and Harriet's rooms were prepared. It left him with plenty of time to settle behind his desk to study *The Art of Begetting Handsome Children*, which turned out to be a thin pamphlet, first printed in 1860, written by Anonymous.

The first page began with frank discouragement:

*It is not unheard of for a new bride to wait months before she feels
inclined to consummate the marriage....*

"What?" He flipped through the pages in search of something
useful.

*When the husband cometh into his wife's chamber, he must entertain
her with all kinds of dalliance, wanton behaviour, and allurements....
But if he perceive her to be slow, and cold, he must cherish, embrace
and tickle her....*

Tickle her. Sounded right idiotic.

*... and shall not abruptly break into the field of nature, but rather
shall creep in by little and little, intermixing more wanton kisses with
wanton words and speeches, mauling her secret parts ...*

Mauling them?

*... so that at length the womb will strive and wax fervent with a
desire of casting forth its own seed. When the woman shall perceive the
efflux of seed to approach, by reason of the tinkling pleasure, she must
advertise her husband thereof that at the very same instant or moment
he may also yield forth his seed, that by collision, or meeting of the
seeds, conception may be made ...*

He threw the pamphlet in the bin under his desk. Kiss her, kiss
her quim, take her slowly—he'd have done so all without the help of
a manual. No, his approach wasn't the trouble—it was him: scarred,
blunt-fingered, lowly bred. And there was nothing he could do about
that other than get on with it. On second thought, he dove under the

desk to retrieve the pamphlet because it said it there, black on white in fancy speech, that a woman should get some *tinkling pleasure* from the act rather than just suffer it if she wanted to get with child. If Harriet wasn't open to enjoying his attentions out of modesty, then perhaps impartial scientific advice could change her mind. He'd find out tomorrow night.

Chapter 10

The night before the wedding, her mother came to her bedchamber looking more harried and tight-lipped than Hattie had ever seen her. She carried a slim booklet, which she waved at Bailey, who was in the process of brushing out Hattie's hair. "Leave us." She proceeded to pace in a narrow circle next to the vanity table. "Bailey shall wake you at half past seven tomorrow."

"Yes, Mama."

"The gown and accessories are ready, the carriage is ready. Don't tarry—we are leaving at half past nine sharp. The chapel is close, but traffic is thick at that time in the mornings."

The wedding was scheduled for ten o'clock and would be witnessed by only her immediate family. The lunch would take place in her parents' lunchroom, and they had *strongly advised* against Hattie inviting her friends. So she hadn't. She felt like hiding from the whole world, in any case. Now her mother was fussing over the hopelessly old-fashioned wedding gown, which was draped over the mannequin at the foot of her bed; she aligned a ruffle here and straightened a capped sleeve there while muttering under her breath.

"Mama."

"Hmm?"

"I know you have always wanted me to have a grand wedding in St. Paul's," she said softly. "And I'm sorry."

A pause ensued, heavy with clashing emotions. Finally, her mother glanced her way. "I advise you to please your husband," she said. "At least in the early days. It should make married life considerably easier on you."

She placed the book on the vanity table next to the brush and left. Hattie waited until her mother's footsteps had faded before she picked up the book.

Instruction and Advice for the Young Bride
by Ruth Smythers
Beloved wife of The Reverend L.D. Smythers

Ah. *That* sort of pleasing her husband. Though alone in her own room, she opened the first page with apprehension.

To the sensitive young woman who has had the benefits of proper upbringing, the wedding day is ironically, both the happiest and most terrifying day of her life. On the positive side, there is the wedding itself, in which the bride is the central attraction in a beautiful and inspiring ceremony, symbolizing her triumph in securing a male to provide for all her needs for the rest of her life. On the negative side, there is the wedding night, during which the bride must "pay the piper," so to speak, by facing for the first time the terrible experience of conjugal relations. . . .

She closed the book, her cheeks hot. She was sheltered but not clueless—she certainly had an idea about the mechanics involved in *conjugal relations*, though it was all rather blurred where the details were concerned. Judging by the stars in Annabelle's eyes whenever her duke was near, she had assumed the experience wasn't too harrowing. This was before she had known who her own husband would be, of course. Too late to run away now. It wasn't just that someone was keeping watch outside her bedroom door at night since the day at the gallery. No guards were required to make her stay; her raging shame saw to it very effectively, for with shame came the fervent desire to undo her mistake, to make everything feel right again, no matter the cost.

She rang for Bailey and told her to please send her married sister to her room. Minutes later, Flossie swept in, with a robe tied loosely over her nightgown and chubby Michael on her hip. Normally, Hattie would have rushed to her baby nephew to kiss all the small fingers and toes peeking from his lacy hems, but tonight she barely raised her head.

"Nerves?" Flossie asked. "Cold feet? All quite normal, my dear. Especially under the circumstances."

Of all her family members, her older sister had seemed the least overcome by recent developments, and Hattie had never been more grateful for her presence.

"Mama gave me this . . . book," she said, and nudged it. "I find it very unhelpful."

She kept her gaze on the wall as her sister stepped closer.

"Oh, that awful thing," she heard Flossie say.

Hattie peered at her. "You know it?"

Her sister skimmed the first page while absently bouncing Michael on her hip. "Hmph," she said. "It's as dramatic as I remember it." She shook her head and pulled one of the chairs from the wall closer to sit. "I was needlessly overwrought on my wedding day because Mama had left it on my bedside table," she said. "I'm glad you called for me."

"So am I." Hattie shuddered with cautious relief. "But should we, erm, speak of this in front of Michael?"

"He's ten months old," Flossie said. "Babies are sweet creatures, but incapable of understanding a thing. Aren't you," she crooned down at her son in her lap and giggled when he waved a fat little fist at her face. "The truth is," she said, "I cannot deny that it will be awkward at first, but I daresay you will soon find it rather funny."

"Funny . . ."

"Perhaps *pitiful* is the better word," Flossie allowed. "Men are very keen on it, and they become, how to put it . . . a bit silly in the process."

Silly? She couldn't envision a silly Lucian Blackstone. He was hard-muscled, steely-eyed intimidation.

"He will groan and pant," Flossie said, "but with a few little tricks, you can hasten it along, reduce it to a few minutes, even."

"Oh, good."

"And never let what happens in the bedchamber ruin your esteem for him outside of it. I confess I still have trouble reconciling these two versions of my clever van der Waal: a cunning man of business during the day, a needy creature at night. Truly, Hattie, we can be grateful to be women and that by nature we aren't afflicted by such urges."

She couldn't comment on this, since her urge to kiss an unsuitable man had put her into this situation in the first place. "How do I . . . hurry it along?" she brought herself to ask.

Now Flossie's cheeks reddened. "Allow him to look at you."

"How . . . could he not?"

"I mean in the nude, dear."

She had fancied herself quite adventurous and open-minded. Now her instincts, rigorously schooled since girlhood to keep her hands gloved, her necklines high, and her legs covered down to her heels to protect her modesty, shrieked in dismay at the word *nude*.

"Don't look so discouraged, Pom Pom," Flossie said. "If your nerves are too shaky, you could try ether to ease you through the first encounter."

Hattie's eyes grew round. "You mean . . . ether?"

Flossie nodded. "I haven't heard much about it in my circles in Amsterdam, but I understand here in London, doctors will sometimes prescribe it for nervous new brides. I feel as though I know someone who knows someone who employed it to great effect, though I can't think of the name. . . ."

"But I would be unconscious!"

"Precisely. You would wake up a wife in all ways and not have felt a pinch."

"Thanks," she said, filled with horror at the thought of Blackstone laboring away over her incapacitated body.

"Whatever you do," Flossie said, "do not imbibe too heavily. Before, I mean."

"Why not?" A champagne haze sounded mightily more tempting than a dose of ether.

"Because the scientific community believes that children, when conceived while husband or wife is intoxicated, will become slovenly and mean-spirited adults."

"Oh." No drink for her, then.

"One last piece of advice," Flossie said, and now she was covering Michael's ears. "When you act as if his efforts please you, you mustn't exaggerate it, or else he might think he married a wanton, and you do not wish to create that impression. And whenever you find it bothersome, keep in mind that you might get a darling baby from it by the end." She planted kisses on top of Michael's lace cap, and Hattie was accosted by the image of a robust toddler on her own knee. Her insides seemed to weigh a hundred stone. *He will give her coarse-looking, disagreeable children!*

"Before I forget," Flossie said, "I meant to tell you—your friends have been writing to you."

"What?"

Flossie nodded. "I assume they were your friends, from Oxford. They sent letters, and a telegram. Mama must have caught them all at early breakfast. She probably burned them."

Hattie swayed from the shock. "Flossie. How could she?"

Her sister weighed her words carefully. "I suppose she thought it would save you distress. She is not cruel, dear. Perhaps I shouldn't have told you."

"No, I'm glad you told me." She had started and discarded half a dozen letters to the girls, only to decide that it would be much safer for their reputations to visit once everything had been put right in the chapel tomorrow. . . . Tomorrow. So soon. Her throat tightened.

Michael sensed her fraying nerves; his small face crumpled and he began making displeased hacking noises.

"Hattie," Flossie said as she stood and rocked her fussy son. "Don't fret so much. A gentleman knows what to do and shall treat you with the respect a wife can expect."

"But he isn't a gentleman."

Flossie's face fell. "Then hold him accountable with unwavering standards," she said after a pause, and for the first time Hattie could remember, her sister sounded uncertain.

The next morning unfolded under a bell jar, with all shapes and sounds strangely distorted. Someone else seemed to be moving her limbs and speaking on her behalf. Someone laced her tightly into the wedding gown. Disembodied hands fixed the orange-blossom wreath to her hair while her reflection in the mirror was a white blotch. She would have been hard-pressed to recount the conversation during the carriage ride to the chapel. In the cramped interior of the coach, the strong mothball smell of her gown mixed with the sweetness of her stephanotis bouquet to terrible effect. Cold sweat coated her face by the time they reached the chapel.

"Harriet." Her mother's disapproving stare was on her left hand clutching the posy. She reflexively switched the bouquet to her right. After today, only Blackstone would be entitled to tell her in which hand she must carry her bouquet, she thought. And he probably wouldn't care about such details. So at least there was that.

She had expected him to wear the black tailcoat and gray-striped trousers of upper-class grooms, but when she spotted him at the altar, he looked surprisingly approachable in a three-piece suit of a warm, sandy color. His eyes, however, held a penetrating intensity that made her feel shy. She chose to focus on the suit fabric when they stood facing each other. Finest Scotch herringbone tweed. Probably from the Isle of Harris. He had pinned a small bouquet in the colors of the Greenfield coat of arms over his heart as was the custom, but he had added a Scottish thistle. The purple hue went well with the blue and yellow colors of her house, and the spikes provided structure amid the soft petals of the blooms. Charming. It was something she would have liked to see on her groom. While she parroted her lines, her breath roared in her ears like a distant ocean. She stumbled over *love*, *obey*, and *until death*, for those were lies, or at least not the truth, and normally she'd never lie in a chapel. She watched, aloof, as Lucian Blackstone slid a heavy gold band onto her ring finger that marked her as his wife.

"You've added a Scottish thistle to the buttonhole," she said to him when the brief, perfunctory father-of-the-bride speech in her parents' lunchroom was over. A string quartet was now playing, filling any stretches of awkward silence with a jaunty tune.

Lucian lowered his spoon and turned to her. "I have, yes."

The strong column of his neck looked positively confined by the cravat and high collar.

"My father mentioned your family is from Argyll?" she asked.

He nodded. "Near Inveraray."

"Which clan presides over that area?"

"Clan Campbell," he said slowly. "But I'm a MacKenzie, from my grandfather's side."

"One of my dearest friends is a Campbell," she said, relieved to hear of a connection even as tenuous as this. "Lady Catriona. Her father is the Earl of Wester Ross."

His brows pulled together. "Unusual. The region used to belong to the MacDonalds. Sometimes to the MacKenzies."

He must have a habit of pulling his brows together; two sharp, vertical lines were forever notched between them. His dark lashes, however, were lush like mink pelt, a precious touch of softness in his face. She would see this face every day now.

"I don't know much about the clans, I'm afraid," she said.

He gave a shrug. "The days of the clans are long gone anyway."

"Because of the Clearances?"

He looked vaguely surprised. "You know of the Clearances?"

"Of course. The Greenfield dining table is a veritable well of political information."

She couldn't recall the context of the Clearances being discussed, but she knew the brutal practice of driving the Scots from the Highlands since the last Jacobite rebellion—she supposed the Jacobites would have called it a bid for freedom—which had been ongoing until recently. Officially, it was to make way for sheep pastoralism; unofficially, or so Flossie said, it was about accumulating land in the hands of a few. She would miss the Friday dinners. Seeing their faces, watching them quarrel. Everyone except Flossie was still acting distantly toward her; Zachary still refused to properly look her in the eye. It hurt. But she had done all she could to make it right. As of today, she lived in another house, and all that remained of her past was Bailey, who had heroically agreed to continue her position as a lady's maid. Without warning, her nose stung with tears. She swallowed hard, to no avail—she was about to sob into her wedding soup.

A light touch on the small of her back made her stiffen, and she glanced up to find Lucian watching her intently. "Are you all right?"

She cast a nervous glance around. He seemed to mean well, but drawing attention to her fraying composure was impolite. Her siblings, her parents, several aunts, and a few cousins her mother had invited were chatting softly among one another, pretending not to notice that she was suffering a bout of nerves.

"I'm well, thank you," she whispered.

He looked skeptical. "Say the word," he said, "and we'll go home."

Home. He meant his house. Her face flushed. Once they were *home*, he would take off collar and cravat and they would kiss again. More than kiss. She was expected to allow this perfect stranger outrageous liberties tonight. As if the stroke of a pen on a formal piece of paper spirited away one's sensibilities and compunctions like a magic wand . . . Lucian's gaze sharpened, as if he had sensed the direction of her thoughts. As they stared into each other's eyes, heat flickered along the peculiar bond between them. She hadn't felt it since the kiss in the gallery, but there it was, still twitching.

Without breaking the connection, Lucian reached into the inside of his jacket and pulled out a small jewelry box. "I had meant to give this to you during our ride here." His tone was wry, and her blush intensified. Her mother had climbed aboard their carriage with Mina in tow and might as well have announced to the world that she worried Blackstone would pounce on his new wife the moment he found himself alone with her.

He took her hand, turned it over, and placed the box into her palm. Well, it would take time to become used to such intimacies.

"May I open it now?" She did like surprise gifts.

"If you want."

Holding the box low between them, she opened the lid. A silver pendant, perhaps half the length of her little finger, rested on a red velvet bed. She picked it up carefully.

"It's a tiny spoon." The handle was intricately fashioned in Celtic knots and finished in a heart-shaped loop.

"It's a love spoon," Lucian said.

She turned it back and forth. "I know of them." Celtic men fashioned them for their sweethearts. It looked freshly polished, but the inner sides of the braided strands were blackened with time, and there was a weight to the piece as though it had a history.

Lucian's expression was guarded. "My grandmother," he said. "She gave it to me, for my future bride. My great-grandfather had once made it for his wife; he was a Welshman." He glanced at it there in her palm. "I suppose we could set it with a diamond, if you want."

Her fingers closed protectively over the small heirloom. "I find it most precious as it is."

He looked at her oddly, then gave a grunt that could have been approval, and returned his attention to his soup.

She emptied her wineglass, the love spoon in her fist. How often had she daydreamed of being abducted by a handsome highwayman or a marauding privateer? She *dared* fate to be consistent and to prove that being ravished by such a man would be as pleasurable as in her fantasies.

Chapter 11

⚜

Awaiting ravishment wasn't quite as pleasurable as she'd antici-
pated. She had taken a warm bath, put on a thickly ruffled
nightgown, and slipped deep under the covers of her new bed. The
scent of clean linen surrounding her should have been comforting.
She was still shivering from head to toe and could not stop watching
the fiery flickers dancing across the door to her husband's chamber.
A tray with two glasses of champagne was on her nightstand, and
once and again her gaze strayed to the silently pearling drink, for she
was parched and her nerves tense enough to snap.

A brief knock, and the door opened. Her belly clenched. Lucian
stood frozen, his face in the shadows. A reddish glow delineated his
still form, and for a mad moment, the Prince of Darkness came to
mind. Then he closed the door and moved toward the bed, slowly, his
expression calm, but she was instinctively pressing back into the pillows. His black silk robe exposed a V of bare chest and she hadn't
expected there to be a pelt. When he sat on the edge of the mattress,
her breathing became embarrassingly loud. He didn't notice. His
gaze was roving over her unbound hair and it consumed all his attention, drew him closer, transfixed. He reached for a lock and lifted it
carefully, his eyes examining the satiny strand as if it were some
treasured artwork, and the unguarded reverence in his expression

stunned her a little. He must have realized it, too, for faint color crested on his cheekbones and he pulled away. He drew the coverlet back from her trembling body and patted the space next to him. "Come sit with me."

His voice was low and husky, and it made her shake harder. She moved awkwardly and settled at a proper foot's distance away from him. With casual ease, Lucian slid his left arm around her waist and pulled her flush against his side as he leaned across her to pick up a champagne glass.

"No, thank you." Her head was already swimming, from the fresh pine soap scent on his neck, from the intimate feel of a hard, warm torso against hers. At least he wore a pair of soft trousers beneath his robe.

He shrugged and returned the glass to the tray. His hand had moved down from the dip of her waist over her hip, and she was acutely aware of the proprietary splay of his fingers on her thigh.

His gaze glided to the flutter of her pulse in the side of her neck. The heat she found banking in the depths of his eyes burned through her courage as though it were paper. She may have made an anxious sound. He brushed a loose strand of hair back behind her ear, then lingered to caress the delicate spot below with his thumb.

"You know what is to happen between us?" he murmured.

His bluntness made her cheeks burn. "Yes." She was still uncertain what to do. She had decided to ignore Ruth Smythers's *Instructions and Advice for the Young Bride*.

Rough fingertips skated along the curve of her jaw, and the gentle friction against her soft skin sent sparks across her vision.

"You're very pretty," she heard him say, the words emerging clumsily and unpracticed. "In the church today . . . when I saw you, I thought you were the prettiest lass I'd ever seen."

She said the first coherent thing that came to mind: "My dress was ghastly."

He stroked her throat. "That so?"

"My mother," she said. "She chose it. She chooses all of my gowns."

"Have new ones made, then," he said. "The kind you like."

His warm hand curved around her nape.

"I should love a few new dresses," she said weakly. The way he was looking at her mouth, dark and intent, made her lips tingle with a phantom touch.

"Order as many as you want," he said, sounding amused. "But try to not mention your mother while we're in bed."

A nervous laugh burst from her. Was laughing allowed in bed? All thinking ceased when he leaned in and kissed her. His tongue lightly moved against hers, the sensation still so alien and intriguing, she held still to absorb it. So silky, so forbidden. His hands felt dangerously strong, but his mouth was soft. She tentatively matched his movements, and his grip on her thigh and neck tightened. It should have startled her, but a part of her liked it; she liked being held so firmly by him, but that, too, was confusing. The kiss slowly melted into another, and another, until a drugging heat sank through her lower body. Somehow, she was on her back, her head lolling in the crook of his arm while their tongues were sliding together. She was half-trapped beneath a heavy, muscled body, but he was intoxicatingly warm and solid, inviting her to cling to him. She didn't; she turned her face away, panting and with her lips sensitive and swollen. He lowered his head to her neck. The featherlight touch of his lips against her pulse point kindled a throb between her legs, an elemental beat that lulled her deeper into hazy stupor. Too late came the awareness that he had undone the bows down the front of her nightgown. His fingertips were grazing over bare skin. She stilled under his explorations, her languor fading. His hand shaped around the heavy round weight of her right breast, and he made a sound low in his throat. His eyes locked with hers. "I want to see you," he said hoarsely. "All right?"

She struggled to fill her lungs. *I advise you to please your husband . . .*

you can hasten it along by letting him look at you. . . . She hadn't wanted to hasten anything along a moment ago, adrift in the voluptuous sensations of his kisses. As the pause drew out, he seemed to sober, and focused on her face. "You want to wait?"

He meant waiting for all of it. His hand was still on her breast, and he probably hadn't planned to ask. She had thought about waiting, but then she had pictured herself wandering around the house in nervous anticipation and with little reward in the end. The truth was, when one's husband was such an unfortunate match, the passing of time would never transform him into the gentleman of her dreams. "No," she said. "I don't want to wait."

He sat up and shrugged out of his robe. She saw pale skin and sculpted muscle. Dark hair scattered across a powerful chest. It took her a moment to understand that the purple and silvery marks on his arms and abdomen were scars. When he turned his attention to undressing her, she closed her eyes. She kept them closed when cool air brushed her bare limbs. In the silence, she heard Lucian breathing harder, and her exposed skin prickled under the heat of his gaze. She had seen bodies like hers in prints of paintings they hid away from the ladies, scandalous works by Falero, for example, who painted his female nudes as lusty witches, with lushly rounded hips and thighs and bellies, and breasts too ample to suit fashion. The unabashed indulgence in feminine curves had enchanted her. Now that Lucian was studying her, a tiny voice amid ambivalence and breathlessness wondered whether he found her beautiful, too. . . . Her eyes popped open when he put his hand on her breast again. He plumped it up with a satisfied growl and dipped his head, and she felt the now familiar silky slickness of his tongue. Warmth flooded her middle and she squirmed. It seemed to encourage him; he used his teeth on the tip, biting gently, then he sucked, and she choked back a moan. He glanced up, his face looking fever flushed. Her nipple was stiff and glistening wet from his mouth. "Make noise if you want," he said.

Unsettled that he could read her when she knew nothing, she

pressed her lips together and only noticed when she saw Lucian frowning at her mouth.

He raised himself up on his elbow. "I don't know what you were told," he said slowly. "But you needn't be scared of me. I won't hurt you."

"I'm not scared of you," she said, truthfully, for what he did was arousing and done gently enough. And yet . . . "I'm uncertain," she guessed, "uncertain about all that is to happen, and how."

"I see," he said. "I . . ." He gave a small shake and began again. "You don't have to do anything. You can, if you want, but you don't have to."

He was absently stroking the soft underside of her breast with his thumb, as if he couldn't quite keep from touching her.

"And you," she murmured, "what will you do?"

His eyes darkened. "I'll lick your cunny in a moment and then I'll come to you."

"Lick me?" she repeated with a mindless stare.

"Well, here." He slid his broad hand down her stomach and rested it between her thighs.

"Oh no," she said quickly. "I wouldn't like that."

His brow furrowed. "How'd you know?"

Because she felt all sorts of emotions at the thought of his soft tongue on her most sensitive place and *like* was not one of them.

"I'd rather we just got on with it," she said.

Lucian stilled. Then he gave a shrug. "As you wish."

He rolled to his side and worked on his trousers, and she tried to keep her gaze averted, but of course, she looked. That was when matters began to go wrong. Something was wrong with him. Or with her. Sweat broke over the length of her body—he had lied; he would hurt her, because there was no part of her anatomy where he could safely put *that*.

He placed his knee between her thighs, and she reared up. "We . . . won't fit."

He looked bemused. "We will," he murmured, "trust me."

She flattened herself back into the mattress. Lucian palmed up her left calf and braced her knee back, and then both his strong thighs were between hers. *Trust me.* He glanced down at her cramped form, at how her fingers were gripping the coverlet.

"Put your hands on my shoulders," he said, and the low, steady timbre of his voice touched on something inside her. She obeyed. His skin was scorching against her palms, the strength of hard muscle and sinew beneath unyielding, and her limbs went strangely loose in response. *Trust me.* His face was tense above her. A stranger's face. And he was about to hurt her, and about to tie her to him. How on earth could she trust him? She felt blunt pressure at her entrance.

"No." She pushed back. "No."

"What?" His gaze was unfocused.

She dug in her nails. "I want to wait; I've changed my mind."

His expression blanked. "Now?"

"Yes."

He held himself above her, their bodies twin mirrors of frozen tension. Neither one of them blinked.

"Right," he said. He sat back on his heels, and the curves of his shoulders were peppered with sharp little white crescents—her nails had bit deep. He turned and faced the wall and locked his fingers behind his neck. A thin sheen of sweat gleamed on his back.

Hell. This was hell; a mortification more broiling hot than she'd ever felt. She had to watch her husband's shoulders rise and fall with uneven breaths, and when she made to speak, he shook his head before a word passed her lips. There was a flash of a very white, muscular bottom when he rose and pulled up his trousers. As he tied the belt of his robe, he glanced down at her, the hollows beneath his cheekbones deeply shadowed. She hid behind her hair, hoping to become invisible.

"I'll see you in the morning, then," he said, and dipped his head. "Good night."

He left through the door leading to the corridor and closed it behind him softly.

Her breath shuddered out of her. She did not inhale for a long moment. She almost wished he hadn't left; the silence filling the room was deafening and made the riot inside her head roar all the louder. She pressed her cold hands to her hot cheeks. There really was nothing to do in such a situation other than have a drink and a lie-down, was there? She took a glass from the tray and gulped the now flat champagne as if it were water. What a disaster of a wedding night. But she could have ogled every artful depiction of the male form and none of it could have prepared her for the chest hair and scars and certainly not his *thing*. Man's anatomy had certainly evolved since the glory days of Olympia. After a brief hesitation, she slid a hand between her legs. It felt slippery, as if her monthly courses had arrived. But no. She carefully poked inside, which she never did. No, not an obvious fit. Why then had she a creeping suspicion now that she might perhaps have reacted rather too dramatically? She put down the empty champagne glass and grabbed the full one.

When her head lay heavy and buzzing on the pillow, she admitted she hadn't just refused him for fear of being hurt. Her life had changed too quickly in ways she had never envisioned, and this now was her stubborn streak asserting itself, that indelible part of her that despite everything a woman was taught from the cradle, made her want to bend the world to fit her feelings rather than bend and bend herself until she fit whatever situation had been inflicted upon her. But now she had revealed that part to her husband. In a most delicate situation no less. It would be . . . interesting to face him come morning.

❧

No. Her rejection should have worked like a bucket of ice water over his head, but here he was, prowling along dark corridors overheated and with a raging cockstand. *No.* She was imprinted on his senses, on his tongue and his palms, salty sweet, arousing, velvet soft. Her *no* was a physical thing, too, jabbing away into his muscles, sharp like needles, and it eventually drove him toward his gymnastics room. He braced his forearms against the door, waiting and breathing while the sweat on his neck cooled. An inanimate sand sack wouldn't do right now. He needed a reaction, the bracing energy of an opponent. He gritted his teeth. Every single person of consequence in England knew he had married Harriet Greenfield today, and if he showed anywhere in London at this hour for a sparring, rumors about a piss-poor wedding night would spread like wildfire among the toffs.

He leaned his forehead against the smooth oak wood. It was his fault. Matters had gone to shit because he had done something he never did—he had dithered. But when he had first seen her on the bed, his mind had blanked. She had looked so fine, with her hair streaming over the pillows like ribbons of red silk. His wife. A visceral feeling had reared its head: *mine*. Followed right by: *not for you*. Like when he had first seen Rutland's estate looming from the mist, both desirable and antagonizing at once. And if he had learned one thing in life, it was whatever he wanted, whatever he needed, he had to take it. Unless he took, he went hungry. But his usual way didn't apply here. Instead, he had made a clueless attempt at tenderness. His hands clenched in frustration, and he went to the washroom for a cold shower.

He returned to his study a while later, frozen beneath his robe and in no better temper. He grabbed the book on flower language Matthews had brought him the day before: *Flower Lore*, written by a Miss Carruthers from Inverness. He flicked through the pages, skipping over chapters on monks and herbs and Ruskin waxing lyrically about filigree petals until he found the alphabetical overview at the very end. Apparently, red chrysanthemums communicated love. They both knew love wasn't a part of this, but she might appreciate the sentiment. Camellias stood for loveliness. Laurustinus, cheerfulness in adversity. Definitely would get a dozen of those. He was disgusted by his own sarcasm—he should be upstairs, tupping his wife to make the marriage contract count, not picking out flowers. He scribbled his selection down on a piece of paper and went to Matthews's rooms on the other side of the house, because it was only ten o'clock. The muffled, mournful melody of Matthews's traverse flute sounded behind his door when he knocked.

Matthews yanked the door open after a minute, still fully attired in an evening suit. He must have expected Nicolas or Tommy the lad, for his stance became submissive the moment he was aware who was in front of him. But as his gaze scurried quickly, furtively, over Lucian's robe and his damp hair, an emotion flared in his eyes. *Raging antipathy.* Odd.

"You were out?" Lucian asked.

A nod. "The opera. Puccini. Magnificent interpretation."

"Right; I need you to go to the hothouse flower traders in Covent Garden at dawn tomorrow," he said, and handed Matthews the folded paper. "Have her lady's maid make them into a bouquet, which she is to put into Mrs. Blackstone's chamber before she rises."

Matthews took the list without looking at it. "Will do, sir," he murmured. The room behind him was bright and golden from the light of two dozen candles. His flute glinted like a silver scepter on his desk.

"One day you you'll burn down the house," Lucian told him as he left.

Chapter 12

Harriet found him in his gymnastics room the next morning while he was busy pounding the sandbag to hell and back. He stopped punching the moment he noticed her, but his labored breathing was loud in the silence between them. The fierce blush rising above her collar was visible from across the room. Rather too flustered by the sight of a half-naked man, considering she had had his hand between her pretty thighs last night. He wiped his forearm across his brow and reluctantly reached for his shirtsleeves, which were draped over the ropes. His back and chest were hot and slick with sweat and the fine cotton garment stuck uncomfortably to his damp skin.

She hovered on the doorsill when he approached, clutching a flower to her breast.

"I came to thank you for the bouquet," she said, not quite meeting his eyes.

Ballentine had it right about the flowers, then—at least she was here and speaking to him rather than hiding in her rooms. She was still a far cry from the perky miss he had first known, and it grated on him alongside his unspent lust. How bloody little he had planned for this, the time and effort it would take to get used to a wife. Specifically, a high-society wife, raised to be absurdly modest when supposedly their main use was to bear plenty of heirs and spares—no logic in that. Harriet wasn't even cold. Last night she had said *no*, but she had been soft and wet, and presently she couldn't keep her eyes off him: her gaze snuck furtively over his shoulders and lingered on the places where his shirt clung. But he reckoned she wouldn't understand why she felt the urge to do so. She was twisting the flower stem between restless white fingers, and her neck was blotchy again.

"You looked very practiced in the ring," she said as she dragged her gaze from his biceps to his face. "Is pugilism a pastime of yours?"

"Yes."

"Is it how you broke your nose?"

"It was, yes."

If she'd ask him how exactly it had happened, he would tell her the truth: it had been a bare-knuckle match against a mean beast of an Irish fellow when he had still boxed for money. He'd make himself decent for her if he must, put on his shirt and such, but this morning, he had decided to give up any pretense at being more refined than he was, because who was he fooling? Right now, he was contemplating stealing a kiss from her, coarse and sweaty as he was—he found he enjoyed kissing her, and in her pale face, her rosy lips drew his attention as though she had painted them.

Her lashes lowered. "I hadn't meant to disturb your exercise," she said. "I shall leave."

"It's no trouble."

He glanced at the clock next to the door. It was surprisingly late, time for lunch soon. He took off his hand wraps and rolled them up, then he untied the leather string that held his hair in a knot at the back of his head. Harriet wasn't leaving; her eyes were following his movements intently, and it occurred to him that she was an artist and probably trained to be far more observant than a regular person. Something to keep in mind.

"Have you eaten lunch yet?" he asked.

Her smile was apologetic. "I had a light breakfast just now."

"You're a late sleeper." It shouldn't surprise him—he'd gleaned that ladies often had a habit of sleeping until noon.

"I am," she said. "I tend to work late and loathe rising early. Do you mind?"

"Nah." An ill-rested woman across the table was hardly a useful addition to his morning, was it? "But I'm taking lunch in the East End at half past twelve," he said. "Accompany me."

She hesitated. "Of course."

Her unenthusiastic acceptance rankled, but he'd take it. He wasn't a patient man, but he knew a thing or two about biding his time.

She was less reserved by the time the carriage pulled into sunny Shoreditch an hour later. "This is far more exciting than the West End," she said, her nose near touching the window glass. Music halls lined the street outside, shoulder to shoulder with colorfully painted coffeehouses, minor theaters, and the few remaining luxury furniture stores in the area, all wrestling for attention from reveling crowds with flags and boldly lettered signs.

"It's the livelier district," he said. "Renowned, too. The National Standard Theatre, which we'll reach in a moment, is one of the largest theaters in London."

"I heard." She turned to him. "Do you enjoy the theater?" Her tone was polite. She'd be making conversation at formal events with newly introduced gentlemen this way.

"No," he said. "Nor the opera," he added to preempt the next question.

She didn't appear rebuffed as much as curious. "Why not?"

He considered it. "I haven't the habit of it," he then said. "One does not need a habit of enjoying unintelligible singing for hours when the same hours could be used in better ways."

"For creating a stock portfolio, I imagine," she said. Was that sarcasm in her tone?

Not for the first time since she had taken her place across the footwell, he caught himself staring at her. It was because her scent filled the small space, burnt vanilla instead of roses today, and every time she moved, it teased his nose and made him look at her. Pink mouth and chocolate eyes. The red curls framing her face bounced whenever the carriage rattled over a rough patch. She had pinned one of the flowers from his bouquet to her bodice, not quite over her heart but not just to the emotionally neutral front, either. Diplomatically adept, his wife.

"Stock portfolios," he finally said. "Among other things, yes."

She smiled slightly. "You sound quite like my brother Zachary," she said. He remembered young Greenfield and his outrage when the marriage deal had been agreed, and he remained silent.

"I'm wondering," she said, "I'm wondering how you obtain the information required to invest as successfully as you do if you keep to yourself so much."

He met her inquisitive look with an ironic one. "I do interact with other men of business, you know."

"I wouldn't know," she replied. "Your name might be in many mouths, but it is rarely in the papers."

"People prefer to keep silent about my participation in their ventures, until recently at least," he said. "So I use aliases for doing business or let my intermediaries handle matters. And a lot of the intelligence I piece together by myself."

"By reading *The Economist*?"

"*The Economist* and trade and science journals," he said. "And by analyzing data from merchant tables and government blue books. Then I extrapolate." He realized he was rubbing his neck as he spoke. Reading for hours made his back feel as if he'd done a shift underground. His body, and his temperament, were more suited for physical labor in any case, but here he was, building his wealth and power on . . . reading. The irony of that was never lost on him. "As for the stock markets, there's no impartial balance sheet," he said. "There's no rule of law, no inevitable logic that governs a stock price; they are beasts, and they'll lash out at you after long periods of pretending normalcy."

She nodded along. "My family has heated debates about the very morality of stock investments."

"And in the meantime, they make profitable use of them."

"What does your regular day look like?" she asked, unperturbed. "I know you rise early and begin with, erm, exercise. What next?"

He said aloud what crossed his mind: "You're very curious."

"I'm afraid so," she murmured, and glanced down at her hands.

"As you said, I rise early," he said, wanting to keep her engaged. "I exercise. Then I read the papers and take note whether there are new companies forming, any consortiums advertising for an investor, or troubles brewing for supply chains. I read my correspondence"—including any information supplied by his spies in various industries and the demimonde—"and I read the analyses from the men I hire to read the trade journals that I can't fit in. Then I make portfolio decisions."

"Where to expand, where to consolidate, where to wait and see?" she singsonged, as though she had heard it all before. Probably at her family's infamous dining table.

He had never envisioned a wife who understood his business dealings. Admittedly, it was a practical thing as far as having a conversation was concerned.

"Then I meet men of business for lunch," he said. "Men who work in iron, or cotton, or mining." Or the lieutenants of shady figures from the art-dealing world, but that was none of her concern. "Probably once a week I travel to some stock exchange city in the Home Counties to tap local information sources," he said instead. "And I visit my factories."

She looked impressed. "I hadn't realized you were so actively pursuing entrepreneurship, too."

"I need to put the money somewhere," he said. "And it makes sense to own ironworks, which are fueled with coal from my mines, which produce railroad tracks and cars for the railway companies where I have shares. I spend a good deal of my time integrating and eventually splitting businesses again." And before she could prod some more, he added, "And, in my evenings, I read the newspaper sections and government white books on economic policies."

Her ears seemed to prick up. "You have an interest in politics?"

"You can't separate business from politics," he said evasively.

"The Duke of Montgomery will introduce an amendment to the Married Women's Property Act in a while," she supplied.

"Ah," he said. "They try that every few years, don't they?"

"Would you say you oppose women's suffrage?" Her neutral expression was fairly convincing, but he knew she ran with the suffragists. His man, Carson, had reported it after investigating her background in Oxford, and he hadn't been surprised at all.

"I don't oppose it, no," he said. "I haven't given the matter much thought."

She failed to hide her disappointment over the latter statement, and he felt the sudden need to loosen his cravat.

"Well, you work a lot," she said. "Perhaps too much?"

He scoffed. "Nah."

"What do you like to do for pleasure, then?"

He gave her a wry look, and when the meaning seemed lost on her, he said, resigned: "Stock portfolios."

She shook her head. "You do work too much."

"Is it work when one enjoys it?" he asked. "I would have thought as a paintress, you'd understand."

Her expression became serious. "I paint because it feels like a necessity," she said. "It can be enjoyable, but it is more a matter of it becoming unbearable when I don't do it."

"Unbearable?"

"It's an urge," she said. "Colors and patterns have an effect on me; it's as though they stimulate my appetite, for lack of a better word. If

I don't engage, it begins to feel like a living thing beneath my skin. Well, I suppose that sounds hysterical—I assure you I'm not. Unfortunately, I'm not nearly as consumed by my art as I should be."

"Should you be?"

She nodded. "I have this notion that proper artists are servants to their inspiration and must constantly create, whereas The Urge aside, I experience long, dull, uninspired stretches and must be disciplined to complete my works. Sometimes, I wonder whether this makes me an imposter. . . ." She stopped herself, seeming to remember whom she was speaking to, and he felt a pang of annoyance. He understood, he did—the urge to strategize his portfolios and maximize profits was a compulsion, too, *alive beneath his skin*, as she'd put it.

"You changed your perfume," he said instead.

She shot him a quick glance. "Do you mind?"

"No." He did mind; she smelled delicious, and he wanted to reach across and pull her onto his lap. Then kiss her. Then fondle her lush breasts. Perhaps put a hand up under her thick skirts to finger the soft skin at the back of her knees, and move up to the softer place between her legs until she was moaning against his neck.

"My mother insisted I wear the rose scent," she said. "But I prefer this."

Her brother, her mother. It proper quelled his surging arousal.

She seemed to enjoy the restaurant; she was still studying her surroundings with keen eyes after the waiter had seated them in his private booth. The first time he had lunched here, he had been reluctantly impressed by the décor, too. The domed ceiling was painted in a fancy white-and-gold pattern, while the large potted fig trees and creeping ivy added a rustic touch. The air was fragrant with the scent of French herbs and spices from the subcontinent. Harriet's family must visit the same old places in Soho if the atmosphere here excited her so. Perhaps she was simply excitable.

"Why do you favor this restaurant?" she asked as she tugged off her gloves. "It's far from Belgravia."

"It serves the best rice and curry dishes," he replied. "The head chef and co-owner is from Gujarat."

She smiled. "Do you prefer your foods sweet or spicy?"

He looked her in the eye. "Sweet. Why?"

"Knowing your preferences would help me with the meal plan."

"Meal plan," he repeated, confounded.

She tilted her head. "For your cook? He keeps a tidy kitchen, but the pantry looked a little bare this morning."

"Right." In any regular household, wives were indeed in charge of the weekly meal planning. He felt oddly relieved when a waiter approached him with the menu.

"Want to take a look yourself?" he offered when he noticed Harriet peering at the menu across the table, and her eyes brightened.

"Yes, please."

He hadn't just offered to indulge her independent streak. In loftier London restaurants the menu was invariably written in French, which was the bane of his lunch experiences, for he didn't speak French, nor had he the time to study it. It had made for some terrible surprises when he had chosen blindly in the past; best to stick to the dishes he knew he enjoyed.

"It seems that except for select Gujarati cuisine, all the dishes are French," Harriet remarked.

"You've no trouble with foreign languages, then, or with reading?"

She glanced up, wariness shimmering in her eyes. "Reading poses no problem."

"What is the problem?"

It was bad conduct to mention her impairment, but he did want to understand it.

"The trouble is the writing," Harriet said. "Even if I were to copy the same lines I just read, I'll likely make an error. The same applies to rows of figures." She gave a one-shouldered shrug. "I don't know why. Words that are spelled similarly apparently look the same to me. Some letters dance."

"Dance?" he said, baffled.

"Yes. Some are more agile than others." She slid the menu toward him. "The baked goat cheese with the pear chutney, please."

Her smile was overbright, like the too-white brilliance of a false diamond. Her affliction troubled her.

"You're up at Oxford," he said, feeling an urge to make it better. "Your brain won you a place, unless that was bought and paid for."

"You can't buy a place at Oxford," she said indignantly.

"So you convinced Ruskin. He's no fool."

Her false smile turned sarcastic.

"You think he's a fool?" he asked.

The waiter returned to take their orders and pour some white wine.

Harriet enjoyed a few sips before returning to his question. "Ruskin is no fool," she said. "He is a titan in the art world, and I idolized him long before I made his personal acquaintance. I first met him for my admission interview, in his office, and he rose from his chair and said, 'Ah, but you look too lovely to be clever.'"

Even he could tell that this was a shite compliment. "Badly done," he said.

"Men say such things frequently, so I'm quite inured," Harriet said, her cheeks turning rosy from the wine. Her skin hid nothing, one of several things that intrigued him about her. "Except that in my family," she continued, "I was the Lovely One. Flossie and Mina were the Bright Ones. I thought it was perfectly fine to be lovely, until Ruskin made me think it was a synonym for *silly.* . . ." She interrupted herself, just like she had earlier in the carriage. Remembering that she didn't trust him yet. Perhaps she never would.

"The male students," he asked. "How do they treat you?"

"Oh, they were rather excited about the female cohort," came the vague reply.

His gaze narrowed. "They bother you?"

She shifted on her seat. "No."

"Not at all? No comments, no staring?"

"Well, sometimes. When I visit one of their lecture halls. Or pass them by on the street. Or bump into them in Blackwell's or the Bodleian. But the naughty comments, they usually say in Latin. Which, admittedly, I understand well enough."

Floppy-haired, pompous little twats. "I see," he muttered, feeling the tension in his face.

Harriet looked alarmed. "You said you wouldn't object to my studies," she said.

"I don't," he replied. "I'll introduce you to Carson later today—your new protection officer."

Her face fell.

"Do you know what happened to your old officer?" he prodded.

She avoided his gaze, as if embarrassed. "I asked my father to write him a reference," she finally said. "I understand he returned to work for the Metropolitan Police."

That had been the decent thing to do, give him a reference, though in his opinion her officer deserved to be fired for his poor performance.

She looked subdued behind her wineglass, so he changed the topic.

"The house," he said. "Is it to your liking?"

She gave a polite nod. "It is, yes."

"Make changes, if you want."

"Thank you." She put down her glass. "May I ask why you don't keep any staff?"

She had noted the absence of regular staff last evening and, to her credit, hadn't fainted.

"Cook and Tommy the lad weren't to your liking?" he asked, for he did keep *some* staff.

"No, they seemed decent," she said quickly, "though Tommy seemed rather young."

"He's twelve," Lucian said. "Old enough. I'll employ a girl to tend to the fire in your rooms but thought you might want to choose her."

"I would, thank you," she said. "But what of a butler? A valet, a housekeeper? Parlormaids? Footmen? Grooms?"

"I've no need for them. I use few rooms, I prefer to dress and shave myself, and I value privacy over convenience." Besides, he hadn't been born into the habit of perceiving other humans as part of the inventory as long as they wore a uniform, and he didn't care for feeling surrounded by crowds. Harriet looked a little nervous, unsurprisingly. The new etiquette book for gentlemen on his nightstand had reminded him that upper-class rules were plentiful and specific. Harriet probably knew the type of velvet a woman was allowed for trimming the lapels of such and such a jacket and all the various ways of how to properly sign off a letter depending on the recipient, and by those standards, his household was barbaric.

"I assume Mr. Matthews is your man of all work, then?" she said.

"Of sorts."

"He plays the flute," she said. "I heard him last evening, and again this morning."

He supposed he'd have to hire more staff so she could organize social events at his house, and he loathed it already. Perhaps he should give her a house just for holding dinners and the like. Then again, making nice with society had been the plan all along. "You'll find he plays obsessively," he said. "Matthews."

"He plays very well," she replied. "He must have enjoyed an excellent musical education. How did he come to work for you?"

He did not, for a while, understand why he told her the truth that moment. "He was in debtors' prison when I found him."

She looked intrigued rather than shocked. "Why?"

"Because he has a gambling problem. Might explain his obsession with his flute," he added. "Obsessive minds tend to obsess about more than one thing."

"I meant why would you recruit your closest assistant from the jail?" she whispered.

"Leverage," he replied. "My assistant knows more about my affairs than any other man in London. Matthews won't blab."

"And how long has he been in your employ?" Her expression was troubled now.

"Three years."

She'd be proper shocked if he told her he had bailed out Matthews specifically because he had been in Rutland's employ as his secretary. A source had alerted Lucian that Rutland had left the man to rot. The information about Rutland's business affairs and weak spots he had squeezed from Matthews during his first week of unexpected freedom had been worth its weight in gold.

Their meals were served, and Harriet ate in contemplative silence while he watched her between his own bites like a lecher. He couldn't help it; she handled her cutlery with an innate lazy gracefulness that a part of him found hopelessly mesmerizing. Perhaps sensing the turn of his mind, Harriet attempted more conversation.

"Why aren't you in New York?" she asked. "I understand the New York Stock Exchange is vastly more developed than the London Stock Exchange."

"It is."

"Is it true that Americans are more appreciative of self-made men?"

"Americans don't care where the money comes from as long as there's lots of it," he confirmed. "So society in New York invented other criteria to create hierarchies—how far back one's ancestors arrived to make their land grab, for one."

She waggled her tawny eyebrows. "I noticed the number of dollar princesses invading London determined to marry a title for prestige grows by the year."

"You mind?"

"I don't mind it at all," she said with a shrug. "But it does strike me as wanting your revolutionary cake and eating it, too."

"Old King George is rollin' in his grave," he agreed, and her small burst of almost laughter nearly made him smile. He felt compelled to look at his plate while her gaze shied to her lap. A strange thought occurred to him as he watched her from beneath his lashes: that he had enjoyed this lunch. An unfamiliar lightness, an ease, had filled his chest throughout. He wondered whether she felt the same. Unlikely. The table separating them was small and yet the distance between them was still palpable. She was like one of her precious artifacts, on display but beyond his touch behind an invisible barrier. His usual course of action was to break whatever blocked his path. *The usual way did not apply.* He needed a tactic. She had already told him what she wanted in the Blue Parlor: to build her own world with a friend. Well, he wasn't the man for that. She was shiny and preoccupied with colors; he had breathed and ingested darkness, had stared at it for so long it had begun to stare back into him. Darkness was a part of him now, encrusted in his soul like coal dust in a miner's skin. But for the last half hour, he had had a glimpse beyond the veil, what it could have been like, and it left him thinking he needed a tactic.

⁓⤫⁓

Her first day as a married woman had slipped into evening, and beneath the quiet of the Belgravia house, tension began to simmer in step with the sinking sun. Another wedding night was looming. Presently, Lucian was ensconced in his study—after he had introduced her new protection officer, a Mr. Carson. Mr. Carson's head was bald and shiny as a billiard ball, and he was larger and certainly meaner than Mr. Graves. She dared not ask in which jail Lucian had found *him*. Safe to say, it would be nigh impossible to run from Carson.

She spent an hour lolling around on her plush new bed, trying to absorb the contents of the new *Woman's Suffrage Journal*, but her focus was too scattered. She wasn't well on her own these days, and had to yet write to her friends. She finally closed the periodical and decided to visit Lucian's private chambers. After the terrible awkwardness last night, she hadn't expected a thoughtful bouquet this morning. Nor a pleasant lunch. Perhaps her husband was hiding other, promising things.

She inched open the connecting double doors and felt pleasantly surprised. His bedchamber exuded warm elegance, with rich shades of burgundy, navy blue, and dark woodworks.

She slipped inside quickly.

In contrast to the rest of the house, the décor here was sparse: an armchair in cognac leather next to the fireplace, a secretary against the wall, a large wooden chest with metal fittings at the foot of the bed. The bed was vast and square and covered by a tartan blanket patterned in earthy browns and greens. The MacKenzie tartan? Looking at the bed made her feel shy, so she moved on to a side door. His walk-in wardrobe. It was spacious and neatly organized: glossy cherrywood shelving from floor to ceiling and an armchair at the center. The lingering fragrance of his shaving soap drew her deeper into the small room. She trailed a fingertip over silken waistcoats. She stuck her nose amid the freshly starched shirts and inhaled. He might not have been her choice of husband, but she would bottle his scent if she could. She pulled out drawers and paused when she found his braces rolled up in neat coils. On impulse, she grabbed a pair and stuffed it into her skirt pocket, but the moment her loot had been securely stashed she felt like a terrible intruder. Her heartbeat picked up as she slid the drawer soundlessly back into place, and she hurried out the door. She screeched like a loon, for Lucian stood next to the bed.

"Good evening." His tone was mild but his gaze was coolly assessing.

"Mr. Blackstone," she said.

He approached, and now her heart was pounding at double speed. He halted with his toes an inch from hers, his expression opaque. "What were you doing?"

She had been in his wardrobe, sniffing his shirts.

"I wanted to see where you sleep," she said. As if that was a less disturbing explanation.

His eyes narrowed slightly. "Why do you want to see where I sleep?"

The beginnings of a beard shadowed his cheeks and jawline. This morning, in his exercise room, he had been perfectly clean-shaven, and it crossed her mind that he must have shaved last night, just before coming to her bed, for his face had felt smooth against hers. . . .

She gave a nervous cough. "I wished to become more closely acquainted with you."

"By . . . looking at my room," he said. "When I'm not in it."

"It does sound rather silly when one says it out loud."

His shoulders relaxed and his eyes were warming. "Learned anything interesting?"

Her wits scrambled. "You hold Scotland close to your heart?" She nodded at the tartan counterpane.

He looked at the bed, then back at her. His eyes were hot. Her heart dropped to her belly.

"You know," he said casually, "there are more expedient ways to become acquainted with one another than snooping through a wardrobe."

"Expedient," she echoed.

He cupped her face in his palm, and feverish heat swept over her skin. His gaze sank into hers while he lightly traced her cheekbone with the pad of his thumb, back and forth, with a deliberate, mesmerizing languor that rendered her mute. Taking her stillness as acquiescence, he slowly slid his other arm around her waist and leaned down. Stubble whispered across her cheek. Her nose was against the warm skin of his neck, right against the source of his delicious scent. Lucian made a low groan when his mouth found the bare inch of her throat above her collar. His fingers delved into her hair and he carefully angled her head back, then she felt the fluid strokes of his tongue below her ear. She sagged against him, her legs turning liquid, and Lucian's hold on her tightened. The solid feel of his chest caused the tips of her breasts to ache with pleasure. She arched into him, seeking relief, as if a reckless woman had slipped into her skin and enjoyed his attentions. He raised his head. His eyes were hazy, and the brush of his breath across her lips made them sensitive. *Kiss me*, she thought. He complied. She felt the flick of his tongue against her mouth like a touch much farther down, and a tiny moan escaped her. He pushed his tongue in deeper, and the embrace lost its restraint. Her hands roamed over hard shoulders and up into thick curls. Her nipples were chafing against the delicate chemise, and as if Lucian knew, his hand slid down to her chest and squeezed. She sighed, and when his thigh pressed between hers through the thickness of her skirts, it felt glorious. Until the edge of the bed bumped against the back of her legs. She broke the kiss and cast an apprehensive look around. They had crossed half the room while locked in each other's arms. She had been as absorbed in his kisses as she became lost in a painting.

She glanced back up at him and found his eyes were black with his pupils dilated to the size of pennies. This was the tipping point, the second between remaining upright and lying down on a bed. For a heartbeat, she saw herself giving over to him, a man she barely knew. Saw herself lying skin to skin with him, his strong body mov-

ing over hers as she cradled his hips with her thighs. . . . She shrank
from him. She wasn't ready, she just was not.

"I'm indisposed," she said, avoiding his eyes.

A quietness came over him. He knew she was fibbing. She didn't
know why she had done it; she must have panicked.

"Why not rest, then," he suggested.

"Yes," she said quickly. "It's late."

They both glanced at the rectangle of afternoon light stretching
brightly across the floor.

When she walked past him, he caught her hand. His gaze was
steady in a way that made her a little breathless. "You needn't lie to
me, you know," he murmured. "I know when you do, anyway. Just
say no."

Heat crept up her nape. He called it lying, when she and every
normal person in London would have called it politely excusing one-
self.

Back in her room, she wandered in circles, wishing Lucian would
heed the unwritten rules that allowed women to safely withdraw
from situations rather than demand that she bare her private thoughts
to him. It made her feel both like a coward and a little rebellious. Her
thoughts were her own; he should not pry. But he wasn't wrong—
honesty was a virtue. Still, *no* was a difficult word when it had to be
said in cold blood. Besides, he confused her deeply. She obviously
enjoyed his kisses, but she also had no notion who she was when in
reaction to his presence. This morning, when witnessing him thrash
his boxing bag into oblivion, she had been alarmed by the raw violence that had guided his punches, realizing that her husband could
kill other men with his bare hands. It troubled her. It had also, per-
versely, enthralled her a little, and that troubled her most of all. She
had thought of herself as impulsive, a free spirit, and yes, a bit of a
coquette. But not as *base*. Not as a wanton filled with *pitiful urges*.
And in the end, none of her compunctions mattered, because sooner
or later, she would have to let him in.

Chapter 13

He sat in the drawing room unshaven, reading the same parliamentary minutes on the Customs and Inland Revenue Act for the third time when Aoife walked in. She must have entered the house with her key, for Matthews was given leave on Mondays. More significantly, her narrow face looked troubled when few things short of murder troubled Aoife, if that. He came to his feet right quick.

"I need a drink," she snapped.

She looked unharmed; her movements were fluid. But she had carelessly plopped a hat atop her cropped hair rather than bother with pinning a braid to the back of her head. Definitely trouble.

"Could you make it a double? That would be charming," she said when he went to the drinks sideboard to select a Scotch. She took the glass from his hand as she paced past with a murmured thanks, and then she said, "My house has been ransacked."

Ransacked. Hell. "Are you all right?" he asked sharply.

She gave a dismissive wave. "Wasn't home. I was at the music hall with Susan and then stayed at hers. When I returned this morning, I found chaos. So it must've happened between eight o'clock last night and nine o'clock this morning."

It was ten o'clock now; she had come straight to him. "How bad is it?"

She half emptied her tumbler with one gulp and grimaced. "In terms of what's been stolen, too soon to tell," she said, "though all the rings and cuff links I kept on my vanity table are definitely gone." She chopped at an imaginary neck with her hand. "Susan gifted me some of these pieces, and I want them back. In terms of damage, now, this is where it's interesting."

"Interesting how?"

"There's two types of break-ins, isn't there: either the place gets smashed up, or it's done on cat's paws and you won't notice until days after the fact. But this—this was a strange one. Looked as though they started out carefully—just delicately sniffing around hoping I'd never know—but then they thought, *Hold on, a proper burglary needs some chaos*. So they knocked over a few lamps and vases and broke open my desk drawers. But the scattering, and the way things were knocked over, was odd. Oddly halfhearted, like an afterthought. I s'pose if I wasn't used to seeing properly burgled places, it wouldn't have looked so off, but to my eyes it was off."

"Could have been a distraction done by an amateur," Lucian murmured, "or someone wanting to appear amateurish. Where was your doorman?"

"In bed, sickly. Makes me think the house has been watched." She finished her drink and returned to him for more since he was still holding the bottle.

"You have anything that could be of particular interest to anyone?" he asked while he poured.

"Always," she said. "But I haven't had any trouble for years. I'm on no one's side, neutral ground. Whoever pays gets information from me. And now this is what I get."

Her anger was palpable. Like him, she was attached to her shiny objects and the absolute privacy of her home.

"I'll put a man on the case," he said.

He sensed the wariness in her sideways glance. "Police?"

"No. Carson."

"Thank Christ," Aoife said. "The peelers make me nervous. Luke, I was wondering if they might've been after something of yours."

He paused with his own tumbler halfway to his mouth. "What makes you think so?"

"Don't bloody know," she said, and shrugged, "just a hunch. Seems odd that it comes right at the heels of your wedding, which was all over the news."

The list of people who knew of their connection beyond that of an informant-client relationship was short; they both diligently protected their relationship from the shadow world. Still, he considered his potential adversaries: the lords who owed him, the crooked art dealers or fellows from Scotland Yard who wanted artifacts in his possession, disgruntled figures from the past he had blackmailed or otherwise harmed . . . none of them a plausible suspect. But not impossible. The murkiness of the situation added fuel to his already simmering frustration, and he set the bottle down too hard. A jade figurine on the other end of the sideboard was shaken off balance, and he had to watch it topple into a crystal decanter and push the decanter over the edge. It smashed apart on the tiles with a terrific noise. He cursed.

Aoife was watching him with growing intrigue. "Why, you're in a mood. It's not all that bad—probably just a regular burglary."

The burglary alone wasn't making him tetchy. "Use my house in Richmond if you'd rather not stay at your current address," he said.

She righted the nearest figurine on the sideboard with deliberate care. "You looked grim when I walked in and hadn't yet opened my mouth. I've a feeling your mood has not all to do with the ransacking."

She was too perceptive. It happened when one's senses had been honed to cutlass precision on the grindstones of the gutter; survival on the street depended on quickly and correctly classing the mad, the bad, the drunkards, and the harmless, even from afar. He remembered there had been a time when Aoife and he had been friends—well, urchins, sharing the same dreary fate during the day and warmth on a pallet at night.

"Aoife."

"Yes?"

"You're a woman."

Her brows rose. "I'm so excited to learn where you're taking this."

He gave a shake, wondering what had possessed him. "Forget I asked."

"Oh, come now."

"It's nothing."

"Trouble with the lady wife?"

"No." Said too fast.

She cocked her head, a sarcastic glint in her eyes.

"Aye," he muttered.

"Well." Delight filled her voice. "I'm all ears."

The words appeared to be stuck at the back of his throat like a fishbone, going neither forward nor back down. "She's not . . . keen," he finally said.

"Keen?"

"Keen on . . ." Astonishingly, getting punched in the sternum felt less excruciating than saying such things out loud. "Never mind."

"Keen . . . ooh. I see." She cackled, all witchlike.

Hot irritation surged through him.

"Keen," Aoife repeated, and crossed her arms over her chest. "You sound like a doctor for female ailments, trying to make it sound all flowery and nice. Keen," she crooned, "why not say *fucking*? Normally, you would've. Interesting."

He realized he was grinding his molars. "What of it?"

"It's interesting, that's all. I thought the marriage business was just a means to an end—"

"It is, but the ends aren't being achieved."

Aoife pursed her lips. "Perhaps she's scared of you."

Scared? She had been chatty enough all day yesterday. She had come to his bedroom. But yes, then she had hared off again rather than finish what they had started. . . .

"I told her she needn't be scared," he said.

"I swoon," Aoife replied dryly. "Well, I never even seen her. How can I know her reasons? I do know you've known how to do your *duties* since you were a lad, and there was happy sighs when the girls talked, not complaints—"

"She's different," he cut her off.

"Different?" Aoife said, sounding hostile now. "Like how? She has gills? Wings? A mermaid's tail?"

Close enough. She had never lifted a finger for any of the meals she ate. She didn't brush her own hair. She was considerably more intelligent than experienced, which made her opining pretentious, and she made him feel brutish just by standing next to him so utterly self-possessed in her ignorance and ruffled gowns. He had known who he was and what he wanted for over a decade, which allowed him to be in charge just as he liked it, and now he was ambushed by second guesses and thoughts he hadn't expected himself capable of thinking. That bothered him more than her reluctance.

"What you mean is that she's a lady," Aoife said derisively. "But I've heard you've knocked knees with those before."

"They sought me out for so-called depravity."

"Perhaps that would be to her liking, too."

Ah yes, he thought, *because new brides crave to be bent over a divan and get their arses paddled.*

"I've known a few mistresses in my time," Aoife said, "and what I heard again and again is that gentlemen rut like beasts because they think they can't inflict it on the wives. Meanwhile, perhaps it's their wives knocking on your door?"

"How is this supposed to help?" he asked, incredulous.

"I don't know," she admitted. "I'm just always tickled when man's division of women into frigid wives and lusty whores slaps them right back in the face."

He growled. "Your advice is right shite."

"All right," she said, sensing that she was pushing him too far.

She put down her glass on the sideboard—gently—and came to him. Lucian watched with a furrowed brow as she took his hand and turned it over.

"I bet you've not lifted crates or broken heads with these in a while," she murmured as she studied his palm. "And yet, they are still so strong." She glanced up. "At the back of her mind, a woman knows she's at the mercy of how well the menfolk in her life can control their hands, Luke. And you have the hands of a brawler."

He pulled the offending extremity from her grasp. "I don't beat women."

"And how would she know, hmm? And perhaps you've been rough and not noticed? Men too often grab a woman the way they themselves want to be touched—stupid. Her skin is so much softer." She raised a hand to his face and he allowed it, only for her to slowly drag a gloved fingertip along his jaw to the rasping sound of stubble against kid leather.

"So whenever you think your touch is light," Aoife murmured, "make it lighter still. . . ." Her voice trailed off. Her gaze focused past him, in the direction of the door behind him, and she withdrew her hand from his face.

He turned. His wife had entered the room, her face more sour than spoiled milk.

Chapter 14

Two days. It had taken Lucian two days to break his word and turn to another woman. And he had invited her into their home. In bright daylight. It made no sense, but there were few other logical explanations for the caress she had just witnessed, and so she stood as if glued to the spot and stared. The woman wasn't good society, and her hair was short and mousy, and the coiled tension in her slender body evoked a spring ready to launch. She still exuded a particular sensuality; it was in the worldly way she angled her chin, in the leisurely, confident manner in which she had dragged her fingertip along Lucian's jaw. She was immediately enviable—Hattie could see her gracing one of her canvases as a heroine. Under other circumstances. She heard her teeth press together. Her stomach was burning with a violent emotion.

"Mrs. Blackstone," Lucian said, and she knew the look on his face: impersonal, aloof—her father used it on her mother when they had company.

"I heard something crash." Her voice had come out feebly. She didn't acknowledge his guest, as the correct course of action was to pretend mistresses did not exist, but she felt the woman's assessment prickle over her skin, and the heat in her veins surged like the tide of a fiery sea. Even a merely vaguely caring husband would exercise discretion. To think she had begun embroidering his braces with Scottish thistles last night . . . Her throat tightened.

"It was an accident," Lucian said. "Don't trouble yourself." He beckoned with his hand. "Allow me to introduce Miss Byrne."

"No." It shot out of her mouth quickly, like a bullet. His face froze. As they measured each other across the room, the air between them quivered like some creature in its death rattle.

The woman made as though to place a hand on Lucian's arm but seemed to think better of it and stepped back. "I take my leave," she announced.

Hattie avoided looking at her when she approached. Still, she saw it, that the woman moved with a slight swagger rather than a sway, and that the corner of her mouth turned up in the tiniest of smirks when she walked past. Then she was gone, leaving a cloud of ambergris and tobacco hanging in her wake.

Lucian's footfall was heavy on the tiles, and her pulse stuttered. She tried ignoring him, too, but he planted himself right in front of her and stood as immovable as a brick wall until she reluctantly met his gaze.

"What was the meaning of this?" he demanded, thunder in his eyes.

He was angry. Immediately, she felt nauseous. "I'm not obliged to acknowledge such a thing," she whispered.

"A thing," Lucian said quietly. "What thing?"

"Your . . . your liaisons."

His face was blank with disbelief. "Since you're not stupid, you can't possibly think that I would introduce you to a side piece," he said, "so forgive me if I assumed you were rude to my friend on purpose."

Stupid. She sucked in a breath. Very well, perhaps she had jumped to conclusions, but his brazen *friend's* feelings were presently his concern? She clasped a hand over her belly. "Unless she is your mother, sister, or cousin, in which case I'm terribly sorry for refusing an introduction, I'm quite certain I'm not obliged to acknowledge an unacquainted woman who is fondling you in my drawing room," she said primly.

"*Your* drawing room," he repeated, amazed.

Apparently, he didn't even regard her as the mistress of the house. Her ears glowed with humiliation. "Insofar as the drawing room is a private area of the home, and usually the wife's area," she muttered. "Which requires any *decent* visitor to at least announce themselves to the wife before they enter it."

The flash of displeasure in Lucian's gaze said he didn't appreciate the lecture on domestic protocol. He leaned down until his nose nearly touched hers. "And as your husband," he said softly, "I won't tolerate you acting like a snooty brat when we have company—even if you think they're beneath you."

His voice was cold. His eyes were colder. She stared into the gray depths thinking the soul behind might well be an arctic desert, hostile to anyone who had made the mistake of daring a foray. Last night, she had fallen asleep wearing the pendant he had gifted her between her breasts and a spark of hope inside her chest. She had slept well for the first time since the calamity in the gallery. *Snooty brat*. He did not like her much at all. Except, and she realized this now, except when he was trying to seduce her into sharing his bed.

"I would like to take to my room," she said shakily.

His gaze searched hers right down to her bones, and whatever he saw made him step back. He speared five exasperate fingers through his hair. "All right. Go, then."

She left with enough verve to make her heels slip on the floor. Halfway across the entrance hall, she abruptly turned left into the corridor leading to the back entrance. The correct procedure would be to ring the bell next to the door and ask Nicolas to please ready the carriage, then call for Carson. Next, Lucian would notice she was absconding, and he would probably put a stop to it. With a quick glance back over her shoulder, she opened the door and bolted into the courtyard. She banged her elbow on the doorframe on the way out, and the dull ache was still pulsing through her arm long after she had left Belgravia behind.

It took her nearly an hour to arrive at the sleek granite façade of London Print at number thirty-five Bedford Street. Both the white-haired receptionist in the lobby and the page boy operating the lift knew her as a friend of the owners of the house, hence they did not dare notice that she was hatless, gloveless, panting, and unsuccessfully trying to hide a limp. Limp notwithstanding, she hurried from the lift to the director's apartment, for in the unlikely event that Lucie had returned from Italy, she would be in the apartment during lunchtime rather than her office. She had so little hope to find her friend, she burst into the room without knocking.

"Oh dear," she gasped, and squeezed her eyes shut. Lucie was here, behind the desk, breaking from a passionate embrace with a tall, red-haired man.

"I apologize—"

"Hattie!" For a beat, it looked as though Lucie considered vaulting over the desk, then she rushed around it instead and flew across the room. She clasped Hattie's hands in a grip surprisingly firm for her delicate frame. Behind her, Lord Ballentine was leisurely straightening his cuffs and cravat.

"My dear," Lucie said, her eyes searching Hattie's with concern, "how do you do?"

Hattie's gaze flicked to Lord Ballentine, who turned to her and dipped his head. "Mrs. Blackstone."

Her stomach gave a tiny lurch, the inevitable effect of the viscount's symmetric beauty on a sentient person. With his soft mouth, high cheekbones, and perfectly cut jawline, his face called the archangels to mind. The devious glint in his eyes, however, said he was as wicked as the fallen one, and women across Britain were undecided whether to envy Lucie her roguish fiancé or to pity her. Judging by the lingering rosy flush on Lucie's cheeks and her kiss-swollen lips, her friend was perfectly satisfied with her choice.

"The lift moved much faster than I remember," Hattie stammered, mortified.

"Well spotted, ma'am," Ballentine said smoothly. "I had the old lift replaced by a hydraulic one."

"That sounds terribly modern."

"Rather, the old one was hopelessly behind the times—this one is, too. Werner von Siemens has just invented an electric lift."

"How fascinating."

"Why don't I send a tea cart up," Ballentine suggested. "Mrs. Blackstone—congratulations on your nuptials. My lady."

He exchanged glances with Lucie—his tender, hers harried—on his way out, and the moment the door had closed behind him, Lucie tugged Hattie toward a green fainting couch.

"We returned as soon as we heard," she said. "But first, our mail delivery was delayed by nearly a week because we had changed hotels—"

Hattie sat down, stunned. "You . . . came back because of me?"

"Of course. But then every single Italian train was canceled or too slow. In France, there was a strike. It took *eight days* to reach Calais. I was ready to take over and drive one of those blasted things myself."

Hattie gave a small moan. "You shouldn't have abandoned your holidays." In fact, her friend was still wearing a gray travel dress.

Lucie took her hands again in an unusually tactile display. "How could I stay? It all came at a great shock. Ballentine tried to reassure me he has never known Blackstone to maltreat a woman, but I had to see for myself."

"But you so rarely take time for your own leisure!"

"If that worries you, look at my desk." Lucie pointed at it, the towering stacks of mail specifically. "I'm dreadfully behind on my correspondence with the chapters in the United States, and Montgomery is putting the Married Women's Property Act amendment proposal to Parliament in October, so I must lobby half the House of Lords by then. Idleness always takes revenge. I would have called on you in Belgravia this afternoon. Catriona shall be joining us here soon."

"But . . . Catriona is in Applecross."

"No, she stayed in Oxford, waiting for an opportunity to ambush you since you showed us the cold shoulder."

"But she mustn't!"

Lucie cut her an exasperate look. "Wouldn't you do the same for us?"

"Of course I would," Hattie said reflexively.

"So there."

"You must know, my mother intercepted your letters," Hattie confessed. "Hence the impression of me showing you the cold shoulder . . ."

"Dear, we aren't cross with you," Lucie said. "We understand. We are worried about you, not put out."

"Well, that's a relief," Hattie murmured. "What of Lord Ballentine? Is he terribly annoyed? You look very dark; it seems you had at least a few days by the sea."

"We did." Lucie touched her fine nose where her skin was peeling. Her blond hair had lightened to a silvery shade of white. "My bonnet, the stupid thing, was blown into the sea during a stroll on the beach in Naples, and I burned despite Ballentine giving me his hat—isn't it odd, you would think as a ginger he would fry, but no, he turns a most becoming hue of bronze. He isn't natural, I tell you. And he isn't annoyed; he's keen on making progress here, too—he has recently taken up with this playwright, Mr. Wilde, and my cousin Lord Arthur, do you remember him? He is determined to include their Decadent Movement poetry in London Print's portfolio. We are becoming a radical publishing house after all, it seems. . . . Anyway, Hattie, why aren't *you* wearing a hat? Or gloves? And why are you hobbling?"

"It's nothing," she said, her smile a rictus grin. "I'm wearing new mules, and I took a wrong turn at Piccadilly Circus. I might have a blister or two."

Lucie stilled. "You walked here. From Belgravia."

"I wouldn't have, but I realized too late I had no coin on me to hire a cab or take the underground." Besides, she had never traveled on the underground unaccompanied.

Her friend was back on her feet, her hands on her hips. "You dashed from the house," she said. "What has that man done to you?"

"Nothing."

"Nothing?"

Hattie groaned. "There was . . ." She had to close her eyes against the shame of it. "There was a woman."

"A woman." Lucie sounded incredulous. "But . . . you have been married only two days!"

"And I regret I ever consented to it."

"The scoundrel!"

"It appears I was a bit hasty with my conclusions, but it revealed that he doesn't care one wit for me, and he was terribly commanding."

"Was he, now?" Lucie snarled. "How horribly provoking."

The display of unconditional loyalty made her nose burn with tears. "Lucie," she whispered, "I wish to apologize to you."

"To me?" Lucie said, flummoxed. "What can you mean?"

She forced herself to meet her friend's gaze. "I don't think I fully comprehended the suffrage cause until now." This had become clear to her during her hour-long, sticky, undignified hobble across London.

Lucie regarded her with two vertical lines between her brows. "Go on."

The words came haltingly. "You see . . . whenever you said wives were rightless and voiceless, I heard you. And I have read many letters of unhappy wives during our meetings, and never doubted the righteousness of our cause. But now I feel as though I hadn't truly understood. Perhaps . . ."

"Perhaps?"

"I suppose it still felt as though these misfortunes were happening to other people. What I mean is, my life has always been pleasant despite me being a woman, and I must have expected it to just continue that way. My father, my brothers, my uncles—they can be pigheaded, but they are good and kind men and husbands. . . ." Or so she had thought, until her father had single-handedly decided her betrothal. "I joined the cause because I wanted to have a cause, too," she said thickly. "I wanted to feel useful. I enjoyed having new friends and being part of something radical. But I understand now. I . . . I was a silly fool."

Lucie was shaking her head. "You are not a silly fool."

"Then why am I so shocked?" She made to search her reticule for a handkerchief, only to remember that she had left the reticule back at the house.

Lucie walked to the desk and fetched a handkerchief from one of the drawers. "You were ignorant," she said as she handed Hattie the neatly pressed white square. "Your personal good fortune has protected you from the consequences of the law thus far. Engaging with politics was a choice for you. For those who live with the consequences of injustice every day, political activism is not a choice. So I reckon the shock you feel now is your ignorance shattering—think of it as growing pains."

Hattie pressed the handkerchief to her nose. It smelled of lemons, like Lucie's soap. "You must have found me very annoying," she murmured.

Lucie made a face. "I'm annoyed when you berate yourself."

"But you must have noticed that I came for the company and cakes as much as for the cause. You were impatient with me sometimes."

"Well, yes," Lucie said, and paced in front of the couch. "Because impatience is one of my many vices. Hattie, I'd never expect your convictions to run as deep as mine."

"N-no?"

"No. You're a loyal activist, you have taken real risks for the cause, and you always cheer the troops. That's plenty. If I expected every suffragist to feel exactly as I do, our army would be tiny in size and insufferable in disposition. Golly, don't cry!"

She couldn't help it: several weeks of pent-up emotional pressure burst out in a flood. Lucie cast a wild look around the room. "Would you like some brandy? A cigar? Ah, I wish Annabelle were here—I'm terrible at handling tears."

Hattie squinted at her through a watery veil. "Lucie. He can do anything to me he wishes."

All motion went out of Lucie then; for a moment, she was a like a statue. She approached slowly and knelt before the couch; her up-turned face was as serious as Hattie had ever seen it. "Hattie," she said, and placed a warm hand over hers. "I must ask: has he hurt you?"

He had. Somehow, Lucian had managed to wound her feelings. But that was not what Lucie was asking.

She shook her head. "He hasn't. But he could."

And he could parade his fancy women around the drawing room if he wished. She understood now that she'd rather bite off her tongue than seek refuge with her family and tell her mother or sisters about the woman in her house. In fact, it was why she had come here rather than set out for St. James's. She glanced down at Lucie's hand, protectively covering hers, and her heart swelled again with the pain of too much sudden gratitude. How fortunate she was to have such friends.

A knock on the door made her freeze.

"The tea," Lucie said calmly.

Hattie glanced sideways at the young woman who pushed the

cart into the room. She wore the neat white-and-blue London Print staff livery Hattie had designed when Lucie had taken over her share of London Print a few months ago. How pleased she had been to have been put in charge of the décor. Then Lucie had said to her, *You have free rein. However, keep in mind this is an office building and not my great-aunt Honoria's drawing room; no chintz, no kitten tapestries, please.* She had quietly crossed chintz off her list of fabric options and decided to forget the hurtful comment because Lucie was brash with everyone. But she remembered it now as she sat here on the fainting couch, in need of advice like a hapless girl. Like a girl who would *lean in.*

Lucie poured the tea. "In summary, Blackstone flaunted his paramour, and he was bloody to you."

"He claims she was a friend," Hattie murmured.

"I still hate him," Lucie said, and added three lumps of sugar to Hattie's cup before handing it to her.

"She . . . she was caressing his cheek," Hattie said, and the memory of it curled her left hand into a claw.

Lucie's gaze briefly lingered on that claw. "I see," she said. "How did you catch them together?"

"They were in plain sight in the drawing room."

"The drawing room," Lucie said, baffled. "Why, then he is either evil, or truly innocent."

"In any case," Hattie said, "I refused an introduction, as is only proper, but then he was put out that I was snubbing his *friend.*" And he had called her a brat.

Lucie blew on her tea. "Do you wish to leave him, then?"

"Leave him?"

"Yes."

"Move to the country, you mean?"

"No. I mean whether you wish to properly leave your husband."

Her mind blanked. "A divorce."

Lucie's eyes were intent. "Assume it would be possible, without consequence to your reputation. Would you leave him?"

"Oh my," she said, and disturbed, "I don't know."

Her answer should have been an unthinking, resounding *yes*. She sipped her tea until the hot, sugary liquid slowed the merry-go-round in her head. "Does it sound terribly indecisive when I say that until this morning, I didn't resent him, only the power he has over me?"

Lucie gave her a rueful smile. "No," she said. "Not to me. I love Ballentine with all my heart—sometimes I look at his beautiful face and can't breathe from how much I love him. I still shan't marry him as long as it would make me his property. But now you are married, and if you don't wish for a divorce or allow me to dispose of Blackstone in cold blood, we must work within those constraints. It is promising that you didn't resent him at first—you normally have a good intuition about people's character."

She stared at the crumpled handkerchief in her lap. "I leaned in for the kiss that caused everything," she said softly.

"So there is an animal attraction," Lucie said, nodding, "however, that alone does not a good marriage make."

"Animal attraction," Hattie repeated. "Is that what it is?"

Lucie regarded her with some astonishment. "What else would it be, my dear?"

A sense of recognition between them, a forbidden pull . . . a warm response of her body to his scent and touch . . . well, yes. Very much an animal attraction. Part of her was intrigued, but her face was red again. Unlike Lucie, she hadn't spent the past decade rigorously unlearning the deeply injected litany about female virtues and a woman's natural lack of desire.

Lucie refilled Hattie's cup, then she proceeded to move around the study, pulling folders from the cabinet and rooting through drawers. "A carnal attraction is a fortunate thing," she said as she piled documents and writing utensils onto her desk. "That said, your husband sounds very unmanageable, while you—your stubborn and inflammable nature aside—are sweet-natured at your core. So, if you decide to return to Blackstone, please keep in mind that 'Beauty and the Beast' is a fairy tale. You do know the tale of the Beauty and the Beast?"

"Of course," Hattie said. "You are still speaking in riddles."

"The Beast traps the Beauty," Lucie said, and sat down behind the desk, a fountain pen in hand. "In the end, Beauty saves the Beast—and herself—thanks to her gentle nature, self-sacrifice, and loving heart—so loving, she becomes smitten with an ugly, probably smelly monster that wanted to murder her father and kept her imprisoned."

"It sounded more romantic when Fräulein Mayer read it to me," Hattie said.

"Ah well," Lucie said as her pen was flying across a page, "it is easy to become distracted by the enchanted castle. But the conclusion of the tale remains: no matter how beastly a creature, a woman's self-sacrificing love shall eventually turn him into a beautiful prince."

Hattie cut her a sullen look. "Why don't you speak plainly?"

Lucie rolled an ink blotter over her lines. "Blackstone won't turn into a prince, no matter how loving and patient you are. Fairy tales express our hopes, not reality. The tale of women being tied to men they don't want is as old as time, so of course we want hope. However, the reality is, a woman's martyrdom will not change a man who doesn't wish to change. Do you remember Patmore's infernal poem?

While she, too gentle even to force
His penitence by kind replies,
Waits by, expecting his remorse,
With pardon in her pitying eyes

"When—if—you go back to him, don't endeavor to shame him into feeling remorse with your pitying eyes, Hattie."

She felt a pang of irritation, for she might have endeavored to do exactly that. "So what would you have me do?" It came out a little petulantly.

Lucie struck a match to melt the sealing wax. "Had Beauty been a man," she said, "he wouldn't have hesitated to kill the Beast rather than fall in love with it. So I say, make your husband earn your goodwill. So few men respect things that are freely given."

"Make him earn it," Hattie murmured. "Easily said, when he has all the men and horses."

Before her eyes, Lucie's elfin face turned into the pointy visage of an evil pixie. "If he can't behave, consider staying with Annabelle," she said. "She would never turn you away, and even Blackstone is powerless against a duke."

She shifted uncomfortably on the couch. Inconveniencing her friends with her self-inflicted turmoil to such a degree felt terribly wrong. The fact that she was currently sharing her marriage woes so freely with a friend already broke a great taboo.

"Montgomery is still recovering from his own scandal of marrying Annabelle," she said. "And Mr. Blackstone has a lawful right to me—he can order me home. And if I refused, they could send me to j-jail. . . . You know this."

Lucie folded the letter into a square and sealed it. "You don't have to make any grand decisions today." She gathered the letter and other documents, tied them with a string, and brought the parcel to Hattie. "Your escape kit," Lucie said. "To Mytilene."

"Mytilene." Hattie took the papers gingerly. "I thought the Amazons were relegated to legend status these days."

Lucie chuckled. "Not these ones. This Mytilene is an enclave run by female artists, near Marseille, and few people know of its existence, because it is also a women's shelter."

"Marseille," Hattie whispered. *France.* "You know I dream of France."

"I do. Now, this one here contains ten pounds"—Lucie tugged at the corner of an envelope—"this here the detailed itinerary of how to reach Mytilene, and this one my letter of recommendation as well as a letter from the British consul granting you an unbothered passage to France from any British port."

Hattie fingers tightened around the stack. "*Merci?*"

"The consulate letter is a forgery, of course," Lucie said, "however, it is expertly done and has never caused any of my charges any trouble."

She had known Lucie had a network of people smugglers at her fingertips, spanning across Europe. Her friend used it to make women disappear if they wished it. Her stomach roiled at the thought. She had never imagined herself being one such woman.

"Would you really have me go and live in France," she said, "forever, and in hiding?"

"Of course not," Lucie exclaimed. "But sometimes, a woman is in need of a ticket—one she may use independently of anyone else's goodwill. This here is yours. You can keep it in a drawer and feel well in charge."

Feeling well in charge sounded too good to be true.

She held the letters to her nose. "Mmm," she said. "It smells like the Montmartre."

Lucie was amused. "Montmartre," she said. "What does it smell like?"

"Like adventure, fashion, and fabulous art."

The one-way ticket seemed to radiate bright like a beacon from its place inside her bodice as she sat in the carriage to St. James's. It would be best to spend the night at her parents' house to make her displeasure known, but when she finally stood on the doorstep of her old home, she felt devious and ill at ease.

"Miss Greenfield—I beg your pardon, Mrs. Blackstone." Hanson's watery eyes had lit with delight when he opened the door, and he stepped aside with an animated flourish of his hand. Her heart ached a little at the familiar sight of the butler's weathered face and severely brushed-back silver hair, and the rigid way he moved, as though his shirt and collar had been starched with iron. . . .

"I'm afraid Mr. and Mrs. Greenfield are not home," Hanson explained as he oversaw the maid taking the hat and shawl Lucie had lent Hattie.

"When shall they be back?"

"Past the time for supper, I'm afraid—they are attending an assembly in Surrey."

A pressure in her chest eased. Apparently, she wasn't at all keen on seeing her father; she would prefer to be safely ensconced in her old bedchamber by the time her parents returned.

"What about Zachary—is he home?"

Hanson's cheerful mood withdrew like a clam into its shell. Impossibly, he carried himself straighter than before. "He is home, yes."

"Where is he?"

"Hmm. I believe in the library, ma'am."

He was walking conspicuously slowly beside her as if to force her own pace to a crawl.

Her pulse sped up. "What is it, Hanson?"

The butler looked pained: "There is a possibility that Master Zachary is not in a condition to receive callers."

"No—has he taken ill?"

"*Ill* is not quite the word—"

"And callers, Hanson? I'm his sister!" She rushed along the corridor leading to the library, not caring that she lost Hanson on the way.

She swung open the heavy door. "Zachary?"

Silence.

She took a turn along the dark, dusty bookshelves lining the walls and mindlessly looked behind the couches and armchairs around the cold fireplace. "Zach?"

"Hattie Pom?" An unsteady figure had appeared in the arched doorway to the adjacent study.

"Zach." She hurried toward him and took his hand.

He looked down and blinked slowly at their clasped fingers, then dragged his gaze up to her face, his expression dumbfounded, as though he wasn't certain she was real. His eyes were unsightly, bleary and bloodshot. "Why are you here, darling?"

She recoiled from his whisky breath. There was a vast liquor cabinet in the library study, and by the smell of it, her brother had drunk it all. "Blimey, Zach—it's barely noon."

He squinted. "I guarantee you, it ish six o'clock somewhere at the moment."

This was unlike him—Zach usually indulged in moderation and handled his drink well.

"What is it?" she prodded. "Are you in trouble?"

He untangled his hand from hers and grabbed her shoulder to hold her away from him. "Lemme look at you." He squinted harder. "Well, you *seem* whole and hale."

A shyness came over her, and she thought how awkward it was to be seen by her brother after a wedding night even if it hadn't taken place. Zachary appeared to have little apprehension of things; he was using her shoulders as a crutch. She wrinkled her nose. "What has happened to you?"

"'Away, and mock the time with fairest show,'" he drawled, "'false face must hide what the false heart doth know.'"

She shook her head. "*Macbeth*, brother?"

"Clever little goose."

"Come now, be good," she tried. "I may need your help: do you believe Papa would object to me staying here for the night— Ouch."

The hand on her shoulder had tightened like a vise. Zachary's eyes had narrowed to dangerous slits. "Fleeing him already," he said. "What has the bastard done to you?"

"Nothing—Zach, you are hurting me."

"Ah well," he said, and dropped his hand. "Either way. I'm of no use here. It's of no use."

She was rubbing her shoulder. "I don't like you much when you are in your cups."

"Neither do I." He turned back toward the study, swaying like a spinning top just before it toppled. "A good thing you never pay attention to business," he said. "Always with your lovely head in the clouds . . ."

She slipped a supportive arm around his slim waist as he was taking course toward the Chesterfield below the window. The crumpled pillow on the seat said he had been resting there before her arrival.

"I do pay attention," she said. "I know more than you might think."

He slumped down on the sofa. "Do you? You read the business section, then?" He gave an ugly laugh, and the fine hairs on her nape stood.

"Very well," she said. Was there a blanket? He was in dire need of sleeping off his debauchery.

"Poor Pom Pom," he mumbled. "It said it right there, black on white, that the Greenfields are now the majority owners of Plasencia-Astorga."

The world became very quiet. Except one voice was loud and clear: Zachary's, when he had told her at the dinner weeks ago that the Greenfields wanted Lucian's share in the railway company. When she spoke, she sounded as drunk as he. "What are you saying?"

Zachary slid down sideways onto the pillow. "You didn't know that, huh?"

She was on her knees next to the sofa and slapped his cheek. "Zach."

A bad premonition crawled up her spine. She smacked him again.

Zachary's eyes slitted open, their depths unfocused. "At half price," he said. "Half. Price. I don't trust that fellow . . . too calculating. Mark me, he planned this through and through."

Her gut clenched as his words began to make sense. A lonely roar filled her ears, like the howl of a storm over an empty plain, as the pieces of her life were pelting down around her all over again.

Chapter 15

Outside her bedchamber windows at Lucian's house, the black silhouettes of London's chimneys pointed at the crimson sky, emitting curls of smoke like pistols that had just been fired. Nightfall was close. He would be here soon, and the churning, nauseous pressure in her belly increased with every heavy tick of the clock. But it had been impossible to stay in her childhood home, the place where her own father had betrayed her.

After sending Bailey away, she had switched on every lamp in the vast room and begun brushing out her hair in a futile attempt to soothe herself. The gaslight gave her reflection in the vanity table mirror a sickly yellow pallor, and she regarded herself with wretched amazement as she worked the brush. Had her face always looked so girlish, so soft? Was it any wonder people believed they could do with her as they pleased—such as pawning her off like a prize calf? This was still a common enough fate for women of her age and standing, but perhaps she had fancied herself exempt. Fatal vanity on her part. Her family deemed her entirely expendable. Well, not entirely—she was worth half price of a railroad investment. She gripped the brush handle tight enough to strain her bones. The wedding ring broke the light and winked at her, evilly, derisively. The white-gold symbol of her childhood dream was to be degraded to a permanent reminder of her stupidity, then. Her hair crackled and rose, and the coil of violent emotions in her stomach twisted and thickened. She gathered her locks over one shoulder and saw that her fingers were shaking.

The rap on the door slammed her heart against her ribs.

In the mirror, her eyes were huge.

She was still wearing her day dress, high-necked and thickly ruffled down the front. Better protection than a delicate nightgown, considering the confrontation to come. She forced a deep breath, and another. The knock had sounded on the door to the hallway, not the one to Lucian's bedchamber.

"Enter." It came out hoarse.

From the corner of her eye, she saw her husband, looking unfamiliarly polished in proper black-and-white dinner attire. A dinner invitation obtained courtesy of the Greenfield name? Acid welled from her stomach, nearly making her choke.

She had meant to face him on her feet, but she couldn't rise from her chair; she sat staring straight ahead with her pulse racing away in her neck as he approached. He halted behind her. His hand hovered briefly, as if to caress her left shoulder, and she glimpsed the heavy gold band of his wedding ring. Unlike most men of her acquaintance, Lucian had decided to wear it beyond the wedding day. To gloat? She wondered if he saw a ticket to power whenever it caught his eye.

"Harriet, I—" She peeked at his reflection and found his dark brows pulled together in a frown. "I spoke harshly to you this morning." He reached inside his jacket pocket and procured an ornate, oblong box. A case for a bracelet or necklace. He leaned over her to place it next to the collection of perfume flasks.

"Thank you." Her hands remained tightly clasped in her lap.

He was too close, muddling her senses with his scent and the heat of his body. And untried as she was, she still recognized the look on his face in the mirror: a muted version of his expression when she had been naked and under him on the bed. Want. He was here because he wanted his wife, perhaps later tonight—and the pretty box on her table fulfilled his side of the bargain. She felt at once tense and soft, hot and cold. Had this day never happened, she might have wanted him back. She had felt an attraction whether she wished it or not. She had become familiar with the strong planes and angles of his face, and had secretly begun to find him handsome, which possibly sprung from the possessive notion that as her husband, he was hers in a unique way, and hers alone. Now the thought of his touch made her shiver with cold revulsion.

He noticed, and straightened, watching her intently now. "You went out today."

"I did, yes." She was breathing too fast.

"Without Carson." His tone was calm, not unfriendly.

"Yes."

He shook his head. "Have him escort you the next time—it's not safe for you otherwise."

The hypocrisy. The greatest threat to her well-being was currently himself. The flash of indignation brought her to her feet, and she turned to him. "I visited my parents."

His eyes revealed no emotion, but an alertness came over him and subtly tensed his shoulders. He might be an unfeeling liar, but like an animal, his instincts were finely attuned to the faintest signs of trouble. She suspected it was how creatures like him survived.

"I know now," she said, unable to stop. "I know."

"Know what?"

"About Plasencia-Astorga."

"Very well," he said after a pause. "It was hardly a secret."

"You bought me."

Her inclined his head in concession. "Why not call it a bride-price? It's not uncommon."

"At half price!"

He blinked. "I can assure you that substantial sums were involved."

Her breathing became labored. "I cannot condemn you for taking what was on offer," she said unsteadily—the *offer* was entirely Julien Greenfield's responsibility. "However. What I must know is whether you manufactured the opportunity for a sale."

He was not so blasé now. He was holding himself too still. "Explain your meaning."

"The kiss," she said. "The kiss—it wasn't a coincidence that it took place in a room with large two-way mirrors behind which a crowd happened to be waiting."

Mr. Matthews must have known, too. If she hadn't been so *lovely*, so *naïve*, so shocked, she would have suspected it the very moment it had happened in the gallery.

"I don't recall stealing the kiss from you," Lucian said. He was as expressive as a stone.

"You didn't," she said bitterly.

"Nor did I prolong it against your will."

"You didn't. My own foolishness compelled me to give it freely."

"Therefore—"

"Please." She gripped his forearm. "Please set aside your cruel ways for once and tell me the truth: have you finagled the situation? If you don't confirm my suspicions, I shall forever question whether I imagined it and it shall drive me utterly mad over time."

He glanced down at her white hand clutching at his sleeve. A muscle worked in his jaw as he deliberated, and finally, he looked her in the eye. "I arranged for the situation," he said. "Then I took the opportunity when it presented itself."

The room was swirling around her in a shrill stream of colors.

"How could you be certain a kiss would take place?" she managed. "And at that very moment? With an audience behind those mirrors?"

"I wasn't," he said, impatient now. "How could I? But at the very least, we would've been observed talking together, and I had planned to further those impressions over time. The kiss just brought everything to a conclusion quickly."

"You should have stepped away," she said thinly, "just should have."

"To what end, when I wanted your hand?"

"I see." Her voice came from afar, grotesquely distorted. "I presume our union is but one step on the ladder of your social climb."

He glowered and plucked her still-clinging fingers off his arm. And made as if to leave.

"Where are you going?" Her hands were on her hips; from somewhere came the urge to yell like a fishwife.

He looked back over his shoulder. "You know all you wanted to know."

"Why me?" she cried. "It was my *life* with which you tampered."

"Because," he said, "you made yourself available. Repeatedly."

It knocked the air clean from her lungs. She tried to breathe and couldn't. She pressed her hands below her breasts. Nothing. Panic turned her cold, as if she had just been thrown hard from her pony and lay staring blindly at the sky, desperately trying to drag air into her stunned lungs. He hadn't set a trap because a sudden bout of mindless desire had compelled him to steal her; no, he would have snatched any available, unsuspecting woman of her station stupid enough to amble into his path. . . . Finally, a breath.

"I want this marriage annulled," she said.

Her words hit him square between his shoulders and he halted abruptly. When he turned back, his thoughts were written plain on his face: their marriage had not yet been consummated—she was free to leave him without much complication indeed. His expression darkened, and her vision wavered. The presence of the vast bed behind her pressed to the fore of her mind. She backed away on shaky legs. "If you force me, I will scream."

He took a step toward her, but stopped. "Force you," he jeered softly. "But yes. You would think that." His voice was icy enough to freeze a sea. "I don't go round violating women, Harriet." His gaze swept over her with such contempt, she felt his disdain in the pit of her stomach. "So I suggest we don't consummate this marriage until you come to me," he said. "And you'll make it so clear that you are willing, even the kind of brute you take me for could not mistake it."

He left, and the chamber door fell shut behind him with a bang.

A high-pitched noise wailed in her ears. In a state of detachment, she thought she should probably fall onto the bed and sob. But she didn't move, and her eyes were dry. He had confessed. It confirmed her role as a silly pawn, but it brought a measure of calm—a cold, brittle calm, but it at least allowed her think. She went to the vanity table and opened the jewelry box he had gifted her. A bracelet, two fingers wide, comprised of four strands of golden chains linking pearls and gemstones. Elegant, yet whimsical. The dull light couldn't dim the rich blue of the sapphires and the glow of the rubies. In the sun, the piece would have shimmered beautifully on her wrist, complementing her coloring perfectly, and the woman she had been five minutes ago would have felt a great twinge of misery in her heart for all the things that could have been. Now, she only saw opportunity. She had never paid attention to the price of things, but she was still aware that she was holding a small fortune in her palm and that the gems and pearls could probably be pried without too much effort from their gold settings. Jewels—a woman's portable bank account since the beginning of time. Or at least ever since they made it difficult for wives to hold money and an actual account in their own name. It was why they bartered their favors or turned a blind eye in exchange for necklaces and rings and diamond hairpins, and endured being called little magpies for hoarding trinkets. Her trinkets would keep her in good stead all the way to southern France.

⁂

The corridors rushed past in silence as Lucian put distance between himself and his wife's bedchamber. *If you force me, I will scream.* He wanted to punch a wall. He hadn't intended for her to find out, and now he knew why: it was ugly as hell. It had sliced any friendliness between them to ribbons just when he had realized it was something he might want. And he'd have her only when she approached him for it? He'd now wait for the next one hundred years to be inside his wife—when the whole purpose of this damned marriage had been the production of Greenfield grandchildren. . . . Just then he caught sight of himself in the large mirror on the wall across from the entrance doors, his snarling visage a feral sight beneath his disheveled black hair.

"Well, fuck me." His first official social function at the exchequer, and he looked like a demon.

"Matthews," he roared.

His voice was still reverberating off the walls as Matthews hurried from one of the corridors. "Sir?"

"Tell Nicolas to get the two-in-hand ready."

"Yes, sir."

"Tell Carson to keep an eye on Mrs. Blackstone's chamber door—if she leaves, he's to escort her."

Matthews's brows pulled together before he schooled his expression to neutrality. "As you wish, sir."

"And have a tray brought to her from the kitchen."

He had time to control his temper during the carriage ride to Westminster. Julien Greenfield awaited him in the pillared reception room of number ten Downing Street, masking whatever grudge or lethal loathing he might still nurse against his son-in-law with a jovial demeanor. He had the cheek to ask about Harriet's well-being as if he cared, and Lucian lied straight to his face that she was doing just fine. The dinner was a success; Greenfield introduced him to Prime Minister Gladstone, who also happened to be chancellor of the exchequer, and they took each other's measure under the pretense of discussing the latest upheaval in the British wool market, forever caused by

Americans imposing outrageous import tariffs on British wool while trying to flood the British market with lower-quality but vastly cheaper wool. But frankly, he gave no damn about wool tonight, and by the time he'd boarded the coach again, his jaw ached from consistent clenching. Lifelong ambitions were coming to fruition as planned, and here he was feeling in a black mood the moment he entered his house. He changed from his dinner attire into his exercise clothes, went to saddle his roan, and took course to East London.

He returned to Belgravia a few hours later, his face and body sore and his mood still foul. He scrubbed himself in the shower, and after half a bar of soap, the water circling the drain still seemed tinged with gray. All the mirrors were blind when he finally emerged from the cubicle.

In his study, he went directly to the drinks cabinet and indiscriminately picked a bottle. His right hand protested the motion with a dull ache. Bare-knuckle brawling and drinking—he could just picture his wife's disapproving face. *One can take a lad out of the squalor, but not the squalor out of the lad.* He took the bottle—whisky, an Oban of good vintage he now saw—to one of the armchairs by the fireplace and settled down with a groan. Squalor or not, he was too old for fights in damp, dim, smoke-filled basements. No one had openly questioned his sudden presence at Macintyre's establishment tonight, but as he had dodged and thrown punches until the floor was slick with blood and sweat and spit, he had felt the room vibrate with speculations. He had wondered whether they'd steal his horse, leaving him to deal with muggers when crossing Whitechapel on foot. He had realized that he thought like a toff and didn't belong in places like Macintyre's anymore. So he had caught a mean upper cut, and still tasted blood.

A knock sounded on the door, too firm to be his wife. "What."

Matthews stood on the doorsill, as usual in his suit. "Sir—you have a visitor."

He straightened. A caller close to midnight was always bad news. "Who is it?"

"Lord Ballentine. He is at the back entrance—here is his card."

Odd. Ballentine hadn't called on him in years. "Bring him here. Matthews—"

"Sir?"

"Has Mrs. Blackstone eaten?"

Matthews's face was unreadable. "Every morsel."

A few minutes later, the viscount's tall, wide-shouldered form appeared in the doorway. His expression was suspiciously pleasant as he meandered in while surveying the study, the stacks of yellowing magazines, the map, the battered desk, the monetary and fiscal policy timeline. "Blackstone," he said. "How quaint you have it here."

"What's your business, Ballentine?"

"I came to congratulate you on your recent nuptials." Ballentine's gaze traveled from Lucian's raw knuckles to the bruise on his jaw. "You look splendid. Married life seems to suit you."

"I could go another round, ye ken."

His lordship raised his hands in surrender. He had a vested interest in keeping his pretty features exactly as they were—one of the reasons he'd always left the dirty work to Lucian during past undertakings. Like the diamond stud sparking on his right ear, Ballentine distracted with a garish glimmer from an impenetrable surface. He was the living embodiment of all the things despicable in a man: privileged from birth, easily amused, and hedonistic, a modern-day male Marie Antoinette, except no one was truly inclined to lop his head off—he was just so terribly charming. And apart from Aoife, he still came closest to what Lucian would call a friend ever since their paths had crossed in a den of iniquity ten years ago.

He gestured at the empty chair across from him. "Take a glass. Have a seat."

"Believe me," said Ballentine as he poured himself a drink and stretched out his long legs to reveal absurdly patterned socks, "your lack of enthusiasm over my visit is entirely mutual. However, given the choice between your wrath and that of my lady . . ."

"Your missus sends you?"

"Of sorts."

Lucian scoffed. "A hen-pecked libertine—pathetic."

"Former libertine," Ballentine said amicably. "I'm hopelessly devoted now."

Had rumors about Lucian's marriage troubles made the rounds already? Appalling, how preoccupied he was with the matter of gossip about his person when until recently he had been free not to give a damn.

"As you know, your wife called on my fiancée today," Ballentine said.

He gave a grunt of acknowledgment, when in fact, he hadn't known that. He needed a word with Carson.

The nobleman gave him one of those bland smiles that hid multitudes. "My betrothed now has a bee in her bonnet about the state of her friend's happiness."

"That so?"

A grave nod. "She thinks she detected a lack of honeymoon exuberance in Mrs. Blackstone."

When Lucian replied, his voice was icy. "Are you here to meddle with my marriage?"

"Good God, no. No, I'm here for old times' sake. In the capacity of a friend."

"The same capacity that made you send me a wedding-night manual?" *Which hadn't even worked.*

Ballentine winced. "In my defense, that was not my idea."

"Were you forced at gunpoint to send a telegram, then?"

Ballentine's silence drew out.

"Hell," Lucian said. "You were forced at gunpoint."

The viscount shrugged. "There was a fair chance a dainty Double Derringer would have come into play," he said, "but the more potent and immediate threat was Lady Lucinda withholding her favors for the duration of the holidays unless I sent *something* your way, so what was a man to do?"

What indeed. "Your purpose," he repeated.

Ballentine swirled whisky in his glass. "Lady Lucinda has a habit of inspiring rebellion in her fellow women. And she is very protective of Mrs. Blackstone, so I reckon she may have done a good deal of inspiring this afternoon."

Grand. The whole half-price debacle had fallen on fertile ground, then. A tension started up in his temples, the dull throb in rhythm with the pulsating pain in his jaw. "So you've come to warn me about mutiny."

"Well—"

"You think I need help with handling my wife—again."

Ballentine made a stupidly innocent face. "I'd never."

Lucian leaned abruptly forward. "Marriage is a simple affair unless you overcomplicate it. She's mine. What can she do, eh? Where will she go?"

His lordship was nodding along, his half-lidded gaze deceptively lazy. "Of course."

Lucian drained his whisky to the dregs. "There's nothing wrong with that approach."

Ballentine shrugged. "Not at all. But . . ."

"But?"

"She could, in fact, go places."

He stilled. "Tell me."

"I know nothing concrete," Ballentine said. "Just that Lady Lucinda can make women disappear when they don't wish to be found. And Mrs. Blackstone is such a lovely, whimsical, overly trusting creature and it would be unforgivable if she endangered herself while, say, traversing the continent on her own."

His hand tightened around the empty tumbler and fresh pain

spiked hotly through his abused tendons. Ballentine was an arrogant git, and the familiarity with which the libertine spoke about Harriet annoyed him, but the accuracy of Ballentine's intuitions was rather unrivaled—he wouldn't have lent the man money otherwise. Well, he had ruffled his wife's feathers all right, and he was traveling to Drummuir the morning after next and couldn't keep an eye on her. What to do, lock her in her room for days? Send her back to her parents? He uttered a profanity that would have shocked a less depraved man. The nobleman just nodded sagely. For a long moment, they sat watching the leaping fire as the burn of the whisky spread through their veins.

"An odd concept, wives," Ballentine finally said.

Lucian said nothing.

"Like no other, they inspire in a man the desire to please them," Ballentine continued. "Pesky, this urge to see them happy, but there we have it—care nothing for their happiness, and you're hurtling toward a cold, cold hell of your own making."

Lucian pushed the Oban away instead of pouring some more. "If you had proper concerns for her welfare, you'd not be here warning me," he said. "You'd be helping her run off."

Ballentine chuckled. "Not as long as I owe you money."

He'd be leading the heist, the liar. Though even he couldn't tell with Ballentine; the man lied as smoothly as he spoke the truth. He had witnessed it firsthand when they both had tried to squeeze business from the demimonde as adolescents. They had joined forces for a while, extracting secrets from intoxicated noblemen during debauched nights in secret back rooms and gambling hells only to sell the information or use it for blackmail. Ballentine had been in charge of opening doors to inner circles with his pedigree, his angel face, and his silver tongue. Lucian had enforced ultimatums or dealt with this or that fellow's henchmen. This had literally sullied his hands, but Lucian had always felt the viscount had done the dirty part, with him slithering among his own like a snake, and seducing and lying so beautifully. It was why he'd never fully trust the nobleman. He did, however, believe the part about the angry wives he'd just heard. He needed a plan. But what was forming at the back of his mind might well send him to *cold hell* without a detour.

Chapter 16

At eleven in the morning, Victoria Station was swarming like an anthill beneath the vaulted glass-dome ceiling. Trains arrived at platforms with an exhausted hiss; luggage carts squeaked past alongside rapidly clicking heels. A sea of hats heaved around Hattie, top hats, feathered ladies' hats, countless dull brown workmen's hats, the caps of station staff. She still felt as exposed as on an empty plain—since climbing from the cab at the east entrance, the back of her neck prickled as if someone was following her. It couldn't be; Lucian had left the house at dawn. The horrid man. He had come to her bedchamber at midnight to inform her that she would accompany him on his travels to Scotland. She had begun packing the moment he had left—the mere thought of being stuck in the Scottish wilderness with the abominable male had greatly hastened her plans for France along. The stale station air coated her mouth with the sweetish taste of coal and steel. Poor Bailey. She hoped there would be no troubles for Bailey, whom she had tricked into distracting Carson so she could flee through the kitchen entrance. Through her netted black travel veil, her gaze clung to the number-seven platform sign in the near distance as if it were a beacon. Her brain played tricks on her; she kept seeing a familiar powerful male shape from the corner of her eye and her stomach plunged every time. She tried pushing faster through the crowd, but her hems were heavy with sewn-in jewelry, and her right arm was burning from the bulky weight of her carpetbag; she had fair overstuffed said bag with spare gloves and chemises, stockings, a nightgown, and a bodice matching her current skirt; hygiene articles; her watercolor case, sketchpad, and sewing kit; the current edition of *Bradshaw's Continental Railway Guide*; her brush; suffrage journals; and some provisions including a large tin with toffees she had grabbed from the pantry. After closing the bag's latches with great difficulty, she had tucked her parasol on top. She would have to visit Marseille posthaste to order new dresses, hats, and gloves. . . . A man stepped into her path, and a scream stuck in her throat. Lucian. His face was as dark as the devil's.

No.

She made to run. "Excuse me," she whispered to the gasps of consternation, "excuse me," as her bag bumped against skirts and knees. But her gown was too narrow for running, and her luggage heavy like a boulder, tearing at her arm. Lucian was by her side in a heartbeat. "Allow me," he said tightly.

She veered to the left. "Let me be."

He snatched the bag from her hand. Her feet kept walking of their own volition. She'd go regardless; she would go without her belongings. . . . Lucian looped his arm through hers; feeling his muscular body against hers was a shock, and she moved blindly for a beat. He was not exerting any force. It then registered; his grip was light, light enough to *dare* her to break free. But she didn't. She didn't. He leashed the raw strength of an ox behind his measured hold, and the people around them . . . their disapproving faces, their shocked exclamations . . . the visions of that kept her compliant. Her ears were hot, and angry tears needled her eyes.

"Let me go," she managed. Lucian guided her straight past the entrance to platform number seven. Dread exploded in her chest. "Let go," she said, frantic now, "let go, you . . . miserable brute."

His lips pressed into a line, and his quiet anger flared around his form, dark like shadows. Farther and farther he maneuvered her away from her platform, and she followed; she was allowing him to drag her to her demise in the middle of a crowd, amid the screams of whistles and blaring announcements. . . .

"*Mademoiselle.*" An older gentleman with a tall hat and thin mustache was strolling alongside them, his tone jovial. "*Mademoiselle, puis-je vous aider?*"

May I assist you?

They had attracted attention. Mortification stung her cheeks, and she knew not where to look. Lucian glanced at the man over her head. "Don't bother my wife."

"Ah, matters of the heart, *oui?*" The Frenchman gave a knowing little laugh. "*Mes condoléances, monsieur—les rousses viennent de l'enfer.*"

A whole barrage of French reproofs jumbled through her mind at that, but the gentleman had already faded back into the surrounding hustle and bustle. She glanced up at Lucian's stony face and decided to beg. "Please—I'm missing my train."

"Your train's right there," he said, and turned onto platform number eleven. A Great Northern train was ready on the tracks and belching plumes of thick black smoke. She moved through the wafting soot in frozen silence—was he abducting her? Sending her to a remote estate? Bedlam?

"Where are you taking me?" It came out as a croak.

He nodded at a young man in station staff uniform while he pulled her up the coach stairs. "To Scotland," he said. Vaguely, she registered the plush splendor of a private railcar. Lucian guided her to the table booth next to a window. "Have a seat."

Dumbfounded, she plopped down on the bench. "Scotland," she repeated when he took his seat across from her. "But your departure was tomorrow."

"That used to be the plan," he said. "I decided to reschedule."

She glared at him in disbelief. "Did you lie in wait, to see whether I was leaving? And had the train readied just in case?" When he was silent, she cried, "What sort of madman does such a thing?"

His elbows came down on the table as he leaned in. "What sort of mad*woman* travels to Europe on her own with nothing but a handbag?"

Europe—how did he know?

A whistle screeched, and a shudder went through the train.

She shot to her feet. "You cannot just abduct me."

He scoffed. "It's travel for business, not an abduction. And we need it."

"We?"

"Our marriage needs it."

"What?" She felt so wholly unmarried to the scowling creature looking up at her, his words triggered genuine confusion.

Lucian fixed her with a dark eye. "We're married," he said. "You don't like it, because you're angry with me, but you running away won't change a thing. We need to . . . we need to mend it. So. Sit down."

She remained standing. "Mend it," she repeated, feeling dizzy. "Mend it—Mr. Blackstone, this is entirely unmendable."

"I hadn't taken you for someone who gives up this easily," came his cool retort.

How dare he. And yet. She had allowed it. She had allowed him to put her onto this train, for fear of causing a scene. A tide of self-loathing made her cringe. She whipped back her veil. "Perhaps," she said, increasingly reckless with emotion, "perhaps I simply don't consider our farce of a marriage worth the effort."

His expression hardened. "All right." He flicked his hand toward the arrangement of red velvet settees, the blue ceiling with the chandelier, the elaborately carved wooden trellis partitioning the car into a dining area and a drawing room. "This is my—our—private car. As is the next one. Yell or throw things if you must. Or you could order some tea and accept the situation."

Yell and throw things? She was too well-bred for such tantrums, and after last evening's revelations, certainly too jaded. She took a deep breath and lowered herself back onto her seat. "You are a horrid, loathsome man," she said quietly.

"And you are my responsibility," he replied unmoved, "So don't expect me to idly stand by while you try to get yersel' killed, robbed, or raped."

Her bland smile did not mask her surging fury. "France," she said, "was a dream of mine. How perfectly safe the world would be for women to follow their dreams if it were not for men interfering at every turn, wouldn't it?"

"And as long as it's the way it is, I'll keep you from traipsing across the continent on your own."

She bit back a screech. "I demand an annulment."

He tensed and jerked his gaze to the window instead of gracing her with a reply.

The train lurched into motion. She stared at his cold profile while her hands were curling into fists to the labored clanking of the wheels. A bruise was smudged across her husband's jaw, making him look terribly common. This man had squashed her one bid at rebellion without a second thought. Because he could. Not a hint of sweat on his brow; it had cost him nothing to bodily drag her from her path. Fire seemed to move through her veins, swelling hotter and higher until a whole blaze was roaring through her and she had never known such incandescent rage.

"Fine," she said. "I shall go to Scotland with you. But I shall be the stone in your shoe."

Lucian continued to look out the window.

"The thorn in your side."

Still he ignored her, so she leaned closer. "The poison in your soup."

This, at last, caused a reaction—he faced her. "Careful, beloved," he drawled. "You'll find yourself sharing every meal with my loathsome person and take the first bite of all my dishes."

"*Beloved*," she said, astonished. "As if you know what love is. As if I could love you—as if anyone could. You are a most wretched soul, one who must resort to scouring the jail to find staff, one who must resort to betrayal to take a respectable wife; you are an upstart and I became a social failure the day I wed you. No, what I would *love* is to see you brought to justice, and the least I can do is promise that I shall never, ever love you."

He was deadly still by the time she'd finished. There was only the sound of her panting, and she had a wretchedly sick feeling in her stomach.

"Are you done, then?" Lucian said. His eyes looked dead, too.

"Yes," she whispered. In her lap, her hands were shaking. The words had shot out in such harsh, clear, rapid succession, surprising her. They must have been there all along, forming a neat queue while waiting for a moment stripped of all civility to burst into the light. This was not like her.

Lucian came to his feet. His shoulders were still tense enough to snap when he disappeared through the partition to the next car. She sat nervously watching the door, the fierce rush of energy abating only slowly. Another husband might have raised his voice or slapped her. She had risked it; she had wished to see him wounded with the fire of a thousand suns, for hurting him equal to her own hurt seemed the only way to make him see. Her attack had failed to inflict even a scratch. He expected no love; of course he didn't.

She took off her glove. The wedding ring had a dull sheen, pretending to be inanimate metal, but she could feel its aliveness, its derision. The finger it encircled felt numb. She gripped the ring and pulled. It didn't budge; her fingers had swelled from carrying the bag and the heat of her agitation. She tugged violently, only to hurt her knuckle. The ring remained in place, and it felt as though she were being choked around her neck. This should have been a symbol of love. Instead, it was her scarlet letter.

Outside the window, the blackened brick walls of slum houses were sliding past, leaning against each other like rotten teeth, like tombstones. In a barren backyard, a woman was beating carpets on a line while children in rags chased a ball through the dirt. *What misery*, Hattie thought, *what misery*. Beneath her feet, the tracks kept slipping away and putting miles between her and life in London, and perhaps in one last bid for relevance, vivid memories returned: Zachary, ever protective . . . her mother, meddling with the minutiae of her life . . . her father, allowing her to go up to Oxford because she was useless at the family business. Chaperones and officers following her every step. Catriona accommodating her foolishness, Lucie abandoning her holidays . . . Annabelle going to the jail for her. . . . Her skin itched as if it were too tight. Protection to the point of asphyxiation. She had once thought this a proof of love, but it was almost certainly a consequence of her being deemed lovely, foolish, and possibly weak. And she was sick of it. She wasn't a mindless young girl. She wasn't a breakable bauble. Now she knew why girls were not allowed to feel anger—there was a reckless hope in it, and power. She would not loathe the compliant woman she had been this morning, oh no; she would direct this precious anger outward, and her gaze forward. *Les rousses viennent de l'enfer*—redheaded women are from hell. Lovely was dead. Enter the witch.

❧

Harriet ignored him for the entire nine-hour ride to Edinburgh. When he returned to her coach to see whether all was in reasonable order, she was lounging on the divan, reading a book, and eating toffees from a tin. She hadn't granted him a glance, so he had retreated to his own car to deal with his correspondence. At noon, he went to ask her to take lunch with him, only to find her indulging in a selection tea cakes she must have packed, and she looked at him wordlessly and with polite disdain until he withdrew. He sat eating his food, not tasting a thing. His chest felt oddly tight, and loosening his cravat hadn't helped. His wife hated him. Worse, she didn't respect him—no woman bestowed wifely affection on a man she didn't respect. He should dismiss her anger as irrational female theatrics like his etiquette handbook advised, for no man in his right mind would have let her go traveling by herself. France. If she wanted to bloody go to bloody France, he'd take her there, Paris, Lyon, Marseille, whatever she fancied. As soon as he had sorted out Drummuir. Until then, it shouldn't bother him. Instead, he was staring at her empty seat while he joylessly chewed and swallowed and acutely felt all of last night's bruises. He must have been looking forward to shared meals as pleasurable as their lunch in Shoreditch. What was wrong with him?

He pushed his unfinished plate away and picked up an article detailing various speculative economic scenarios following an income tax reform. The words on the page failed to sink in.

As if I could love you—as if anyone could.

Well. He knew he wasn't lovable, not since he'd been a boy, anyway, and he had only known it then when Sorcha had put her sticky little hand upon his cheek and told him she loved him, so he had no expectations in that regard. But hatred?

During the stop in York, he sent a telegram to the hotel to order a coach to Waverley Station at eight o'clock. When they reached Edinburgh, the sky was the color of lead and proper fat splats of rain were drumming on the ribbed glass ceiling of the railway station. A gust of wind near ripped the umbrella he was holding over Harriet from his hand when they stepped outside. "Welcome to Scotland," he murmured. The air was damp on his face and tasted fresh. An illusion. To the left loomed the turreted silhouette of Edinburgh in dark uniform color as though the whole city had risen from the same giant rock, for soot and smoke had coated the soft sandstone of every house with the same black stain. Farther to the east, the old castle kept watch over the city through the mist as it had for the past eight hundred years. He felt a yearning pull deep in his chest and a sorrow at the sight, a blend of emotions expressed best by the lone skirl of a bagpipe. This was why he disliked going north.

Once settled in at number twenty-five George Street, a town house hotel where Robert Burns had purportedly liked to take rooms in his day, Harriet immediately made to flee his small chamber through the door that led to her room.

"Tea is downstairs in half an hour," he said to her back.

She stiffened, halted, and turned to him. "You mean supper."

He took a deep breath. "You'd call it supper."

"I'm not hungry."

"I'm requesting your company."

Her mouth flattened. "I have nothing to wear."

She looked fatigued, he now noticed, with curls of her hair loose around her face and faint blue smudges beneath her eyes. He wouldn't relent; he would take hatred, but no more disrespect. He untied his cravat. "You should find a trunk with dresses in your room."

She gave him a suspicious glance. "You had a trunk packed for me?"

He began unbuttoning his waistcoat. "It seemed sensible."

"When?" she demanded. "When did you have my clothes packed?"

"Matthews picked some up at Harrods while they readied the train."

Her eyes were slits. "Gowns off the rack?"

"They'll do."

She muttered something under her breath.

"The train to Fife leaves at eleven o'clock tomorrow," he said grimly. "Purchase whatever else you need in the morning."

She pursed her lips. "No doubt you think Cockburn Street *will do*."

He stopped unbuttoning at hearing the word *cock* from her mouth. "What?"

"Cockburn Street," she enunciated slowly. "The street where one can find the finest supplies in all of Edinburgh, according to *Bradshaw's Travel Guide*."

"Aye," he said, feeling heated. "It's pronounced Coburn Street, but yes, you'll find everything there."

"Are lady's maids for hire on *Coburn* Street?" she said. "I require one, since you forgot to invite Bailey along."

Uppity brat.

"Say the word," he said, and dragged his gaze over her disheveled appearance. "I'll undress you. Assist with your bath, too."

He pulled his shirt over his head, unwillingly aroused by the thought of her soapy, slippery body beneath his hands, and wasn't surprised to find her gone when he reappeared.

Though she looked very pretty in the russet-colored gown the Harrods shop assistant had suggested, dinner would have been more palatable without her company. The small dining room should have attracted her attention; it was underground with low vaulted ceilings, whitewashed walls as thick as a castle's, and torches burning in iron-cast sconces, but she was very much preoccupied with examining her fingernails after taking off her gloves. She did smile at the waiter, a wide, sweet smile that left both Lucian and the lad a little stunned.

"Is the lobster very fresh, I wonder?" she said.

"Yes, ma'am," the young man replied, his gaze flickering uncertainly between her and Lucian. "It's fresh from the firth every day, ma'am."

"Lovely. I so love a fresh lobster." Her smile sparkled in her eyes, and the waiter blushed.

"Bring the lobster for a starter," Lucian said. "And the lamb for the main course."

She was so outrageously clumsy in her attempts to provoke him that it shouldn't have bothered him, not one bit. He still felt as irritated as if the place were swarming with midges, because despite the clumsiness, it had worked; he knew he'd commit a minor crime in exchange for such a smile from her.

She seemed to enjoy her wine and drank rather much of it, and later, she deftly plundered the fat lobster tail with her utensils. "I was wondering where you put me in your ledgers," she said, glancing up as she pulled the soft white meat apart on her plate. "On the one hand, your return on me should be immense. On the other, I suppose I'm a depreciating asset since both my looks and my ability to bear you children shall fade with time."

His etiquette guide for the discerning gentleman recommended a man stoically endure any mean-spirited remarks and unreasonable demands a woman directed at him, as those were the only weapons she was permitted, and in any case, her weak mind and volatile sensibilities weren't her fault but a lamentable consequence of the nature of her sex. That had sounded like bollocks to him, for he had seen women chase after men while brandishing a skillet, and he had witnessed them stoically clean up tragedy and bring whole families through winter on their own. But now, faced with this sweetly smiling creature dissecting a crustacean on her plate with merciless precision, it all made sense. He ate in silence. Time was on his side. The law was on his side. Those were still the facts. It was but a feeling that the playing field had leveled today.

Chapter 17

When they resumed their journey the next day, the sky was a blustering display of dramatic white and gray swirls on blue, an El Greco the size of infinity. The Firth of Forth flowing alongside the railroad tracks sparkled like silver coins in the sun, another lovely sight over which to ignore a husband. The husband sat across from her, wearing a well-fitted navy tweed suit, a gray paisley waistcoat, and a deeply brooding expression that would have been alluring had she not resolved to despise him. At least he was keeping his word: he hadn't made any attempts to claim husbandly rights last night. And he hadn't as much as blinked when she had purchased half of Cockburn Street right under his nose this morning. Four large crates with costly frippery she had no intention of ever using were now on their way to Belgravia. She couldn't bankrupt him this way, but it had been quite enjoyable to try.

She glanced at him. His shoulders were relaxed and the dark fans of his lashes lowered against his cheeks as if he were dozing. He never slept enough; he went to bed late and rose too early, that much she had learned about him. A loving wife would fuss over this, and she felt fresh resentment rise because he had forever taken such small, caring rituals from her.

He woke when the train rolled right down into the bustling harbor of Granton and came to a halt at the waterline.

She pointed at the large sign looming on the banks: *Granton–Burntisland Ferry Service.*

"Do they mean to move the entire train onto a boat?"

"It's a roll-on ferry," Lucian said, his voice distractingly scratchy.

"I see."

His bleary gaze fell to her hands, clamped around the edge of her seat. "It's been running well for thirty years," he said. "It won't have its first capsizing today."

She reluctantly released her grip, determined not to show him her apprehension. How infuriating, she thought as the ferry carried train and passengers across the firth, that for thirty years such masterful feats of engineering allowed people to move freely and quickly across vast distances and uninhabitable terrains, and yet a woman must not go shopping or to a gallery by herself. It was too dangerous, they said, for her reputation, her virtue. But who did the endangering? Men. How convenient for men as a group that the misdeeds of a few elevated each one of them to the status of protector and rendered women dependent on them, so that in turn they could legitimately drag them along to Scotland whenever they saw fit. Proof that progressiveness wasn't a matter of possibilities—who and what was to be included in the progress was a matter of will. Man would probably circle the globe in a flight apparatus before women had power over themselves.

In Burntisland, they changed into a battered-looking old train to continue the journey away from the coast, up north. The scenery soon changed into sweeping green valleys dotted with sheep and crofters' cottages, and there was a vastness to the land that made the observer breathe deeply. Still, when they finally alighted at the one-track station stop in Auchtermuchty, she was exhausted. Her pocket watch said it was close to five o'clock, and she stood by despondently as two young Scotsmen loaded their trunks onto an old-fashioned black coach outside the station. She endured another hour of being bounced around on a badly sprung seat before the vehicle gradually creaked to a halt on an abandoned plain—in front of the only building far and wide. The Drover's Inn. She eyed the place through the window with growing alarm. The gray stone building was two stories high under a dark slate roof, an irregular patchwork of old, weathered features and newer extensions, which gave the impression the house had somehow organically grown by itself over time. There was an aliveness about it; in fact, the entire structure was leaning to the right with some urgency, as if it had at some point been frozen during an attempt to flee.

She shuddered. "Something is wrong with this house."

Lucian leaned forward to look more closely. "Appears to me like most of the inns I've known in Scotland."

His face was so near hers she could smell the shaving soap on him. She pulled back, and he shot her a dark look and opened the coach door with a vigorous push. She followed him to the entrance of the disturbing building on stiff legs. Next, she screamed and jumped with great agility as she found herself under attack by clawed, swiping paws. A black bear, rearing on its hind legs in the corridor, its maw forever open with a silent roar.

"It's quite dead," Lucian remarked, and she realized she was pressed up against his side.

She quickly stepped away. "A very helpful observation." She still had a hand over her hammering heart when a short, stout woman hurried toward them from the shadowy depths of the corridor. Her brown hair was streaked with silver, and the corners of her eyes were furrowed with lines from frequent laughter and squinting. "I'm Mrs. Burns," she told them, a little breathless, "I'm one of the proprietors—the other is my husband, Mr. Burns, who awaits you inside. I hope your journey was uneventful; we've been having lots more rain than usual at this time of the year and the roads are all muck. My sons will bring your luggage straight to your room, sir." She looked at Hattie, then she nodded at the bear. "Don't let Alistair frighten you, ma'am; he's a good lad. Follow me, if you please."

The low black ceilings and wooden walls of the inn were coated with dust. Antiquated gas sconces lined the narrow corridor and spilled orange light over antlers, wings, and paws—stuffed woodland animals were stacked atop one another in glass cases and on shelves mounted on the walls with little space between them. By the time they'd reached the reception desk, Hattie felt weak and haunted by undead creatures. The tall, bald man behind the desk greeted them with great enthusiasm. Probably not many guests ever found their way to this forsaken place or stayed for long. Perhaps they never left?

"The telegraph I sent yesterday mentioned my wife needs the service of a lady's maid for the duration of our stay," Lucian told him as he signed the ledger. "I pay London rates."

"Of course," said Mr. Burns. "I'll fetch my daughters. One wee moment."

He disappeared through the heavy curtains to a back room.

The silence was as absolute as at the bottom of a lake. A stuffed raven sat on the desk next to the bell, its head bent at an inquisitive angle.

She turned to Lucian. He was looking straight ahead, very stoically.

"Whatever made you choose this peculiar place?" she hissed.

"It's the only one there is near the mine."

They stood intimately close together, but given their strange surroundings, she was reluctant to put distance between them.

"It's ghastly," she said. "I expect the bear Alastair and his friends will all come alive at midnight and feed on the guests."

Unexpectedly, he placed his hand on the small of her back and urged her a little closer. "There's an etiquette guide that says a woman's vocation is to be amicable, admirable, and delightful," he murmured into her ear, his voice deep like a distant roll of thunder. "Consider reading it."

"Hmm," she murmured back, "sounds crusty—I'd consider burning it."

Her pulse was high from his touch, but he withdrew his hand and his jaw clenched, very satisfying to behold.

Mr. Burns returned with his wife and two young women barely out of girlhood. Their brown hair hung in thick plaits over their shoulders and they regarded her with overtly curious blue eyes. "Miss Mhairi Burns and Miss Clara Burns," Mrs. Burns introduced them. "At your service."

Lucian turned to Mr. Burns. "They speak English?"

"They do," said Mr. Burns. "The Drover's Inn is frequented by international guests."

Miss Clara Burns had a dusting of flour on her forehead, and Miss Mhairi's hands were still red and damp from scrubbing something. How dreadful, to be adding to their chores.

She addressed the one who had been introduced as Mhairi. "You are the elder one?"

"Yes, ma'am." The girl performed a wonky curtsy.

"A pleasure, Miss Burns," Hattie said. "It is our honeymoon, you see, and it shall be so much more convenient with your assistance."

The girls' faces fell. "A honeymoon." Mrs. Burns looked put out. Even Mr. Burns seemed taken aback. Lucian was looking at her warily from the corner of his eyes.

"Well," Mr. Burns said brightly. "This is a first-class establishment. It is run very orderly, it is very quiet, very unique. An excellent choice for a honeymoon."

His wife shot him a sour look.

He closed the ledger. "We're at your service."

"Wish you hadn't forgotten there was a bride," Mrs. Burns said to him. "We would have put a basket together."

"Yes," Mhairi said. "Ma'am should've had a newlywed basket."

Hattie gave them all a tremulous smile. "How terribly kind."

The women rallied. "It's a delicious basket," Miss Clara said enthusiastically. "We'll add the best shortbread."

"And blueberry jam."

"And cured ham."

"Well, go on, then," Mrs. Burns barked, "don't just stand there discussing it." She turned back to Hattie. "Apologies for the delay of the basket, ma'am. Had we known there's a bride . . ." She shook her head.

"You've the best room, with the best view." Mr. Burns joined the collective effort to comfort her over her dismal honeymoon, inflicted upon her by a no doubt dismal husband, and to her dark delight she felt Lucian's temper beginning to broil.

"We'll add a bottle of Auchtermuchty, best vintage," said Mrs. Burns.

"Auchtermuchty." Mr. Burns gave Lucian a conspiring nod. "Best whisky in all of Fife."

Their room upstairs was possibly the least best in all of Fife. It was small and tired and smelled like a basket full of old linen. The right side was occupied by a lumpy bed and a wardrobe. Straight ahead was a single window with a patched armchair underneath; to the left, the fireplace and a curtained side entrance. At the center of the chamber, a scarred table wrestled for space with their luggage. A black folder lay atop the table, and Lucian went to pick it up with a keen expression that said he had been expecting to find it here.

Hattie went to the window and pushed aside a careworn curtain. The view was drab: a dirt path winding through a heather field, and in the near distance, a double row of gray-stone cottages and what looked to be industrial structures. It was doubly drab because if it weren't for her husband, she would now be overlooking the roofs of Paris or romantically fading lavender fields in Provence. *You shan't take France from me forever*, she vowed silently.

"I had hoped for vast, proper mountains in Scotland," she said out loud. "This looks like East Anglia, flat as a crumpet."

"Fife is part of the Lowlands," came Lucian's voice.

"How dull." She peeked behind the curtain of the side entrance. The room was barely more than a cupboard: a few square feet in size, containing only a footstool and a washbasin with pitcher. The window was up high and narrow like an arrow slit. She supposed the water closet was downstairs—a severe inconvenience.

A jolt of an entirely different apprehension went through her then. She turned back to Lucian, who was leafing through the folder.

"There is only one bed."

"Yes."

She crossed her arms over her chest. "I require my own room."

"I'm sure you do, love, but there are none."

"An inn with only one room?" she said, agitated. And the way he called her *love*—like a northern shopkeeper addressing patrons.

"There are three other guest rooms, and they're all taken," Lucian said coolly.

"All taken—but who in their right mind would want to linger in this godforsaken place?"

"A mining engineer, a civil engineer, and the future mine manager. They're here on my behest."

They must have left the folder for him, then.

She turned to the small fireplace, eyed the mantelpiece, and sniffed. While the badly stuffed animals seemed to be confined to the ground floor, ugly wooden gnomes had gathered on the shelf, their hair and beards made of tufts of graying sheep wool. A Black Forest cuckoo clock modeled after a railway house was affixed to the wall right next to the mantelshelf, richly ornamented with carved leafy vines—charming in its own right, grotesque in its surroundings.

She swiped a finger over the mantelpiece and held up her hand as she turned back to Lucian. "The room is dusty, and there's a draft."

Lucian rubbed his neck but appeared otherwise deeply immersed in his reading.

She repeatedly stabbed her fingertip at the long arm of the cuckoo clock until it reached the full hour, which forced the small green window shutters of the railway house to open and the mechanical bird to shoot out to give seven hectic, tinny squawks.

"You can't expect me to abide this every hour," she said when the window had fallen shut again. "I'm returning to London tomorrow."

Lucian glanced up from his documents with hooded eyes. "Harriet. How would you like a spanking to settle you down?"

She blinked. She grabbed one of the wooden figurines off the mantelpiece. "How would you like a gnome to your head?"

His lips thinned. Then the corners of his mouth twitched suspiciously. "It's not a gnome," he said. "It's a trow—wee beasties from the isles that don't appreciate being thrown."

She put it back down fast, fair loathing his lopsided smirk.

⁓⦁⁓

They went to the dining area downstairs for tea, or *suppah*, because Harriet preferred eating in public over a more intimate meal in their room, no surprise there. A handful of patrons who had the seasoned looks of regulars were scattered along the poorly lit bar, eyeing them curiously through curls of cigarette smoke, but the waitress led them to a booth at the window front.

"What may I bring you, sir?" The waitress was smiling and addressing him in English.

"What's your recommendation?"

"We make the best haggis in the Kingdom of Fife," she said, "served with mashed potatoes and well-cooked turnips."

"Well-cooked, you say."

"Then there's the beef-and-potato stew—best black Galloway beef from the West Country."

He glanced at Harriet, who seemed apathetic, then back at the lass. "You have a menu?"

"Not on my account," came his wife's soft voice. "I'll take the recommended dish."

He gave her a skeptical look. "It won't be to your taste, I reckon."

"Well-cooked turnips," she said blandly. "Why, I crave them."

The kitchen is lacking, was what she really said. She knew without seeing the menu; the place was lacking, Scotland was lacking, *he* was lacking. He ordered haggis, stew, some wine, and ale, thinking a wooden trow to his head would have been well worth it.

Time passed slowly here in the middle of nowhere. The rack on the wall held the newspapers from three days ago. It felt like eternity until the steaming dishes were placed before them, compounded by the glum silence coming from the woman he had wed.

"You like the haggis?" he said as she ate her meal with a passive expression.

She gave a one-shouldered shrug. "It reminds me of black pudding, but the taste is more severe. What is it?"

"Sheep's stomach," he said, "stuffed with chopped sheep innards and gruel."

She put down her fork. "Very nourishing, I'm sure," she said faintly.

She didn't pick up her cutlery again but kept drinking her wine in tiny sips.

"I can order you a new dish," he said after a while.

Suspicion flickered in her eyes and his fingers tightened around his spoon. He should be wholly unaffected by her moods and lack of trust, but she had introduced a hitherto unknown complexity to his life: he found he was holding multiple contradictory thoughts—or worse, feelings—at the same time. Her mistrust, her sniping, the sullen, petulant curve of her mouth, bedeviled him very effectively, and yet he still wanted to lean across the narrow table and kiss that mouth. Her expensive burnt-vanilla scent was mixing with the smell of smoldering coal creeping in from the pits, a bizarre, sensual clash of his old life and the new that unmoored him in some fashion.

She finally continued to eat, and once and again her gaze strayed out the window to the dark outline of the far hills gradually fading into the night.

"Were you really hoping to see mountains?" he said, because apparently, he was perverted and craved rejection.

"Of course." She sighed, her wistfulness sincere. "Looking at them elevates the soul. 'What are men to rocks and mountains?'"

"That's from a poem?"

She regarded him with a carefully curated look of pity in her brown eyes. "It is a line by Jane Austen."

"Ah." He'd heard of Jane Austen but knew nothing of her work.

"Of course," she said. "You wouldn't know—you don't read novels. In any case, you could not be farther from a Mr. Bingley if you tried."

He had no idea how to reply to such a thing, so he took a long draft of his ale.

"You are beyond even a Mr. Rochester," Harriet said, and he didn't know that fellow, either, but he deduced he was odious so he pinned her with a look over the rim of his glass.

"In fact," she said, her eyes widening with shocked realization, "in fact, you—you are a Heathcliff."

Perhaps—and this occurred to him for the first time—perhaps she wasn't just trying to provoke him; perhaps she was genuinely unhinged. She didn't speak for the rest of the meal, and when they had finished, she asked to be excused and he had barely nodded when she had already fled from the booth.

The waitress took Harriet's departure as the signal to approach to clear the table and inquire whether he wished for more ale.

"Who, or what, is Heathcliff?" he demanded.

"Heathcliff—why, he's a bit of a villain in *Wuthering Heights*, sir," she supplied as she leaned in close to collect his plate. "It's a novel."

"The villain, eh?"

"Well, he's a brooding, ill-bred man who moons after a fine lady."

"Is he, now?" he muttered.

"Then he makes a fortune but is still obsessed with revenge and ruins everything."

Lucian was quiet.

"Some of the lasses quite fancy him," the waitress said, and glanced at him from the corner of her eye.

Heat washed over his neck in response. The glance could have been anything; innocuous, pitiful, or a flirtation. He looked away. This was the state of things now, was it, him becoming randy the moment a woman *glanced* his way? It had been too long; he hadn't sought out female company since he had struck the deal with Green-field, and it had been a while even before that. Now he had a wife around who smelled like something edible when he couldn't taste her, whose skin was glossy and smooth when he couldn't touch her. He wanted to follow her to their room, peel off her prim dress, and push her down on the creaky bed. He would run his ill-bred, villain-ous Heathcliff hands all over her soft curves while she was looking up at him with a sweet smile and desire in her eyes; She would ea-gerly open her legs for him . . . and she would be impossibly snug and hot and he would fuck her so slowly, she would soon whine for him to do it harder. . . .

"Whisky," he said hoarsely. "More whisky."

It was well past midnight when he returned to their room. She seemed asleep. He quietly undressed and washed, then fumbled his way toward the bed. He paused next to where the cuckoo clock had hung and found the spot on the wall already empty. Harriet must have tossed it out the window, and she'd probably done it with a pout and shrug, just how she would do such a thing. He was drunk. He was never drunk. Except for those few days a year. . . . She made a breathy little noise when he came to bed. He carefully pulled the covers up to his shoulders and lay quietly on his side. Her warm body was curled up just inches from his back, and despite the drinking, his muscles were hard with a yearning tension so thick a knife wouldn't cut it.

She rustled softly in the sheets. "It is so dark," she mumbled. "I have never seen such darkness."

Indeed, there was little difference between his eyes being open or closed. No man-made light polluted the depths of Scottish nights.

"Don't be afraid," he murmured. The dark and he had a history;

he knew all the different sorts, and this one now lying over their bed like black velvet meant no harm. Her breathing settled, and it occurred to him that he had had this soothing effect on her, and that despite all her misgivings, she was here, in this bed. That was a start, he supposed, one he would use to his advantage.

Chapter 18

He set out to inspect the mining hamlets right after drinking a bucket of strong breakfast tea. The night had been short; at some point Harriet had left her side of the mattress, possibly in search of warmth, and he had woken to the soft weight of her breasts pressed against his back. He had lain staring at the wall, the world reduced to the sensation of her breath brushing over his neck in gentle puffs. The memory of her shape was still hot like a lingering burn on his skin as he joined his party in the Drover's Inn coach: his new mine manager, Mr. Stewart—a tall, clean-shaven Scotsman from Dundee whom he'd met before in London—and taciturn Mr. Wright, a civil engineer who was originally from Surrey but now resided in St. Andrews. The mining engineer's expertise was not yet needed, hence the man had stayed back to leave room for one of the lads from the inn, who was to carry Wright's camera equipment.

Spraying rain shrouded the valley, and when they descended from the coach at the village entrance, they were greeted by chilly blasts of wind cutting through their robust tweed coats. The settlement stretching before them would have been miserable even under a cloudless sky.

"As you can see, the road is raised above the house entrances," Stewart said, wrestling with his papers while also trying to hold the umbrella over his long body. "This is not the case in Heather Row—

out of the two hamlets, this one here will require more significant improvements."

Heather Row was located within walking distance from the inn, but Lucian had decided to start their inspection on the far side of the mine at the smaller colliery and the older settlement, Drummuir Grove. It matched the mental image he had developed based on the maps Stewart had left for him back at the inn: a crooked chapel to their left, and thirty old stone cottages each on either side of the straight dirt road. The road was in bad condition and riddled with black puddles; and yes, its higher elevation meant rainwater flowed straight into the lodgings to the left and right.

"What about the refuse ditches?" he asked.

Mr. Wright took a pencil and notebook from the inside of his coat. "They're too close," he said. "Will be a nuisance whenever temperatures are warmer," he added, and smoothed his ruddy mustache. "I suggest a greater distance by at least six feet."

"So we are redrawing the ditches."

"Correct."

He had suspected as much from the map.

They were being watched; while the rest of the community was at work over at the mine, the elderly would be home, minding the toddlers and keeping an eye on any suspicious activities from behind the curtains. Memories encroached, of the day when he arrived back in Argyll to fetch his grandmother. The once familiar cottages had seemed smaller, the few stray sheep sicklier, the winding path muddier. No one had recognized him, aged nineteen and wearing a fine coat, and the lads he had approached had been wary of his clean skin and the London vowels that had crept into his speech. Nanny MacKenzie? She had died in February. Blinding agony, to realize he had been too late by a month. A month. After seven years of waiting. They had buried her in the graveyard of their old hamlet, her spot marked by an already rotting wooden cross. Had she been waiting for him by the window in her patched shawl, her tired gaze on the village road, holding on to hope until the very end?

He blinked against the rain in his eyes. "How bad is the damp?"

"Much worse here than over in Heather Row," said Stewart. "Half the older miners appear afflicted with rheumatism. The road is the main culprit, but the roofing contributes its share."

The bloody roofing looked as though it hadn't been touched in half a century. Curse Rutland. Curse the consortium that had taken the mine off Rutland's hands and continued to charge rent for these hovels. He'd call in the earl's debts, then use the money for renovations.

Doors were opening; people were emerging to inspect them more closely. Young children soon stopped hovering behind their minders and came running to circle Mr. Wright as he readied his camera to photograph the ailing water tank. Lucian approached the nearest cottage, where an elderly woman stood leaning against the doorjamb. She had tied a red handkerchief around her hair, but the few tendrils that had escaped were still sooty.

"I'm Blackstone," he told her.

Her watery gaze took stock of him; he felt her assessment go through his bones. "They told us you would come," she said in Scots. She revealed all her remaining teeth in a smile. "They say you visit the hamlets."

"May I look inside your home?"

She nodded and stepped aside. He knew from the blueprints that the cottages here had two rooms, a kitchen and a bedroom. When Wright joined him, Lucian toed the flagstones with the tip of his boot. "Stone floors," he said. "Make a note, I want wooden floors with the proper insulation underneath."

Mr. Wright was scribbling diligently.

"I want a larder added to the back of each house—after the ditches have been redrawn, that is."

The woman followed him around in the small space, careful to

balance her obvious pride in her meagerly supplied but tidily organized kitchen with harried sighs acknowledging the damp and missing larder and badly done ditches. No need; he saw how dire it was.

"What happened?" he growled when he was back outside in fresh
air. "Accommodation was more humane in the sixties."

Wright and Stewart looked away, embarrassed, as though they
could sense the emotion beating through him. *Are you a violent man,
then?* Harriet's face was tied to the question; he could see her, wide-
eyed in her parents' parlor. He was, at least, an angry man.

The smell of poverty hung in his clothes and hair after visiting the
cottage, this distinct blend of damp walls and stale cigarette smoke,
of the watery stew that always simmered on the stove, of sweat and
clammy woolen clothes that were never given the time to fully dry
after washing because they were needed for wearing again. It smelled
like all the evenings when he'd come home as a boy after the shift.
Hours later, while they were shuttled to Heather Row, he was still
contemplating razing Drummuir Grove to the ground.

They ate their packed luncheon in the empty classroom of the
village school before the next assessment. The situation here was indeed better: dry brick houses, most of them boasting a parlor and
decently sized windows. They finally ended the inventory in the
kitchen of Mr. Boyd, the community spokesman. Boyd's lined face
gave no clue about his age, but he had a head full of thick chestnut
curls and all his teeth in a row. A recent accident with a runaway
wagon had put his arm in a sling, so he couldn't go underground, but
his wife and daughters were out on the field sorting coal.

"Here in Heather Row, it's the water for the households that's the
main problem," he explained while his mother was serving them
oversweetened tea. *See here*, said that tea, *we have the means for sugar,
and lots of it*. "The water comes from the newly opened pit, but there's
something wrong with the filtering process. If you'd look at the
pump well here, you'll find lots of matter in the water and there's
bouts of dysentery in the community." Boyd's uninjured hand was

broad, callused, and forever dusty, and it rested perfectly motionless on the table surface as he spoke. A calm man. He was also deeply wary of Lucian; the look in his habitually squinting blue eyes made no secret of it.

"Mr. Wright here will look at the water," Lucian said.

Boyd's practiced gaze measured the engineer, who was presently eyeing the contents of his tea mug with great suspicion.

"I'll be blunt," Lucian said, "we've work to do. The first thing I must ask of you is to talk to the men about joining the region's trade union."

Boyd's lips twitched, as if suppressing his impulse to spit. "No worries, sir. We've no intention to unionize."

"You mistake me," Lucian said. "I want you to put it to the men to join the union."

Boyd regarded him with a poker face and said nothing; Stewart and Wright were puzzled; the lad carrying the equipment was watching him with blatant astonishment.

"You didn't consider it before because Drummuir is on its last legs?" Lucian prodded.

Boyd gave a huff. "Oh, we considered it, but it was made very clear that if we joined, we'd be shut down," he said. "Drummuir, she's become a tough and stingy old mistress, isn't she."

That was one way to sum up a bad investment. "She is."

Resignation warred with stubborn pride in Boyd's expression. "Durham, Northumberland, the south of Wales—that's where the pliant fields are these days, I understand."

"I intend to revive Drummuir's profitability by investing in transport infrastructure and new cutting technologies, and not by working miners into an early grave for a pittance," Lucian said. "So put it to the men—unionize."

"All right," Boyd said after a long pause. "I'll do that."

"And I want the accommodation communally owned. Discuss that, too."

Boyd was left bewildered by these developments, but his wide shoulders relaxed and he became talkative, first about the weather, then about the idiosyncrasies of the different coal seams that couldn't be found in the ledgers and official reports. He was eventually interrupted when the kitchen door behind him opened and a black-haired child entered, a boy. He was five or seven years of age, impossible to tell, stunted in growth as he was. At the sight of the visitors, he dropped the bucket and the contents spilled across the floor. Turnips, thin and pale like bones.

"Och, Ruri," said Boyd, and shook his head.

The lad didn't move; his eyes locked on Lucian and Lucian instantly knew what he saw: a man in a fine suit and a tall hat, with a thick silver pocket watch chain on display, flanked by other men who looked to be from the city; a picture that spelled trouble—a mum walking on eggshells for days, perhaps, or an angry da, or less food in the larder. Lucian's chest tightened with resentment, and it worsened while he watched Boyd's gray-haired mother pick turnips off the flagstones. Absolution came from the clanging of a distant bell—five o'clock. The shift was over for the day, and they took their leave.

Outside, the weather had turned, and beneath the coal odor the refined air smelled like soil warming after the rain. Boyd walked with them, demonstrating his approval. "My eldest daughter's wedding is in five days' time," he said, nodding and raising his healthy hand in greeting at some of the miners returning from the field.

"My congratulations," Lucian said. It was a request for him to pay for the festivities, which boded well. Boyd wouldn't take his money if he still distrusted him.

The next moment, he did a double take. A vivid flash of red had drawn his attention to the bench in front of the last house in the row. His wife. Sitting at the center of a pack of small children like a happy hen in a nest. Briefly, it was so silent in his head he thought he could hear the clang of the chisels from under the rocks.

Chapter 19

Earlier in the Day

She had stood by the window for an hour, watching the purple hues of the heather field change depending on the shifting afternoon clouds, and when the sun finally broke through, she examined the dresses Lucian had purchased for her more closely. Save the russet silk gown and one in emerald green, her trunk contained plain wool dresses in earthy colors. Which, admittedly, were perfect, since given the choice between waltzing into the village like a Marie Antoinette in fine silks or staying in the room, she would have elected to stay in the room, where she would have gone mad. If she couldn't create, she had to move. She picked a plum-colored dress, laced up her boots, and with her sketchbook satchel and her parasol, she went downstairs to request Mhairi's company. This put Mrs. Burns in an embarrassing position, for Mhairi was quite indispensably at work in the kitchen, until Hattie suggested one pound for the service, which was an offer Mrs. Burns thought unwise to refuse. Then, on a whim, she requested pen and paper and wrote a note in passable French, which informed the mistress of Mytilene of her arrival as soon as next month, and that she would make herself useful in the community in whichever way required. She knew the address by heart—a safety measure she had taken before setting out for France—and offered Mrs. Burns another pound for discreet delivery of the note to the post and telegraph office in Auchtermuchty.

"It's peculiar," she said to Mhairi, as she strode briskly along the path toward the village a while later, "I keep expecting the air to smell fresh in a valley and yet my nose tells me I'm in the middle of the city."

"It's the coal field, ma'am," Mhairi supplied after a pause. "There's an open seam and there's always small fires."

"Have you been to London, Miss Burns?"

Mhairi glanced at her sideways, clearly amused. "No, ma'am. I've been to Dundee."

"Charming—and I suppose this is Heather Row." Entering the village felt like walking into a Dutch Renaissance painting: all colors had a brown tinge to them and a somberness lay over the scene. The two rows of houses would have appeared abandoned had it not been for a group of children chasing a hoop down the road.

"I suppose everyone is at work."

"They'll return very soon," Mhairi said, nodding at the furnaces steaming in the distance. "At five o'clock."

"Would they mind if I sat and sketched the lodgings?" She pointed at the wooden bench in front of the first cottage in the row, from where she could conveniently sketch the cottage across.

"I don't think they'd mind, no," Mhairi said, "Hamish's mother's lives there, Rosie Fraser; I know her well."

She looked on curiously as Hattie unpacked sketchbook and pencils.

"Sit with me," Hattie said, and with an embarrassed giggle, the young woman settled next to her, and was soon watching intently as the house across the way began to appear on the page.

It took not long for the children to find them more interesting than their hoop, and for Hattie to find them more interesting than her sketch. Their little group brought field mice to mind with their round eyes and dull brown coats. One of the girls was chewing on a strand of blond hair. Hattie smiled at her. "Hello, angel."

Encouraged thusly, the children encroached. Grubby little hands were touching the shiny blue silk of her folded parasol. She laughed when Mhairi tried batting away the boldest ones. "Let them," she said.

The blond girl promptly climbed onto the bench between them and cuddled close to study the sketch. Then she said something incomprehensible in Scots.

Mhairi snorted.

"What did she say?" Hattie asked.

"Anne's being daft, ma'am. She wants you to draw her."

"Anne." The girl's eyes were wide and blue, and eerily serious. "Would you like me to draw you, Anne?"

A nod.

"You would have to hold still for a while," Hattie said. "Can you do that?"

"A shilling that she'll not last a minute," Mhairi said.

"Why don't you hold her on your lap?"

Bemused, Mhairi hoisted the girl onto her apron, and the pen flew over the paper again, easily capturing round, dirt-smudged cheeks, a pouty mouth. . . . The challenge was always the eyes, and in this case they held a very complex little soul. . . . When Hattie finally glanced up, she found several elderly women had joined the circle and were craning their necks.

"It looks like a photograph," Mhairi said, amazed.

She shook out her hand. "It's just a sketch."

Anne seemed sufficiently smitten with her likeness; she gripped the sheet and held on tight.

"I suppose you shall have to take it home to your mama, hmm?"

The cozy atmosphere shifted as the miners were returning to the village, groups of men and throngs of children, and judging by their overt stares when they noticed Hattie, the curiosity was mutual. But when she comprehended what she saw, her stomach sank. "The children," she murmured. "Were . . . they working, too?"

Mhairi followed her gaze to a couple of boys trotting past. "Yes, ma'am."

They looked not much older than little Anne. Her next shock followed right at their heels—the women streaming in . . . were wearing trousers. They wore a sort of loincloth on top, the hems of which didn't even reach their knees, and they were linking arms and chatting as if they weren't practically in the nude. Outrageous. Intriguing. None of it half as startling as her husband moving into her field of vision. A hat covered his shaggy hair, but his purposful stride was unmistakable. Her belly clenched with a visceral emotion, and the elderly women who had been studying her sketch exchanged glances, grabbed the children, and dispersed.

"Um," said Mhairi.

"Why don't you return to the inn," Hattie suggested. "It appears I have an escort."

The girl had disappeared by the time Lucian reached the bench.

He was glowering down at her in a by now familiar manner. "Mrs. Blackstone."

"Sir."

"Will you accompany me to the inn?" Why did he even bother phrasing it like a question?

She collected her pencils. She had woken this morning with the strange notion that his presence in their bed had ensured her warmth and safety in those bizarre new surroundings. She was most powerfully deluded, for he looked moody and not at all pleased to see her.

He noticed her troubles to adjust to his pace as he steered her toward the dirt path, and he slowed at once, but he made no effort to make conversation.

"There were women coming from the mine in trousers," she tried, because the silence felt awkward. "Is this commonplace?"

"Pit-brow lasses," he said, keeping his eyes on the inn ahead. "They're very common. They all but run the coal fields down in Wigan."

"I must tell Lucie," she murmured. "She leads our suffrage chapter back in Oxford," she added. "I wonder if she knows—"

"I assure you they're not motivated by politics."

"What do you mean?"

He finally halted and looked at her. His expressing was grim. "They don't wear trousers to make ladies clutch their pearls or change laws, but because it allows them to work," he said. "They aren't freaks for you to gape at and find exotic."

She gasped. "Is that how you think I think?"

"And those children," he said, "they're not your playthings."

He resumed walking, the matter settled. For him.

"But of course," she said, keeping up with quick, angry steps. "You think I'm a snooty brat."

"Don't worry," he said, "you've announced yourself as such by showing with a parasol." He cast the pale blue contraption she was holding over her head a contemptuous glance.

His low regard stabbed her right in the heart, when his cruelty should no longer surprise her.

"My skin cares not where the sun happens to shine," she said, shaking with distress. "Would you rather have me burn as proof of my good character?"

His face fell, as though he had heard impending tears in her voice. "No," he said gruffly, "no, I—"

"Well, I think you would. You have no desire to mend a dratted thing between us."

She hurried ahead, the path swimming before her eyes. She shouldn't care; she shouldn't, and comprehending that she did doubled her misery. At the inn, Mhairi was manning the reception desk and greeted her with notable wariness, which Hattie tried to assuage with a wide smile while storming past. Her blood was still rushing in her ears when she reached the dreadful little room. She dropped the parasol and ripped off gloves and hat. Mr. Blackstone better have the decency to go elsewhere—preferably straight back to his empty throne in the land of the dead.

The door flew open, and she was stunned to the spot by the smolder in Lucian's eyes. He came to her; he didn't halt until his knees pressed into her skirts. Her hands fluttered up, but he grabbed the thick fabric at her hips and pulled her flush against him, and her thoughts flew apart. His gaze searched her face so intently, as if he wished to see right into her soul.

"Much that I despise," he said hoarsely, "and all that I desire, meets in you. And it frustrates me beyond reason."

She felt the erratic thud of his heart beating through her chest in counterpoint to her own, and a different kind of agitation gripped her.

"That's not my fault," she whispered.

"It isn't."

Her fingers curled into the lapels of his coat. "It isn't an apology, either."

His thumb was against her mouth, lightly pressing on her bottom lip. The brazen caress flashed through her body like a shooting flame, and his eyes lit up at her soft mew.

"I don't know how to do this right," he murmured. He took off his hat and tossed it aside. "I don't know what to make of you. I know I'd rather my skin burned than yours."

He would kiss her now. Had he been angry, she would have resisted. But she sensed a need singing through him, deeper than desire, and it harmonized with a fiercely frustrated cry in her own soul. She raised her chin. His fingers slid into her hair, and their mouths met. A hot touching of tongues, and she headlong drowned in him—smooth lips, sugared tea, thick hair between her fingers. She indulged in mindless groping and heated closeness until she felt his urgency, hard and heavy against her belly, a reminder that kissing was not where he might wish to stop. As if sensing her surging apprehension, he eased his hold on her. Everything gentled and slowed. His hand slid from her hair and smoothed a warm path down her spine, then up again, wooing her to remain in his embrace. He cradled her cheek in his other hand, mindful of the sensitiveness of her skin, and brushed his thumb at the still damp corner of her eye. She leaned against him, trembling, unable to stop feeling him, and a last tension in him melted.

When he deepened the kiss again, it felt like an apology: deliberate and tender, seeking and somewhat humbled, an unfamiliar taste on his lips. It rendered every sensation acute: the carefully coaxing slide of his lips against hers, the intimacy of tongues teasing each other, the caress of his breath across her cheek. It made her swoon. She broke away with a gasp.

Lucian made no move to retrieve her, he was watching her, almost warily. Their breathing was shaky. The place between her legs ached. She shifted uncomfortably, and he tipped back his head on a dark laugh. "Supper is at seven o'clock," he said. He left without his hat.

⁓

Dinner was a tremendously awkward affair. The sudden outburst of mutual lust joined them at the table like an ill-behaved inebriated uncle: avoiding addressing it felt wrong, but doing so also felt quite impossible. Lucian appeared fairly at ease, considering; he ate with appetite and he had loosened his cravat to a scandalous degree so that one could see the hollow at the base of his throat. Harriet kept sneaking glances at it, and eventually, he caught her doing so. His half smile made her feel hot in all sorts of ways, and she dropped her gaze back into her stew. Could one despise a man and still crave his kisses?

"You're getting on well with the lass, then?" he asked.

He meant Mhairi, she assumed. "She is wonderful, thank you. I'm indebted to her by an additional two pounds."

Lucian's spoon stopped on the way to his mouth. "Whatever for?"

"Her accompanying me to Heather Row today."

"That's more than a maid's monthly wage in London," he said, comically outraged.

"Oh, I know," she said, "I was trained in household management."

Whatever his response was to that, he swallowed it with a big gulp of ale.

"Some of the children I saw coming from the pits today can't have been older than eight or nine years of age," she ventured.

"They'd be that, yes," he replied.

"That's rather young."

He gave a shrug. "Old enough to work as a trapper. If not a hurrier, when they're boys."

"A trapper?"

"They open the trap doors for the coal tubs coming through. Or to ventilate the shafts. Children much younger than the ones you saw today used to do this." He was rolling his right shoulder while he talked until he became conscious of it and stopped abruptly.

"Much younger?" She was thinking of Michael, sweet cherubic Michael bouncing on Flossie's knee. Sending him to work in such frightening conditions in five years' time? Impossible. "How could any parent inflict this upon a little one? Isn't it terribly dark in the tunnels?"

Lucian's features hardened. "Yes. It's dark. So dark you can't see the hand in front of your eyes sometimes. But every child in a working family is one more mouth to feed; it's best if they learn early and earn their keep."

She drew back. "At that age? You don't mean that."

"You seem to believe in the goodness of my heart despite much evidence to the contrary," he remarked.

It seemed so. She had been temporarily swayed by the tenderness of his kisses and claims that he'd rather see his skin burned than hers.

She put down her spoon. "I'm certain that it is unlawful for young children and women to work underground."

"Aye, there was a law passed in the early forties. The Mines and Collieries Act."

"That's it," she said. "And doesn't it prohibit women and children from working underground?"

He nodded. "No more women and girls in the tunnels. Boys must be aged ten and older. They mustn't work more than ten hours a day. Officially." His voice was caustic irony.

"I presume women and girls are still going underground," she murmured.

"Here in Drummuir?" he said. "Yes."

Her appetite left her altogether. "Will you put a stop to it?"

He gave a curt nod.

"I'm glad."

"The women won't be," he said. "Often enough they're the ones breaking the law on their own accord."

"Why is that?"

"This notion that women are delicate creatures who should idle the hours away with letter writing in a parlor is a reality only in your circles, you know."

"*Our* circles," she said mildly.

He looked surprised for a beat, then picked up his ale again.

"I'm aware that most women work," she said. "Bailey works with me every day, but she earns a wage she finds agreeable. Why not pay the miners a decent enough wage for work that is safe? I doubt the women here break the law because they crave being in a tunnel."

"Aye, I could raise their wages until they are all very nice and comfortable on ten hours a day aboveground and raise the boys' age to fourteen," he said. "You know what would happen then?"

"You would have less profit?"

"In this case, I wouldn't have a mine anymore—because other mine owners wouldn't follow suit, so they'd be pricing Drummuir coal out of the market. And if they don't have Drummuir, where will they go? Seen any factories nearby where they could make a coin?"

"No," she admitted.

"Even if there were," he said, "ask any pit-brow woman, and they'll tell you they prefer the coal field over inhaling fluff all day in a hot cotton mill."

She digested this while drinking wine, then she said, "Something is not right when the viability of a mine depends on the lowest pay possible for the workers."

His dark smile went through her bones. "You have that right," he said. "Something is very wrong with that."

"I should have paid more attention to Lucie's work with the women's trade unions," she said glumly.

"I'll tell you what they say," Lucian said. "They usually object to women worker protection coming out of Parliament, because it always aims to keep women from working. All right if they're married and their husbands earn well, but what of the single women and widowed women? Wives of poor workingmen?"

"Or the ones who desire to be independent in any case?" she said pointedly.

"That, too," he said. "And forbidding women to go underground was never brought on by concern for their health. The public and the church wanted it so for moral reasons. Can't have women in the nude, they said. I say let the church compensate for the difference in earning, but they don't."

If he was trying to shock her, he had succeeded. "In the nude," she repeated.

He took the bread from his plate and tore off a chunk with strong teeth. "It's hot as hell underground and often wet," he said when he had swallowed. "Stripping off makes it more bearable."

Much as she was reeling from this news, it was remarkable that he knew such details. There was a lot of talk at the Greenfield dining table, but her father probably knew little of the conditions in the mines where he owned stakes, and even Flossie, for all her fervor, had never set foot in a tunnel. Hours of clever discussion and snarling at the ills of the world suddenly rang hollow.

It felt strange to pay Lucian a compliment, but she did try to be fair in all things, and so she said, "I find it commendable that you took care to learn such a great deal about the plights of the communities."

He paused. Studied her more closely. Then he shook his head. "I thought you knew by now," he said. "You've a very keen eye, after all."

Her nerves shrilled with alarm. Quite like when he had been on the cusp of kissing her for the first time next to a pair of Han vases.

"I used to be one of them," he said. "I'm Argyll mining stock."

Chapter 20

Judging by his wife's blank expression, she hadn't had a clue. Ah well. He supposed if she had married him knowing he was illegitimate, she would in time come to terms with this, too.

"You said you worked for an antiques dealer near Leicester Square," she said, sounding shaken. "And that your mother was employed as a maid in a manor."

"I said I was thirteen when I took up apprenticeship in the shop. I lived on the street for nearly a year before that. I had come down to London from Inveraray when I was twelve."

"The street," Harriet whispered. "You were alone in London—what of your parents?"

"Both dead at the time," Lucian said, and she flinched at his harsh tone.

She took her napkin from her lap, folded it into a sharp triangle, and put it aside on the table.

"Please, do tell," she said.

"My mother was from the mining community," he said. "She had a rare flight of fancy and thought to better herself by taking a position at the manor. Well, she soon returned to the pits, but in the family way." He realized his hands were in fists, and he could relax them only slowly. "After she was gone, I stayed with her husband until the man who had sired me died. A cousin of his took over his estate; he was of the zealously religious sort and made the rounds through the county to collect all his cousin's bastards, to shorten his time in purgatory, I reckon. He meant to send us all to a religious boarding school in Kensington."

Harriet's eyes were huge. He wondered what possessed him to speak of these things. The coal-infused air, the boy Ruri spilling the turnips, her soft mouth beneath his, salty with tears his rudeness had caused. A potent mix, enough to make a man talk about himself.

"I thought your stepfather had given you his name," she said. "Why would they care to take you from him?"

"They knew who I really was. Everyone did. My mother had worked at the manor until her condition became impossible to hide; she had stayed for the richer food and lighter work, you see, for as long as she could. They knew, and they came for me."

He remembered the day clearly. The weather had been cold and windy, properly dreich, and still the mountain slopes had glowed with the fiery red colors of mid-autumn. He had just been brawling with a lad who had tried to settle some disagreement by calling him a bastard; hence the most vicious punches had been thrown until someone had separated them—a regular occurrence in that community, where they had had to settle after the mine accident. The men had arrived on mud-splattered horses and had sneered down at him from their saddles while his stepfather had held him before them by the scruff of his neck. His clothes had been dirty and his nose had still been clotted with blood. "You're certain that's him?" one of them had asked, and the other one had laughed.

"Of course. Same face as his old man and same temper, too, by the looks of it."

He had been outraged to learn that he took after a man he had never met but loathed all the same. Meanwhile, his stepfather wasn't objecting to him being taken but to him not getting adequate compensation. "Look at him," he had said to the men in his nasal voice, "look how strong he is for his age. Can't do without his wages."

When the haggling had been done, Lucian had resisted. He had indeed been strong for his age, and he had fought like a cornered animal, inflicting bruises and kicking at soft parts with good aim until his grandmother had emerged from the cottage and trudged through the mud to reach him. She had taken him back to the kitchen and broken his defenses in ways violence never could. There was nothing for him here, she had said. Everyone in the new place knew he was a bastard and would never let him forget it. Besides, the miners died young, and in life they had nothing but the mine and their pride. His mother had tried, but being a woman had betrayed her—but he, he had a chance; if he went to London and studied, he could have better things. He had fallen to the floor and put his head on her knee and sobbed, not wanting to leave her. *Then you come back for me*, she had told him and stroked his hair, *you come back a fine man.* She had given him his grandfather's *sgian dubh* and the love spoon he was to gift Harriet many years later, and sent him on his way.

He became aware of Harriet's probing gaze and of the long pause he had allowed to stretch between them. "They came for me," he repeated. "And I went with them."

"I see," she said. "But if you had a home in Kensington, why would you live . . . on the streets?" She whispered this, as though it were literally an unspeakable horror.

"Ah well," he said. "The school's headmaster wasn't a good man."

After barely a week of classes, the rotter had tried to put his hand between Lucian's legs after a caning, and Lucian—prepared by the hints of the other boys—had grabbed the heavy paperweight off the desk and put it to the man's head. He had never seen so much blood pouring out of a human, and after tiptoeing to the dorm to snatch his belongings, he had run all the way to the docklands in East London, uncertain whether he had committed homicide. Aoife had found him a few days later, starved and hiding in a corner. It was the day he had named himself Luke Blackstone and Lucian Stewart had joined the mass of missing children.

"The street didn't suit me, either," he said.

"Unsurprisingly, I would think," Harriet said faintly.

"There's hierarchies, and if you want shelter, people force you to join this group or that," he explained. "Life is cheap there, and someone always has trouble with someone else and makes you stand with them even if you're not interested in the trouble. Half the time, it's stupid trouble." The same held for more elevated underworld activities, which was why he had withdrawn from those, too, many years later, one by one while he still could without too great a cost. "I used to be good at working with wood," he told Harriet, "doing carvings and such, so when I saw the sign in the antiques shop window, I tidied myself up and applied."

He had risked the jail by stealing a pristine shirt and cravat off a washing line to present himself to Mr. Graham, the antiques dealer and owner of the shop. Sometimes Lucian wondered what his old mentor would say were he alive to learn that his bit of trust in the scruffy boy had been a cornerstone of said boy's ascent to the top of London. . . .

"Since this seems to be the hour of truth," Harriet said, "who was the woman in the drawing room?"

Her lips were pale, but there was unexpected steel in her gaze.

"Aoife Byrne," he said easily, thinking, *Of all the things she could have asked*. "We met on the street. She set my nose when it was cracked. And she saved my hide several times while we were both homeless urchins." After which she had soon become a ringleader in the smuggling operations at London Port, but that wasn't for Harriet to know.

"You are not urchins now," his wife remarked. "Yet still acquainted."

So she had done away with the polite stance of not acknowledging her husband's *liaisons*. Only here her efforts were wasted; Aoife would never bed a man, and since she had found her Susan, not even other women, but that, too, was not for Harriet to know, at least not from his mouth.

"I gave you my word that I wouldn't take a lover," he said instead.

Harriet promptly made a bored face, as if she couldn't care less. Fickle creature. "Miss Byrne shares your interests," he said. "She's often up at the Royal Academy or with the Decadents, sitting for paintings. She enjoys the opera."

"How thrilling," Hattie murmured. Her shoulders were drooping and shadows had appeared beneath her eyes from nowhere, and his fingers flexed on instinct, to take her somewhere where she could rest. But he'd be damned before he lost his composure and fell on her again. The memory of their kiss promptly seared through him. He tried to block the phantom feel of her warm, wet mouth and eager tongue.

"Would you like a bath?" he said, and when her gaze flickered to him uncertainly, "I have to deal with some business affairs—I'll do it here."

She hesitated. "You would work here—in the dining area?"

"Has anything been done by protocol lately?"

A tired smile tugged at her mouth. "No," she said. "I do love a bath." He rose when she did, but she shook her head. "Please, stay. I should like to go alone."

He was aware his gaze was following her swaying skirts like a hungry dog going after a bone, and he didn't like it. It felt as though she had a part of him on a leash. *I don't know how to do this right.* The tops of his ears felt warm when he recalled his heated words earlier. He couldn't remember the last time he had admitted cluelessness to another person. First, there had never been a need for it—as Aoife had pointed out, there was no one around for him; second, he was hardly ever clueless. And his men of business didn't cry, no matter what he said; all they wanted from him at the end of the day was profit. What did Harriet want from him?

He ordered another ale to his booth and assessed his financial due diligence reports. It demanded near inhumane discipline. The moment he put the pen aside, she invaded his mind again. How at ease she had looked among the children. Her keen interest in . . . everything. Her tears. Her soft, soft kisses. He neatly stacked his documents as restlessness took hold of him. She was sweet. Genuinely sweet and unassuming. Spoiled and ignorant, too, but her cheerful disposition was rooted in something deeper; there'd be some whimsy in her even had she been raised in a beggar's hovel. It was reckless to be this way, in a world such as this; she could be hurt in all sorts of ways. He felt a knot in his stomach as a cold sensation seeped beneath his skin. He hadn't felt moved to keep a particular woman safe from . . . everything . . . in over ten years. Now the long-buried instinct rattled its cage at the bottom of his soul. Unless he kept it buried, it might swell with the force of a tidal wave and take the ground from under his feet.

Harriet was left to soak undisturbed in the metal tub next to the fire for a long while, but she was barely conscious of the soothing heat of the heather-scented water. Her mind was too deeply preoccupied with Lucian's revelations.

When he finally returned to their room, her hair was nearly dry again and she was huddled in the armchair, hugging her knees against her chest beneath a double layer of tartan blankets. He washed behind the curtain in the side room, cursing softly as he maneuvered in the small space, and finally he emerged wearing a soft black cashmere robe that outlined his strong shoulders to great effect. She studied him as he sorted his papers on the table, trying to superimpose all she now knew over the man she had thought he was.

"Is that what you do?" she said. "Acquiring ailing mines to improve the communities?"

He glanced up. "When I can, yes."

"I thought the mining commission takes care of such matters."

"It should. It does. But laws are only ever as good as the will to enforce them."

"What about the miners' unions?"

A sardonic glimmer lit his eyes. "Tell me—who still owns the mines in Britain, the slate mines, the coal mines? Or who steers the consortia that own them? The unions?"

"No," she said reluctantly. "Dukes and earls and wealthy men of business."

"That's right."

"They are not above the law."

He gave her an incredulous look. "When have you last heard of an earl brought to justice for his crimes against the working classes?"

She touched her aching temples. "I haven't."

"Drummuir here's been owned by Rutland," he said. "It's why the conditions are so dire."

This shocked her a little. "I did not know," she said.

"He cooked the books, too," Lucians said. "Consequently, the consortium buying Drummuir formed the wrong conclusions from their due diligence. When they noticed this mine will yield only low profits even after the necessary investments, they sold it to me at a loss. Will there be consequences for Rutland? Doubtful."

"The lords you have ruined," she said slowly. "You did not choose them at random, did you?"

"No."

Gooseflesh spread down her legs. She hugged her knees more tightly. "You are taking the law into your own hands, one reprehensible nobleman at a time?"

He cocked his head. "You disapprove."

"Tell me," she said, "have I married an anarchist?"

"Hell, no."

"Well, that's a relief," she said, and then, suspiciously, "Why aren't you?"

His mouth twisted derisively. "You know what anarchists do?"

"Contemplate the demise of the monarchy?"

"They sit around all day and talk a whole lot," he said. "And under this pretense of avoiding authority by talking a lot about everyone's ideas—when in the end, there's always a leader and group coercion, anyway—they achieve bloody little."

"Oh."

"I don't care much for authority," he said. "So I won't suffer inefficient authority exerted by hypocritical chatterboxes."

"Understood," she soothed. "Are you a communist, then?"

He shook his head. "Though I support a few financially—William Morris, for example."

"*The* William Morris?" she asked, amazed. "The wallpaper designer?"

"Yes."

"I had no idea."

"Now you know."

"Yes," she said, "you're a socialist."

He gave a shrug. "I want to turn people in power; I care little about how."

"Turning people in power," she murmured. "I suppose that is my role, then. Or rather, my father's."

He gave a nod.

She felt numb. "I'll have you know that my father hardly has a magic wand to wave," she said. "And he is bound by the law, too."

He leaned back against the table and crossed his arms over his chest. "Do you deny that he has influence? Could open doors?"

She put up her chin. "Why not begin bettering the world by giving away your vast wealth to those in need?"

Lucian made a contemptuous sound. "Charity? No. I want lasting change. Remember the trouble of raising wages to a living wage as a single entrepreneur? I want a restructuring of government expenditure. A systemic redistribution of wealth—*that* is what I want."

"Right."

He was right fired up. "Take a guess how much of public spending is allocated to the British military every year."

She gave a tired shrug. "Twenty percent?"

"Thirty," he said, "thirty percent of central public spending for infernal imperial wars. On the other hand, nothing for health or education, not a shilling. Which very nicely maintains the oversupply of poor, uneducated lads to the front lines and mining pits. There's more dignity in bullets and rocks than in begging for alms in a rotten London ally."

He sounds like Lucie, she thought as she watched the room's shadows play over his hard face; the strength of conviction, the focus, were the same.

"What do you propose?" she asked softly.

He uncrossed his arms. "We'll never see money diverted from the imperialists," he said. "They'd rather devour the world than feed the people of Britain. I'm looking at the revenue side and currently the most effective lever is to increase the income tax."

"I had to study Gladstone's voting records for my suffrage work," she said. "I'm fairly certain that for the last twenty years he continually advocated for abolishing the income tax altogether."

"Och, but he never did, because it's baseless pandering," said Lucian. He was pacing in front of the table now in a rare agitation. "The budget relies excessively on customs and excise duty when trade conditions are continually worsening, and American imports are able to undercut British products at every turn."

"Sounds logical," she allowed. "Still implausible."

"Gladstone knows there's no alternative," he said. "Income tax is applied at a rate of less than one percent, and most citizens are exempt—it must be increased and expanded, also to include corporate profits."

She snorted at the absurdity. "A corporate tax?"

"One day," he said. "You'll see."

It struck her then that she had been tricked into a marriage for the purpose of British fiscal reform. She narrowed her eyes at him. "Why can't you buy members of Parliament to do your bidding, like a regular industrialist?" she demanded. "Or form an opposition party? Why must you become one of them?"

He smirked. "Trust me, these strategies aren't mutually exclusive. But the strongest fortresses don't fall under siege. They need to be hollowed out from the inside."

"And once the walls fall, you will give away your excess wealth?" Her tone was sweet.

"No," he said, grimly.

"Still not?"

"A wealthy man has the ear of powerful men; a poorer one doesn't. We only hear of a lowly worker if he dies some violent death and is put on his company's record, or if a journalist cares to make him a headline for a day—either way a poor man is usually heard louder in death than in life."

"How convenient for you."

He came to an abrupt stop and glared. "I'll never go back to the pits," he said, and pointed at her. "I'll never again degrade myself for food; I'll never again be held in the same regard as a sewer rat."

"All right," she said soothingly. "All right."

He glanced away, a little shaken, presumably at having lost his composure, at having revealed some of the shame in his past. Her heart, tired and bruised as it was, went out to him then, because that was what it did: it flung itself toward the hurt of other people, not caring whether it was deserved.

"I was provoking you," she said. "I know the difference between change and charity well from the suffrage movement. Our leader, Millicent Fawcett, is a socialist."

He pondered it for a moment. "I suppose there's much in common," he then said.

"Injustice is injustice," she replied. "It occurs to me that it might be inconsistent to acknowledge merely the injustices that suit."

Their gazes held across the room, and an understanding passed between them that made her defenses rise once more, to shut him out.

"My father sacrificed me for his business interests before," Harriet said. "What makes you think he'll support your politics when it begins to hurt his pockets?"

He came to her with heavy steps. He looked at her upturned face with eyes as deep as the dark night outside the window, then he slowly went down on one knee. "Will you ever stop being angry with me, you think?"

She contemplated him, on his knee on the floor. "I cannot say," she finally said. "It is certainly a bit less ghastly to have been used for good, a greater cause than just for your individual gain."

Lucian winced.

"But it's also more tragic," she continued, trying to match her words exactly to her thoughts for once. "I would have greatly enjoyed joining forces with my husband for a just cause. But the manner in which our betrothal came to pass . . . your callousness and deceit . . ." She shook her head. "For all your talk of justice, you have used me badly."

The corner of his mouth curled in a humorless smile. "Would you have accepted me," he asked, "had I wooed you the normal way?"

She knew the truth to that. "No," she muttered. "Nor would my father."

His expression remained unchanged; he had expected this. "I never planned on forcing your hand in the manner our kiss in the gallery forced it," he said.

Perhaps unwisely, she believed him. "Your actions still describe a devious man," she said. "How can I possibly trust you now?" Her pulse sped up again. He had ruined something that could have been a dream come true. "Yes, I *am* angry," she said thickly. "And I'm not certain how to make it stop."

He shifted slightly as though he had noticed the worn floorboards pressing into his knee, but his gaze never left her face. "For what it's worth, I respect that," he said. "I respect your anger."

"Well, I think an annulment would put a swift end to all the angriness."

He was quiet for a long moment.

"Could we discuss that after we return to London?" he then said, his voice surprisingly tired. She felt the same fatigue, deep in her bones.

She sighed. "Very well." She rested her forehead on her knees, overstimulated and exhausted.

"Allow me to carry you to the bed," she heard him say after a pause.

She raised her head warily.

"I'll not bother you with my attentions," he said, sounding sarcastic, but the expression in his eyes was sincere.

"I'm so tired," she murmured. "Being petty is surprisingly taxing—I've tried my utmost in the past few days, but I don't think it suits me much."

"Believe me, you were a natural."

She avoided looking at his face when he scooped her up. Secretly, she marveled at how effortlessly he carried her, and why a deep, instinctual part of her would be so at ease in his arms.

Chapter 21

The next morning, Harriet woke when Lucian exited the side room, fully dressed and prepared to begin a productive day. She threw back the covers and jumped out of bed. "I should like to come along."

He halted in his tracks, his gaze roaming over her nightgown. "Whatever for?"

"To talk to the women," she said, crossing her arms over her breasts. "I thought about it, last night before I fell asleep."

His dark brows rose. "Why?"

She yawned behind the back of her hand. The room was filled with the bright light of a sunny morning, but it was far too early for her liking, no later than seven, surely. "Because I trust that the women are responsible for the household and the children."

"They are, yes."

"We must speak to them, not just to the menfolk, to know how to assist the community."

Lucian's brow furrowed in a frown. "We talked to a few women yesterday, Wright and I."

She padded closer, aware that she was in her nightgown and that her hair was spilling down to her waist in tangles. "Our suffrage work shows that women are more inclined to talk about *female issues* to other women," she said, "and female issues are family issues, and families make a community."

Lucian seemed to attempt to hide some displeasure, and he at last achieved a merely mildly surly expression. "I tried to explain it yesterday but I didn't do it well," he said. "These women, you see, they, too, are not your playthings. They don't exist for you to feel useful . . . or for you to indulge in the warm glow of your benevolence."

It stung. She had to swallow hard before she could speak again. "Am I to not have any purpose, then?" she asked in a low tone. "Because I happened to have been born Hattie Greenfield, I must forever be idle?"

This seemed to take him by surprise. "No," he said. "But what do you offer that they couldn't do better themselves? They'll have to take precious time out of their day to explain their circumstances to you."

"I know how to organize," she said quickly. "I help Lucie prepare suffrage meetings and demonstrations, so I could conduct a survey of the women's needs and orderly collect and record opinions. I'm acquainted with the leaders of charities and societies in London that provide funds and expert knowledge."

He still looked skeptical. "You said you aren't good at writing—how would you take notes?"

"I can write, Lucian," she said, although the mere thought of standing at a blackboard made her die a little inside. "Or do you think the women here will do it better?"

"No," he admitted.

"Unless they are union members?" She only thought of this now. "In which case, they would know all about organizing themselves."

"They're not, but I'd like them to be," he said, looking quite keen now. "Why don't you speak to them about that, joining the union."

She eyed him curiously. "Wouldn't that run counter to your interests?"

A cynical look passed behind his eyes. "No. I like to know when enough is enough."

What a strange man she had married. "What of recruiting the women to the suffrage cause?" she asked.

"They'll let you know what they think about that," he said with a smirk.

The shadows were lengthening and the air had cooled by the time she went to the village. Mhairi had suggested visiting community spokeswoman Rosie Fraser after the day's shift to request a meeting with the women of Drummuir. To Hattie's embarrassment, the main door of Mrs. Fraser's cottage opened straight to the small kitchen, and they barged right into communal cooking activities. A wall of warm, damp air greeted them, and the chatter of seven or eight women and the rapid chopping of vegetables around the crowded table ceased. Assessing eyes narrowed beneath sweat-gleaming brows.

"Good evening," Hattie said, her voice sounding high-pitched to her own ears.

A teapot whistled faintly into the silence. Outside the kitchen window, a red-haired young man swung an ax with fluid grace, followed by a dull thud.

Thankfully, Mhairi stepped forward and explained. Unlike Gaelic, which was spoken in the Highlands, the Lowland Scots had a fair semblance to English on paper, but hearing it spoken was confounding.

Rosie Fraser had a neat kitchen: tiled walls, pretty ornaments on the dresser, dried herbs hanging in bunches from a polished rack. . . . A middle-aged woman who wore a blue handkerchief around her head detached from the group. "Welcome to my home, Mrs. Blackstone," she said in English as she wiped her hands on her apron. "I'm Rosie Fraser." Her cheeks were ruddy with webs of fine red spider veins; her green eyes were sharp and clear.

"How do you do, Mrs. Fraser."

"You did a drawing of wee Anne yesterday," Rosie Fraser said. "It's a lovely drawing. Her mum was well pleased. Would Ma'am like some tea?"

There was a sudden explosion of activity; some women cleared a part of the table and urged her to sit, while another took the teapot off the stove and Rosie Fraser disappeared into the adjacent parlor to fetch a finer china cup.

"We can do an assembly after mass tomorrow, after the lunch," Mrs. Fraser suggested while Hattie politely sipped the scalding brew. "We're cooking the lunch now, you see. But what I'm thinking is, could you perhaps do some more sketches?" The women flanking her nodded.

Hattie put down the cup. "I suppose so?"

"Of my Hamish," Mrs. Fraser said and tipped her chin at the young man who was working in the yard. Mhairi had been craning her neck in that direction for a while; now she quickly looked away.

"If you'd be so kind, Mrs. Blackstone, I'd like one of my Archie and my Dougal," said an older woman who was clasping her tea mug to her chest with raw hands.

"Certainly?" Hattie said.

Mrs. Fraser looked at the other woman askance. "I think Mary Boyd should have one before you have one."

The woman made a face. "Och."

"Mary's only got one left," Rosie said, and the others murmured in acquiescence.

"One left?" Hattie asked.

"One son," Rosie explained.

"Oh. I am sorry."

A solemn nod. "Her Domnhall was hit by rocks last year."

"I'm sorry," Hattie stammered. The women were deliberating in hushed voices, and while some were speaking Scots, she gathered they were discussing who had suffered a loss and how long back various accidents dated, to determine who was to be prioritized for a sketch. She had a sinking feeling in her stomach by the time Rosie Fraser turned back to her and said, "So we have an assembly tomorrow, and get some sketches in return, aye?"

"It's a deal," she replied with forced cheer.

Her mood was subdued on the way back to the inn. "Do they not have photographs?" she asked Mhairi, who had a spring in her step and swooped to pick sprigs of heather here and there to put them into her apron pocket.

"Photographs," the girl now said, her blue eyes surprised. "You mean of the dead?"

"Or the living."

Mhairi laughed. "But no. They'll keep locks of hair. Having a photographer come here, to photograph the dead, all the way from Auchtermuchty? Too expensive, ma'am. But of course"—and now she became serious—"of course a lock isn't the same, is it? The truth is, the memories of a face fade no matter how badly you want to remember, don't they? Then you feel bad, for forgetting."

What a harrowing visit it turned out to be. "Are accidents in the mine commonplace?"

"I s'pose?" the girl said. "If you count the small ones, yes. Explosions, not so often these days."

"What counts as a small accident?"

Mhairi thought about it. "I'd say, fingers getting crushed, and arms breaking. Not fatal but puts you out of work. Then there's deadly missteps when going up or down in the heapstead, or stones falling off the ceiling. Or tubs breaking loose from a pony and going over someone who wasn't in a safety hole fast enough."

Before her mind's eye, she saw the scars on Lucian's body. Perhaps the silvery ones across his abdomen were from his harness, when he used to pull the tubs as a boy. . . .

"But most miners don't die from accidents," Mhairi said. "The black lung gets them, with them breathing in coal dust all day long."

"I imagine so," Hattie said, when truly, she couldn't fathom it.

Mhairi hummed an incongruously merry Celtic tune until they reached the entrance door to the inn. "Mrs. Blackstone?" she then said.

"Yes?"

She hemmed and hawed. "You think you'd have time to draw Hamish Fraser?"

"The lad who was chopping wood?"

Mhairi's cheeks turned pink. "Aye."

"Do you worry for him?"

Mhairi's gaze dropped into her heather-filled apron pocket. "No, ma'am. No harm will ever come to him."

Hattie wrung her hands. "How many miners work in Drummuir?"

Mhairi glanced up. "Three hundred or thereabouts?"

She tried to envision herself setting up an easel and a case full of water or oil colors in the damp school and have the villagers sit for her, one after the other. Impossible. The miners had little time to themselves during daylight hours except Sundays, and she'd have to stay here for months to paint them all. She supposed she could have them sit only for sketches, and then color them in at her studio. . . .

She shook her head. "I might have a better idea." And it involved speaking to Lucian.

She took her leave from Mhairi and rushed up the stairs and barged into their room, propelled by brightly burning determination. She came to an abrupt halt. The tub was back in the room. And Lucian was in it. His naked wet shoulders and his knees loomed over the rim; he fair overcrowded the vessel with his size. Her eyes squeezed shut reflexively.

"Sorry, love," she heard him say, his voice a relaxed drawl. "I stop short at taking a bath in the dining area."

Heather-and-pine-scented heat wafted toward her from the tub. Well, drat. She could flee and return when he was no longer so very naked. But her excitement would not be contained, and they were married, after all, were they not?

She opened one eye. "Do you mind?" she said.

His chuckled. "No." Steam was rising off his skin in lazy swirls.

With his thick hair wet and slicked back, nothing softened the hard contours of his face. He had never looked more like a vagrant, and rarely more intriguing. She gave a shake. "I need a camera," she remembered.

He slanted his head. "What for?"

"The miners," she said.

"The miners."

"They don't seem to have the habit of keeping photographs of their loved ones."

"In a community remote and impoverished like this?" he said. "Not usually, no."

She was trembling a little. *How dramatic you are, Pom Pom.* She paced a circle before the tub. "Imagine working in such a dangerous profession and then living with the added guilt of forgetting your loved one's face."

"Yes, imagine." Lucian adjusted his position, sending water sloshing over the tub rim. "What did the women do to you?"

"Nothing," she said defensively. "They were perfectly amiable."

He was contemplating her with a mildly amused expression. She thought of his scars, below the waterline.

"The black lung," she said. "It's why you don't smoke, isn't it?"

"You've noticed."

It had occurred to her during the walk back. "I have. I have not once smelled smoke on you." It was probably why his scent was always fresh and his teeth still white. "Nearly all the men of my acquaintance are partial to cigarettes. They even claim they are healthful."

He huffed. "Easy to claim anything. I've seen what breathing in black smoke does and I doubt there's much of a difference in different kinds of smoke."

She wondered whether being coated in dust and soot for years was the reason why he kept himself so fastidiously clean. He washed in the morning and at night, and the shower in his house in Belgravia was state-of-the-art.

She pulled a chair away from the table and sat, feeling overwhelmed.

Lucian was watching her closely now. "I'll ask Mr. Wright," he offered. "He has a camera."

She shook her head. "I want a portrait of each one of them, and I'd rather not have the pressure of someone waiting for their camera. It's over three hundred portraits."

"You know how to operate a camera?"

"No. But I can learn. I feel . . ." She hesitated. "I feel this is something I must do myself."

"I see." There was a splash when he fished for the flannel. She watched from beneath her lashes, how he languidly drew the wet cloth over his skin and the muscle beneath—forearm, shoulder, chest, the back of his neck—and her mind stilled. Her eye, trained to analyze the composition of objects and the human form, was hopelessly riveted, for while Lucian had a brawny rather than an elegant build, the details of him were wonderfully, precisely done: the distinct lines of the pectoralis, the clean curve of his deltoid, the finely tuned interplay of his biceps and triceps as he worked the flannel. She wanted to paint him. Not as Hades, but as Hephaestus, god of the precious metals and mines, as he swung his hammer to forge weapons for the righteous . . .

"Why don't they leave?" Her voice was scratchy. "Do something else?"

Lucian's eyes were heavy-lidded. "It's difficult to leave all you know," he said. "Even if it is what kills you."

"You have done it."

"Yes, and I was dragged away from it kicking and screaming," he said. "You'll find no greater brotherhood than in a mining community. They'd share their last shirt with you and their last penny when hardship strikes, 'cause no one outside gives a damn. But try stepping out of line. Try eating your porridge differently, wearing your cap differently; think of extracting the coal differently, and your own people will knock you about and mock you, afraid you're better than them, that you have ideas above your station. Then the upper classes won't have you because you eat and dress and think differently, and because you have ideas above your station." He flicked his hand dismissively. "Nah, don't blame anyone for not leaving; blame the circumstances that make staying hell."

She flushed. "I wasn't apportioning blame."

She had, however, made no secret of her concerns over his lack of manners and breeding and his detrimental effect on her social standing. She had done it partly because her base attraction to him had disturbed her. Was disturbing her still. She had tried to make him feel less than over her own lust. Shame.

"Wright is off to St. Andrews on Monday to purchase parts for the water tanks," he said, commanding her attention back to his face. "If you like, we'll go, too, and have him advise you on a camera that's right for you."

"Yes," she said quickly, "yes, I would like that very much."

He smiled, faintly but it was there, and she realized she had forgotten that she was angry with him. Instead, she remembered clutching his nape and how exciting his tongue felt in her mouth. Her limbs became very warm. He carelessly rose from the tub, and she looked away.

⌀⋯⌀

That night, Harriet dreamed she was watching Lucian chop wood on the street of Heather Row, or perhaps he was throwing punches at a sandbag. His chest was bare and glistening with sweat in the sun, and when he noticed her, he paused and wiped his brow with his forearm. She knew she was dreaming because next, they were in a bedchamber and she opened her nightgown at the front to show him her breasts. She would never do that, awake and of sound mind. She wouldn't cup and lift them for him, and revel in the fullness spilling over her small hands and the velvet-soft feel of her skin. But in the twilight? She arched her back. *Do you like them?* She knew he did. She knew he was starving for her. It was in the way he looked at her throughout the day when he thought she took no notice, and in the deliberate care he took not to touch her. She wanted him to touch her now. She sank back into the pillows. He stood at the foot of the bed, hungry and waiting. *Come to me.* He crawled over her, his shaggy head bent, and the feel of his hair trailing over her bare chest sent heat fanning through her belly. His teeth grazed the tip of her left breast, and she arched up against his lips until he gently bit down. She moaned, in her dream, or in truth, who could tell? She writhed beneath the wet, hot pull of his mouth. Her hands settled on his hard shoulders and she pushed him down, and lower. . . . She felt him nuzzle her where it ached. *Do you want this?* he asked. She made a fist in his hair. *Kiss me, Lucian.* At the first soft stroke of his tongue, she gasped with relief. He did it again, gently. Too gently; it was light, fleeting licks until she canted her hips, seeking more friction. He wouldn't give it. When she made to clamp her thighs around his head, her touch went through him as if he were smoke.

"Harriet."

He was dissolving; she could merely hear him. She let out a sob of frustration.

"Harriet."

She emerged disoriented, damp and prickling from her lips to her toes. Sheets had snaked around her limbs as though she'd thrashed around in her dreams. His voice still rang in her ears, very much real.

She must have woken him.

The awareness came over her bright and terrible. Save her erratic breathing, the room was too silent. He was indeed awake; his gaze penetrated the dark with such focus, it tingled on her face.

Her mouth went dry. "It was a dream," she said.

He was quiet, in the controlled, drawn-out way that made it meaningful.

She licked her lips and tasted salt. "A nightmare."

"I must have been bloody to you, then." His voice was raw.

"You were not in it."

A pause. "You were saying my name."

Moaning his name, rather. *Kiss me, Lucian.*

She shivered.

Sheets rustled as he rose on his elbow. "Are you cold?"

She couldn't tell—goose bumps were prickling over the surface of her skin, but inside she felt heated. "A bit," she said.

He was more shadow than solid form, his eyes a faint glitter in the dark. "Lie closer to me," he said. "I'll warm you."

She gave a shaky huff. "That's not all you want."

"No," he said after a moment. "I want to touch you."

She couldn't seem to catch her breath. "Just touch me?"

He held himself very still. She had breathed the words so softly she had not expected him to hear them. "It's all I'd do," he murmured. In the velvety dark, still humming with unspent desire, his ragged words promised pleasure. The dull ache between her legs became a yearning pull.

Slowly, slowly, she rolled to her side to face the wall.

Lucian was silent.

She inched her hips back toward him.

It was the only invitation he needed. He embraced her from behind; one strong hand slid under her chest, the other over her, his fingers spreading over her belly as he pulled her against the hard length of his body.

She gasped—he slept naked. "I don't—"

His hold on her eased. "I heard you."

Her heart still beat rapidly beneath his palm. She was aroused by transgression and risk; it was the only explanation for why she had pushed her backside up against a naked, virile man. His hair tickled her cheek, then he lightly kissed the side of her neck. At her soft sigh, his hand on her belly slid up over the curve of her hip and lingered, and when she remained still in his arms, he stroked slowly down her thigh. Heat bloomed beneath the warm pressure of his palm, then all attention pooled where his fingers inched under the hem of her gown. The wicked touch moved over her bare leg, up, and up. He gently kneaded her breast that filled his other hand, and her cheek was hot against the pillow. No thoughts, just sensations. The steady flow of his breath. The rustle of her gown. Her body gathering pleasure wherever he moved his confident fingers. He caressed the downy-soft skin high on the back of her thigh until she shifted to ease the building tension. From behind, his hand slipped between her legs. She was panting when he rubbed over the most delicate spot.

His warm lips brushed her ear. "Does it feel good?"

She couldn't speak. His hand was working small, firm circles. She could barely hold on to thoughts. "Y-yes."

A twinge of pleasure-pain stung her nipple and her back arched, pushing her breast more fully into his palm. He pinched her again, and down below his fingertips sank into her as if through water. Dangerous. Delicious. She still disliked him, but images flashed of him naked and aroused with his knee between hers on the bed, and her body clenched over dissatisfying emptiness. They would have fit very well indeed. Her nails dug into the mattress.

His finger entered her, slid in smoothly. "Yes," she heard herself say. He wouldn't be hurried, but he gave it to her, in a leisurely, steady rhythm, winding her tension tighter with each push of his fingers until her hips were moving, chasing the promise of a pulsing release. . . . His other hand stroked from her breast down her belly and lower, and then he pressed with his fingertips in counterpoint to the plunge of his fingers from behind. A powerful rush of heat overtook her, and she gave an anxious cry. She felt his teeth graze the side of her throat. Then he bit down. The tension between her legs snapped in a shower of stars, and she cried out again.

She lay wrung out in his arms, feeling both light as air and heavy as lead. Her mind was reassembling slowly, one breath at a time. She became aware of Lucian's need, simmering beneath his warm skin, seductive in its leashed urgency. She supposed she could roll onto her back and open her legs. He could enter her relaxed body easily, not causing her much discomfort, and he could take his pleasure, too. For a moment, it was tempting. But he was a man of his word, and unless she asked him for it as he had told her she must do, he'd probably not do it. He'd rather endure his unspent lust. That, too, was tempting.

"Do you remember?" she said drowsily.

He shifted, carefully withdrawing his hands. "Remember what?"

"On our wedding night, when I said I wouldn't like it if you kissed me, down below."

Her eyes were drifting shut by the time he said, "I remember."

"I said I wouldn't like it."

He was quiet, allowing her to return to sleep.

"I think I have changed my mind," she whispered.

The bed creaked as he rolled away from her. "Noted."

The dark warmly welcomed her back.

⚬≈⚬

He lay next to her, motionless while a hard pulse beat away in his neck. When her breathing had become even and deep, he rose and went to the washroom. He sucked her taste off his fingers, then wrapped his wet hand around his cock. He kept his eyes on the stars winking through the window slit as he worked himself. It took only moments until his vision blurred, for the long-held tension to coil tightly at the base of his spine. Her wet heat, her throaty cries. He hovered in perfect stillness for a second, then hot release exploded through his body with such mind-obliterating violence, he gritted his teeth and slapped his other hand against the stone wall, once, twice. He came to hoping she had slept through it, oblivious.

Chapter 22

The next morning she woke to mild cramps and the arrival of her courses, which she should have expected had she not lost track of time during the emotional whirlwind of the past few weeks. Lucian had already gone, and a note lay on his pillow informing her that he and the mining engineer would spend all day examining the tunnels. That was a relief. The memories of their debauchery last night intruded, and in the light of day, it made her head red-hot.

She felt improved enough around noon to go and hold the women's assembly.

The small classroom was crammed with approximately fifty women lining the walls and sitting behind the small worn desks. Rosie Fraser took her seat next to Hattie in a chair in front of the blackboard. She wore her Sunday finery today: a white blouse and blue wool and no handkerchief to protect her hair. She had flaming-red locks like her son, Hamish.

She seemed intrigued enough by the idea of joining the trade union, but some of the other women grumbled. "It'll put us up against the men before it protects us or our wages," an older woman in the first row said. "It's our own menfolk that thinks we're the competition."

"Not all of our own," Mrs. Fraser said with vehemence. "Most are sensible." But there were still some dark faces in the crowd. "I for once want the same pay," said the blond woman who had asked Hattie for a sketch of her two sons the night before, and that elicited ambivalent murmurs. The final vote, however, revealed that a majority of women wanted to join, and Hattie scribbled the result onto the blackboard with a squeaky piece of chalk.

On the matter of joining the suffrage movement, they laughed uproariously. "Should we come down to London on Sundays and hand out pamphlets, then?" Rosie Fraser asked. "I'm all for it," said another. "I'll leave my fellow to change the baby and to bake the bread while I'm gone having a lark." This started a good five minutes of hilarity, where they envisioned their husbands doing this or that around the house. "We can try to improve our pay through the union," Mrs. Fraser concluded after restoring order. And that was that, women's suffrage dismissed with a wave of her broad hand.

"But if you had the vote, you could hasten all these decisions about pay and working conditions along," Hattie tried, "by voting for a party that works for precisely those interests. And you don't have to come to London; you can sign petitions. You could influence the movement itself with your sheer numbers."

"Precisely, eh," Mrs. Fraser drawled. "But we're not eligible for the vote. Our *men* aren't eligible, ma'am. We don't own property, nor do we run expensive households in a city."

Nodding all around. This was not going well at all. "There shall be another reform act to enfranchise the workingmen," Hattie said. "The property qualifications shan't last forever."

"Do you know that for certain, ma'am?"

She didn't, and she felt some disappointment in the crowd when she bit her lip and shook her head. Her proposition was voted down.

Her palms were damp and her pulse high by the time she explained her idea about the photographs.

"Photographs," Rosie Fraser repeated, her eyes narrowing. "Like they did in Yorkshire?"

"What happened in Yorkshire?"

"People went there and took photographs of the lassies in their working clothes a few years back," Mhairi said from her seat in the front row. "Turned them into postcards."

"Scandalous ones," Mrs. Fraser added derisively. "The people selling them made good coin."

Murmur rose again.

"Well, these portraits would be yours," Hattie said. "Free of charge and for your personal use."

Rosie Fraser contemplated her with an unreadable expression. "Why?" At least she didn't flat out ask, *What's in it for you?*

Hattie replied the one thing that came to mind. "Because I can."

The vote to have the portraits done was unanimous.

"I should like to have the vote," Mhairi told Hattie an hour later as they walked back to the inn. Her plaid-patterned Sunday skirt was swinging in step with her thick braids. "I'll have my own business one day and then it would come in handy."

"Will you take over the Drover's Inn?"

"Oh no. My sister, Clara, and I—we'd like to train as soap makers. The inn will go to my brothers."

"Soap," Hattie said, nonplussed, "why soap?"

"We thought people will always need to wash, won't they? Drummuir will stop yielding one day, and then what's left for the inn? Did you like the heather soap in your bath?"

She hadn't paid much attention to the soap. "It smelled wonderful," she said truthfully.

"It was us, suggesting heather to the soap maker in Dundee," Mhairi said with obvious pride. "Now we have heather scent yearround from the linen. Would people in the cities want to buy it?"

Impulsively, she wanted to make exuberant promises. "When the time comes, you must send me a note," she said instead. "I'm an esteemed customer in two fashionable perfume shops in London." At least she would be again, once the scandal prompting her wedding had waned. Mhairi's steps turned into a skip for a few paces, and

Hattie's chest felt tight with an emotion. A foot in the door, Lucian had called it. There needed to be more of it.

She returned to the room feeling both restless and exhausted. It was advised that a woman rest during this time of the month, and here she was holding assemblies and walking across heather fields. She wished her friends were at the inn so she could think out loud in front of them to organize her mind, which was a riot of flitting thoughts and hatching ideas. Eventually, it overwhelmed her innate reluctance to pick up a pen and write words. It was just a letter to Lucie, a friend.

My mind is turning at double the normal speed because I have so many thoughts, and only some of them are fully formed while the rest shall plague me with half-baked conclusions for weeks. I know you are busy with lobbying the House of Lords for the amendment hearing, but I wish you could meet the women at Drummuir so we could think together. My impression is they share a great camaraderie and possess a stubborn cheerfulness despite their daily hardships. They would make a formidable army for the Cause if we could convince them to join. They laughed at me today when I suggested it, since they don't meet property qualifications; even if they did they'd have no spare time on their hands. They work on the coalfield like men, then they come home to babies, cooking, laundry, and scrubbing. I can't see their men taking on these domestic chores so that they might go picketing or liaising, and for nothing.

My second impression is that we are committing a serious error by focusing so strongly on the lamentable lack of employment for women of our class, when there is a large group of women that has rather too much work on their hands all while receiving inadequate compensation for it. Legislating against their work in the name of protecting them ignores the reality of their families needing to eat.

Finally, I feel a strange unease, or perhaps a sense of guilt, that I can safely walk away from Drummuir and forget all about its exis-

tence when Rosie Fraser will continue to live this life every day. I have read about mining accidents in the papers, so it was hardly a shocking revelation that they exist; I have just never shared a table with the potential next victims before. I know most would argue that there is a natural order to these things, that we are born into our station in accordance with a higher plan, but as suffragists, we reject the same kind of thinking in regards to our sex, hence I feel quite encouraged to reject this way of thinking entirely.

I feel more acutely than ever an obligation to put whatever talents and good fortune I might possess to the best possible use. I'm not sure yet what best *means, but I shall accompany Mr. Blackstone to St. Andrews tomorrow in search of a camera. . . .*

Regarding Mr. Blackstone,

she wrote, and paused for the longest time.

I'm quite well.

He has revealed himself to be part Robin Hood rather than plain villain.

She crossed out the last sentence so thoroughly, it was a black bar across the page, and Lucie would find it very strange indeed.

A glance out the window said the sun was still high in the sky, but already butterflies swarmed in her belly at the prospect of facing him at dinner. Half dream, half shadows, their erotic intimacy last night appeared in soft focus now, but, oh, it had definitely happened. His fingers inside her, his teeth against her neck. She gave a nervous little huff. Her current condition would keep them on separate sides of the bed for a few nights. A *no* would suffice to deter him in any case; she knew this now. The trouble was, she might not say no. She could feel herself waver. And he knew. In the controlled, patient way a confident man could afford to wait, Lucian was waiting for her.

Chapter 23

Harriet hid behind *Bradshaw's Railway Guide* during the train ride to St. Andrews. A sharp new awareness loomed between them since their erotic interlude two nights ago, and she was shying away from the edges. He was keen to repeat the experience, but he was wary of it, too—his chest warmed and his mind muddled whenever he looked at her. She had borrowed an old-fashioned straw bonnet in anticipation of the seaside, and looked too young to be his wife with the large green silk bow beneath her chin. Yes, warm and muddled. Drunk people made bad decisions.

When the train rattled through the small town of Strathkinness at noon, the coach waiter served some sandwiches, which Harriet seemed to enjoy, and instead of picking up her *Bradshaw* shield again after the meal, she acknowledged his presence: "The women of Drummuir," she said, "one of their worries is that their clothes don't dry properly on time even when they put them through the mangle, especially during the rainier seasons."

"Year-round, then," he said, and it summoned the ghost of a smile.

"A building with a heating system where they could hang the woolen clothes to dry would greatly help reduce rheumatic troubles in the community," she said.

A shockingly obvious solution. "I'll have one built," he said. "Thank you."

"They also complain that their pay is lower than the men's."

"That's not uncommon."

She was watching him alertly. "Will you raise their pay?"

"Yes."

"Equal to the men's?"

"Not quite, no."

Her face fell, and he felt her disapproval like a too-tight cravat round his neck.

"They should be paid more than the men," she said. With her belligerent face beneath the feathered crown of her bonnet, she looked like an angry titmouse. "They work double: both in the colliery and in the home."

"Agreed," he said.

Her hostile expression softened.

"Their fellas wouldn't like it," he explained. "And the more frustrated they are, the darker their moods get around their women."

She drew back. "But it's the women demanding it," she said. "Surely they know their own mind?"

"But was it all women demanding it?"

"No," she admitted after a disgruntled pause. "But it's still a poor reason."

He nodded. "Don't mistake me—I'm not approving of it."

"But accepting it?"

He remembered the fists to his face when he had stood between his mother and her husband as a lad. "No," he said.

"Oh, how frustrating," she said, "to keep a woman's wages low to soothe a man's vanity."

"It's not just vanity," he murmured.

"Cruelty, then."

"For some it's that. Mostly, though, it's pride—"

"Pride!" she cried. "What is there to be proud about?"

"Very well, a fragility, then, masking as pride," he said grimly. "The sort you have when you have little else."

She kept shaking her head. "Upper-class men maltreat their wives, too," she said. "I helped compile a report about this very thing. What is their excuse, then? I shall tell you what I think it is: it's a contempt for women ingrained in some men, an innately low regard for wives. Just last month, the fines for a rabbit poacher were five pounds and one month in prison, and for a wife beater it was ten shillings and a fortnight in prison. One concludes that regardless of circumstances, even the law holds the health of a wife in lower esteem than that of a rabbit—a fine example to the public, is it not?"

"Ten shillings," he repeated, baffled. "How do you know this?"

"From the *Women's Suffrage Journal*," she snipped. "It lists these cases in every edition. Lest we forget."

He shifted on his seat to accommodate the sudden weight of discomfort in his stomach.

"I don't know what a toff's excuse is to be mean to his woman," he said, "and I'm not making excuses for it; there's never an excuse for such a thing. I tried to explain something I've seen growing up: a boy in Drummuir learns that a good man provides for his wife and keeps his family safe. When he becomes a man, he's usually proud of his work, proud of being a miner. But he also realizes that he'll never offer his sweetheart more than the damp hut and a lifetime of backbreaking work, and no jolly song, no camaraderie, can change that truth. Money might be tight all the time. He needs her to work to make ends meet. Makes some men angry, that. And the wife, she knows every fellow with a tall hat and a cravat can grind her husband into the dust with his posh heel if he wants, yet here she's to submit to her husband's authority. It's never said, but you know, deep down. It can cause bad blood."

Harriet wrinkled her nose, as though it were causing her brain some physical effort to accommodate his perspective. "I suppose injustice in one place is usually linked to injustice elsewhere," she finally said. "A ghastly web. One more reason for men and women to be coequals in a marriage—there, no bad blood over failed duties and expectations."

"Logical," he conceded, which made her look half-satisfied.

"Who's more hard done by, then," he said, "a poor man, or a rich woman?"

"The rich woman," she said easily, "for her oppression before the law and in the home always depends on her being a woman, regardless of her circumstances or position in society."

Logical again.

"I suppose," he said. "But there's oppression in never having a day without worries about tomorrow's bills. Where the next hot meal and warm coat comes from. In having to run up and down the heapstead over and over like a rat in a drainpipe just to feed your family, until you finally turn up your toes."

"Indeed," she said, looking vexed. "But working on improving one ill doesn't preclude paying attention to another, I'm certain of that."

He liked having a companion for debate in his wife, he realized, even if to date, he had never cared much for debating. A ghastly web, she had called it. She had words for things he usually only felt intuitively.

Harriet was contemplating him curiously now. "What would your mother say?" she asked, blindsiding him.

"What?" He sat frozen in his seat.

Her smile was a little uncertain. "Your mother. Would she have wanted equal pay?"

He kept his eyes on the green pastures rolling toward the horizon while he collected his thoughts. "I don't know," he said. He focused on his breathing; his chest felt tight.

He didn't want to speculate about what his mother would've thought or said; he never did, for it sufficed that whatever memories he had of her kept spurring him on to reach his goal. Any thinking beyond that, and anger began crawling through his gut. Or he remembered how young she had been when she had died. Seven-and-twenty. Too young to die, too young to have an eleven-year-old son. This realization had struck when he had gone to the graveyard to find his grandmother. He had visited his mother, too, and when seeing her birth date on her stone, he realized that she would have been fifteen or sixteen when she had returned from the manor to the colliery. From all he'd heard, his father had been ill-tempered and older. Money made a man look good, often enough, but he was still hardly the type a proud young miner lass would fancy. So he couldn't know. He couldn't know with certainty whether he had been forced into existence through an act of violence. The thought had brushed his soul cold like a wintry breeze while he had stood by the grave, doing the math, and he had avoided thinking of it since. Something inside him shut down fast and brutal like an iron portcullis at the thought of Harriet knowing. She had only just begun to look at him with a blush on her cheeks instead of an angry, wary, or contemptuous glitter in her eyes, and he'd do more than lie to keep it that way.

"I don't know what she'd want," he repeated.

"What was she like?"

His hand moved to his chest. His brow felt damp. "I remember that she loved the sun. It was probably what she loved best in the world. Sunlight."

"That's a lovely memory," Harriet said, and the warm, interested expression on her face kept him talking.

"When it was bright in the morning or after the shift ended, she was at her happiest, I could feel it," he said. "I remember thinking . . . I remember thinking that she belonged in the light, not underground. Her hair was the color of ripe wheat, you see. It always made me think of summer."

A small pause ensued. "What happened to her?" Harriet asked quietly.

"She drowned," he said. "In an accident. With my sister, Sorcha."

Harriet touched her throat. "I'm sorry."

Just like that, his body felt icy on the inside. He hadn't said Sorcha's name out loud since the day they had buried her, and now it had scraped out, unplanned. Across from him, his wife's brown eyes were soft and shiny, as though she were about to cry. He glanced out the window again, because her tears unnerved him, and because he had nothing to add. There were some emotions that couldn't be spoken, and that fateful day was shrouded in mist in any case.

"I'll think about the women's wages, how to make them stretch as much as the men's," he said, cutting off whatever she was making to say. She returned to her book for the remainder of the journey.

St. Andrews awaited them beneath turbulent skies, the gray above mirroring the low gray cottages and cobblestone streets below. Seagull cries filled the air and a salty wind relentlessly beat away at the university towers and crumbling abbey ruins. The only dots of color were the billowing scarlet gowns of the students who were promenading along the quay down by the beach. Harriet seemed excited by the rustic surroundings and wanted to dawdle and look at oddly unremarkable things—a weathered gargoyle here, a breeze-ruffled gull there—but Mr. Wright had rejoined them at the railway station from his coach and was making straight for the camera shop.

"It's right near to the studio of Thomas Rodger, the first professional photographer in St. Andrews," the engineer explained. "You shall see some very fine Rodger portraits on the wall behind the counter."

The shop was located between a bustling post office and a bookstore. It displayed three cameras on tripods in its window, and the sight of them made Harriet balk. "Good grief," she said. "They look awfully big."

She changed her mind quickly inside the shop when the elderly owner tried to give short shrift to her with a very small-looking model.

"Has it any flexibility to bring a motif closer?" she asked.

The man had been showing the camera to Lucian, but at her

question, his attention briefly shifted to her. "You are referring to the option of different focal lengths, ma'am?"

"Probably?"

"Yes, but because of its size, the range is limited."

"Hm. And what about the lighting?"

The man's gaze flickered back to Lucian. "She means the aperture?"

"If it determines the brightness of the image, yes," said his wife, unperturbed.

"It does, as does the shutter speed. I'm afraid there is little variability. But this model is light and conveniently portable for a female hand."

"Well, I need it all," Harriet said, "all the trappings."

"I assume ma'am is referring to all the *movements*," the man said, and, to Lucian, "You'll be looking at the large whole-plate cameras, then, sir." He gestured at the models in the window display.

"They look as though they should fold up neatly," Harriet said cheerfully. "Like an accordion."

"Quite—would ma'am prefer wet collodion plates, or gelatin dry plates?"

"I'm uncertain about the difference."

The shop owner looked between her and Lucian with a frown furrowing his brow. "The latest, more convenient alternative to wet plates. Madam knows how to calotype?" And, at her silence, "The chemical process of making the images on the plates visible?"

"Chemistry . . ." She shook her head. "But I'm proficient at mixing colors. I'm certain I'll learn this in no time."

"Hmm. Certainly."

"Mr. Wright here will teach me," she said.

"Erm," said the engineer, who had been hovering in the back, and he shuffled his feet in embarrassment, for Lucian stood right near him, which made it difficult to refuse.

"If you are content with finding your perfect model with

Mr. Wright's competent assistance," Lucian said, suppressing unexpected amusement, "I have a few telegrams to send. The post office is right next door."

He'd have to telegraph Aoife to inquire about any findings about the burglary, and Matthews, because he had to extend his stay here in Fife if Harriet wished to photograph three hundred miners and was completely clueless as to how to go about it. Vastly inconvenient on the one hand, but on the other, it might be his one chance to consummate this marriage after all. He had an advantage here in the wilderness of Scotland where there was only one bed, while stuffy, snobby London only emphasized the gulf between them and would remind her of all the reasons why she hated him. Besides. She looked . . . happy here. Her eyes glowed and her skin shimmered at the prospect of learning something new, of doing something for the people of Drummuir, and her excitement made him feel all sorts of ways.

She pulled a letter from her reticule. "Would you post this for me?" she asked. "And would you terribly mind bringing me a penny dreadful from the bookshop?"

When he returned after successfully completing all errands not half an hour later, Mr. Wright and the shop owner looked harried and sweaty, but a camera had been selected: a whole-plate model using dry plates, at the price of sixty-eight pounds when including all required equipment and accessories. The apparatus, tripod, plates, plateholders, protective gloves, and bottles of chemicals would have to be meticulously wrapped for secure transport.

"My head is buzzing like a beehive," Harriet said as he was signing the check. "I should like to go to the beach and have the wind blow the cobwebs away while everything is being readied."

They left to take a stroll to the castle ruins, where a ramp led onto the beach. The sea in the bay below was in uproar and the slate-gray line of the horizon blended water and sky. The damp breeze blew unhampered here and filled Lucian's mouth with salt. Next to him,

Harriet gasped and threw her arms wide open. "Isn't it vast—isn't it beautiful!"

"It is," he murmured, but she was already dashing toward the shore. By the time he had caught up, her hems were soaked with sea spray. The pebbles and shells that lay scattered along the waterline soon snared her like a will-o'-the-wisp: she stopped and stooped every other yard to pick something up, held it up for inspection, put it into her skirt pocket, and hurried on toward the next, and was soon ahead of him again. She was light-footed despite heavy hems and pockets, and her ribbons and tendrils of her fiery hair were dancing in the breeze.

He had grown up in Argyll, close enough to the sea to know all about selkie lore. His grandmother had told the stories at night, about these creatures who lived as seals in the sea but shed their skin to take the shape of a human when they wanted to be on dry land. Selkie females in their human form were said to be enchanting.

"Lucian!"

She was coming toward him, and his heart was in his throat. "Yes?"

She held up a brownish stone. "I believe this is amber?"

He forced his attention away from her rosy-cheeked face to the lump she was waving at him. Her white gloves were covered in sand. "It is," he said after a brief examination.

She gave a small whoop of delight and resumed her hunt.

A female selkie in human form better not stumble across a man. She would be naked with only her long hair to hide her charms while her sealskin was tucked away safely under a rock or in some cove. In the legends, the man set out to find her pelt so he could keep it and force the selkie to remain a woman and to become his wife. When Lucian had heard the stories as a boy, he hadn't yet felt the desire to steal; he had had a child's simple sense of justice. He had felt a noble rage on behalf of the creature who was now forever trapped on land, in a fisherman's hut, with only memories of her freedom. Granted, the selkie was a female, whose natural lot seemed to be to eventually become stuck indoors with a brood no matter her species, but he had known unfairness when he saw it. He supposed he hadn't been born bad. He had become that way.

On the train ride back, he was reading the book he had purchased in the bookshop, and Harriet was ignoring her new penny dreadful and spread her beach loot on the table. Glancing over the top of his page now and again, he soon noticed that she was arranging it first by material—stone, beach glass, fossilized squid—and then by color. She seemed especially fond of the beach glass.

"Why did you collect those?" he finally asked, and nodded at a pile of unremarkable gray beach pebbles rattling on the polished wood.

She looked up, vaguely confused, as though he had pulled her from the depths of some meandering thoughts. "Those?" she said. "So that they wouldn't feel left out."

His brows pulled together. "They are . . . stones."

She gave an apologetic shrug. "Yes, but I don't think anyone ever picks them."

Somehow, no sarcastic answer came to mind. Instead, his throat felt strangely constricted as he watched her sort the unloved pebbles into an orderly row.

He was in dangerous territory. Like a hunter who had been too focused on chasing his prey and suddenly found himself on very thin ice indeed. Dangerous, because the legends about the selkies never ended with the trapped female living out her days with the man who had stolen her. Inevitably, someone always found her skin, and she would slip it on and leave her husband and family to return to the sea without a backward glance.

Chapter 24

H er first attempt at photography in the village school the next day was discouraging, a disaster, a chagrin. Mr. Wright explained the camera's different movements to her, but he used a lot of terms she had never heard before, and she barely got to touch the camera, for he kept doing everything himself. The children of Heather Row, among them little Anne, sat patiently when she first tried to immortalize them on a gelatin plate, but the image on the focusing screen was very dim and upside down, and by the time she had found her bearings, the children were bored and moving. When Mr. Wright suggested she practice on an inanimate object for a few weeks and learn the theory behind dry-plate emulsions, she fled. The children liked her much better without a dark cloth over her head and ran alongside her on her way back to the inn. Anne insisted on putting her small hand in hers, and Hattie felt strangely guilty for not having brought any boiled candy. "I shall be back tomorrow, and bring some toffees," she told the girl when the Drover's was in full view. "Will you sit for me again?" Anne regarded her with serious blue eyes, giving no indication whether she had understood, but then she nodded. She gave Hattie's brown wool skirt a covert little stroke and dashed after her friends back toward the village, her braids bouncing on her small shoulders.

Hattie lingered on the path, breathing in the sweet scent of heather and coal, and wondering whether the idea forming at the back of her mind since leaving the St. Andrews camera shop was genius or deluded tosh.

Lucian was in their room, in the armchair, using the evening light to read the book he'd been reading on the train the day before. At her entry, he raised his eyes from the page immediately and his gaze swept over her. She raised a hand to her hair—the dark cloth had left a strange smell on her skin and disheveled her coiffure.

"What are you reading?" she asked, strolling closer while pretending nonchalance.

Lucian had shed both his jacket and his waistcoat and looked rakish, sprawled in the chair with his braces on display.

He closed the book and put it aside on the windowsill. "Something on peat."

Sounded boring. "And how was your inspection of the shafts?" The map of the mine's bowels—tunnels, pits, drainage channels, and ventilation shafts—was spread on the table, a vital piece in Drummuir's safety plan as well as a tool for gauging the remaining yield.

Lucian's gaze narrowed. "Is there something you want?"

She clasped her hands before her. "I had an idea."

His mouth quirked, but not in a mean way, and so she continued. "I would like to take artistic portraits of the people of Drummuir, in addition to functional ones."

"What for?"

She pulled a chair away from the table and sat down with a sigh of relief. "I have a documentary in mind. An artistic exhibition—to raise awareness in London. All proceeds of tickets and pieces sold would fully be passed on to Drummuir."

"Awareness," he drawled. "An artsy documentary . . . Love, in case it's slipped your attention, this is the time of the Decadents. People want to read and look at beauty, sensuality, pretty things.

Life's too grim for art to be grim, even for those higher up on the ladder."

"It's the right thing to do," she said firmly. "I feel it in my belly."

"Ah," he said. "How was your first lesson?"

She hung her head and rubbed her temples. "Horrid."

"So naturally it made you want to do more of it, and to critical acclaim no less."

The lesson hadn't made her want to do it. Feeling Anne's small hand in hers had. Seeing Rosie Fraser in her Sunday finery, easily confused with any other respectable matron in the city.

"I know nothing," she said.

Lucian's expression was a careful blank.

She gave him a sullen look. "Mr. Wright tried his best, but he has a way of making it all sound dreadfully complicated—he lectured about focal point calculation for thirty minutes, and I nearly cried with frustration because I don't want to invent new cameras, nor build them myself. I just want to use them."

Lucian shrugged. "He's an engineer."

"But I am an artist. And I require a teacher who understands my artistic ambitions, and then offers the technical solutions."

"If you find him impossible, we'll find you someone from London."

That was her next problem. "I don't have enough time in any case," she said. "Delusional of me to think I could manage it in three days' time."

"You can't," he agreed. "I already sent word to London that we're staying awhile longer."

She sat up straighter. "When?"

"Yesterday, in St. Andrews."

When her silence drew out, he added, "I telegraphed Matthews, instructing him to come up to Drummuir and bring a few documents I need for my own affairs of business."

"I see."

"He's also bringing a book with prints by Julia Margaret Cameron."

"Her name sounds familiar," she said, still coming to terms with the news.

"She was a photographer, one of the greats," Lucian said, "one of the first and few to blend art and photography. She knew some of the Pre-Raphaelites."

Was it a trap? A kindness? She fixed him with a distrustful stare. "Why?"

He gave a shrug. "I thought her work might interest you."

Whatever his motivation, he had shown great foresight in anticipating her desires. *I don't want to*, she thought, *I don't want to like him so*. She had barely slept last night, as if his nearness beneath the blanket set all her cells alight with heated yearning. She felt a little molten inside right now; it must be her old, unbetterable self, feeling pleased that someone was pleasing her.

A man would have killed the Beast.

She wrestled with the words before forcing them out: "I would appreciate it had you consulted me before prolonging our stay," she said. "Particularly in a place such as . . . this." She nodded at the tired little room.

Lucian tilted his head. "You prefer to leave?"

"No! I still—I'd still appreciate being asked."

One black supercilious brow went up. "Noted."

See there. She had made her point in cold blood, and nothing terrible had happened.

Perhaps she should kiss him. Under normal circumstances, one would kiss a husband who had put thought and effort into a surprise.

Lucian's smile was crooked. "You're wondering if you should kiss me as a thank-you."

She started. "What?"

"It's what a good wife would do," he said, and spread his knees.

"She'd come and sit in my lap and kiss me." Wicked laughter was dancing in his eyes now, and heat spread in her middle. So he possessed some humor. The darkly sarcastic kind.

His mocking smile faded when she rose and went to him. By the time she was perched on his hard thigh, his features were tense.

"Like this?" she said, her heart beating wildly. He had spent the day outside and smelled deliciously earthy. The shirt buttons at his throat were undone, low enough to reveal the dark dusting of hair on his muscular chest.

"That's good," he murmured. His arms were locking around her waist. She had walked into that snare with eyes wide open, in search of something, her boundaries, her powers. She kept her eyes on the V of his bare chest. A very fine chest. She put a fingertip against it. Lucian's throat moved, the rest of him was still as a rock. She stroked, lightly, over warm skin and soft-crisp hair, then slowly trailed down toward the top button. There she lingered. Lucian broke first; he clasped her chin and kissed her full on the mouth. Need barreled through her at the intimate contact. A soft flash of his tongue against hers, and she had to pull away, needing air. The surface of her skin was hot from head to toe.

She looked out the window, where the sun was sinking in a liquid glow. "It's so . . ." She shook her head. "Confusing," she whispered.

His dark gaze traced her profile, assessing. "Perhaps because your mind is telling you one thing when your body is telling you another," he said in a low voice. "Might be less confusing if you stopped thinking of it as a reward for me, but as taking pleasure for yourself."

Well, that only went against every tenet of a woman's education.

Her confusion changed direction when she recognized the spine of the book he had placed on the windowsill.

She turned to Lucian in time to see a flash of *oh drat* pass behind his eyes. "This," she said, "is *Wuthering Heights*."

"Aye."

"*Something on peat*, you said!"

He shifted beneath her. "There's lots of mentioning of the moors in it."

"Where did you find this?" The book looked new, the spine just broken.

Lucian took it from her and held it against his chest. "In the bookshop in St. Andrews."

Silence, except for the tapping of his fingers against the book's jacket. Nervous—he was nervous for having been caught reading a novel, the silly man.

"And are you . . . enjoying it?" she ventured. "The read?"

He gave a shrug. "I suppose."

"So you do."

"I do, yes. And turns out you're wrong. About everything."

"What? I am not," she said. "What do you mean, *everything*?"

"To start with, the *villain* of this book isn't Heathcliff, but Nelly—"

"Nelly!"

"Someone should stick a boot up her meddling old arse."

"I can't believe you are singling out poor Nelly—why, Hindley would be a far more obvious villain than her."

He scoffed. "Hindley, sniveling bastard, needs a good beating, but he's not who kept interfering between Cathy and Heathcliff with such great effect."

"Nelly did what she thought was right to protect her mistress."

"Nah." He shook his head. "She's a servant reveling in her ill-gained powers like a hog in the mud. And Cathy didn't want protection; she wanted Heathcliff. Here—she says . . ." He settled her deeper into his arms, opened the book, and riffled through the pages until his fingertip found the line he was searching for. "She says, 'My love for Heathcliff resembles the eternal rocks beneath: a source of little visible delight, but necessary.'" He looked up at her with heated eyes. "*Necessary*. Those are her words."

She'd never last through a Sunday evening of him reading to her, she realized. As he had drawled those *words* with his Scottish burr, her heart had fluttered like a butterfly under an unexpected sunbeam.

"And another thing you have wrong," he said, his gaze boring into hers. "I'm no Heathcliff."

Her pulse still high, she slid a poignant glance over him. "You're not?" With his glower and curling black hair, he looked like the Yorkshire winds were still howling around him.

"First," he said, "I'd have never killed that dog; it hadn't done a thing."

"Poor Fanny."

"Yes, Fanny. Second, Heathcliff was indecisive. Which I'm not."

"You're not," she acknowledged.

"A disloyal creature like Cathy wouldn't be worth the efforts of a revenge," he continued. "I'd ne'er return to that place to flaunt my new wealth and position only to torment her. But *if* I were fool enough to pine so after such a woman—nay, any woman—if I thought the very beating of my heart was compelled by her existence, and knew just a sliver of this sentiment returned, I would take her. No running away in a sulk after hearing things I don't like, no idly standing by while a whey-faced gent weds and beds her. I'd have crossed the moors with her thrown over my shoulder if need be."

"No doubt you would," she breathed, aware of his arm tightening around her waist. "And naturally you would think nothing of forcing her to live in squalor with you."

"Ah, but there was no squalor—he was clever, and fortune smiled upon him, didn't it?" He was smiling, too, exposing his chipped tooth and looking like a gleeful wolf.

An agitation crawled beneath her skin. She shook off his arm and stood. "She was compelled to choose Linton by economic realities and propriety—most women would have done the same; it was her one sensible choice."

Lucian shook his head. "She had too little faith in the man she needed, so he hated himself even more and she chose a puny groom for her bed instead."

"Puny? You hate the poor man."

He made a face. "He near faints when Heathcliff glares at him. *Faints* when he *glares*. Which woman who says, 'I *am* Heathcliff' could be well pleased with *that*?"

Her lips parted before she had an answer. Before she realized she had, in fact, nothing to parry this. Her mind was wiped clean. Instinctively, she understood why such a woman couldn't have been pleased. Her gaze fled to the vast expanse of heather outside the window, then to the low line of hills on the horizon. A woman like Cathy would have pined for passion until the end, beneath whichever glossy veneer of social respectability she had painted over her loss, because the truth was there—down deep where the rocks might be, but it was there. And so hidden in the dark and gradually compacting beneath layers of self-deception and pretenses, truth could turn to rot and eat away at the very roots of one's existence. That's why some women went mad and haunted the moors. Some hearts strove for the mellow pleasures of kind and steady things, and some beat for the heat of passion even when they knew they'd burn. *I'd choose the blaze*, she thought. The clear recognition of her own essence cut at something inside her, sharp like teeth. *I could have never loved Clotworthy Skeffington*. And he could have never loved all of her. Imagine, the fine-faced lord's reaction to her wayward thoughts, her desire for more, her gloriously helpless cries when Lucian had slid his fingers into her. She blew out a breath and touched her cheeks. Her hands were icy. Odd, how the truth pounced into plain view after being there all along. She wasn't *lovely*. That's why she had such a strong reaction to the word; there was nothing wrong with lovely, but it was not her. Beneath lace and silk, she was a wild and dangerous creature.

When she turned to Lucian, his eyes widened. "You're smiling."

He said it in the same tone as a man would say, *I have just seen a pig fly by*.

"Because I believe we are discussing literature, Mr. Blackstone," she said.

A look of surprise stole over his face. "I believe we are."

"Romantic novels, no less."

"This isn't Florence, though," he said, and glanced around their bleak abode.

"No," she said. "It's a haunted inn in a desolate wasteland."

He barked a laugh, a rusty sound, but his eyes gleamed bright and he suddenly appeared close to his true age of nine-and-twenty. Her heart gave a palpable *thump*. This was how he could have been. He could have been *fun*.

The twinkle in Lucian's eyes faded. "You all right?"

Coming from him, the hint of worry in his tone felt more intimate than an openmouthed kiss. She glanced at the chamber door. "I must go and inquire after our laundry."

He studied her for a moment, then he released her with faint reluctance. "You do that, then."

As she made her way down the creaking stairs, watched by dead-eyed waterfowl, she wondered whether the truth gained layers over time and was never just one thing. Perhaps Linton had been kind and appropriate, but was still utterly wrong for Cathy. As for Hattie's own husband . . . he was wealthy and ruthless now, but which of the lines on his face had been carved by the hardships of his youth? Had the seeds of his callousness been planted when he had been six years old, forced to sit alone in the dark? He would have grown taller had he been better fed as a boy. He would be softer had he lived in the light. He could have discussed novels with refined speech had there been learned minds to teach him rather than the cruelty of the colliery. She pictured him laughing, in his fine cotton shirt and a spark in his eyes, and she was struck by his good fortune and the magnitude of his achievements. What sheer force of will had to be driving him every hour of the day to defy all the odds stacked against him? It made her feel nervous and hot. *I crave him*, she thought. She shouldn't, but it was no use—the passionate part of her desired him exactly for who he was. But while she wanted the heat, would she have the strength to suffer the burn?

Chapter 25

Mr. Matthews's arrival at noon the following day brought memories of London, of a previous, now strangely nebulous life. As usual, Matthews was meticulously dressed in a well-fitted maroon travel jacket, speckless gray trousers, and paisley waistcoat. The man himself looked frazzled; he must have packed and left Belgravia the moment he had received Lucian's telegraph two days earlier.

"I cannot thank you enough for your troubles," Hattie told him when he presented her with the box containing the portrait book of Mrs. Julia Cameron.

"My pleasure, Mrs. Blackstone." His bleary gaze slid discreetly over her appearance from head to toe. "I hope you are in the best of health."

She had dressed without giving any thought to her accessories this morning, she realized—perhaps it was obvious. She smiled vaguely. "You are in Mr. Stewart's old room—I shall show you the way."

"Meet me in the dining area in half an hour, and bring the documents," Lucian said from behind them, and his coolly commanding voice came as a small shock. It was his voice from the days when she had first known him, and she realized that she had become used to a much softer tone since. Matthews simply acquiesced. He was murmuring at the overabundance of stuffed animals and the precariously creaking stairs when Hattie guided him to his lodgings.

"One grows used to the menagerie," she reassured him, "but I so look forward to all the news from London—the papers here are two days behind the time."

Matthews absentmindedly replied that it would be his pleasure. When she took the book off him and left him to settle in his new lodgings, he raked her with another glance, and his scrutiny left an uncomfortably prickling sensation on the back of her neck.

Back in her room, however, the photography book soon consumed her attention entirely. Julia Margaret Cameron had mainly photographed women and children, and what portraits they were! Her lens was soft without sacrificing sharp, meaningful details, and it had made the simple ethereal and the static emotional. There was no denying that looking into the expressive eyes of these strangers gazing from the pages was moving. This, this was life! Incomparable to her own amateurish attempts at putting meaning onto canvas. When Hattie turned the last page, she sat in quiet turmoil. Lucian had been right all along: it was possible to make art with a piece of technology. Her mind galloped ahead; after the miners, she would photograph the suffragists. How often were they subject to ridicule and spite, were they reviled as ugly, mannish, angry creatures? Daily. She'd dare any critic to look at Annabelle's Pre-Raphaelite beauty, or Catriona's quiet depths, or Lucie's elfin face, and not feel silly for perpetuating such prejudice. . . . She excused herself from lunch and began analyzing the images to understand the elements that in sum created something so wonderful.

"What is the current state of color photography?" she asked Mr. Wright a few hours later. "Is there any interest in developing colored photographs?"

Wright's bushy brows rose. "I assume so. The industry employs legions of miniaturist painters."

"I don't mean retrospective coloring by second parties," she said. "I'm interested in transferring the color straight from the scene to the plate."

Because Lucian was working in the main room, they were in the small side chamber, which Wright had turned into a tiny laboratory by adding a narrow side table the day before. Her camera was on that table, with all the accessories laid out around it like the innards of a thoroughly dressed kill. Mr. Wright, in his calm yet insistent manner, had already made her memorize the name and function of each of the parts and probably meant to test her.

"I'm not an expert on physics," he now said, frowning. "However, color is nothing other than a material's reaction to light. And as Newton found out . . ."

"I was hoping there would be some research on it in this century," she said quickly.

"Maxwell's research might be of interest to you, then," Wright said after a pause. "He proved that technically, you can create any color by mixing red, green, and blue light. I suppose one could experiment with colored lenses . . . but the photographic emulsion would also play a part . . ."

"Mixing light," she murmured. "Like mixing pigments . . ."

"Why not focus on the things we understand?" Wright suggested. He pointed to the small portable blackboard he had procured from nowhere. "There are two chemical processes involved in developing a photograph—one to prepare the plates with a silver-bromide gelatin emulsion—this here is a silver nitrate molecule, by the way," he said, and drew some threatening-looking structure on the blackboard, "and one to develop the images on the plate."

The words *chemical processes* made her break out in a cold sweat; the whole situation with the blackboard already harkened back to her school tutorials, which had usually ended with her in pain and feeling stupid. She let out a shaky breath and thought of Mhairi's sweetheart, Hamish, and of Anne's little face, and slowly released her death grip on her notebook.

". . . Mr. George Eastman's recently automated the coating

process, so we don't have to trouble ourselves with the preparatory emulsion. . . ."

They were halfway through the lesson when the skirl of a bagpipe filtered into the room, and at first, Harriet thought she had imagined it. But then the old floorboards vibrated with the rhythmic stomping of feet and a distant roar of voices raising as one.

"Oh dear," said Mr. Wright, and cast an alarmed glance around the walls.

"How exciting," said Hattie. There was most definitely dancing and singing. There were people in this inn who were actually enjoying themselves as opposed to feigning enjoyment over tangential plate-coating history. "I wonder what they are celebrating."

She stuck her head through the curtain gap to where Lucian sat at the table, working through his freshly delivered folder. "Do you know—"

"A wedding," he said without interrupting his note taking.

She stepped into the room. "How do you know?"

He looked up. A feral curl fell distractingly over his left eye. "I paid for food and drink," he said.

"That's kind of you," she murmured, surprised. "Whose wedding is it?"

"Boyd's daughter."

She glanced back over her shoulder at Mr. Wright. "Would you mind finishing early?"

The engineer stroked his mustache, looking resigned. "No, no. Seems quite impossible to work with such noise in the background."

He gathered his belongings and took his leave, and Hattie slunk around in front of the table. "Is it considered rude in Scotland to join a wedding celebration uninvited?"

"As rude as anywhere," Lucian said, his eyes back on the page. "But since I paid for it, I received an invitation."

"Then why are we here? Don't you wish to go?"

And there it was, his exasperated nape scratch. "I'm working," he said.

Working—when there was music, and merry people, and in immediate reach! "I bet Mhairi and Hamish are in attendance."

Lucian looked up. "Who is Hamish?"

"One of the lads from Heather Row. Should we not go downstairs to congratulate the couple?"

He gave a small shake. "I'm working."

"Surely I don't need an escort here," she said. "You wouldn't mind if I were to join them, would you? I should love to see the bride."

Lucian studied her with an opaque expression. "No," he then said. "I wouldn't mind."

She did a little hop of excitement. "I shall be back before dinner."

As she freshened up in the side chamber, she wondered which of her hair combs would most delight a bride; she couldn't decide between the silver one with jade stones and the rose gold with amethysts. The obvious solution was to simply gift them both, but once Lucian found out—and he would—he would harp about her ignorant ways again.

When she passed the door to Mr. Matthews's room on her way downstairs, she paused. Matthews had seemed a little peculiar earlier, but he had lunched and perhaps napped by now, which surely had restored his good spirits. And after the taxing journey inflicted upon him at short notice by her husband, he was possibly in the mood for some diversion.

She knocked.

Matthews looked indeed well rested; his hair was neat with a fresh side parting and his mustache freshly waxed. His surprise to see her quickly turned into concern. "Mrs. Blackstone—are you well?"

His eyes were searching her face with an overly familiar thoroughness.

"Certainly," she said perkily.

"Oh, well, I'm glad . . ." He stuck out his neck and looked left and right down the murky corridor. "It is a rather ghastly place, isn't it? And for a lady of quality . . ."

"I was wondering whether you should like to come to the community's wedding celebrations downstairs," she said, "to acclimatize you."

He blinked. "A miner's wedding—is that what this racket is?"

He really could do with a drink and a dance, the man. "It is, and I reckon there are plenty of lasses in need of a dance partner," she coaxed.

"Dancing," he said, recoiling, "with miners."

For a moment, he appeared not like Matthews at all; the polite, nervous man had been replaced by a sneering one.

She had taken a small step back. "I intended no offense."

He ran a hand over his hair, and his solicitous expression slid back in place so naturally she wondered whether she had imagined the sudden change in his mood seconds ago.

"Very gracious of you to attend, ma'am," he said. "It should be quite interesting, anthropologically speaking."

"Anthropologically?"

"Well, this whole place—it brings Samuel Johnson's observation about Scotland to mind there for a moment, doesn't it?" he said with a low laugh. " 'The noblest prospect which a Scotchman ever sees, is the high road that leads him to England!' "

An uncomfortable feeling came over her. "I'm afraid I don't understand."

"Ah well," he said, smiling nervously. "You know how I mean it."

She wasn't sure, but she suspected it hadn't been well-intentioned. She did recall imagining Lucian as a sword-wielding, kilted barbarian, and her cheeks flushed. Part of her had found it titillating to imagine him so, but now it felt as though she had done him an injustice to reduce him to such a character.

She gave Matthews a nod. But no smile. She had given thought to her smile lately, because she had consciously withheld it from her (then) undeserving husband, and it had occurred to her that she smiled more often to preempt someone else's displeasure than to express her joy. Any remotely self-determined woman should claim control over the curve of her own mouth.

A swell of warm, damp air and raucous laughter greeted her in the downstairs room and swept the odd encounter with Matthews to the back of her mind. All movable tables and chairs had been pushed aside to make space for the punishing rhythm of a reel and the dancing crowd. She stood back against the wall at first, searching for familiar faces, bobbing along on the balls of her feet to the fiddle. It was how Mhairi found her, and the girl took her to the bride, a dark-haired young woman who, radiantly happy and overwhelmed with her day, just laughed and accepted the gift as though Hattie were any regular guest, and gestured at her to join the dancing.

She should leave. Mhairi looked lovely tonight, in a bluebell dress that matched her eyes and with her braids pinned in a coronet around her head, and she should be shaking the floorboards with some good footwork, not feeling obliged to cater to her. She allowed herself one longing glance at the intriguing figures the dancers were weaving right in front of them. The bride was dancing with her father, Mr. Boyd, and he was laughing while they spun. Rosie Fraser's red hair flashed in the fray.

"Would it be difficult to learn a reel, you think?" Hattie asked, leaning in close.

Mhairi gave her an odd look. "You've never danced at a ceilidh?"

"What is a ceilidh?"

Mhairi burst out laughing. "It's a gathering, of course. Hamish!" She stretched out her arm and tapped the shoulder of a red-haired lad who was in a shouty conversation with a group of young men.

When he turned, a glass of ale in hand, Hattie recognized the man behind Rosie Fraser's kitchen window. His eyes were a striking, rich, cornflower blue. And he had discarded his jacket. Who could blame him, she thought, the inn was dripping hot.

"Hamish, imagine," Mhairi yelled over the bagpipe, "Mrs. Blackstone here's never danced at a ceilidh before. She doesn't even know what it is."

"Of course not," Hamish said, but he said it with a smile dimpling his cheeks, and she found she was smiling back. Lucian must have gained the respect of the men, for smiles were hardly required.

Hamish gently nudged Mhairi's shoulder. "I reckon Ma'am has never had whisky before, either."

"I have not, in fact," Hattie confessed.

Mhairi's eyes widened. "Never had a wee dram?"

"No."

"Haven't you tried the Auchtermuchty? From the basket?" The girl looked disappointed.

"I'm saving that for a special occasion," she said quickly. "I have had plenty of sherry, however. My aunt is very partial to it."

"Sherry," Hamish drawled, and said something in Scots that made Mhairi thump him in the chest.

"Very well," Hattie said. "I shall try it." What harm was there in one *wee dram*? It sounded quaint enough.

"Guest of honor, guest of honor," Hamish was shouting on his way back from the bar, holding three tumblers up above his head. "To your health."

Hattie drank. Fire. Her mouth and throat were on fire, and she was coughing and wheezing like an old woman.

"Be good," Mhairi said to Hamish, who had swallowed his Scotch in one smooth gulp. "Go and fetch Mrs. Blackstone some ale."

"Ale?" Hattie croaked, fanning herself.

It turned out to be a dark ale with a creamy top, and it did soothe her throat. After a few sips, her head was spinning, but she was no longer coughing and could finish her whisky.

"How about dancing?" Hamish said.

"Oh, you must," Mhairi said. "I shall dance with you."

Hattie's gaze flitted between Mhairi and the whirling, stomping, clapping couples. "Now?"

"Nah, the next one. Hamish, why don't you go and ask Archie what dance is next."

Hamish tipped two fingers to his brow and winked. Hattie watched as he made his way through the crowd, and she liked how the sweat-dampened linen of his shirt clung to his straight shoulders. She swilled beer around in her mouth, feeling breathless and depraved to be standing around drinking ale and ogling men. Would Lucian know how to dance?

"Do you think me too forward, asking you to take a spin?" Mhairi yelled into her ear, her breath smelling of sugar and spirits.

Hattie lowered her glass. "I'm very pleased that you asked me."

Hamish returned with more whisky, and he said something guttural in Scots.

Mhairi squealed. "Oh, that one is a favorite. May I, ma'am?" She took Hattie's hand. Both their palms were damp, from the condensation on the glasses and because they were overheated.

"I'll tell you the steps now, so you're prepared," Mhairi said. "Do you see how all the couples are lining up, facing each other?"

"I do, yes."

Mhairi's fingers felt rough in places. *I have forgotten to put on my gloves,* Hattie thought. How could she have forgotten her gloves? She sipped whisky while Mhairi talked about spinning and kicking feet and changing partners at a turn.

"Are you following, Mrs. Blackstone?"

"Not at all." Her brain was tied in knots from the Scotch and the instructions, so when it was their turn, it was a disaster; she spun in the wrong direction, stepped on toes, and some long-forgotten ballet classes resurfaced and made her footwork look so strange that Mhairi and her friends were falling over each other, howling with laughter.

When it was over, Hamish presented her with a refilled tumbler, and she shook her head. "I shouldn't."

"But, ma'am," he protested, "this one's been sent to you by Boyd, father of the bride."

She really shouldn't, but the roar of the bagpipe derailed her reasoning.

"What do you do, Mr. Fraser, when you aren't corrupting ladies into drinking?" she asked.

His blue eyes lit up. "I'm a getter," he said. Getters were the men at the coal seam, she had learned, working the coal loose with their pickax.

"And he's writing a novel," Mhairi said proudly.

"Och," Hamish said, and ran a hand over his hair.

"A novel—wonderful. About what?" Hattie prodded.

"About being a coal miner in Fife, ma'am."

"There's lots of novels about mining communities these days; I heard it in Inverness," Mhairi said.

"But they're all written by Methodist ministers and other do-gooders," Hamish said. "Wouldn't know an ax from their arse, those people."

"Hamish!" Mhairi cried.

"I should love to read it," Hattie said earnestly, and Hamish chuckled. "My friends own a radical publishing house," she added, and now he looked startled.

Another aisle was forming on the dance floor as men and women lined up to face each other, heat and unspoken promises swirling between them. Hattie raised the glass to her lips. The drink did not burn half as badly now. The warmth spread pleasantly; it seemed one felt less intoxicated the more one drank. *Clap clap clap*, *stomp stomp stomp*, round they went.

"I'm claiming the next one, if I may," Hamish said to Mhairi, and offered Hattie his arm. His eyes were glassy, and she doubted he'd have dared otherwise, but the Scotch in her blood agreed that this was an excellent idea. She danced better this time, or she cared less, and another ale was pressed into her hand afterward. One reel blended into the next. Sweat glued her chemise to her breasts. She allowed Hamish to put his hand on her middle when it was his turn again because Mhairi seemed well fine with it.

It was how Lucian found her: galloping down the aisle with Hamish holding her at the waist while the other guests were cheering them on as if they were horses at a race. She nearly took a tumble at the sight of the familiar dark figure against the wall; Hamish, with his back turned toward the intruder, hoisted her off her feet for the last swing-around, then nearly dropped her when he saw. Then the musicians spotted him and ground to a halt, one after the other, until the bagpipe petered out like a sad trombone. Her stomach sank. For how long had he been standing there with his bland expression, watching her fraternize with the miners, frolicking with another man?

Lucian detached from the wall and raised a tumbler up high. "To the health and a long life of happiness of the bride and groom," he said, the deep timbre of his voice carrying to the edges of the room. "*Slàinte mhath.*"

The whole party eased up again as one. "*Slàinte mhath!*"

He was coming toward her, stopping here and there to shake a hand and reply to a quip, but he was coming for her. For a brawny man, he had a sinewy quality to the way he moved, and she felt thoroughly stalked by the time he was in front of her. Mhairi and Hamish had disappeared like fairies in the mist. Her head spun, from the Scotch, or the penetrating look in Lucian's eyes. The music had started up again, and so he leaned in close. "Amusing yourself, Mrs. Blackstone?"

Now she remembered. "I've forgotten to return before dinner, haven't I?"

"You have, yes."

"You ate alone?"

"I did."

She looked up at him, sideways through her lashes. In the thick air, his fresh scent was a delicious respite, and the relaxed fullness of his mouth said he was in a—suspiciously—good mood.

"I suppose I must pay a penance," she said. Her tongue had felt unwieldy in her mouth since her last pint, but *penance* still came out clear as glass.

"You do," he said. He slid his arm around her waist and pulled her close. "You'll have to dance with me."

"Is that a euphemism for being put over your knee?" He had offered to do so once, and feeling his strong thigh against her own brought his words back.

His surprise gave way to a low laugh. He lowered his head and nosed her temple. "I'd put you over my knee all right," he murmured, the velvet of his lips soft against her ear. "But you would have to ask me for it, and nicely so."

Oh. "I had some whisky," she said, feeling overheated.

"I know," he said. His grip on her tightened, and he took her with him among the twirling couples.

He could dance. Rather well. Really well. She could dance, too, guided by his hands.

"I thought you were a pugilist, not a dancer," she yelled as they spun.

"It's very similar," he replied, "boxing, dancing, in Scotland. Look at the footwork—it's useful to practice for a sword fight, for close combat."

"Sword fight," she echoed. Was he jesting with her? This dancing, laughing version of him was unfamiliar and difficult to gauge. It was also a dangerously attractive version.

"I should like some fresh air," she said. The room was broiling, blurred, and loud.

She hung on his arm as he guided her out the side door near the bar. The cool night air was reviving, and she inhaled greedily. Her stomach roiled in response, so she breathed through her mouth.

"The bride's hair comb looked very similar to one of yours," Lucian said casually.

"It did?" she said. "What a strange coincidence."

"Och," he said. "What will she do with it, wear it when doing the washing out back?"

"Lucian," she slurred, and placed her hands on his chest. "You must understand: every woman needs something that serves no purpose other than that it please her eye. Or something that makes her feel pretty. There is a lot of pleasure to be had from being frivolous."

His hands were on her waist. "I wouldn't know."

"Aye," she said. "And I know you think me terribly frivolous, but don't spoil my otherwise splendid evening by telling me so."

"All right," he said. "I'll not say it."

Across the black sky behind him, the Milky Way arched white and billowing like a giant bridal veil. She was certain that it shouldn't be billowing to the bare eye. "I think I'm a trifle intoxicated," she mumbled.

"A trifle," Lucian said, urging her closer into the shelter of his body, and she leaned against him with a sigh, because his chest felt wonderfully solid and he could make stars explode behind her eyes with his fingers. Lucian's shoulders went rigid. She realized her head was on one of the shoulders.

"Do you own a kilt?" she asked.

"What?"

"Do you?"

"Yes," he said after a moment, "why?"

She snuggled closer. "Why did you not wear it for our wedding?"

He took his time to reply. "The queen wears tartan now," he finally said. "It's hardly the rebel fashion of my ancestors anymore."

She rose to her toes and nuzzled his warm throat. No reaction.

She pressed her breasts against him, because she was young, and curious, and filled with a newly roused passion that had nowhere to go, and because she could not seem to get close enough to him. She touched the tip of her tongue to his skin, just where his collar met his neck. He shivered and pulled back. "Let's take you inside."

He walked her round the inn, to the main entrance. She was giggling and silly when he maneuvered her up the dark stairs with his hand on her bottom. She thought Mr. Matthews was in the narrow corridor when Lucian guided her past, and she tried to behave, with no success: the moment he had closed the door to their room and flicked the light switch, she clasped the lapels of his jacket and rose to her toes.

He turned his face away, and her eager mouth met his cheek.

"What?" she murmured. "Look, I'm quite willing."

"Good," he said, his eyes searching hers. "Now you only need to be conscious."

"How rude, sir." She grabbed for his cravat. "I am consh—consc—"

He caught both her groping hands in one of his and stilled them. He was rejecting her.

She hadn't expected it, and the humiliation felt like a stab to the gut, which was also unexpected. Her nose burned with a salty surge of tears.

"You very arrogantly told me to ask for it," she said, accusingly, aware that she had left her dignity on the dance floor. "Is this just a sport to you?" He released her hands, and she touched her wet cheeks. "And why am I crying?"

It took her a moment to comprehend that Lucian was *chuckling.* "Because, *mo chridhe,* you are pissed," he said.

"What?"

His hands framed her face, steadying her. "You've had too much whisky." He was enunciating every word. "You are deep in the cups. And it appears you're a crying drunk."

"Cruel of you to acknowledge a lady's incapacitation. I don't want to be a crying drunk."

"Better than a mean drunk," he offered.

Her head was heavy despite his warm hands holding it. She squinted at him. "Are you one of those? A mean one?"

He gave her a wide smile, and her belly flipped at the sight of his broken tooth. "I'm always mean," he said. "You know that."

She desired a mean man, then. It made no sense.

"I'm not feeling too well," she said thickly.

She sat on the bed, and Lucian was on his knees before her and unlaced her boots. She sighed and wiggled her toes, and then she felt ill again and lay down.

"I'll loosen your clothes, all right?"

"Please."

He turned her to and fro, unfastening and unbuttoning her, the front of her dress, the clasps of her skirts, the ties of the gauzy petticoat. He made quick work of her stockings, the touch of his fingertips against the sensitive backs of her knees fleeting as he untied the bows supporting the elastics. *He must have done this many times*, she thought as she felt the deft tugs and subsequent loosening of her front-lacing corset around her belly and ribs. *But with other women.* A sob racked her when he pulled the corset from beneath her.

"Here, now," Lucian said gruffly. "It'll be all right."

"Will it, though?" Tears had streaked down her cheeks and soaked her hair, and the wet strands clung to the sides of her neck.

"Aye." He tucked the blanket around her shoulders.

"I don't know what has come over me," she said. "The wedding was wonderful. I was so happy."

"You've had a rough time of it lately," he replied. Then he left, and returned with the washbowl from the side chamber. He put it on the floor next to the bed. "If you're ill, try not to miss."

"Oh," she groaned. "I'm dying."

A glint of teeth. "No," he said. "But tomorrow morning, you'll probably wish you were dead."

Alarmed, she tried to raise her head. "What do you mean?"

He was holding her face again, his thumbs brushing beneath her eyes. "Rest now."

Her eyes closed. She was half-asleep when she felt his lips press softly against her forehead. "What spell have you put on me?" he murmured.

She was spiraling, upward or downward, impossible to say.

~~~

He cooled off outside the inn, his eyes on the shadowed outlines of the valley before him, thinking if he were in the habit of smoking, he'd be lighting a cigarette now. His hands were shaking slightly, and it couldn't be from the one Scotch he'd had. Flickering light and the sounds of drunken revelry spilled through the inn's dining room windows behind him, compelling his mind to replay how Harriet had mingled among the miners, laughing, carefree, exerting an electrifying bodily pull on him. They made an uneasy picture, his old life and the new one in the same frame, but for a moment there she had danced on the edges of both worlds as though one could do just that: belong neither fully here nor there but right in between.

The noise rose, and a couple stumbled outside through the side door. ". . . he's quite all right, isn't he?" someone slurred in Scots.

"Too soon to tell," came a female voice, "but I do like how he's besotted with his wife."

"I like how he didn't rip Fraser's bollocks off for him putting his paws on the wife. . . ."

Besotted.

"Mrs. Blackstone will publish Fraser's novel . . ."

Besotted. That's what it was, then, the trembling hands, the restlessness, the heat in his veins. How could she not affect him? His cold bed was now warm and his usually fractured sleep calm. His solitary hours were filled with her clever, womanly scented presence. He rose in the mornings with an unfamiliar lightness in his chest, and the only thing that had changed about his routine was . . . her. It was high time to bring his attraction to his wife to its natural conclusion before he went soft in the head. Had he been a more philosophical man, he'd have wondered whether that would indeed be the conclusion, or the beginning of something rather more complicated.

Chapter 26

I shall never drink again, she thought as she crept along the path toward the village, *not a single wee dram*. The sunlight that brightened the valley shone right through to the back of her skull, hurting her. Holding her parasol was exhausting, though sipping a pint of salty broth for breakfast as Lucian had suggested in his morning note had much improved her. Lucian. *I shall never be drunk like a sailor in front of my husband again . . .*

A small figure came running toward her, her pale blond hair flashing in the sun. Anne. The girl must have lain in wait for the toffees she had been promised yesterday. The tin was in Hattie's satchel, rattling against a flask with chamomile tea that had been provided by a pale but smiling Mhairi.

Her little friend halted at a respectful distance and ducked her head.

"Good afternoon, angel."

A gap-toothed smile spread over Anne's face. Hattie offered her hand. "Shall we have a picnic?" She gathered up her skirts and steered them off the path over hunks of heather toward one of the gnarly trees that were scattered across the plain. They settled in a sun-dappled patch, and Hattie opened the satchel and took out the tin. "Here you go, dear." The girl took a long time to select a toffee, but then she grabbed one, unwrapped it, and stuffed it into her mouth rather quickly. She also took the parasol and put it over her shoulder to sit under it as though it were a tent.

"Shall I photograph you like this?" Hattie murmured. "With a parasol?"

Anne just looked at her while toffee ran down the corner of her mouth.

"Oh dear." Hattie tugged off a glove and wiped with her thumb. "But yes, that is exactly what I shall do. And you could bring a toy. You have a toy?"

This invited a high-pitched explanation about a doll in half-comprehensible Scots, and Hattie nodded along as images took shape in her mind.

Anne left with her cheeks and pockets crammed with sweets, and Hattie rested against the tree. A gentle breeze rustled the leaves and carried the spirited song of a skylark across the valley. She curled her bare fingers into warm earth. The sweet scent of sun-dried heather rose from the soil. *How simple*, she thought, rubbing grains of sand between her fingertips, *how simple to just* be *here under this tree*. She did not even feel tempted to send her mind wandering off to Paris. And much as she loved and missed Oxford with its honied walls and domed lead roofs, the stained-glass windows and quaint parks, the punting and the Pimm's and the leisurely strolls in the botanical garden, she couldn't remember the last time she had had the pleasure of seeing such a pure, blue sky. The breeze had driven all fumes from the colliery away to the east. Lucian would have known such pristine skies as a boy. How did he bear London now, a city forever shrouded in smoke?

Lucian.

Hazily, she remembered her whining and groping the night before and she wanted to expire. But there were other memories, too. Warm, careful hands undressing her. Callused fingertips grazing the sensitive skin at the backs of her knees. Lucian's lips, soft against her brow. A tender pulse began to throb between her legs. She was no longer indisposed, nor intoxicated. In several hours, her husband would return from his excursion.

In the near distance, the lark ascended toward the sky in an arrow-straight line. Hattie watched the small body hover in midair, teetering as if holding the balance on a precipice, and how it sang through the inevitable fall back to earth.

The sun was low on the horizon when she returned to the inn. She found fresh towels and heather soap on the bed, and she indulged in a lengthy sponge bath. She settled in the armchair wearing a clean chemise beneath her robe and waited.

Lucian's heavy footfall announced his arrival, and her breathing turned shallow when he stepped into the room. His hair was damp. The hard look in his eyes diffused when he took in her state of undress, and her skin warmed beneath his gaze.

"Your hair is wet," she said, and it came out too high.

He ran a hand over his head. "I went for a swim after the inspection. There's a small loch near the north face."

A vision of his naked white body parting the dark waters made her shift in her seat. "I trust your inspection went well?"

He shrugged out of his dusty overcoat and hung it on the clothing rack next to the door. "It didn't."

"Oh no."

He took a medicinal brown bottle from his trouser pocket and placed it on the table. "Two of the newer tunnels along the northern coal face have unsafe ceilings," he said and sat down heavily. "It appears Rutland had coerced the miners into pillar mining. Seems like dancing at the wedding sealed their trust in me enough to share this information," he added cynically.

"I don't understand pillar mining," she said, "but I'm sorry you are encountering trouble."

He began unbuttoning his waistcoat. "Pillar mining means advancing a tunnel into the coalface to extract the coal, and when it is time to retreat again, miners also get what they can from the pillars that were left to ensure the static safety of the tunnel," he explained. "The tunnel collapses as the miners withdraw."

She felt herself pale. "That sounds dangerous."

"Gets most of the coal, causes almost half of all fatal accidents," he confirmed. "It also means the mine is even less viable than I thought, because much of the yield stems from an extraction technique I'll not support." He tossed his waistcoat onto the next chair and attacked the knot of his cravat. "And to conceal the low yield, Rutland hadn't even had the tunnels mapped."

"Please don't enter these tunnels again," she said. "Please don't make the men go in, either."

He paused, the cravat ends trailing around his neck. "Why?"

"Because it is dangerous."

"Ah." His smile was crooked. "Don't fash. The men who go are experienced." He pushed his braces off his shoulders. "And I would leave you a very wealthy widow."

Her stomach clenched with a visceral emotion. His wickedly handsome face gone forever, his gravelly voice no more . . . He gripped the back of his shirt and pulled it over his head, and the sight of hard muscle and soft chest hair quieted all thought.

Lucian uncorked the bottle and poured oil into his palm. The scent of rosemary filtered through the air. He reached back, and the slide and flex of his biceps while he massaged his neck was a work of art.

"Do you need assistance?" Her voice came out husky.

He paused. The knowing darkening in his eyes knocked the breath from her.

She went to him on unsteady legs. He hadn't moved; when she assumed a position behind the chair, his hand was still curved around his nape. He bared it to her with a slight hesitation, and her fingers hovered. He smelled of herbs, of fresh water and the hills, like a creature from the wild in the shape of a man. A well-made man. She touched him, causing a slight ripple of tension. His skin felt slippery and cool beneath her fingertips. She gave a tentative stroke toward the curve of his shoulder, leaving a glossy sheen. A scar marred the back of his right biceps, and she moved her hand down and stroked the twisted skin with special care. Stories were mapped out on this body. If she took Lucian inside her, she would know him in ways that an exchange of thoughts alone would never afford her.

She reached over his shoulder to pick up the bottle, and he leaned back, against her breasts. The room swam before her eyes. She straightened and poured more oil, and pressed her palms into heavy, knotted muscle. "You're impossibly hard," she said.

"You could say that," came his dry reply.

Oil welled between her fingers; heat welled in her belly. Her massage unraveled into an aimless, mindless caress. Lucian reached back and caught her wrist. He pulled her hand down to his chest and held her there, and the fast thuds of his heart beneath her palm quickened the yearning beat of her own.

"I'm not making it any better, am I?" she whispered.

His voice was dark and low. "You have made everything better."

He laced his fingers through hers and guided her to his side, then onto his lap, until she straddled him. She took him in, the smoky gray of his eyes, and his curls, black-blue like Scottish nights, and she knew it would be like riding a storm.

He dipped his head. It was a careful contact, a light bump of his mouth against hers, searching, like a question. She parted her lips in answer, and then she was lost in a slow, openmouthed kiss. Her fingers sank into his hair, reveling in the thick, silken texture. His hands were on her body, gliding over delicate fabric in warm, soothing strokes until she softened. He held her in his gaze, reading her, when he put his hands under her hems and palmed up along her thighs.

She said out loud what crossed her mind: "You are very good with your hands."

Dark delight sparked in his eyes. He settled his good hands on her bare bottom and squeezed, and rays of heat fanned through her thighs down into her toes. She arched with a sigh, and he leaned in and pressed a kiss to her throat. "You're very good to touch," he said.

He ran his hands up her spine, taking her chemise with him, and the robe, and briefly, the world was a cloud of muslin. She should have felt shy, but Lucian's gaze drifted over her soft naked shape with such hunger, it made her want to lean back and purr. When he passed his hand over her breasts in a gentle reacquaintance, she pressed a little closer. Feeling the strength in his hands made her feel weak, a new kind of weak she knew only with him and the only type of which she desired more.

Unexpectedly, he rose with her, and she gave a squeak when he sat her bottom down on the cool wooden surface of the table. He stepped between her thighs.

She glanced up, vaguely alarmed. "What are you doing?"

He leaned over her and swiped across the table, sending notebooks and folders clattering to the floor.

"Appreciating you," he murmured, and urged her back until she rested on her elbows. The next kiss wasn't gentle; it was carnal and deep, making her feel how well their mouths fit together, how well *they* would fit together. She was gasping for breath when he released her, her body rosy and shimmering with heat.

His warm lips skated along the curve of her jaw, then his tongue glided down over her neck.

"This is hardly decent," she stammered, a farce of a protest.

"What part of it?" he breathed against her ear. His warm chest was pressed against her breasts, and it felt delicious and she couldn't think.

"I'm not a . . ."

He dragged his hot mouth lower, over the slope of her breast.

"I'm not a . . . ahh."

Her tender nipple was clamped between his teeth.

". . . banquet," she said weakly.

He released her and followed the sting with a soothing lick. "And yet I want to relish you," he said, his voice like smoke. "Devour you, if you let me."

It sounded dangerous, so naturally, she ached for it.

He brushed a kiss between her breasts. "Will you?" he asked, looking up at her. "Let me?"

The place between her legs ached for it, too. It felt slippery and empty.

His hands were on her hips, his thumbs stroking lightly. He was well in control of himself.

"Yes," she whispered, uncertain whom she wished to unleash more.

She watched his eyes darken before his lashes lowered.

He grabbed her hips harder as he put his mouth back on her, and she sank onto the table, her limbs loosening and spreading in an erotic surrender that somehow felt like victory. Lush kisses on her belly, strong fingers pressing into her thighs, opening her. A gentle roar filled her ears like the crash of distant waves. Lucian pulled her thigh over his oil-slick shoulder and buried his face in her lap. She stopped breathing. The first hot swipe of his tongue made her see black. He did it again, leisurely and with a hum in his chest, and her nails scraped across wood. She was writhing; he was unhurried, shamelessly relishing her as promised. By the time he was stroking a finger into her, then two, she was dissolving in dizzying heat. The only way to stand it was to moan, and to move against his mouth, his face, and on his sliding hand. She thought she felt him smile. When his fingers curled inside her, she clamped her thighs around his head and screamed.

She came to, trembling and with energy crackling over her flushed skin. She was still on a table. Sitting up. Lucian was leaning back into the chair, looking deceptively idle, with hazy eyes and a smug edge to his mouth. His mouth. She stared at it until it pulled into a faint smile.

"Welcome back, love."

Golden flecks still danced across her vision. He had propped her left foot onto his knee, she realized, covering it with his warm hand.

"Sir, are you mocking me?" she said. Her voice was pliant like velvet. If she moved, she might float off the table.

"Mock you." He slowly shook his head. "Did it feel like mockery to you?"

She had felt glorious. Worshipped and taken and set free. The key to Lucian was to feel him, she realized, not to think. Her natural inclination was to feel first, to rationalize second, in any case. Feeling his essence beneath layers of unfavorable appearances had drawn her to him since they had first locked eyes next to a Han vase.

Her gaze fell to the bulge straining against the front of his trousers, and longing stirred and mingled with the last ripples of her release. It was a longing she would carry until she sated it.

She looked her husband in the eye. "I want you," she said.

He gave a soft huff. "You don't owe me favors. I've wanted to work you over like this for a long time."

"I want you."

His gaze became alert. "It would make an annulment more complicated," he murmured.

"Do you wish for me to beg?" she asked, and leaned forward. His eyes followed the sway of her breasts before he looked back at her face. "Because I won't," she said.

His features sharpened. "Well then."

He extended his hand and helped her off the table.

Now she felt shy, naked in front of him, while he sat there in his trousers.

"We could do it like this." He gestured at himself on the chair.

It took her a moment to envision the logistics of such a thing. "Why?"

"It might please you better," he said, "to just take however much you want."

His hands stilled on his buttons when she gave a small shake. Her body wanted his to cover her. "I trust you would stop," she said. "You did before."

A rueful glimmer in his eyes said he remembered their disastrous wedding night. "Yes," he said. "I would stop."

On the bed, their bodies seemed shaped to fit the other perfectly. Her own soft form seamlessly molded to the heat and weight of his, and when he finally eased into her, he held her, patiently, until she gradually shaped herself around the heavy warmth of him inside her, too. Then their joining became a blur of sensation. Warm skin tasting of arousal, muscle rippling beneath her palms, the guttural pleasure groans of a man enjoying himself. She opened her eyes when his movements lost their measured rhythm. She watched his face turn feral when he gave a last deep thrust and held himself inside her with his head thrown back.

*   *   *

He lay against her from behind with his thighs drawn up against the backs of hers, his body warming her like a well-heated brick. They were married, in all ways now. In her sated lethargy, the realization merely rippled through her.

"We must make haste, and prepare for supper," Harriet finally murmured without any discernible enthusiasm. "We asked Mr. Matthews to meet us at seven o'clock."

"Supper can go hang," came Lucian's deep voice.

He nudged her backside with his hips. He was hard again. More outrageously, she felt she would not refuse him.

He sat up, and she glanced at him, and her breath caught. His expression did not match his tone, or his crude nudging: his face was soft: eyes, lips soft, his hair deliciously rumpled. Her heartbeat stuttered. *I could love such a face*, she thought; *I could love him badly*. Goose bumps spread on her skin. She had always assumed that loving someone came first and desiring closeness followed. With Lucian, the urge to feel him inside her had come first, a risk she had taken. She felt very, very naked before him now. It seemed lust alone made for a flimsy blanket.

He had been stroking her hip; now he stopped. "Too sore?" he asked, his eyes searching hers.

She blushed. "No."

He traced the color on her cheek with a tender fingertip. "If you'd rather not, tell me."

His caress unwound something in her. She rolled onto her back. It might not be love, but whatever it was, right now, she wanted it, and needed him again, if only to douse the unexpected flicker of panic. Lucian spread her knees with an expression of restrained greed in his eyes that heated her core. Whatever *it* was, he badly wanted it, too. He made a noise in his throat when he entered her, an instinctive sound of almost pain, and she understood. Feeling him return to her was so good it hurt.

He slept a little afterward. She listened to his even breathing, thinking that the only time love had been mentioned between them had been the moment she had vowed to never, ever love him, and how this had not fazed him in the least.

Chapter 27

"Must you look at me . . . there?"

Lucian raised his chin from her bare thigh to meet her gaze. "Yes."

They had woken late. Cool daylight filled the room, rendering visible freckles, creases, and scars, every secret of a naked body. And she was lying back in the pillows and allowing him liberties. She was far, far gone from the shores of propriety, adrift on a sea of passion, lost in a haze of lust. The weather had changed for the worse after their first night together, so Lucian had decided it was best to stay inside and keep warm, and since she had promised to honor and obey, she couldn't very well object, alas. Over the past four days, her world had shrunk to a creaky bed, the sound of rain tapping against a window, and the addictive sensation of her husband's hard, hot body easing into hers. When she was exhausted, she curled up and slept. When they were hungry, Lucian ordered a hearty meal to the room. They ate while wearing nothing but their robes. His had a habit of falling open at his chest and attracting her eye to exposed muscles, and that was when Lucian would put down his cutlery and drag her back to bed to slake more urgent appetites. They were creatures in a burrow, mating, eating, sleeping, becoming more instinctively attuned to each other as the physical boundaries posed by their bodies lost significance one heated encounter at a time.

Presently, Lucian's desire was leashed, but his deliberate languor held its own lasciviousness.

"I want to look at your cunny all day," he said, his deep voice husky with longing. "You are very pretty here." He stroked softly with the pad of his thumb. "Like a flower."

Delightful warmth bloomed under his caress, and her feet flexed restlessly. "Flower," she said. "I like that much better than that other word."

He lifted his head again. "I still can't believe you didn't know the name for your parts."

She gave a shrug. "It's not considered appropriate to know the names," she said. "In any case, I prefer *flower*."

He gave a shake. "What did you call her? Until today?"

"I didn't."

"But . . . how do you even think about a thing when you haven't a word for it?"

She gave him a speaking glance. "One doesn't, which is the point, I believe."

He rolled to his side and propped up himself up on his elbow, his eyes narrowing at her. "But you must have thought of it."

"It's difficult to avoid," she admitted.

He placed his big hand on her belly. "What of touching yourself?"

Well. "I think it would be considered sinful." She must have looked shifty as she said it, for he raised a knowing brow. "So you do it, then feel ashamed," he said.

"Possibly," she muttered.

He moved his hand lower and began a gentle massage with his three warm middle fingers, and she gave a small moan. Yesterday, they had refrained from intercourse to treat *the flower* with some care, and Lucian had brought her to a lovely climax with his mouth. Then he had wrapped her hand around his thick length and she had satisfied him with her hand. It had been very wicked and exciting, but now she clenched around emptiness and yearned for the sensation of him inside her. Hopelessly debauched, after less than a week.

Lucian encouraged her moral decay. "What's on your mind when you do it?" he asked, his eyes darkening by the moment.

"What a peculiar question." Her voice was shaky. He was expertly skilled with his fingers.

"Tell me," he murmured, "and perhaps I can make the bedding better for you."

"I'm well pleased," she assured him, but he smirked.

"There's more."

More. Her siren call. As luring as the caress of his now slippery hand.

"I thought of pirates."

His hand came to a halt. "Pirates," he drawled.

"And highwaymen. Sometimes Vikings." In for a penny, in for a pound.

"Right."

"Now you know."

His smirk widened. "You like a bit o' rough. I knew that already. We'd not be here, like this, if you didn't."

Perhaps she did. Perhaps she did like a bit of rough, as he put it, though she would have called it dark, determined, and a little dangerous. Someone bold and carnal enough to not drown in her desire for *more* but to match and master and pamper it.

"I thought about it," she said. "And I think it is because a woman's life in London . . . is complicated. Even the part where we lounge in a parlor and read books—they have to be the correct books and they have to be read at appropriate times. Propriety and etiquette rule every step we take, every word we say. . . . One should think we habituate to this constant implication of potential slander, but I don't. Every day I feel one fateful, clumsy misstep away from scandal. One slip-up and I'm losing my worth. The awareness is always present, a current in the back of one's mind no matter how happy the days. I hadn't ever seen it clearly until you brought me here . . . because what can I do wrong, here on the heather field, or in this strange inn? It's dreadful having to live under someone's eye, being steered toward the same things everyone should like and do. It feels like a constant pruning of my self. So occasionally I cannot stand it and I run away from Mr. Graves."

"There are no pirates in this story," Lucian said.

"A pirate is free," she said. "He has seen the world and does bad things and doesn't care. He just does and takes as he pleases; it's who he is. There'd be no rules with him."

Lucian cocked his head. "Not sure whether you want to be the pirate or want to be ravished by one."

She closed her eyes. Thinking was difficult with need pulsing away between her thighs.

"Perhaps both," she whispered. "But most of all, I thought of ravishment."

"I see," he murmured.

"I imagine them handsome and dangerous and undone with want for me. There'd be no choice but to surrender if a ruthless man stole me, would there? Who would judge me?"

He was silent, his fingers at rest, and she kept her eyes closed, certain she had said too much. The erotic exploits of the past days had made the bed a place where the rules did not apply, either, and it had loosened her tongue.

Lucian moved, and she sensed his face was level with hers. His breath was soft on her cheek. "Look at me."

She peered up at him.

The quiet intensity of his gaze turned her limbs as weak as water. He had looked at her like this once before, during their wedding night when he had ordered her to put her hands on his shoulders.

"I can do that," he said. "Take you without asking, without stopping. Have you submit to indecencies. Do you want me to?"

She swallowed. The look in his eyes, the undertone in his voice, felt like a key sliding into the lock of a secret box harboring unspeakable desires. All she had to do was lift the lid . . .

"You're hardly a marauding stranger," she said. *Not anymore*, she added silently.

Lucian smiled faintly. Unexpectedly, he turned her over on her belly, and his hair-roughened thigh grazed over the backs of her legs and pinned them down. His arousal pressed hard into the side of her hip. "It's good that you know me," he said, his lips warm against the side of her neck. "You don't truly want to be hurt, do you?"

"N-no." He had slipped his right arm under hers and reached up, and he let his fingers play over her throat. "I think it is about the desire . . ." she stammered. "I want to feel madly desired and not be blamed for my indulgence."

"Hmm," he said. "And I could make it feel as though you didn't know me much at all."

Her pulse throbbed against his stroking thumb, her thoughts too scattered for her to speak.

His hips gave hers a nudge. "I could take you from behind," he murmured. "I could hold you, just so." His hand closed around her throat, lightly, but the suggestion made everything go still inside her head. "You wouldn't see my face," came his dark voice. "You could imagine some Viking in my place."

She was panting and confused. Vaguely she realized she was rhythmically pressing her thighs together. Lucian's fingers left her neck and glided up into her hair. He made a loose fist at the back of her head and tugged until she faced him, her lips aligned with his. "Though I'd rather you imagined me," he said against her mouth. His eyes were flinty. "I'm not sophisticated; my tastes are base. I don't share. I'm afraid any pirate making to touch you would live to regret it."

She wanted to touch herself, right now while on her belly, trapped by the weight of his leg and his hand in her hair. Her tastes were base, too; how reckless, how wonderful.

"Yes," she breathed.

"Yes what?"

She held his gaze. "I want you to do it."

He studied her, taking in her flushed cheeks and damp lips ripe for kissing. "All right," he said, and released her. "Then we'll do it sometime."

She blinked. "Sometime?"

He nodded. Sudden outrage crackled along her overwrought nerves. His touch, his husky murmur, the forbidden images his words had painted, had stimulated her to aching point. The soft bedsheet felt abrasive against the overexcited tips of her breasts. She made an angry sound.

He stroked her shoulder. "You're still new to this," he said. "Perhaps your tastes are yet to change. And I'd want to read you better. And you'll need a good grip on a word other than *no* for when you do want to stop."

When she did not reply, he made to kiss her, but she pulled away. He gave a low chuckle.

"I've angered you."

"Yes," she snipped, feeling the chasm in experience between them and not in a titillating way.

Lucian rose and sat back on his heels. "I'd rather take your anger than your regret." He surveyed her dissatisfied naked form. "Roll over."

She gave him a sullen sideway glance. "Why?"

The amusement faded from his eyes and his features set in hard lines. "Because I'll fuck you now," he said calmly, "and I want to see your pretty face while I do it."

A hot thrill shot through her center. "But you just said—"

"I know what I said," he said. "I'm offering a taste—if you want it: on your back, miss."

Trembling, she obeyed.

"Good." His stern expression hadn't changed. He shifted his position until he knelt right at her feet. "Now spread your legs, nice and wide," he said. "Knees up."

Her muscles locked. She had let him look his fill just a minute ago, but he felt different now, looming and unyielding. She had always sensed such a side in him, but seeing it emerge made her heart race.

Briefly, his mouth softened. "Too much?"

She gave a small shake.

"Well then." He tapped her ankle with two fingers. "Open. That's good. Wider. Ah, no hiding." She had put a hand between her charms and his penetrating assessment. "You know, hidden things only invite a more vigorous chase," he said. He palmed his heavy erection, and his biceps flexed as he did it. She removed her hand very slowly. She wanted him vigorous.

"Will you hide again?" he asked, the steady steeliness of his voice seeming to reach her deepest places.

"No," she whispered.

"We don't want you tempted," he said. "Put your arms above your head."

After a moment's hesitation, she did, and it lifted her breasts, presenting them to him. Her toes curled when the heat of his gaze brushed over her tender skin and she heard the steady rhythm of his breathing fracture. She had to make quite the picture, a luscious offering for him with her legs spread for his pleasure and her nipples red from days of his attentions.

"Cross your wrists," he ordered hoarsely. She wanted to squeeze her knees back together, to hide and to soothe the ache between her thighs, but then he might do something outrageous and she didn't feel that brave. She crossed her wrists.

"Difficult?" Lucian's tone was faintly derisive, but he was watching her face carefully.

She licked her lips. "Yes."

His gaze dropped back to her cunny and he gave himself a lazy stroke. "Lucky it's just me enjoying the view, then, and not a whole crew."

The thought of another dozen pairs of hungry eyes appreciating her most intimate place, the pretty place she was to keep concealed, nameless, and forgotten, made her face flame. She felt a rush of warm liquid to her entrance, and Lucian let out a low laugh. "You're greedy, my love." His hand settled heavily on the top of her thigh as he looked at her with his stranger's eyes. Pirate, outlaw, thief. He slid his thumb through her softness, and she groaned when he rubbed over the sensitive spot at the top.

"Please," she heard herself say.

His cool mask cracked.

She squeaked when he grabbed her bottom, pulled her up, and entered her. He didn't pause; he held tight while he eased forward, and her breath came in erratic gasps. In this position, every minute nudge sent heatwaves through her limbs until she lay molten and boneless in his grip. She felt the rough hair of his thighs against her bottom. The press of his fingers into her hips. His labored breathing while he moved. He was looking down where their bodies were joined, and the dark intrigue on his face alone urged her onto a path straight toward bliss . . . until he stopped. Her indignant cry made him smile. "Now touch yourself," he said.

"What?"

"Here." He pressed his thumb down, sending a jolt of need through her. "Put your hand on yourself, the way you do it."

He was mad.

Apparently, she was mad, too, for she put her hand where he had ordered it. She closed her eyes, but she still felt him watch, then adjust his own movements, until he took her in a glorious counterpoint to her own efforts, and it set the world on fire.

She couldn't speak for a long time after the embers had settled.

"You all right?" Lucian was stretched out next to her, on his back, lazy and sated. Sweat had glued a curl to his brow. "No bashful thoughts?"

Thoughts? Her mind was quiet. She was glowing and alive. She smiled.

"Good," he said, and the corner of his mouth tipped up.

This was why they kept young women in fearful ignorance. She would do reckless things for the rush of bliss that had just swept her away.

What change a little brazen honesty could bring. Lucian's reaction to her fantasy had been unexpected and thrilling, like stumbling upon a hidden door that led to a vast, secret garden where she could breathe, even within the cage of matrimony. . . . It had brought her closer to him. She had just learned as much about him as he had learned about her. Apparently, he didn't mind a wanton wife.

"I wonder," Harriet said drowsily, "if it were women who held all the power in this world, and not because of our pretty faces . . . what would I have imagined in place of the pirate?"

He turned his head toward her. His eyes were heavy-lidded. "Whatever else you were taught to worship," he said. "Or a thing you'd want solely for itself."

"Does such a thing exist, you think?"

He glanced away. "I used to think it didn't," he said.

"You're a powerful man. What do you dream of?"

"I don't dream," he said. "I plan." He fell asleep.

⁓

Because they could not while yet another day away in a lustful haze, not even a Sunday, Lucian worked on his list of MPs he wanted to lobby for tax reform after lunch. Hattie waited until Mhairi was free, and they paid a visit to Rosie Fraser to acquire her permission to use the miners' photographs in an art exhibition.

"Art, in London," Mrs. Fraser said, one hand on her sturdy hip, the other on her gleaming kitchen counter. "About us." She exchanged a glance with Mhairi. "Who'd want to look at that?"

"Plenty of people as long as tickets are terribly expensive," Hattie said. "They all have to have one then."

"Pfff." Mrs. Fraser shook her head. "And all proceeds would go to Drummuir?"

"Yes," Hattie confirmed. "Including any money paid for the pieces."

Mrs. Fraser considered it while she poured tea into mugs. "I'll ask round," she then said. "I'll have a list of people who gave permission. But there's one thing that I'd like to say, ma'am."

"Of course."

"How did you arrive here at Drummuir?"

"Why, by coach."

"And before that?"

"By train."

"Aye, and there's a ferry, too, across the firth, isn't there."

She nodded. "Indeed. A feat of engineering."

Mild sarcasm crinkled the corner of Mrs. Fraser's eyes. "And all fueled by coal," she said. "As are the factories that make the iron and steel. More than half the homes in Britain are kept warm thanks to coal. They say it'll even fuel electricity one day. Mhairi, what do you put into your clothing iron?"

"Hot coal," said Mhairi.

"So even our clothes are nice and smooth, thanks to coal," Mrs. Fraser said, sounding satisfied. "You see, we rarely leave the collieries. But the fruit of our labor is in every house in Britain and out on the railway tracks and the high seas. Without these"—she held up her hands, raw and cracked—"there'd be no modernity. So, indeed it's fine to have an exhibition, ma'am. But don't make us a freak show."

"I couldn't," Hattie said hastily. "We shall use your words, if you like. No, I shall hire you as my consultant while I'm working."

Tawny brows pulled together. "Hire me—what for?"

"It's quite simple—you think of the message you wish to communicate to the Londoners, and I shall put it into practice."

"And how much does it pay," Rosie Fraser said, "the consulting?"

"I have a generous budget," Hattie said, thinking of her two thousand a year. "We could have a photograph of your hands, too. Next to the portrait. What do you think?"

Hamish ambled into the kitchen from the parlor, his blue eyes sparkling first at Mhairi, then at Hattie. "You've my permission to exhibit this perfect mug, Mrs. Blackstone," he said, and stroked his angular jaw. "Watch out, Michelangelo."

"Aye, it's the perfect mug," his mother said, "for a cartoon."

Back in the inn, Hattie's imagination was spurred to great heights. She was mixing silver nitride solutions with the help of Mr. Wright's written instructions, because the engineer had returned to St. Andrews. She experimented with different light and aperture settings on her camera in the main room—the brighter the light, the better, she found, but then she had turned to practicing on her parasol instead of breathing, twitching subjects, so who knew how it would be once Anne held the parasol? She worked on mastering the exposure time, which required her to monitor her pocket watch while moving the lens cap from the lens and back again at the right interval, over and over, until the watch became superfluous.

"I shall master this," she told Lucian, covered in chemicals and sweat, with the smell of dark cloth cloying her lungs.

He looked up from his two-days-old newspaper. "Of course you will," he replied, and she detected no hint of sarcasm.

The following day, she paid one of the Burns sons, Calumn, to help her carry her equipment to the village school, and while he set up her camera, she went to visit Anne's house. Anne's mother answered with a naked, dribbling toddler on her hip. She barely reacted to the large tin of shortbread Hattie had purchased from Mhairi to bring along as a gift; she was not unfriendly, but rather harried and exhausted. She called over her shoulder for Anne while the toddler drooled stains onto the already dirty blue bodice.

"I thought it time you and I practice together, don't you think?"

Anne was more interested in the peppermints Hattie had ordered from Auchtermuchty.

"Angel, why are you hobbling?"

The girl had been skipping alongside her; now that she moved normally, her limp was plainly visible.

"Is it your legs? Your feet? A blister?"

A shrug.

As soon as they were in the classroom, she ordered Anne onto a chair. "Let me see."

The girl stuck out her leg, dispassionately watching Hattie's examination as she sucked on her candy. The problem was quickly determined. "Your shoes are far too small, my dear."

In the left shoe, the girl's toe was about to break through the careworn leather. On the right, the shoe had won. The removal of the dirty stocking revealed small toes, curled and bruised.

She looked down at the pale little foot in her hand and fought the urge to kiss it better. Anne didn't need sympathy. She didn't need shortbread or photographs, she needed shoes. New stockings. A warmer coat. Her mother needed a week of leisure by the sea.

She was unfocused under her dark cloth, wasting dry plates with poor exposure timing. She wanted to take off her pearl earrings and send them home with Anne, but she couldn't just dispense random charity. She gave Anne the whole bag of peppermints.

That night, she couldn't sleep. Lucian was behind her, holding her and dozing after exhausting himself over her. Her mind was going in circles.

"Lucian," she whispered into the dark.

A grunt was the reply.

"Am I a hypocrite?"

Her question pulled him back from the brink of sleep. "What can you mean?"

"I like to be warm and have lovely things," she said. "But I cannot stand for children, or anyone, working themselves to death for my comforts. And . . ." Her breathing was shallow. "I think I'm afraid—afraid of what will become of me if I don't wish to be a hypocrite."

"Ah. You're afraid of becoming a radical."

"Is that what it is?"

He gave her a light squeeze. "Afraid of having to live naked in a barrel to not feel guilt?"

"It almost appears to be the most consequent consequence."

His chest shook against her back, as though he was laughing quietly. "Nah."

"But isn't it? What good is frippery when there is misery?"

"Wasn't it you who said every woman needs something just because it's pretty?"

"Perhaps I was misguided," she whispered.

He rose on his elbow and looked down at her in the dark. "If no one purchased frippery anymore, how would the seamstress make her bread?"

She considered it. "Perhaps she wouldn't have to work for her keep if we all lived in a barrel."

He scoffed softly. "You think everyone living off the land, hand-to-mouth, like the days of the clans, was an easy life, or a good life?"

"Probably not?"

"Trust me, it's not," he said. "You know what drives inventions that keep everyone warm, not just the inventor? Or the progress in the medical sciences? Or systems that govern groups of people beyond family size?"

"Clever minds?"

"Time," he said. "Spare time. Because the clever mind can think and tinker instead of foraging for food and doing battle with other clans who try to steal your cattle all day long."

She contemplated it. "The same is true for the arts," she then said. "Written stories and music . . . paintings."

"Yes," he said. "So, I cannot think of a division of labor or owning the means of production as the root of evil."

"But some people paint," she said, "and others are stuck in a tunnel."

"You'd be worse at wielding an ax than Boyd, just like Boyd wouldn't have patience with a brush or camera," he replied. "But you enjoy a warm hearth, and Boyd will enjoy your photographs. What you must do is pay a fair wage and provide good working conditions. When your seamstress loses her eyesight because she works long hours without pause to put food on the table—then you should feel guilt. That's something you shouldn't stand for."

"I don't," she said. "But who decides what's fair?"

There was a long pause. "I don't know," he finally said. "I tried to read the works of men who are more educated than I to understand it when I first owned property. Locke and Coleridge and such. What I know is that market forces alone are never fair. Which is why we need regulation and systemic wealth redistribution."

"What about Marx?" she murmured. "He'd say you're so wealthy because you keep your workers poor. Have you read his work?"

"Some of it," he said. "Agreed with his criticisms, disagreed with his premises. But even he'd say there's room between a hypocrite and living in a barrel—what was his name, the philosopher's name, who did this?"

She smiled. "Diogenes."

"Right. Well, what ills of the world did he solve, there in his barrel, celebrating poverty?"

"None, I presume."

She felt his hand on her hip, heavy and warm, and her body softened in response. How fortunate, to have a husband who knew how to settle her.

Anne's bruised little foot flashed before her eyes. She raised her head. "Do you really believe a nation can abolish poverty?"

"Relative poverty?" His arm tightened around her. "No. But absolute poverty? The destitution on every street corner, the workhouses, the slums? Piss-poor housing for workers? Yes. We will make it so."

A warm emotion welled from the depths of her and spread and spread until it felt she might burst from it. Her chest ached. Her lungs burned. She was trembling quietly in the dark. *I'm in love with him*, she thought. *Help me, I'm in love with him.*

Chapter 28

⁂

They both rose early the next morning because Hattie had decided it was important to breakfast with Mr. Matthews, since the poor man was still stuck at the inn after the constant rainfall had flooded the southbound railway tracks. She looked civilized for the first time in five days, neatly dressed and coiffed thanks to Mhairi's help, though Mhairi kept biting her cheeks to keep from smiling as she twisted and pinned the braids into place. Clearly the entire inn had taken note that the Blackstones had finally begun their honeymoon in earnest. There were more covert glances when the blond waitress served them breakfast, and Hattie wanted to disappear under the table. Mr. Matthews, thank goodness, seemed oblivious, and simply ordered some smoked salmon and black coffee. Treacherously ravenous, Hattie ordered a full Scottish breakfast—scrambled eggs, mushrooms, cooked tomatoes, bacon rashers, and spicy sausages. . . .

"The lads brought the mail from Auchtermuchty," the waitress said when she returned with the laden tray. "There was a letter for you, ma'am." She took the small envelope from the tray and placed it on the table.

A thrill of excitement rushed up Hattie's spine. "A reply from Lucie," she said. "Gentlemen, do you mind?" She was already breaking the seal.

Oxford, October 4th, 1880

My dear Hattie,

Your letter filled me with relief, pride, and contrition; relief because you are well; pride because you are promoting the cause in a place as remote as a Scottish coalfield; contrition because indeed, we must make a greater effort at approaching the women's labor unions.

Here are my thoughts on the matter, for now: You call the mining women a formidable army, but an army marches on their stomach. We cannot, with good conscience, rouse those women of Britain who live hand-to-mouth and then demand they spend their wages on train fares and meals away from home to take part in gatherings and picketing campaigns. We must not even expect them to pay for stamps. If we want an army, we need the funds for such a thing. Hence, the first task would be to devise a campaign for raising the money to pay for our troops' logistics and meals, at least hot tea and rolls upon their arrival in a place of action. Is there a campaign possible and grand enough for such a thing? We must put our heads together, but I can tell you now that it shan't be easy. Nevertheless, it shall be done; it is necessary for our greater vision—equality for all women before the law and in marriage.

It is an odd thought, isn't it, that there are specific rules for us women just because we are women, only for the rules to differ again depending on the clothes we wear and how much wealth we have to our name. If I were to leave a carriage as Lady Lucinda, men would rush to lift me from the vehicle; if I were to dress in the pit-brow clothes and went by plain Miss Lucie, they wouldn't worry too much about having me pull coal tubs like a pony. It reminds me of a letter from one of our American sisters, who realized this after reading a speech by a Black American suffragist called Sojourner Truth—Mrs. Truth, rightly, pointed out that some of the same men who insisted on carrying some women over ditches would not do the same for her because of the color of her skin—to which she purportedly said, "and ain't I a woman?" Hattie, never doubt that how women's bodies are prized and categorized depends on their social standing, and, accordingly, the different uses (think: brood mare, mistress, or workhorse) our men, or even our fellow women, have in mind for them.

I must stop now because the amendment will be introduced in two days' time, and I haven't convinced half the men we need on our side yet.

London, October 5th

The lobbying continues to be as tedious and painful as pulling teeth. Ballentine is helping me by way of shady maneuvering, but after the liberals' recent shift into power, it seems the conservative MPs we require for a sound majority are doubly stubborn on the issue.

London, October 7th

I am still too furious to write much—you probably saw it in the papers: we lost! The text has been rejected soundly! And the entire Home Rule Party voted against us; bloody hypocrites—independence for them only, it seems. . . .

Heat, then cold, washed over her. "Oh no," she said, "oh no."

"Is anything the matter?" Lucian and Mr. Matthews were watching her, alarmed.

She tried for a neutral expression. "Some unfortunate news from my friend," she said, "nothing too serious."

She ate her meal, but she could barely swallow. They had lost, again. Lucie had to be crushed. And she, Hattie, was the worst—she hadn't properly thought of the amendment introduction in days—she had been too busy frolicking in the nude.

She managed to last through long minutes of stuffing the heavy food down her throat and listening to Mr. Matthews make small talk about London, the latest gossip, the weather there . . . unbearable, when one's right to remain a person after marriage had just been pushed down the list again.

～◈～

Lucian knew his wife was deeply troubled despite the polite front she put on, and he followed her to their room instead of going over his white paper on the income tax reform.

She stood at the window with her back turned.

"What is it?" he demanded.

She faced him, her fingers against her lips. "They rejected the text for the Married Women's Property Act amendment."

"I see." He had been unaware the amendment had been introduced.

"You don't understand," she said shakily. "The Duke of Montgomery wrote the text—his bills always get passed—always."

"Hasn't he made a crowd of enemies since he married his mistress and switched sides this spring?"

Harriet went red in the face. "She wasn't his mistress. Besides, the liberals have the majority in the House, and he left the Tories—none of them want us to be people." She was pacing, her hands on her cheeks. "It was only the First Reading," she murmured, "there will be the Second Reading."

"So not all's lost," he ventured.

She looked at him bleakly. "No," she said. "There's a committee stage, the report stage . . . a Third Reading—it will take a year or two, of course, if the first text is already rejected. But yes, there is hope." She attempted a smile, and it was a gut-wrenching sight. He was mentally listing the members of Parliament and Cabinet he had in his pocket, via either debt, or greed, or incriminating personal information. If he could force improved workers' rights, he could try to force women's rights, too.

Harriet was mumbling again. "Of course, the House of Commons could then still turn it down after the Third Reading—"

"Right," he heard himself say. "Let's . . . let's have an excursion."

She stopped in her tracks. "An excursion—when?"

"How about now?"

"Now! To where?"

"The Highlands."

"I don't understand."

Neither did he, but he knew he hated seeing her in distress; it made him want to take action. "You once said looking at mountains lifts the spirit." He glanced at his pocket watch. "It's just past eight o'clock. We could be in Auchtermuchty at half past nine and take a ten o'clock train."

Her eyes began to shine despite herself at the prospect of an adventure. "But the railway tracks are flooded."

"The southbound ones."

"I hadn't realized we were near the Highlands."

"It's a good sixty miles to Lochnagar," he admitted, "and we'd arrive well past lunchtime. But we could stay in an inn, in Braemar, for the night."

She seemed hesitant, but then she straightened her shoulders. "Very well."

Unexpectedly, the prospect of seeing the mountains heated his chest as if a beacon fire had been lit inside. He cleared his throat. "Good," he said. "You'll meet some proper Scots, then."

Her brows pulled together. "What is wrong with the local Scots?"

"Lowlanders," he muttered. "They're as good as English."

Higher powers approved of his ad hoc plan. The weather was unpredictable in the mountains, but the sky was blue and the breeze mild and dry when they arrived at Braemar rail station. A hackney stood in the coach area, and the driver knew an inn that had spare rooms and promptly took them there. The inn was located at the outskirts of the small town, and it was rustic but tidy, and the thick wall-to-wall tartan carpets at last coaxed a sign of interest out of Harriet. She had been silent during the train ride, lost in her own head.

"They recommend we take the pony wagon to the main trail in Glenmuick," he informed her after discussing it with the inn's receptionist. "The trail begins sixteen miles from here, and we can take a pony along on the walk, in case you feel tired."

Hattie eyed the two shaggy ponies skeptically when the wagon pulled up in front of the inn's entrance steps. "They are rather small."

The booted, bearded Scotsman holding the bridle patted the brow of the animal closest to him. "Each one of them can carry a whole big stag down a mountain," he told Lucian in Gaelic. He assessed Harriet with a practiced glance. "They should carry her."

Lucian translated, and his wife cut him a dry look. "I'm so relieved."

They ate a late lunch during the ride, sitting in the back of the wagon and helping themselves from the basket Mhairi Burns had packed before they had dashed to Auchtermuchty. There were apples and fresh hunks of bread with thick slabs of cheddar cheese, and the tea was strong and sweet, but despite that and the open views, Harriet was still quiet. It grated on him. He wasn't used to her being silent anymore, not with the pillow talk they now shared and the conversations they had over their meals.

"Remember our conversation about fairness a few nights ago?" he said.

She granted him a distracted glance. "I do."

"I had mentioned reading learned men's thoughts on the matter."

"Yes."

"I came across a theory by Locke that I thought made sense." The wagon wheels bumped over a rough patch, and he caught the apple that rolled from her lap and handed it back to her. His gloved finger-tips grazed hers, and the fleeting contact immediately swelled to need, as though he hadn't just felt her around him this morning. He gave a small shake.

"Locke," he said. "Locke says a man has a right to appropriating and owning the land or a resource once he has mixed his own sweat and labor with it. I liked that. I thought no one had given me any-thing and I had sweated and bled a whole bloody lot to own what I own."

"No one did give you anything," she said quietly.

"Perhaps not," he said, though there had been lucky opportuni-ties. Graham and the antiques shop, for one. "But I had also worked underground. And it occurred to me that miners literally mix their sweat with the coal seams, but they don't own them—men who never step into a tunnel do. Where, then, does Locke take me?"

Now he had her full attention. "What do you mean to do?"

"I've been thinking about giving Drummuir to the miners."

She considered this while nibbling on her apple, and he felt strangely tense while awaiting her verdict.

"A communally owned mine?" she finally said.

He nodded. "There have been experiments of the kind—Robert Owen tried it both in the States and here in Britain, in Hampshire. I'd have to do all necessary investments first, though, else they'll be bankrupt in a week." He shook his head. "Probably the worst mine I ever bought."

"Hmm," she said. "What happened to the man who fills his rooms with priceless trinkets just because he can?"

He showed her his teeth. "Can't I be both?"

"I'd say you could," she said after a pause. "But I'm the wrong person to ask such a thing; there is little linearity to my thinking. What were the results of Robert Owen's experiments?"

"They failed. Dismally. Apparently, the communities lacked dis-cipline or the interest to organize any effective management. Then there was too much infighting among the workers—many felt they worked harder than the rest and resented that everyone still gained the same benefits."

"Oh dear."

"Every child knows that a common enemy is the easiest way to keep men united."

She raised a tawny brow. "The enemy here being colliery owners. Men like you."

"Men like me, or what we represent." He shrugged. "More important, you'll never work as hard as when you work for your own clear gain and glory first. Human nature."

"Unless you are a woman," she said bitterly. "Then you are taught that spending your every breath on others *is* working for your own glory. A rather sly appropriation of surplus labor if you ask me."

He nearly choked on his sandwich. "You receive two thousand a year. In addition to all essential expenses paid. That's one hell of a wage."

"And in return, you receive all of me, with no end to my work-day," she replied, "while the women in Drummuir are expected to do it all for no coin at all, a whole second shift. It seems that labor, once it crosses the door into a home, is magically transformed into a price-less act of love or female duty—meanwhile, women's hands are raw from very real chores."

He had nothing to counter that. "Your thoughts are wild, lass," he said instead.

Again, her brow went up. "As wild as handing a colliery to its miners?"

He laughed out loud despite himself. Her expression remained cool. "All right," he said, sobering. "I'll do what I can. About the bill. For the Cause. For you."

She dipped her chin. "Will you? Do what you can?"

"My word on it."

"Through honest means?"

"And dirty ones."

"Good." There was a hard edge to her mouth.

He nudged his knee against her skirts. "Now my murky ways suit you, eh?"

Her gaze strayed to the driver's back. "I'm afraid I have been quite thoroughly corrupted by my husband," she then murmured softly.

"Your husband is a fortunate man," he said in an equally low voice. "I reckon he's keen on thoroughly corrupting you again tonight."

She blushed, and heat washed over him when her lovely lips relaxed at last. Had they been alone, he would have pulled her onto his lap for some kissing. Instead, he contented himself with watching her finish her apple with delicate bites. She wrapped the gratings in her handkerchief. "For the ponies," she clarified. "I'm wondering: Why would you communalize Drummuir if the other experiments failed?"

He had wondered the same. "I suppose sometimes, all one can do is try again," he said. "To learn some more. Ah, now, what's this look?"

The corners of her mouth twitched. "Nothing—it just sounds unlike you."

"Unlike me—how?"

"A little vague," she said. "Soft, almost."

He didn't like the sound of that, not at all.

They continued the journey in silence until they reached the Spittal of Glenmuick.

The sight of the sunny valley stretching before them left him feeling unexpectedly breathless. Distracted, he helped Harriet from the wagon. Lochnagar was part of the Cairngorms, the eastern mountain chain the Highlanders would call Am Monadh Ruadh—the red hills. Beneath clear skies, the majestic slopes honored their name and appeared in reddish-brown hues, and the usually gloomy moorlands were a muted patchwork of browns, green, and tufts of heather. A heavy feeling spread from a dark place in his chest, and he drew the peaty scent of the glen deep into his lungs to ease it. One couldn't behold the austere splendor of the land without noticing how empty it was. He had never known it otherwise; when he was a boy the Highland communities had already been reduced to a tenth of their old numbers. But he had been raised on the stories and legends predating the Clearances, and that part of him could sense the ghosts lingering on this plain.

Harriet was walking ahead, her back stiff like a board, propelled by continued frustration over the failed amendment, he assumed. He nearly called after her: *You can't outrun it.* Funny, how it was she who could toss big words like *surplus labor appropriation* at him because she had been educated better than most men in Britain and could read Marx. *Marx* would say that the same forces that had helped him, Lucian, become outrageously wealthy had also been behind the desolation of his homeland—in Marx's essays, the Clearances were called *the last great expropriation.* An expropriation supported by plenty of Lowlanders, as it was. Now Lowlanders were working for Lucian and their entire livelihoods were lawfully in his power. Where, then, in all this should a man who came from nothing and now had everything position himself? Damn how conversations with Harriet tied his brain into knots.

He spoke to the driver, who was walking two steps behind him with one of the ponies, then he caught up with his wife. "This path brings us to the banks of Loch Muick," he informed her. "We could walk around the loch or could climb up the first slope."

"I don't mind either way," she said, "as long as we move."

They walked in silence for a mile. The path ran parallel to a murmuring stream, but the peaceful sound of water was soon disturbed by guttural roars echoing across the valley. Harriet finally slowed. "Of course," she said. "It's rutting season." She shielded her eyes with her hand and searched the barren ridges flanking the valley. "There is one!"

It took him a minute to find the stag—he was but a dot against the sky. "He'll have a rival right across," she continued, and searched the opposite slopes. He supposed her family were hunters. They were at the heart of Balmoral estate, prime hunting ground for the high and mighty, if invited.

Harriet dropped her hand and let her gaze roam across the vastness before them.

"'Yet, Caledonia, beloved are thy mountains,'" she said. "'Round their white summits though elements war; through cataracts foam 'stead of smooth-flowing fountains, I sigh for the valley of dark Lochnagar.'"

When she fell silent, he asked, "More Jane Austen?"

She laughed. Her first laugh all day. "No," she said, her brown eyes shimmering with mirth. "Lord Byron."

The amused curl of her lips transfixed him. He had actually taken a step toward her.

"Imagine being a stag," she said, staring at the small silhouette on the left-hand ridge. "You would enjoy this sweeping view every day and could roar your lungs out, and no one would think it's odd."

"A good life," he said. "It's healthy to have a decent roar now and again."

"I wouldn't know."

"Well," he said. "Now is your chance."

She looked around. Save for the stags' mating cries, silence hung over the valley, tangible like mist.

"There is always someone near in the city," she said. "There is always someone even when I walk in the meadows."

"Go on, then," he said.

"You just like hearing me scream," she murmured with a sideways glance.

Lust licked through him. "I do," he murmured back. "I'll make you, back at the inn."

She bit her lip and shifted slightly on her feet. "What of the gent and the ponies?"

"He'll just think you're an unhinged Sassenach."

"Fine." She faced the valley, took a deep breath, and gave a hesitant cry. "Well," she said after an awkward pause, "that was pathetic."

"It was sweet," Lucian said, "like a wee lamb."

He grinned at her annoyed little huff and turned to the driver. "My wife will be a bit loud in a moment," he said in Gaelic. "It's for some art exhibition in London."

The man muttered something into his beard that sounded like "Unhinged Sassenach."

"He says it's not uncommon for visitors to scream across Glenmuick," Lucian told Harriet. She narrowed her eyes at him; she wasn't daft. Still, she turned and let out a scream. It was a bridled, nervous sound, as if it felt watched and judged by a hundred pairs of eyes.

"Better," she muttered.

She tried again, angrier. The pony danced on the spot. Her next shout sent a raven fluttering up from a nearby boulder. And then the mechanisms that kept a woman quiet must have broken inside her, for she screamed—drawn out, angry, raw, and loud—pouring all she had to give into her voice, as if she were the last person left on earth.

As Lucian watched her rage, he realized that he couldn't lose her. Not because it would hurt his political ambitions, but because it would hurt. The thought of a life without her, of having the warmth in his chest ripped from him again, felt like the ground beneath his feet giving way, like darkness itself.

He turned away and took a deep breath, shaken by his bodily reaction. He had trouble with accepting loss; he was aware enough to know as much. But how to keep her? Some good loving could make a woman soft, but *his* woman was stubborn and had vowed never to love him barely a month ago. Once the drugging effects of pleasure wore off, she might remember. And while the dank inn in Drummuir kept out the world with an old magic spell, their stay there was coming to an end—London beckoned, and there the memories of the social gulf between them lurked in every corner.

Harriet was panting. "I think I chased the stags away," she said, hoarse like an old man.

"They ran scared," he acknowledged. "You have a mighty roar."

Her gaze locked with his, and it was one of those transcendent gazes that look inside a man and see him, while letting him see her in return, and the sense of connection turned his knees soft. An old reflex stirred in him to raise an ice wall against such weakness.

That evening at the Braemar inn, Lucian persuaded her to try the Royal Lochnagar whisky, and when she felt overwarm and giddy, he escorted her upstairs to their room and carried her over the threshold to the lumpy bed. He did not make her scream. He loved her slowly, tenderly, and held her so tightly, every inch of his hot skin was pressed against hers as he glided in and out of her, causing her to overflow with longing. When she ran her hands down his back and urged him closer still, a wild look entered his eyes, and he kissed her deeply until all she felt, heard, and tasted was Lucian, until she cried out with sweet relief while her peak pulsed around him in never-ending lazy waves. She watched with some confusion when he abruptly withdrew from her and spent himself against her belly with a groan.

Later, he stretched himself out on his side and drew idle circles around her navel with a calloused fingertip. "Your belly is the softest thing I've ever felt," he said.

She raised her head, pleasantly lazy. "Softer than silk?"

"Yes. As soft as flour."

"How romantic."

His expression was serious. "As a boy, I sometimes stuck my fingers into the flour when the women were making bread, just because it was so whisper-soft. But this. . . ." He pressed down lightly, sinking his fingertips into the pliant curve.

"Bread making," she said feebly. "I have thought that sometimes, you look at me as though I were something to eat."

A dark emotion was banking in his eyes. "I've known hunger," he said. "And I have never been as starved as I am for you."

She wanted to make love all over again when he said such things. They *were* making love now, she felt, though it made her anxious to think that word. Lucian still hadn't said that he loved her, a fact that kept advancing on her bliss like an enemy determined to conquer.

She placed her hand on the cool, smooth skin of her belly. "Why did you finish here?"

His voice was drowsy. "If I keep spending inside you, I'll put a babe in you sooner rather than later."

The thought of growing round and encumbered with his child brought an unexpected, deep sense of satisfaction, the primitive kind that defied logic and resided purely in the body. The moment her mind worked again, a twinge of uncertainty curled in her chest. She would be thoroughly bound to him. Her throat tightened.

"I thought you wanted an heir," she said, looking at the ceiling.

"I don't want to share you," came his reply. "Not for a while." Then he leaned over her, his gaze alert. "Unless you hope to be a mother soon. I should have asked, shouldn't I?"

"Yes," she said softly. "But it's sweet, being wanted just for myself."

He rolled over, and they were both looking at the ceiling. The back of his fingers grazed hers. "I want you," he said.

It was almost an *I love you*. The curl inside her chest became a knot. Sometimes, the almost things and phrases only drew attention to the fact that the ultimate gestures and declarations had been avoided. She lay stiffly by his side, her neediness grating on her. It reminded her of Hattie at the Friday dining table, eager for approval. Besides, she had been the one who had sworn to never, ever love him, so she could hardly nurse grand expectations now. Yet here she was, nursing these very expectations—and they were already big and looming. She had thought being in love would be a warm, joyful state of being. Now she found it could also feel like balancing on a ridge in high winds, where she felt breathless and too uncertain where to step or what to say lest it all came crashing down.

Chapter 29

B ack in Drummuir, she was running out of glass plates, distilled water, and chemicals. She would have to pay another visit to St. Andrews to purchase more supplies before she could complete her project.

She had spent her last three plates on Anne holding her parasol, and she was washing said plates in the solution beneath the special red-light lamp in the side chamber. Her heart was beating as fast as though she were six years old again and unwrapping Christmas presents.

"Lucian," she called. He was in the main room, poring over his tunnel map.

She heard the curtain rustle a moment later.

She refocused on the plate, where Anne's face materialized below the solution's surface like a ghost turning flesh.

"It's perfect," she said. "Look, just look!"

A strong arm wrapped around her middle from behind, and Lucian glanced over her shoulder.

"It's good," he said after a pause.

"Good? It's marvelous!"

"It is very good," he agreed. "But bows and parasols?"

"You are still grumpy about the parasol," she said mildly.

"Och no," he said. "But how will you rouse people's pity if the bairns don't look like miners' children?"

She carefully placed the plate onto the table and pulled off her protective gloves. "I don't want people's pity," she said. "Women like Rosie Fraser don't want it, either."

"I like that," Lucian murmured. "It just isn't what I had expected."

She turned in his arms and looked up at him. "Do you think people who visit exhibitions in London don't know that young children toiling in mines still exist?"

"We all know," he replied.

"We all know," she agreed. "Just as we all know that there are people forever bonded to the workhouse and children and elderly people starving on our street corners. But we have learned to ignore it most days—worse, to accept it—and you know what I think makes it rather too easy to do so?"

"Struggling from day to day in one's own life," Lucian suggested, "or not giving a damn."

She shook her head. "Possibly, but another reason is that sometimes we look at fellow humans who suffer and see nothing like ourselves. It is too tempting to believe that hardship is something that only happens to others. The children at the corner are others. A lady who sees a miner's girl, looking exactly like she envisions her, might feel pity. She will also feel quite safe in the knowledge this would never happen to her own little girl and she'll remain quite unmoved beyond the pang of pity."

"Whereas if the girl looks like her little girl . . ."

"Precisely."

Lucian was quiet for a moment. "You truly believe that people can be moved to care, and trouble themselves with change, with such a soft touch?"

"Yes," she said firmly. "I believe most people wish to do right by others."

"Wish that I had your enthusiasm," he murmured.

"You must have some of it," she said. "Else you wouldn't try to change the way of things."

He laughed softly at that.

She laid her fingers against his chest, feeling for the beat of his heart.

He covered her hand with his. "Have you ever wondered why there's been two Reform Acts by now, enfranchising more working-men?" he asked. "While there's been no concession for women who want the vote?"

"I have thought about it," she said, wondering what it had to do with her photographs. "I think it is because people are used to men voting."

"It's because men are violent," Lucian said, "and aren't afraid to be violent. Parliament isn't concerned with fairness, they just don't want open bloodshed and bursting prisons. It's why every time the mood turns proper ugly, a small concession is made to keep everyone sweet."

"Don't tell Lucie," she said. "She will bring the canons."

"Perhaps she should."

She tugged at his lapel. "Are you discrediting my idea?"

"No," he said after a pause. "I think it's a very good idea. As long as one believes people are fundamentally good."

"I do believe that," she said. "I must."

He raised a hand to her cheek and stroked softly with his knuckles. "One way or another, you'll make quite a few people uncomfortable with your art, *mo luaidh*."

She leaned into his touch. "I hope so."

He looked like a thing of darkness with his brooding air and the red glow of the lamp spilling over his shadowed features.

"I should like to photograph you," she said.

His mouth pulled into an ironic smile. "A study of a white knight, aye?"

"No," she said, absently. "A portrait of a Scotsman."

He chuckled to himself as he returned to his desk beyond the curtain.

She spent the evening working with a lack of focus, as Lucian's quip about the white knight buzzed at the back of her mind like a pesky fly. She had hoped for a white knight not long ago, and for good reason: a Sir Galahad was pure and steadfast and could be counted on for noble conduct in all circumstances. Lucian . . . well, he was capable of goodness, but he would doubtlessly do something outrageous if he thought it necessary. Still she wanted him; a glimpse of his bare shoulders, an errant curl, or a flash of gray fire in his eyes, and she became weak in the knees. This was doubly dreadful for as long as she felt alone in this vulnerable position. Lucian desired her, but did he . . . care for her? Love and adore her? A white knight would have left no doubts; in the legends, they took on grueling tests to prove their love to their lady. Hattie wasn't unreasonable; she would have settled for the more realistic version: a man who went down on one knee and asked with a tremble in his voice whether she would be his wife. His ring would have sealed his devotion. She had a ring. A golden reminder that the man who held sway over her heart had tricked her.

As she readied herself for bed that night, she knew what she had to ask of Lucian to assuage the nagging anxiety that dogged her steps these days. When he joined her under the covers with an intent expression she now knew all too well, she stayed his advance with a hand to his chest.

He gave her a searching look, and her heart was in her throat. How tempting, to just indulge in the pleasure he was offering . . .

"I must ask you something," she said.

His eyes became alert. "What is it?"

Her breathing became shallow. "It is about the Earl of Rutland."

And icy wind seemed to blast through the room.

"What of him?" Lucian asked coolly. Beneath her palm, his chest had turned hard like rock.

She swallowed. "Is he the last man on your list?"

"What is it to you?"

"You must know that calling in his debts would not endear you to society," she ventured.

"What is it to *you*?" he repeated. His eyes were onyx, black and impenetrable.

How dark he was inside! This, this was precisely why she had to address the matter.

"I was thinking you should let him go," she blurted. "I would very much like for you to let him go."

He was looking at her as though she were a stranger. "You surprise me."

"I sense a terrible mood in you whenever his name is mentioned, whenever you think of him," she said. "It worries me, it does. You have plans that require a rehabilitation of your reputation, and our marriage shall only advance your standing so far. Besides, it can't be good for your health. Or your soul."

"My . . . soul," he said, astonished.

She nodded. "Grudges are a weight the grudge holder carries, and you already carry so much." And she would rather he felt free. Free to love her, and safe, safe for her to love him back.

"A grudge!" Lucian thawed from his sudden rigidity. "Right now, I have men in possibly unsafe tunnels he asked them to dig into the northern shelf," he said. "And you don't know what else he has done."

"I don't need to know what he has done," she said, "for no man's character should determine your character."

"Too late," he said. "He owned the mine where I worked. He owned much of me."

At her shocked intake of breath, his cold expression suffused with a dash of pity. *Presumptuous girl*, said that face, *don't ask for things you know nothing about.* A thick lump formed in her throat. When Lucian wore this face, she knew men had reason to fear him. How very little she knew of him yet.

"Since you have plans for which you need to be in the good graces of society . . ."

He gave an annoyed shake. "Harriet. Are you so naïve to believe the good men win? No. I don't need to let Rutland off the hook anytime soon."

Naïve. She scrambled to refocus. "I can't fathom the injustices to which he has subjected you, but I understand your hatred for him is at odds with your plans. And I understand his wife is unwell. And your anger frightens me."

"You're changing your narrative, love," he said, not sounding loving. "What is it, concern for my plans, my health, his wife, or your feelings?"

Her reply congealed in her mouth. What was it, indeed? But wasn't it self-evident that he shouldn't torture people?

"Must you make him pay more?" she said. "Even if it costs you a wider success?"

"I can do both," Lucian said. "Am I not allowed satisfaction?"

"I worry," she whispered. "I worry it shall not satisfy you the way you hope."

His eyes became vacant, as though he wasn't seeing her at all. "You don't know what you are asking," he finally said.

Something crumpled inside her chest. Hope? Her self-esteem? Her gaze dropped as her composure slipped.

Lucian touched her chin and made her face him. His face was unreadable. "It would mean a lot to you?" he asked.

"Yes," she said, reflexively.

He released her. He stretched out on the mattress and stared at the dark ceiling with his jaw clenched and struggled terribly with himself for long minutes, which made her want to squirm on the spot. But it had been a good and necessary request.

When he raised his head again, a cool glitter shone in his eyes. "All right," he said. "I'll try."

A weight lifted off her whole being, and the sudden lightness left her disoriented. He was trying. Trying for her. "Thank you," she murmured.

"I'll try," he repeated.

He did not make love to her that night. It was she who approached him in the morning, with a shy hand and her eyes closed, uncertain whether he would respond. He was on top of her very swiftly, coaxing her to look at him, and when she did, his face was his own again and etched with tender greed. She wrapped her legs around his hips and urged him closer.

Though oblivious of the fact, Mr. Matthews had become their guardian of decent conduct, with his presence preventing them from spending their days in bed. Good manners demanded they share meals with him at the regular times, which forced structure upon their newly married life.

Matthews always joined them looking very well groomed and dressed and made conversation about the happenings in London. It was how she learned that her sister Mina's engagement had been announced in "the very best spot" in the *Times*, which shocked her. She hadn't cared to inform her family about her whereabouts after her father's betrayal, but hearing the engagement news from a third party hurt. She missed her siblings. She missed her friends. Mr. Matthews turned into the harbinger of realities she did not yet care for, and she'd breathe a sigh of relief to see him return to London.

"Mr. Matthews is so well informed about society gossip," she told Lucian when she lay sprawled across his chest later.

"He's aristocracy," Lucian said. "He makes a point of being interested in society."

She was aghast. "He's a lord?"

"No, youngest son of a baron, but fallen on hard times. Secretly, he thinks my current position in the world is an abomination."

She nestled more closely against him. "You could be kinder to him," she suggested.

"I'm as kind as I can be. I suspect he's done some bad gambling in my absence."

"I admit I'm slightly relieved to see him leave," she confessed. "I can't shake the feeling that he has been scrutinizing me ever since he arrived." She smiled. "He probably thinks you are a barbaric ravisher and I suffer in your clutches."

Unexpectedly, her banter hit a mark deep inside him—she felt him flinch beneath her palm. She glanced up and found his expression was tense.

"I would never hurt you that way," he said. "You must know that."

She gave him a confused smile. "I know."

The tension in him didn't ease. She cradled his jaw in her small hand. "You are my dark knight," she said. "My cruel prince. And I'm not nearly as scared of you as you would like me to be."

"I don't want you scared at all," he said, annoyed. "If I'm too demanding—tell me so. I can't read minds."

"Is something the matter?"

"No."

She felt his fingers in her hair, stroking absently while something turned and twisted inside his chest.

"My mother," he finally said. "Sometimes," he tried again, "sometimes I can't be certain whether she much liked the man who fathered me."

She pressed a tender kiss to his ribs. "She loved you very much," she said.

"How would you know?" His tone was defensive. She still heard the flimsy, reluctant flicker of hope, and her heart ached for him.

"Because you said she loved the sun most of all," she murmured. "And she named you Lucian."

His eyes narrowed to dark slits.

"Lucian means *light,* or *light bringer,*" she said gently. "Don't you know that?"

He lay perfectly quiet for a moment.

"I suppose," he said. "I just never . . ." He gave a hoarse laugh. "My sister's name, Sorcha . . . it means *light*, too. She definitely loved wee Sorcha. Christ. I just never made the connection." His chest shook with a silent chuckle. "You're brilliant," he then said, his eyes shiny with unfamiliar mirth. "I'm a dunce."

Her smile faded, because he wasn't a dunce, he was wickedly clever. That he hadn't seen the connection was owed to how he instinctively felt about himself. Unlovable. The realization made her breathless with protective anger.

He pulled her up to bring their mouths level and kissed her. "Thanks," he murmured against her lips, so softly she barely caught it.

"My mind is funny like that," she said. Flitting around and cobbling seemingly unfitting things together only to blurt them out loud. Lucian's arms locked around her and squeezed hard enough to make her squeak. "Your mind's bloody brilliant," he repeated firmly, and now it made her glow as warmly as a good loving. Almost as good as an *I love you*. He still had not said the three words, but he had given up Rutland for her, and she clung—yes, clung—to that as a token of his love.

⁓⁂⁓

His wife had morphed from miserable bride into a bewitchingly enthusiastic companion, both in and outside the bedchamber, and it made Lucian nervous. The pleasure between them came at a cost. The urge to please her forced his hand, no matter how outrageous her demands—see the matter of Rutland, the whoreson. Naturally, she had sniffed out what mattered to him the most and had fixated on it. *I'll try*, he had said, for it had felt impossible to promise her anything less. That wasn't all. She demanded more, that he share of himself, not explicitly, but he had noticed she was especially receptive when he did, so he tried. Talking of himself felt rusty and cumbersome, like operating outdated machinery, and sometimes a vent broke and he couldn't stop blabbing. One by one, she drew secrets from him.

Last night, she had asked if he had truly purchased his first properties from the proceeds of the antiques shop sale on Leicester Square. "It was part of the budget," he had said, his fingers playing over her hip, trying and failing to distract her. So he had admitted to stealing valuables from posh houses, and that he had been boxing for money in East London for a while, too. And when she hadn't fled the bed after those revelations, he told her about Renwick, the noise-sensitive artist she had met on their first day. "He came to Graham's shop to collect some old chest," he had said, "and in passing, he pointed out that one of the Louis XIV tables was a forgery. Now, Graham, the owner, who was a decent fellow, had been really troubled that his own keen eye hadn't spotted it."

Lucian had noticed things about Renwick instead: the man's gaunt cheeks and scuffed boots, that his shirt had been turned inside out and was still dirty. The look of a man who might be interested in making coin. "I followed Renwick through the alleys and made him a proposition. If one could recognize a well-done forgery, just like that, one could probably tell how to create really well-done forgeries, too." During the negotiation, he had understood Renwick's problem: the man had no notion how to interact with fellow men, was blunt to the point of rudeness, and had no patience for business affairs. He had been sent down from the best art school in Florence despite his remarkable artistic talents. "His rudeness didn't bother me because he was always right on the facts. He wasn't even keen on coin; he liked making excellent forgeries and having clueless toffs pay for them."

As an artist herself, Harriet had disapproved, but then she had pressed herself against him and fallen asleep with her sweet head resting on his shoulder. It seemed the shagging fogged her brain as much as it clouded his. It had to be the shagging that made him so careless, so eager. Admitting that he was madly, brutally, in love with her would open Pandora's box; it would hold him somewhat accountable to his promise about Rutland, for once, even when the promise had been vague. Besides. Everyone he loved was eventually lost to him.

This night, she was curled up by his side and playing with the silvery scars that snaked across his abdomen. She was tracing, kissing, gently nipping. "It's from the girdle, isn't it," she had asked a while ago, "from pulling the tubs?" He had confirmed it and had explained that they had ponies to do the pulling these days. He hadn't told her about how the girdle had caused him blisters that would hurt like hell before they broke, how the harness would stick and his shirt would be blood soaked by the end of every shift, over and over, until the tender boyish skin had hardened enough to stand it well most days. Something told him that she knew; she made a point of lavishing attention on these ruined parts of him, as though she were trying to kiss them better. . . . He didn't particularly enjoy it; he wasn't a bairn with a scraped knee.

She flicked her soft tongue a few inches below his navel, and his nerves lit with awareness. All right, so he enjoyed some of it.

"You'll be flat on your back again if you keep doing that," he murmured.

Another flick. Cheeky chit.

"When you kiss me," he heard her say, "down between my legs . . ."

He raised his head. "Yes?"

Her eyes were hazy with erotic mischief. "Is it something a man would enjoy, too?"

"Can't you tell?"

She rolled onto her side and rested her chin in her palm. "I meant when he receives it."

A white roar filled his head.

"It's considered a perversion," he then said.

"But would it please you?"

"Yes. But it's not something one would ask from a wife." He added this with reluctance.

She rested her hand high up on his thigh. "If a wife were to want to do it," she whispered, "would a husband think very badly of her?"

His mouth was dry. The pause stretched long enough to make her eager expression falter.

"No," he said. "He would buy her a castle."

Her brows rose. "A castle."

"Wherever she wanted."

She came to her knees and bent over him, and the loose strands of her hair trailed over his sensitive parts. His fingers dug into the mattress.

She paused. "Lucian," she said sweetly.

"Yes?" His cock was so heavy it ached.

Her gaze locked with his. "Why don't you raise your arms above your head."

He tensed. This was not his usual way; he very much preferred to do the doing. While he deliberated, she lowered her head, and the first silky-wet touch of her mouth sent a bolt of heat straight to his spine.

"All right." He raised his arms above his head.

She licked, the way she had felt him do it to her.

He glanced at her, and the picture of her small hand wrapped around him incinerated his shaky attempt at restraint. "Take me in your mouth," he said, his voice breaking. "Then suck, up and down. Use your hand, too."

When she did, he moaned and saw stars. He hadn't expected to feel this particular sensation again. He hadn't expected to indulge in any of his inclinations again, and yet there she was, wanting him rough, and the next day, putting her mouth on him. . . . And it was different. Not just because he surrendered, but because it was her mouth, her hands, her sighs. One by one, his muscles relaxed. His mind emptied. For the first time in his life, he gave all of himself up to tenderness.

A while later he lay flushed and panting in the sheets. He felt undone, rearranged, as if something solid inside him had broken open, as though a storm were howling over the exposed plain of his soul. It hurt.

Harriet was sitting back on her heels and surveyed him with the satisfied expression of a cat presiding over its latest kill. "As for the castle," she said, "I should like a quaint, pretty one. Preferably in Tuscany."

He nodded. He'd give her anything.

She laughed. "I jest." She kept touching her fingertips to her lips, smiling as though she liked the feel of it. "I enjoyed it," she said. "Truly, I did."

"I wasn't jesting," he said. "Tuscany it is."

Anything for her, if it kept her looking at him as though she loved him, too.

Or so he thought.

Chapter 30

Their drowsy morning was interrupted by the sound of a bell clanging hard and fast in the distance.

"It sounds like a fire bell . . ." Hattie murmured, and turned in Lucian's arms. She faltered. Lucian's whole body had gone still and his stare was vacant. He did not seem alive.

"Lucian—"

He was on his feet like a shot and grabbed his robe.

"What is it?" She detangled herself from the sheets and joined him at the window. He didn't acknowledge her; his eyes were searching the horizon in the direction of the mine. "An accident," he then said, his tone cold as a tomb.

Mhairi came into view below the window, running down the path toward Heather Row with her apron strings flying behind her. She was moving at the reckless, mindless speed of someone running for her life. Then Miss Clara was following her. And Mrs. Burns. All the while, the bell kept tolling.

Hattie felt nauseous. "We have to help," she said, and pulled her chemise from the back of the armchair. It released Lucian from his numbness. His hand clamped around her arm hard enough to startle her. He released her at once, but his face was white as bone.

"Stay here," he said.

"But—"

He shook his head. "Trust me."

He began to dress, his movements quick and mechanical, as if he were an automaton.

She reached for her chemise. "I'm coming with you."

His head snapped toward her. "Unless you want to see things that will haunt your nights, I advise you to stay here."

She felt sick. She kept getting dressed. Lucian clenched his jaw. "Very well," he bit out. "I cannot stop you. But forgive me—I'll get one of the horses and ride ahead. If you must go all the way to the site of the accident, try and get one of the pony wagons."

She was still wrestling herself into a walking dress when she heard the thunder of hooves, and a glance out the window confirmed that Lucian was galloping toward the village.

She arrived at the village entrance light-headed and with her lungs burning, but there were indeed a few pony wagons to take the elderly who wanted to look for loved ones. She recognized one of the women from the meeting she had organized and was given a space next to her on the back of the wagon.

She clasped the older woman's hand. "What happened, Mrs. Mac-Tavish?"

"Collapse," Mrs. MacTavish said, her face pinched with worry. "Tunnel collapse at the north pit."

"How many men in the tunnel?"

"Don't know."

The twenty minutes it took to reach the northern shelf at a quick trot were spent in tense silence.

Men and women had gathered around the redbrick building covering the heapstead of the north pit. The first person she recognized was Mhairi, sitting with a blank expression and her knees hugged to her chest against the brick wall. Her sister was next to her and had put an arm around her shoulders, but Mhairi gave no sign of noticing her. A few paces away, Mrs. Burns was holding Rosie Fraser. "Dear

God, it's Hamish," Hattie said, to no one in particular, and her heart turned cold like a lump of ice.

It was Hamish, Mr. Boyd, and another man. It had been their final day of charting the pillar mining tunnels Rutland had ordered them to dig off the existing maps, and the ceiling had come down, separating them from another pair of workers on the other end of the tunnel. The pair had made their way back to the cage unharmed and come up to ring the alarm. Now they flanked Lucian, who was studying a map. "I propose we drill a shaft, aiming at the original path of the tunnel," he said and tapped his finger on the map. "There is a chance they are trapped inside an air pocket."

"But if that part of the tunnel's still intact, won't the ceiling come down if we drill through from above?" one of the younger men objected.

"It will, in part," Lucian said grimly. "But if we don't do it, they are lost with not even a chance. If you vote in favor, I'll have the engineers ordered here by afternoon."

After some discussion, the miners voted in favor of the risky rescue attempt, because there was not much to lose. Judging by the looks on the women's faces, no one expected anyone to come up alive. Shock lay over the scene like fog, numbing all sound and the senses. Hattie wanted to go to Mhairi, but she was in her sister's arms, and words seemed inadequate. Lucian strode past her with his face in harsh lines; he appeared not to see her.

"Lucian." She recoiled when he turned to her. His eyes were wholly different, as though the man inside had been replaced with a coldhearted stranger. He had the same inhuman coldness about him when Rutland was mentioned, and it scared her.

"What will you do?" she whispered.

Lucian was looking past her at the horse he had borrowed. "I must go to Auchtermuchty. Will you be all right for a few hours?"

"Yes," she said, feeling wretched. "Would it be useful to organize a soup kitchen here?" she asked. "Or at the site where you'll begin to drill?"

"Meals, ale, and blankets near the drill site are useful," Lucian said. "The community will know what to do. Give them a hand if you wish."

He galloped off, and watching him disappear, she had to battle a rising panic. She must breathe. She must be calm. She must make herself useful and forget that they were all powerless now. She must not think of Hamish and the men fifteen feet below ground in the dark. *He will dance with Mhairi again*, she thought, and pictured him spinning the girl, their blue eyes laughing. He had to finish his novel. She turned and blindly searched for Mrs. MacTavish. *I should have sketched him and Boyd while I still could.* Her knees felt weak and she moved on to the next pony wagon slowly as if through treacle. The mining women's pain surrounded her and squeezed her chest, and there was nothing, nothing she could do but to keep calm and carry on. She knew that if it were Lucian in the tunnel, ripped from her forever, she wouldn't bear it.

⁂

The small telegraph office in Auchtermuchty was empty except for the clerk dozing behind his windowpane. The screams and the sound of women crying had to be inside Lucian's head. The feeling of rocks crushing his chest—in his head. So he breathed, in and out, by sheer force of will.

"A telegram to Dundee," he said.

The clerk was young, his upturned face pale and soft. It morphed into a dead, pale face with a halo of blond hair, and Lucian blinked, and blinked again.

"Sir?"

He focused on the painting on the wall behind the clerk. A glen, sweeping hills, open spaces. He dictated the message to Mr. Stewart, a mining engineer. Then he requested the name of a physician in Dundee, one who had experience in bone setting.

The white fingers of the clerk leafed through the ledger.

White hands, palms up in the mud. Dead eyes, facing skyward. Sweat ran down his face, and his collar was sticky.

The clerk nervously licked his lips.

"Do you hear a bell?" Lucian asked him.

"N-no, sir."

He kept breathing. It was all in his head. That was the problem. After years and years, the lid had lifted, and he remembered—no, he was not remembering; it was as though he were there, as though it were happening. The accident, the way they had looked, the sense of terror—and the problem was, he couldn't stop. He couldn't beat back the visions, or the noise, and his body had to just endure it. He unlocked his jaw and gave up the message to the physician.

"Would that be all, sir?"

His heart beat too fast; he was aware of that. He was aware the way a bystander might be aware of someone else's pulse. He refocused on the painting, the ridges and the sky. He thought of the day in Lochnagar, of Harriet screaming her rage into the world. Would that his own rage could have been relieved in such a way. But it wasn't just his rage; he carried the unheard screams of dozens, and he had worked, all his life, to give them a voice. There was no peace without justice. *Harriet,* he thought. *My Harriet.*

He pulled another shilling from his purse. "No," he said. "I need to send another one, to London."

⚬⚬

When Lucian returned, he seemed more withdrawn than before. Since the miners had agreed on a digging point, he stayed on the site of the accident to help supervise the early stages of the drill-tower erection and did not join Harriet at the inn until two o'clock in the morning. She watched when he emerged from the side chamber, his steps heavy in the shadows. Grooves bracketed his mouth. He looked a decade older, and it near brought her to tears.

"It's not your fault," she told him when he joined her under the covers.

"Try to sleep," he murmured, then turned his back to her. His body was tense, as if to safely lock his distress in his muscles, but it still seeped from his silent form and deepened the darkness in the room.

The following day, she was busy with cutting vegetables, clumsily peeling potatoes, handing out bowls with stew, and holding Mhairi, who was now alternating between openly weeping on people's shoulders and sitting around immovable like a statue. She tried not to think, not to feel. Once and again, she was overcome. Then she sought out Lucian among the men, and he acknowledged her, but she sensed a coldness in him that made him an unsafe place for her grief. So she returned to the cooking pots. In the near distance, the drill was eating into the ground, at this point a potential savior as much as possibly the final nail in the coffin.

He slept with his back turned to her for the second night, and she was afraid to ask him why.

On the evening of the second day, the drill broke through the ceiling into an air pocket, and a man was lowered down in a cage. When he was pulled back up again, his fist was raised toward the blustering sky in victory—all men were alive. The relief was so overwhelming, Hattie broke into tears, and she cried harder as she watched Hamish and Boyd stagger into the arms of the women who loved them.

Lucian had looked ready to fall to his knees with gratitude when the first man, smeared from head to toe in black, had appeared aboveground. This would remain his only display of emotion, and by the time they returned to the inn later that night, he had withdrawn back into his peculiar cold shell.

Again he came to bed and got under the covers still wrapped in his robe, and Hattie knew she would find no comfort in his embrace. He lay stiffly by her side and stared into nothingness.

She raised her head from the pillow. "Lucian," she whispered, a knot in her throat.

His gaze flicked into her direction. "Yes?"

Her heart cramped. Such a dispassionate yes. "What have I done wrong?"

He was avoiding her eyes. "Nothing."

"Everyone is safe," she said.

He leaned over and kissed her brow, and his lips felt cold.

She tried falling asleep, hoping he would not notice the tears trickling across her cheek. Surely he loved her. Surely she hadn't imagined the bond between them, or the warmth in his eyes when he looked at her. Perhaps this was his regular reaction to great adversity. But the situation had passed; the men lived. Perhaps he was plagued by guilt since he owned Drummuir; he did seem to feel guilty about something. Surely none of this meant that her secret fear, her deepest fear—namely that he enjoyed her but didn't truly love and respect her—was true.

When she woke late the next morning, Lucian was at the table with his back turned to the bed, and he was writing something. The sight of the turned back immediately dampened her overall sense of relief.

"Would you like to join me at breakfast?" she asked when she was dressed.

He glanced up. "I'm not hungry," he said. "Would you mind ordering something to the room?"

"I think a change of scenery shall do me good," she said, suddenly impatient with his abrasiveness and how needy and unloved it made her feel. "I shall go alone."

She ordered a full Scottish breakfast despite her lack of appetite. She listlessly leafed through the paper with yesterday's news while waiting for her meal. Until one of the headlines made her blood freeze in her veins. She sat in quiet shock for a long moment before she could fold the paper and make her way back up the stairs.

Chapter 31

T he Earl of Rutland is dead."

Her voice was accusing. That, and her pointing the newspaper at him like a judge would point his gavel, left no doubt whom she blamed for the man's death.

He put his pen aside. "I know."

A telegram from his lawyer had told him as much earlier this morning.

Her mouth was trembling. "Please tell me it was not your doing," she said. "That it is a coincidence."

"Does the paper indict me?"

She gave an indignant gasp. "They would hardly put it in the papers that he turned to his gun," she said. "There are no details beyond a sudden departing, but I have a hunch."

"I called in the debts," he said, "yes. That doesn't mean his death is my doing."

She hugged herself. "When?" she whispered. Her eyes were swimming in misery.

And yet her distress touched no part of him. He felt nothing at all; he had not felt in days. The news of his nemesis's death, the fruit of his life's labor, had effected but a faint ripple of emotion. That, in itself, had numbed him.

"The day the tunnel collapsed," he said. "When I went to Auchtermuchty to telegraph for help."

Harriet's chin quivered. "You promised," she said. "You promised me to leave him in peace. Now you didn't even tell me when you broke your word, leaving me to find out like this." She crumpled the paper in her fist.

"I promised I would *try*," he said. And that had been before the clanging of the bell. He wiped his forehead with the back of his hand. His fingers had been shaking all morning; his letter was barely legible. He kept seeing bodies, lined up . . . clammy and wet, arranged from tallest to smallest. . . .

"What have you done?" she said. "Lucian, I know you blame him for the accident, and I'm angry, too, but how has this now improved our life?"

She was looking at him as if he'd done her some great personal injury, and his head was empty. He rose from his chair. "Why the hell are you taking that man's side?"

She threw up her hands. "But I am taking *your* side," she cried. "Can't you see?"

"No," he said. "What I see is my own wife condemning me for a weak man turning toward his gun instead of accepting his lot and living on."

"This was not about Rutland's character, but about yours," she choked out. "It was about you—and the goodness of your soul—and your standing, our reputation, our future plans. . . . The papers won't report details, to spare his family the shame, but people will talk. I fear you have done yourself a disservice."

"Really?" he said. "Is that the true reason why you're put out with me?"

"What else?" Her voice was high and thin.

"Forgive me, but I had the impression Rutland was a test of sorts," he said coldly. "A test for you to gauge whether I could be good in the way you wanted me to be good—domesticated, a gentleman." He shook his head. "Well, I am not a gentleman, Harriet. And I can promise—actually *promise*—you one thing: the lily-white creature you fancy drinking hot chocolate with in Italy? I'm not that man. I'll never be that man. The sooner you understand that, the less disappointed you'll be."

Her lips were white as bone. "I could not be more disappointed in you than I am now," she said softly. "You think I'm a silly girl."

His chest tightened as if in the grip of a vise. He hated disappointing her, but he couldn't change that, so he hated how she carried on with this righteous, breathless fury. He did not comprehend her motivations, so she seemed erratic to him, and as such he did not feel safe with her. *He killed them*, he wanted to say, if only he could make himself say such words out loud, but then she already knew that Rutland meant death. Yet here she was, carrying on. If he were to try to tell her of his shame, and his pain, and she still insisted he be her pious version of *good*, he might not find it in him to forgive her. Then he would lose her, and he couldn't. He could not lose her.

"This is not about you," he said. "You don't understand. For now, just trust me that he has done things to my community and my family—"

"Trust you?" she said, her disbelief plain. "I did trust you, and look how it ended. But of course," she added, an odd gleam in her eyes, "I don't understand, I can't, I'm just a brat. I still believe you could have chosen us, and your future, over your past."

"Oh Christ," he said, "do you even hear yourself?"

Her face turned ashen, and the newspaper slipped from her fingers. He watched as she paced, and he began to feel sick. "Harriet," he said.

She turned to him. "Do you regret it?" she whispered. "Do you at least regret what you have done?"

"I regret disappointing you," he managed.

"But do you regret causing the death of Lord Rutland?"

Bodies, lined up, tallest to smallest . . . wet blond hair spread out in the mud . . .

"I can't," he said thickly. "I can't regret it."

A shiver visibly ran through her, and for a moment, she looked afraid. He was irretrievably crushing whatever knightly version she had constructed of him, and knowing he couldn't stop it from happening jammed his throat with lumps of ice.

Harriet straightened, and she faced him with her chin put high. "I trusted you," she said. "When you showed me exactly what you were when you tricked me into marrying you. And then struck a deal with my father. And pretended to be doing the honorable thing in my parents' parlor while I was so afraid, I could barely think straight. All that I knew, and yet I resolved to trust you—more fool me. I have no choice: I must return to London."

The words reached him muffled, as if from underwater.

"I don't want you to leave," he said.

"How could I stay?" she said, her gaze already bouncing around the room, locating her belongings.

"It is unsafe for you, on your own."

She looked him dead in the eye then. "The truth is," she said, "I feel even less safe with you."

Her words sliced at something vital in the very fiber of his being. For a moment, he couldn't breathe.

Later. He would approach her later, when they were both in possession of all their senses.

"If that is how you feel about me," he said, "it would indeed be best if you left for now."

He walked out the door, because watching her pack made him want to howl.

Chapter 32

⟡

At first her thoughts had raced along the same old tracks: *Silly, stupid, silly, stupid*, in rhythm with the speeding train wheels. She had felt grubby, in need of a thorough scrubbing, for every hour she had spent in lustful intimacy with Lucian had itched like a blemish on her body. Had he laughed about her gullibility, about her naïve attempts at *testing* him, behind her back?

To round it off, a man was dead.

He did not hinder me from leaving, she thought when she boarded the early sleeper train in Edinburgh. She would have resisted any attempts on his part to keep her at the inn, and yet, recalling his apathetic face during her departure made fresh tears spring to her eyes. Was there a greater loneliness than to lie in a dark, flimsily locked sleeper compartment with only a carpetbag for company? As she drifted between fitful sleep and waking, guilt crept into her sorrow. A whole mining community had begun looking forward to their photographs, which now would never come. At least not from her camera. *I shall send someone*, she thought, *I shall send them someone who actually masters the craft.*

She climbed the stairs to her Belgravia home with her knees buckling beneath the weighty burden of three sleepless nights and days spent in emotional terror over men lost underground. Her chest ached, as if all vital organs inside were inflamed. Perhaps it had all been too much. Perhaps her exhausted brain had played tricks on her, mixing acute worries and old grievances and wholly unrelated matters, and the result had been a harsh attack on her husband and a mindless flight. . . . A woman opened the door, slender, sharp-eyed, with mousy hair curling around her ears. Aoife Byrne.

Hattie squinted at her. She considered reaching out to see whether her hand would go straight through the woman. "Are you a mirage?"

"Good Gad," said Miss Byrne. "What's he done now?"

⁓⁓⁓

Twenty minutes later, Hattie sat on the drawing room settee, clutching her hot teacup as if it were a buoy on the high seas. The roles of hostess and guest had clean reversed: Miss Byrne had taken her coat and carpetbag; Miss Byrne had told her to rest in the drawing room while she fixed some tea in the kitchen. Miss Byrne looked very much at ease, sprawled on the divan opposite, as though she had a habit of sprawling on it. Hattie was still glad for her presence. The woman was Lucian's age, and she was Lucian's friend. It was like having a small part of Lucian near without all that was horribly aggravating, hurtful, and confusing about him.

"I've been trying to reach him," Miss Byrne told her. "My wires have gone unanswered, so I thought I'd pay a visit. I let myself in; they've all flown the coop. I'm afraid I took rather too long a nap on this very plush divan." She petted the upholstery. "Sorry."

"There was an accident at the mine," Hattie said tonelessly. "The past three, four days have been tremendously busy.

Miss Byrne had gone very still. "Any fatalities?"

"None. But it took over two days to free them."

The woman still looked deeply worried. "Must've shattered him."

Hattie swallowed hard. "The truth is," she said, "I did not much recognize my husband after it happened."

"So that's why he pulled the rug from under old Rutland," Aoife

Byrne said, nodding. "I saw the headlines of his sudden demise and I had my suspicions."

"I understand Rutland coerced the miners into using a risky extraction technique," Hattie explained. "A tunnel collapsed because of it."

"Poor Luke. That would do it."

Hattie clutched her teacup more tightly. "Everyone seems rather cavalier about his lordship's untimely death." There was quite a bite to her voice considering she was more of a disembodied mind hovering about.

"Probably as cavalier as his lordship was when he killed Luke's family," Miss Byrne said with a shrug. "And I'd say they're still far from even, considering Rutland got off easy. A nice, quick bullet on a day of his choosing instead of drowning unplanned."

"What?"

The woman looked vaguely contrite. "My—he didn't tell you."

The tea churned in Hattie's empty stomach. "He told me they drowned in an accident," she said. "He told me Rutland owned the mine where he worked as a boy."

"They did drown," Miss Byrne confirmed. "In the mine. Because of Rutland's criminal negligence."

The drawing room wobbled before her eyes as if the whole house had been shifted onto quicksand. Two decades of rigorous breeding kept her sitting composed and upright. *Why*, she wanted to cry, *why did he not tell me? Why does a stranger know these things?*

She placed her cup on the table. "Miss Byrne," she said. "Would you be so kind as to tell me what happened in the colliery?"

The woman contemplated her. "I don't know if it's my story to tell," she then said. "If he's not told you, he might've had his reasons."

"I believe his reasons," Hattie said, "are that he suffers from stunted emotional growth and finds it easier to build a business empire from nothing than to share relevant stories with his wife."

A snort of amusement burst from Miss Byrne. "I'd like to speak in his favor here," she then said. "I've never known him to be a chatty fellow in any case, and sometimes . . . sometimes there's a sorrow that can't be spoken. Hmm." She plucked loose one of the lavender sprigs she had pinned to her bodice and brushed it under her nose while weighing her decision. "It's in the archives of any newspaper, I suppose," she finally said. "I'll tell you what I know, ma'am. The mine where Blackstone used to work had a large stream flowing nearby. And it should've been secured against flooding by a wall—it rains a lot in Scotland, you see."

"I noticed," Hattie muttered.

"But Rutland, the miser, didn't build a wall. And one day, during an unusually dry season, a lot of rain fell unexpectedly during a thunderstorm. And since Rutland hadn't built a building over the heapstead, because as I said he is—was—tight-fisted, the rain extinguished the boiler fire of the steam engine that pulls up the cage with the miners and tubs. Everyone working underground was stuck. I understand Blackstone was in a different pit that day, but his mother and his sister were in the tunnel because Rutland didn't care about no women and children being allowed below the surface. Anyway, while his mother and sister were waiting in the tunnel for the lift to work again, the runoff rainwater from the surrounding hills swelled the stream that went past the colliery to a torrent, and it rapidly went over the banks . . ."

Goose bumps rushed over Hattie's skin. "Go on."

"The miners in that section of the pit had been underground for over twelve hours already because Rutland worked them like pit ponies and cared nothing for working hours. So, tired and hungry, they decided to exit on foot through a ventilation shaft. At first, they seemed to make headway, but just as most of them had made it through the air door into the drift, the stream water came pouring down the slope of the shaft with such violence, it knocked them off their feet and washed them all back against the door—see, air doors, they open up away from you when you leave a tunnel, and so the water pressure kept the door shut and the water kept rising . . ."

"That's quite enough," Hattie choked out.

"Two dozen miners, all of them women and children, died that day," Miss Byrne said. "And Rutland washed his hands of it. Hadn't ordered anyone to enter a ventilation shaft, he said. Higher powers, the thunderstorm, he said. So he was cleared. Refused to pay compensation to the grieving families, then evicted everyone from their cottages who couldn't afford the rent. Well, I say, who could, with one working spouse dead in the ground? Luke had to settle in a new place, where they called him a bastard." Miss Byrne shook her head. "And that is how he came to hate the Earl of Rutland."

The tea surged back up Hattie's throat, bitter like bile. She had been a fool. "I asked him to give up his vengeful designs on Rutland," she said.

Miss Byrne looked surprised, then impressed. "You've some guts, ma'am."

"And he said he'd try, and then, when he didn't, I—I was ghastly to him."

Miss Byrne dropped her lavender sprig. "He said that? That he'd give up Rutland?"

"He said he would try," Hattoe whispered. "Oh. Oh, I wish he had told me. I wouldn't have approved. What good can come from vengeance? But I would not have spoken so harshly to him." The memory of his blank, pale face while she had railed at him stabbed into her stomach, and she buried her face in her hands. "I was a sanctimonious toad," she moaned.

Through the fog of self-loathing, she heard Aoife Byrne clear her throat.

Hattie glanced up. "Yes?"

"Perhaps he couldn't tell you," the woman said. "Even if he wanted to. Even if you'd done everything right."

"He told you, did he not?"

Miss Byrne smirked at the poorly bridled jealousy in Hattie's tone. "The truth is, I'm not certain Blackstone has a proper memory of it when he's conscious," she said. "He told me everything in the days when we still shared a pallet—nothing naughty, we were only children then. Luke—Blackstone, I mean—is a poor sleeper, and he'd sometimes wake me by thrashing around and whimpering. But he never said a word, until one day, he got hold of a bottle of gin. I hadn't taken him for a drinker, but there he was: blue ruin for a week. I thought I had picked up a drunk, and after a few days of him nursing the bloody bottle, I gave him a good kicking. That's when he told me all I just told you, but he was stone-cold drunk. It was the anniversary of their death, you see, and he feels it in his body every year. That year, he didn't want to feel it, so he got pissed. He's done it every year since. He couldn't remember that he'd told me anything after he had sobered up, but I never forgot." She tapped a finger against her forehead. "It's not a tale you forget. What I meant to explain is, it's not easy to say words such as *My kid sister is dead. My mum is dead. They lined them up in the mud, arranged by size, tallest to smallest. They were dead and I lived.* These aren't easy words to say. Not for a man like him, not in front of a wife he's sworn to protect. He's very protective. And he failed them; he didn't keep them safe."

I feel even less safe with you. For a beat, her chest felt icy cold. Her parting shot must have hit the mark. A strangled sob made it past her composure. "Thank you for telling me, Miss Byrne."

Miss Byrne's angular face softened. "Destroying Rutland was what he lived for, Mrs. Blackstone. And he was prepared to try to give him up, for you. I'm no fortune-teller, but I think he'll forgive you."

Hattie knew she had some forgiving to do, too. She clearly still harbored resentment over how her marriage had begun. And she hadn't forgiven herself for her stupid conduct in the gallery. The haze of passion blurred these ugly, festering emotions, but they had never been properly drained. He was right, she thought, it had been a test in part, asking him to let go of Rutland, her attempt to reclaim a sense of power by turning him from dark knight to a Sir Galahad. What if this simmering resentment would bubble over whenever something unrelated stoked her temper?

Miss Byrne finished her tea, then she pulled a small envelope from her reticule and said, "I had come to give him this—could you keep it safe until he arrives?"

"I can't make any predictions as to when he will show," Hattie said. *If he will show ever again*, she added silently.

Aoife chuckled. "I can," she said. "Again: he was willing to give up Rutland for you. You cannot run from him, I'm afraid. In fact"— she pulled out her pocket watch—"I'll expect him to be here by early afternoon, for I doubt he gave you more than two trains' head start."

Hattie's stomach fluttered, first with giddiness, then apprehension. The mountain of unresolved troubles between them was staggeringly high.

Aoife Byrne, knowing her letter was in safe hands, was taking her leave. Hattie accompanied her to the back entrance, her movements clumsy. She could have fallen asleep standing up; learning the truth about Lucian's family had sapped the last of her strength. Miss Byrne took her hat, gloves, and coat from the servants' clothing rack. In a moment, her competent presence would vanish, leaving Hattie alone in a house full of ghosts.

On the doorstep, the Irishwoman turned back. "If I may," she said. She pulled another lavender sprig from her bodice pin and presented it to Hattie. "They say the scent is soothing."

Hattie took the flower, puzzled. "Thank you." She instinctively raised the purple blossom to her nose and inhaled. Yes. Soothing. Reminded her of Catriona's lavender soap, too. As if by magic, the pressure in her chest eased a little.

"There," said Miss Byrne, and winked at her. Or perhaps she had imagined that.

"I did not think you liked me much," Hattie said, feeling half-delirious and emboldened. "You seemed quite amused by the incident in the drawing room when we first met."

Miss Byrne smiled, rather roguishly. "I *was* amused," she said. "It was obvious that Blackstone had saddled himself with a proper trouble 'n' strife, one who'd give him lip."

"Oh."

"It's what he deserves," Miss Byrne said. "Probably what he needs, too. Do you like music halls, Mrs. Blackstone? You should join my friend Miss Patterson and me sometime; we know the best shows. And we live near the grandest theater of the East End."

Hattie broke the seal on Miss Byrne's letter while she crept up the stairs to her private chambers. She liked the woman now, and she knew she should respect her husband's privacy, but secret messages? She had had quite enough of secrets.

News about the burglary: evidence is inconclusive but there is a solid hunch it may have been your weasel of an assistant. If he was the culprit, I want my cuff links back. Also, in your absence, his gambling took quite the turn. I understand Ritchie's put his henchmen on him— if you don't get to him, they will.

AB

She paused on the landing, clutching the railing and feeling faint. A burglary? Henchmen? The weasel assistant had to be Mr. Matthews. His twitchy smile appeared before her mind's eye, and a cold shiver raced down her spine. Where *was* Mr. Matthews? The house suddenly felt yawningly empty, the silence menacing. A surge of energy made her rush to her bedchamber and slam the door shut. Then she turned the key.

Her room smelled stuffy, but the glossy mahogany furniture and soft blue tones of wallpaper and drapery were exactly as she remembered. It still felt alien, as though she had returned from a yearlong voyage after which the old places looked tired and smaller. On her vanity table, the perfume flasks and pots with potions lay scattered, bowled over by an angrily tossed jewelry box. A lump formed in her throat. She placed Miss Byrne's note on the table and picked up the box with shaking fingers. A pang of misery went through her chest at the sight of the silver love spoon on red velvet.

"Oh, Lucian," she whispered. The pendant felt solid and warm in her palm, much like the man. She pressed her lips to the heart-shaped loop. *Please come home*, she implored him. *Strange things are happening with Mr. Matthews, and we have much to discuss.*

With the spoon in her fist, she staggered toward the bed. Presently, only a nap could save her. Afterward, she would wash, change into a day dress, and call on Lucie, Annabelle, or Catriona. She would be safe with any one of them. She was asleep before her head met the pillow.

She woke to dreary afternoon light shining through the windows, a disappointing return to reality after the French lavender fields rolling through her dreams. Sluggishly, she slipped into a pair of soft slippers and made her way to the shower room downstairs. As she passed the door to Lucian's study, the ache in her chest flared up. And then she heard a muffled sound, a *thump*. As if a book had been dropped. Her heart leapt with excitement—Lucian was here. He was already here. She turned back to the door and made to knock, when something stayed her hand. If Lucian had followed her as Aoife had predicted, why had he not come to see her first? He must have found her sleeping and decided to let her rest. . . .

She opened the door and promptly froze in unpleasant surprise. The slim, well-dressed man behind Lucian's desk was not her husband.

Chapter 33

"Mr. Matthews."

Lucian's assistant stood motionless behind the desk, staring at her as if she were an apparition. Then he straightened while furtively closing a folder.

"Mrs. Blackstone. Forgive me, it completely escaped my notice that you were to return today."

His hair was lank, and his features were slack. In the smoky gaslight of the windowless room, he looked like a wax figure that had been held too close to a flame.

Then she noticed the papers, scattered on the floor.

Burglary.

Henchmen.

Aoife's suspicions were correct. And she was alone in the vast house. Her heart began pumping, dangerously fast.

She feigned a smile. "Don't trouble yourself," she said. "My arrival was unplanned."

"Yours?" Mr. Matthews said quickly. "Mr. Blackstone is not here?"

Ice slid down her spine. She had made a mistake. She kept her gaze on Matthews's face, on his feverish eyes, pretending not to see the open briefcase on the desk, nor the broken hinges on the doors of the large cabinet behind him.

"He is following closely behind," she said. "He should be here any moment."

"Ah." Matthews's forehead gleamed, slick with sweat.

"I shall leave you to your task," she said, and took a small step back. The man's expression turned strangely flat. "I shall ring for some tea," she added, her voice sweet, her pulse pounding, *run, run, run*.

"I'm afraid I can't let you do that," Matthews said, and reached inside his jacket. The metallic glint of a pistol flashed.

Her mind blanked. *Run, run, run*. Her feet were rooted to the floor.

Matthews approached like something from her nightmares. "Come in," he said, turning the black eyes of the pistol on her. "Close the door."

Her voice sounded mechanical in her ears. "If it is money you want—"

A muscle began spasming beneath his left eye. "Close the door, please."

She obeyed, but her hand was shaking so badly she could not grip and turn the doorknob properly.

"Oh, get on with it," Matthews snapped.

She redoubled her efforts, and the moment the door clicked shut, Matthews's rigidness turned into nervous, erratic movement. Keeping the shaking pistol pointed at her, he strode aimlessly around the room, muttering under his breath.

She mustn't scream. That was one of the cardinal rules during a kidnapping: no screaming.

"I'm in possession of several pieces of jewelry," she said. "If you need them, they are yours."

"Hush." He ran his left hand through his hair, gripping and pulling, whispering to himself. He spun and snatched a chair from the wall and dragged it in front of the desk, then he fixated on her with bloodshot eyes. "Sit."

She couldn't feel her legs when she walked to him and sat.

He stood so close she could hear his breath rattle in his lungs. He smelled pungently of sweat and smoke. He wasn't well.

She looked up at him. "I'm willing to help," she said quietly. "And I shan't say a thing."

"Hmm?" His gaze was flitting over the paper chaos on the desk. "And why would you do that, Mrs. Blackstone?"

"I . . . I am not fond of my husband," she said. "Surely you know that he tricked me into a compromising situation."

Matthews's lips twisted with contempt. "Ah yes. And I would feel great outrage on account of any decent, gently bred lady trapped in the clutches of this villainous cad. You, however . . ." He looked at her, and his tongue slid out to wet his bottom lip. "You leaned in," he said. "I furthermore witnessed your behavior at the inn. It is obvious to even a negligent observer that you have fully yielded to his corrupting influence. One can practically smell it on you. Don't try me, madam."

Any retort died in her throat. He had all but called her a tart.

"Hence, I hope you understand that while I shall accept the offer of your jewelry, I shan't trust you to keep quiet." He pushed the heavy typewriter toward her. "Load it," he said, and nudged one of the crumpled sheets closer.

The more nervous she was, the clumsier she became. Her muscles were cramping. She fought for movement, one finger at a time. Sweat slid down her back as she flipped the paper lock and tried to force the sheet behind the roller.

"Now type," Matthews said, and she briefly felt the hard press of the pistol against her shoulder. "Husband," he dictated. "What's this?" he then said, leaning down. "What are you doing?"

"I'm sorry," she whispered. She had missed the *H* key and typed a *G*.

Matthews's left eyelid was twitching furiously. "Are you trying to play me for a fool?"

"N-no. I have trouble t-typing."

"For Christ's sake." He ripped the sheet from the machine. "Get up. Move." He took her place and put the pistol onto the desk. "Don't do anything reckless," he said. "Stand there nice and still. Don't compel me to do something drastic."

Nice and still. She stood like a puppet, but anger began broiling beneath the icy sheet of fear. How dare he wreck Lucian's study and try to steal from him?

Matthews was typing, and after a few moments, he murmured, "Apologies. I forgot myself. Of course, you do not grasp the severity of the situation."

It had to be the gambling henchmen on his heels; it was the only explanation.

He hacked away at the typewriter, humming through clenched teeth. Schubert, she thought numbly, he was humming Schubert's "Ständchen."

He pulled the sheet from the machine and placed it before her.

It was a letter—a letter as if written from her own hand. Telling Lucian that she had gone to stay with family on the continent awhile, and that she wished to live separately. . . . Her stomach clenched with fresh panic.

"No," she said, shaking her head. "No—"

Matthews picked up his pistol again. "Sign it, please. Here is a pen."

She looked him in the eye. "Why are you doing this?" she whispered.

"To buy us time," he said tightly. "Since you interrupted me, and he should be here soon, I can hardly leave you here to tattle. You must understand that."

Us? The letter swam before her eyes. The note would send Lucian in a wrong direction. She would be alone with a bungling criminal. Worse, after their row at the inn, Lucian would think she had indeed abandoned him, that she still loathed him. . . . Perhaps he would even think she had taken Matthews for a lover, and she'd never have the chance to tell him otherwise. The pen slipped from her damp fingers.

"Mr. Blackstone will never believe I ransacked his office and left," she said. "You said it yourself: I have become his creature, and he knows this—"

A metallic click, then Matthews's arm jerked up and he fired. Wood and plaster exploded above, and Hattie screamed as debris pelted her.

"He shall believe it because females are fickle creatures," Matthews murmured, his voice trembling, "and you were morally loose enough to enjoy London unchaperoned even before you wed him. Sign. It."

She signed it. Her fingers were gray with plaster dust. Red bloomed on the back of her hand from a shrapnel cut. She hadn't felt the splinter strike.

"Good," Matthews said when she put down the pen, "good. Now sit down again, on your hands. No, first, put your earrings and your necklace in here." He pointed the smoking pistol at the open briefcase. "Your brooch, too." He hastily began gathering papers and folders.

"Have you any knowledge where he keeps his ledger of debts?" he asked as he flung the contents of Lucian's drawers into the briefcase.

"No," she said.

His gaze narrowed at her. "The book where he keeps incriminating secrets of the ton."

Her cheekbone felt oddly numb. Perhaps she had been hurt there, too. "Why would I know such a thing?" she whispered.

Matthews muttered something.

Then he froze and dropped the papers.

She had heard the fall of footsteps, too.

When the door behind them opened, Matthews was already next to Hattie, gripping her arm and yanking her in front of him. The cool pressure of the pistol touched her temple. But something colder and deadlier had entered the room. Lucian. He was holding a revolver and wore an expression as dark as the devil himself.

Harriet was bleeding. The red rivulet streaked from a gash that ran from her cheekbone to her jaw and pinkened the lace at her throat. But it was the flash of hope in his wife's eyes that unleashed something terrible in Lucian. A crimson haze washed over his vision. Matthews was a dead man walking.

It must have been plain on his face, for his assistant flinched and folded himself more tightly into the shelter of Harriet's body.

"Your revolver," Matthews said. "Put it down, on the floor. Then . . . put your arms behind your head."

Matthews's pistol was cocked, and his trembling finger was curled around the trigger. An accidental slip—and it would be the end. Of everything. Lucian went light-headed for a beat. He took a sobering breath.

"All right," he murmured.

He lowered his arm, then he carefully placed the revolver on the floor. While he straightened and raised his hands behind his head, he took a small, seemingly incidental step toward the desk.

"What's your plan, Matthews?" he asked. "A double murder?"

Matthews's face was shiny like a pork rind. "It shan't come to that as long as you are sensible," he said, quite haughtily.

"Sensible," Lucian repeated, nodding. "Sensible sounds good."

His pulse was too high. Something needed to be between Harriet's soft temple and the gun. A double-barreled pocket pistol. Two shots in total, one already in the ceiling. There'd be no double murder today. Only the justified killing of a rat.

"You seem to be in trouble," he said to Matthews. "Care to explain?"

Matthews shook his head. "Just follow my orders—"

"I have experience with trouble," Lucian said and shrugged, gaining another inch. "I might know a better way."

An angry emotion flared in Matthews's eyes. "Don't treat me like a fool. As if you would let me walk from this."

Correct, Lucian thought. He tsked. "I think I already know what your troubles are. You played too deep at Ritchie's in Covent Garden."

Matthews's surprise quickly slid into a thin smile. "Of course," he said. "You put spies onto your own spies. Watching the watchmen."

"Nothing personal," Lucien said mildly. "And I settled the accounts the first time round, but during my absence in Drummuir, you had little to do and no one to hold you accountable here. You returned to Ritchie's, didn't you, and played a losing hand."

Matthews's gaze flicked to the left, confirming the suspicion.

"Then I ordered you up north," Lucian continued, "where you were held up, unexpectedly, due to the flooded tracks. Ritchie became impatient, since you hadn't paid, and I wasn't here to settle it for you."

"That's quite enough," Matthews said, and yanked Hattie's arm.

Lucian bored his gaze so deeply into the mind behind those bleary eyes that Matthews was hooked. "You returned to the den and thought to win your losses back," he murmured, the shrug of his raised arms distracting from the advance of his feet. "Instead, it all spiraled deeper and deeper, toward the bottom pit of hell—"

"Stop," Matthews snapped, and now the gun was pointing at Lucian's chest.

A tension unfurled in him. Point-blank to the head, the Remington was deadly, but if shot from several yards away, a man might be lucky, might stand it long enough to attack and win.

Harriet made a sound of distress. He shut her out. Kept his mind cold and clear.

"What I cannot piece together is: Why ransack my study?" he asked. "Did you suspect I'd refuse to settle your debts forever? That would have been correct, but it wasn't imminent. Did you think you could steal incriminating information from me?" He surveyed the chaos on the desk. "Yes, I think that was your plan: to run, and to then blackmail me to keep settling your bills from afar."

Matthews blinked. Sweat was running into his eyes; it had to be burning him.

Lucian tilted his head. "And you searched Miss Byrne's house, too, didn't you? The question remains: Why now?"

"The truth?" Matthews snapped. "You were becoming too big for your boots. All my attempts to mold you into something other than an uncultured beast were failing, and I knew it was a lost cause when you married a Greenfield." He wiped his sleeve across his brow. "And now you have killed Rutland. I would have refused another day in your service regardless of my pecuniary situation. I could not fathom taking a single order from a scoundrel like you."

Two paces. The man was two paces away. So close, yet so far.

Cold and clear.

"Odd that you should have a fondness for Rutland. He left you to rot in the jail."

"His *lordship*," Matthews corrected, "would not support my vices; he was a morally upright man. You, however, are corrupted to the bone. You feed my weaknesses. All this," he cried in sudden agitation and waved the pistol, "is your fault." He pushed Harriet aside and took a step toward Lucian, the flicker of anger in his eyes flaring to a blaze. "Look at you," he said. "A lowly upstart, playing God. Killing noblemen because you can. How dare you?"

"My sister, Sorcha, was eight years old when she drowned in a ventilation shaft," Lucian said. Still a foot too far. If he lunged now, the answering bullet would be fatal. His heart beat a slow, labored rhythm. "My sister died thanks to your moral man Rutland not giving a damn about his workers."

Matthews licked his lips. "Regrettable, but if they were workers, then this was always a risk, wasn't it? You scurry around in mills and

among dangerous machinery and belowground, and accidents happen. It's natural. Do you know what is not natural? A man of your
breeding living like a prince. A man like me, whose family owns a
four-hundred-year-old estate, being sent to fetch your flowers and
lurid pamphlets." He thrust the pistol forward. "But your kind shall
not succeed. There are too many of us who won't tolerate this dis-
integration of order, of every wretch pushing above their station. Our
lines harden with every strike that sabotages a cotton mill, whenever
there is a new labor union; yes, the more severely Parliament is be-
leaguered to enfranchise the have-nots, the women, the anarchists,
the more firmly we stand. . . ."

"Watch out," cried Harriet behind Matthews's back, and fell to
the floor with a *thud*.

Matthews's gaze slid sideways, toward the disturbance.

Lucian charged.

Screams and a feral snarl rent the air, and a shot rang out.

For a distorted second, the world was white light and the sound
of someone breathing.

When all snapped into focus, Lucian found he was on the floor.
Matthews was pinned under him, emitting a wheezing sound. The
pistol lay empty and useless on the rug, the bullet lodged somewhere
in the walls. Next to them, Harriet rolled onto her side, brushing her
curls from her eyes. Her face was frozen. It was the loveliest, loveliest
face he had ever known, and she was alive.

Alive.

His heart was pounding so hard, it would break through his ribs.
"You all right, love?" he asked.

Her lips moved, but no word came out.

Beneath him, Matthews moaned.

The cold cage around Lucian's mind splintered apart, smashed by
a wrecking ball of wrath. Energy burst through him like a firebrand.
In place of his body was a force.

He was on his feet, his hand a fist in Matthews's collar, and he dragged the man across the floor like a sack of spuds as he strode toward his revolver.

"Lucian, no."

Her cry in his ears, he scooped up the gun and cocked it.

"You bloody bastard," Matthews said softly.

Lucian pulled him up onto his knees by his cravat and twisted his fist into the fabric. Matthews made a satisfying little choking sound, but he stopped scrabbling when Lucian pressed the revolver muzzle between his eyes. He did not move at all then. He did not even breathe.

Lucian stared into the frozen eyes. "You," he said. "You made her bleed." His voice was torn up, barely recognizable; it came from the rawest, darkest place of his soul. "You scared her. You could have killed her. For that, I should send you to hell." He yanked Matthews forward as he leaned down. "I should send you to hell just so you can't ever hurt her again. No one would find it *regrettable*."

Matthews's scent hit his nose. Pure fear. The type of fear Harriet must have felt when the gunmetal had pressed into her downy skin. When she had been alone with a man who wanted to harm her . . .

A tear slipped from the corner of Matthews's eye. Lucian bit back a growl and shook the man. But the longer he held on, the quicker the primal ecstasy of surviving battle was cooling and fading, and the hot roar of fear simmered down, too. A hot glow lingered; then there was only ash.

A tremor ran through his body. He could have lost her today.

The world would have been empty.

But he hadn't lost her; she was still there, a quiet shape in the corner of his eye.

He lowered the revolver and loosened his grip.

He took a breath, and another.

He couldn't. He badly wanted to hurt the man, but he shouldn't, either. It wasn't his place. And while Rutland's ruination was the only measure of justice his victims could expect to receive, it hadn't brought him any joy. And it had nearly cost him his wife. His wife.

This, here, was not what she'd want or need from him; this was what he needed. Perhaps he didn't even need it himself. Perhaps he didn't even want it. More rage, vengeance, and death—when would it stop? Rutland was gone; he could stop being that man. He could stop. He could try.

"Fuck," he murmured.

He gave Matthews a shove.

Matthews fell back onto his bum, a disoriented expression on his face.

Lucian raked a hand through his hair, then he crouched, bringing their eyes level. "You're unwell," he said.

His former assistant blinked, slowly, like someone just returned to the living. "I know," he finally said.

The door opened, and Lucian was upright, the revolver at the ready again.

Carson's bald head poked into the study. "Boss," he said, the deep bass of his voice resonating in the savaged room. He whistled through the gap between his front teeth as he looked around. "I heard a shot."

Lucian pointed at Matthews, who still hadn't moved. "Take him to the basement. Bring him water and bread and stay with him."

Disheveled and bloodied, Harriet stood amid the debris, watching him with a blank look in her eyes. He went to her, wrapped her in his arms, and held her so close. He felt every precious breath she drew against his chest.

✦

She came to him later, when the sky outside his chamber windows had turned a pale rose and he was stretched out on his bed, capitulating to the effects of hot whisky and crushing fatigue. She wore one of her thickly ruffled nightgowns and her red hair loose around her shoulders, and wordlessly she crept onto the mattress. She lay down beside him, so close the whole short length of her was touching him.

He embraced her eagerly, enjoying the tantalizing feel of her soft weight in his arms. She smelled of warm skin and finely milled soap after her hot bath. She was still shaking, as if frozen to the bone. He made a soothing sound.

"We had a terrible row, you and I," she said, her voice muffled by his chest.

He stroked her hair. "Under the circumstances, I call a truce."

She burrowed into him, and he held her more tightly. There was only one way to be even closer, and she did not seem in the mood for his attentions. Well, there *had* been a terrible row.

"I keep thinking," she said, the words coming haltingly, "I keep thinking: What if you had read Matthews's ghastly note and thought I'd run away, and I would have died before I could tell you the truth?"

His shoulders shook with a quiet laugh. "Nah," he said. "I read the note. Obviously, you hadn't written it."

"How would you know?" she said. "I left you before, in Drummuir."

"I'm aware," he muttered. The memory was a dark smudge on his mind, like something singed. His latent fear of losing his selkie had roared to life when she had begun packing.

"Matthews's note was written flawlessly," he said. "You can't write straight for the life of you."

"Oh," she said. He stroked the dip of her waist, then her hip, sensing how her mind was roiling. "Saved by word blindness," she finally murmured. "Who would think?"

Her breathing was still erratic, her teeth still chattering, and so he held her, comforting himself by comforting her.

"How did you know to bring your revolver?" she asked.

"The house felt strange when I arrived," he replied. The very air had felt disturbed; he had a sense for such things. "I came to your chamber and found Aoife Byrne's note on your vanity table. So I prepared myself."

Her breath struck his neck in erratic little puffs. "I keep seeing him pointing the pistol at your chest," she whispered. "I keep feeling how I felt that moment."

He kept seeing it pointed at her head. "We're alive, love."

"Even so," she said in a low tone. "I shall now forever live with the knowledge that without you in it, the world would be a strange place, and I should never be at home in it again."

The world would have been empty.

Giving voice to her fears seemed to ease her anxious mood. She was softening against him and eventually became heavy with sleep. She didn't wake when he undressed, nor when he returned to her side in his robe. He lay awake and watched her breathe.

He dreamed he returned to Inveraray with Harriet, and his grandmother was sitting on the bench in front of the old cottage, enjoying the sun. Her hair was gray and her face lined, just as he remembered, but when she saw him and laughed, she sounded young, a version of her he had never met in life. She looked wholly unsurprised and happy to see him, and the warm sensation of a deep peace settled in his chest. But when he made to introduce his wife, Harriet had disappeared.

Chapter 34

~·~

He woke to the pleasurable sensation of a soft hand on his hard cock and drowsy kisses trailing down the side of his neck. He was dreaming, undoubtedly. He reached for her and gave a soft grunt of surprise when his palms met bare, sleep-flushed skin. She was naked under the covers with him.

"In need of affirming life?" Lucian murmured, still finding his bearings.

"Yes," Harriet whispered, warm and breathless against his ear. "Please affirm." A flower-scented strand of her hair brushed over his nose.

"Wait." He turned her in his arms and pulled her back into the curve of his body, relishing the feel of her skin against his from his chest to his toes. She rolled her hips in the loose yet deeply needy way inherent to pleasure in the twilight hours, and his sigh of relief mingled with hers when he gave her what she wanted. He nipped at the soft curve of her neck. "Lift your thigh and rest it on top of mine."

"Why?" she asked, and a moment later, she gave a happy moan as the shift in position did the answering.

He loved her slowly, never once easing his embrace, and he held on tighter when she came apart around him.

As the glow of languid ecstasy faded, a gray morning crept through the curtains and the events of the previous days claimed their space between them. They lay at a silent little distance from each other, listening to London waking.

Lucian propped himself up on his elbow. "In the study yesterday," he said. "How did you know to drop to the floor and cry *watch out*?"

Harriet shuddered, and she rolled onto her back as if to bodily evade the memory. "I trusted you would do . . . something," she said. "I thought if I could give you a second, you would put it to good use."

"I'm glad you trusted me," he said gruffly.

She looked up with an opaque expression in her brown eyes that he couldn't place.

"I spoke in anger in Drummuir," she said.

"You had reason to be angry," he said, eager to forget the unpleasant episode, and made to kiss her.

She stayed him with a hand to his chest. "What will you do with him?" she said. "With Matthews?"

"Hand him to the sheriff," he said. "Why?"

She hesitated. "He might hang."

"Yes," he said, "there is a good chance of that." He took her chin between his fingers and turned her face to examine the scratch on her cheekbone. It looked to be healing well.

"Must you notify the sheriff?" she asked.

He released her, astonished. "What else do you propose?"

She gave a small shrug. "He said and did horrid things. And yet the thought of him hanging feels wrong."

"He meant to abduct you. He could have killed you; he certainly was moments from shooting me," he said, and when her mournful expression did not change, "He was too pathetic to make a success of his plans, but he did have those plans."

She plucked at invisible specks of lint on the bedsheet. "I know."

He couldn't quite believe it. He was within his rights, if not obligated, to hand a criminal to the police.

But it was also true that the raw, broken place inside him where his scruples used to go to die had changed shape. The jagged edges had smoothed; the pits had filled up. It made sending people to their death a bothersome affair. And Matthews . . . try as he might, he felt no hatred for his former assistant. His only concern was for his wife.

"If I don't hand him to law enforcement, the gambling establishment will send men after him because I no longer pay," he said. "That's rough business."

Harriet tilted her head. "Hence, sending him to the gallows would do him a kindness?"

"No," he said. "But I want to know you're safe."

She was silent.

"I could offer him a check and a one-way ticket to a place outside Britain," he said, "and if he ever sets a foot on British shores again, I'll kill him. Or Ritchie's men will. Does that agree with your conscience?"

It seemed it did, because she leaned in to kiss his chest, then his mouth. Then she said she wanted breakfast. He wanted to make love to her again, to fill her so completely that it would drive away the lingering, preoccupied expression at the back of her eyes, but she slipped from his arms and left.

⌒∞⌒

The next day, she emerged from her room late, nearly at noon. She looked well rested and was in a bright mood, because she had arranged to visit her friends in Bedford Street, and so he decided to use the day to gain control over his neglected business affairs.

His thoughts began straying to her in the afternoon, and when the hours passed into evening and she didn't show, he went into her bedchamber, just to stand in a place where he could feel her presence. He was quickly disappointed: she had spent few days in this room throughout their marriage, and it showed: she wasn't visible in any of the details; there were no personal touches such as her choice of paintings or pillows or vases full of her favorite flowers. However, her scent lingered around the vanity table, and it stopped him in his tracks. He closed his eyes to breathe in the sweet, mouthwatering fragrance, and it was as though he were inhaling sunlight. *What grace, to be alive*, he thought. That he could still smell, see, and touch. That he could still touch her.

When he made to leave, a glint of silver amid the papers strewn across the vanity table caught his attention. He smiled. On one of the papers lay the love spoon he had gifted her, attached to a sturdy chain. She must have decided to wear it at last.

The warmth in his chest dissipated when he realized the nature of the paper underneath the pendant: it was a letter of passage from the British consulate. Allowing Harriet free passage, to France. The icy blast of a premonition hit him. Indeed, there was a one-way railway ticket to Calais. And a list of items to be packed, in Harriet's hand. His stomach lurched. He backed away from the desk as though it held a poisonous snake.

It was late evening when Harriet entered his bedchamber, rosy-cheeked and a little tousled, as though she had rushed up the stairs to reach him quickly. She looked confused when he remained in his armchair instead of rising to greet her, and her gaze fell on the grate next to him, where the fire had long gone cold.

"Did I keep you waiting terribly long?" she asked, out of breath. "I had such a lovely time, I forgot the hour."

He held up her ticket to France. "Are you planning a holiday?" he said. "Or are you planning to leave me?"

Chapter 35

S he recognized the ticket, and froze as if caught mid-crime.

"I see," he said coldly. And here he had thought they had reconciled. Instead, there had merely been a delay.

Blood roared in his ears when she approached with a guilty look in her eyes. Nah, she was not planning a holiday.

He stayed her advance with a shake of his head. "Explain."

She nervously knotted her fingers together. "It's true," he heard her say. "I must go to France."

"*Must*, you say—in what capacity?"

Her shoulders drooped.

His pulse was racing. The ever-lurking whispers at the back of his mind became a roar: the stolen selkie always got her justice . . . the stolen selkie always returned to the sea.

He came to his feet. "Why?" he bit out. "One day you're terrified of losing me, and next, you're scheming to run?" His voice was raw, exposing the clash of emotional front lines inside his chest. His selfish, possessive side would prevail; it must, or else he'd lose her.

Harriet pressed her fingers to her temples as if to block him from her mind. "I'm not running—I have thought of France for years, if counting my girlhood dreams," she said. "Now I have important reasons to go."

No, he wouldn't be interested in her reasons; reasonability could go hang. "Were you planning it yesterday, while in bed with me?" he demanded. "At the time, you seemed pleased enough."

She blushed. "It was very pleasurable, and we both needed it," she said. "But it also confirmed that it would be right to leave."

"You confuse me, Harriet."

But she hasn't surprised you, not really. As denial raged, that realization kept hovering quietly and clearly like a sublime line in the skies above the carnage. It had been a superficial ambush; his shock was halfhearted. The fear of losing her had always been there. Out of sight. Beneath the rocks. But there. The truth always was.

She ran her hand over her face. "I must leave precisely because whatever bliss we share doesn't silence the nagging voice telling me to go. That is why I cannot ignore my desire. It's not a whim. It's not impulsive. My mind has returned to it over and over since we married, certainly because of how we began. And there are other reasons wholly unrelated to our marriage. My heart—"

"Your heart," he interrupted, "your heart has a duty to me."

He cringed and wanted to yank the words back the moment they had left his mouth, because they sounded both commanding and needy, and Harriet had gone white.

Her gaze lingered on his chest. "I'm aware," she murmured. "I'm aware."

"What does that mean, now?"

"It means," she said bleakly, "that you were willing to take a bullet for me."

"And that troubles you?" he asked in disbelief. "You were the one who said we should all have someone worth taking a bullet for."

Her knuckles were white, her nails restlessly biting into delicate skin. "Yes," she said. "And I feel immeasurably cherished. I'm also acutely aware that my being indebted to you in such a way has made your hold over me even more powerful."

What of your power over me? he wanted to say. *I'm a fool for you!*

"I was speaking of your marriage vows," he said, trying to restore calm. "Nothing else. Wanting to draw Matthews away from you was pure instinct, I could have told you that. So there. Does that absolve you?"

She searched his face and a hesitant smile curved her lips. "A little, I suppose."

His muscles, coiled for battle since she had walked in, relaxed a fraction. "Good," he said. "As for France. Why can't you just take a holiday, why such secrecy?"

Her face shuttered again. "But it isn't a holiday," she said, "first because I don't know for how long I need to be gone—"

"Oh, but I need you to know this." For the first thing that sprung to mind was that if she stayed away for more than two years or so, she could properly divorce him on grounds of abandonment. . . .

"But I don't know how much time I shall need," she said, stubborn now. "More importantly, I must feel certain you cannot just order me back."

"I wouldn't," he said. "Why would I?"

She gave him a speaking glance. "You bodily dragged me from my path to France once before."

The crowded platforms at Victoria Station flashed before his eyes. He had grabbed her, and she had called him a miserable brute. *But that was different,* he wanted to say . . . though it would not look to her that way, would it? And would he really stand by and let the time lapse until she could properly divorce him, should she fancy it? As her husband, he had the right to demand she live where he lived before it came to that; he could enforce it, too. . . .

"Then what do you propose?" he said, and the glinting edge to his voice made her hesitate.

"A separation," she finally said. "*A mensa et thoro.*"

There it was.

"You are asking for a divorce, love."

She shook her head. "It merely entitles me to be absent from your bed and the marital home."

Merely. "You would call that semantics," he said, and she shrank a little from the bitterness in his voice. *A mensa et thoro*, "from bed and board," was granted by the church for all he knew. She would be free to stay away if she wished, and there'd be nothing he could do. She could take lovers . . . yes, his selkie was flying toward her freedom. And in every legend, all good people would rejoice for her. It felt as though his lungs were on fire. Breathing hurt.

"What about Oxford?" he asked.

"I sent a note today that I'm taking a sabbatical," she replied. "I have missed a few weeks of term already."

She had planned it through and through.

"And what of the scandal," he managed, "of being legally estranged?"

She raised her chin and seemed inches taller. "I shall weather it," she said firmly. "After having a pistol pointed at my head, and seeing it pointed at you, I shall weather slander."

He took her in, how she was standing up to him, with the proud tilt to her head, with red hair moving around her face like liquid flame, and he could not contain his emotions.

"You must know that I love you," he said. "Deeply."

The slight quiver of her soft lips betrayed her feelings, but there was steel at the bottom of her eyes. "What I know is that I wish to be courted by the man I love," she said. "I wish to be wooed. I wish for him to go down on one knee and have him ask whether I would grant him my hand in marriage. I wish to live without a single doubt that I did not fall in love with my captor because I had no other choice, but that I am freely, truly loving my husband. Marriage costs me my rights. If I were to give them up, I need a choice."

A choice. Clearly, she had not forgiven him their crooked beginnings. *Is da thrian tionnsgnadh*—well begun is two-thirds done. He gave a hollow laugh. "I've spent half my life making the impossible possible," he said. "What I cannot do is turn back time."

"I know that," she said. "But you never even once said you were sorry."

His smile spread over his face, black and viscous like tar. "Because I cannot find it in me to regret it," he said. "I was a captor to you, but you have given me my only hours of true happiness." His hands clenched by his sides then, as if to hold on to the stolen bliss, but his fingers curled over emptiness. "To me," he said, "you were the light in the dark place to which I'd bound myself."

Her determined expression faded into compassion. "You were not my only jailer," she said. "I'm standing up against everyone who forced my hand: my father; my mother, my sister, a whole society that colludes and agrees that it is morally better for a woman to be chained to a stranger than to be forgiven for leaning in for a kiss. I'm taking a stand against this mortal fear they ingrained in my bones, a fear that something terrible would happen if I refused you." An exhausted smile tugged at the corner of her mouth. "And now I have taken a lot of time out of my day to explain my situation to you."

The words were familiar, and he recognized them as his own when she had been eager to make herself useful in Drummuir. The ghastly web. She was caught in it, too. And he was holding the strands that bound her. He swallowed. He was falling now, grasping for straws as they flew past, and none of them held.

"You felt like an outcast in your clan, but you're your father's daughter," he finally murmured. "You appear so unassuming, but you'll strike when it is least expected." And he didn't know whether to feel bloody proud about this or to damn it to hell.

She came to him then, and her cool hand pushed into his. He looked down at the familiar shape covering his hot palm, at the intriguing aesthetic of her tapered pale finger. Her hand, unique in the world. An ache tore through in his chest. Only minutes ago, it had felt just like his hand, accessible like his own body, for this was what lovers became for each other when they loved. Now all was changed.

Because she was right. He ran his thumb over the silken skin of her wrist. "I hate this," he whispered, because he couldn't say *I'm hurting.* Ironic, that the right thing inevitably crushed his heart when he had only just unearthed it.

"Lucian." He reluctantly raised his gaze back to her face. Her brown eyes were warm with compassion, a bloody unchangeable sentiment. "Even had you and I begun properly, it would still serve me well to go," she said. "You see, I was very angry at you after I read the news about Rutland."

"I recall," he said. "I thought we had made good."

She nodded. "We have. But one reason why I was so angry was that I felt stupid. And fooled. I lashed out. If not then, I would have lashed out some other time, because you were right: part of me was testing you. I wanted you to change, to sacrifice, because I had paid such a price. And I wanted proof of your love, because our vows meant nothing, and because I had stupidly traipsed into a trap—"

"Stop saying that word," he said, his impatience flaring back to life. "You're not stupid; you're anything but."

Her smile was achingly sad. "But I have heard that word, in various guises, for half my life," she said. "I know it isn't true, but I don't *feel* it. I worry for myself. I have realized that outwardly, I'm well accomplished, but inside, I harbor a version of me still at boarding school, full of old insecurity, and I recognize it now as a breeding ground for odd behavior, for me saying and doing things I don't mean, for turning to other people's opinions before consulting my own too often, for feeling unnecessarily hurt because I mix an actual issue at hand with old, still bleeding grievances. I know a few women with such a split disposition—they successfully run a home, but they can't even make a simple decision without their husbands. Or they insist on controlling meaningless details just to feel in control of *something.* And what chance did they ever have to be different? We pass seamlessly from father to husband with no opportunity to know ourselves without interference. We are kept childlike in our dependence, in our small world, and in our continued focus on others, and those others keep telling us what we are. But I'm still young. It's not too late, I can still learn. I already care much less for the opinions of people, and I want more. I need to go to France."

He signed the papers that brought his authority over her to an end in an ecclesial courtroom in Westminster. Harriet wore a somber gray dress, but her hair glowed like rubies in the drabness of the chamber, and it took effort not to stare at her. Whenever he did look, three distrustful stares skewered him in return, for his wife had gathered her friends around her for support: the Duchess of Montgomery, Lady Catriona, and Ballentine's dainty missus, Lady Lucinda. That daintiness was a trap; the pointy-faced madam looked ready to tear his throat out with her teeth whenever she caught his eye, and she'd do it gleefully, too.

Outside the courthouse, a blast of cold wind froze his face. Raindrops drizzled into his collar and the cool, wet touch sent shivers down his spine. He glanced at Harriet, who somehow had drifted alongside him through the wide wing doors in the protective circle of her coven. Now she paused and raised her chin at the plaza before them as if to steel herself. Through his frozen dread, he felt a stab of guilt. Their union had begun and ended with headlines in the scandal sheets, when all she had dreamed of had been a rose-tinted production straight from a romantic novel.

He cleared his throat. "You'll leave soon?"

She turned toward him, and his breath caught. With the soft white fur framing her face, she looked like an ice princess. "Yes," she said. "Tomorrow."

She didn't wish to share her exact destination with him. He supposed it hardly mattered where she went. He could have reached out and touched her pretty face, but there was already an insurmountable distance between them. Bewildering, how one could lie entwined, skin to skin, breathing each other's breaths, only to become strangers again.

"*Turas math dhut*," he said. "Safe travels."

An emotion flickered in her eyes. Disappointment? But she graciously inclined her head. "Come, dear." Lady Lucinda clasped her elbow, and Harriet made to follow her.

It tugged inside his chest, as though his heart was still leashed to hers. "Harriet."

She turned back. "Yes?"

He took off his hat. "I am sorry."

She bade her friend to wait. Now four pairs of eyes were staring at him. He only really saw one of them; he sank his own gaze into Harriet's as if intent to reach her very soul.

"I am sorry," he repeated. "And I'm sorry for not saying it out loud any sooner. I suppose voicing it would have meant admitting to some fault. To the injustice. And I wanted to keep you."

Behind Harriet's shoulder, Lady Lucinda snarled.

"I'm sorry," he repeated, "sorry that I kept you when I didn't know how to care for you. The truth is, loving you took me by surprise. The way love feels ambushed me. It feels brutal. Like an unstoppable force. It demands to be accommodated, against reason, regardless of all that might have been before, and I had too little practice to master it well. I suppose I thought I could remain who I was, and still begin anew with you, but that was wrong. You did right, asking me to let go of Rutland. But I had lived with rage for so many years I saw it no longer; it was part of me, and had I let it go—well, you might as well have asked me to let go of my heart, or some other vital part, perhaps the legs I stand on."

When he had reflected on whether he had anything to tell her before they would part, he had thought about his rage—the force that had given him so much: his wealth, the strength to persist when the odds were against him. It had occurred to him then that the emotion driving him hadn't simply been rage—some of it had been hope, too. And perhaps much of it had been grief. Rage had been simpler, an emotion he knew and could name. Grief . . . grief would have implied that he was suffering. Vulnerable. An accursed feeling, like showing a pink underbelly to a world that was waiting to rip its claws across anything soft. And yet, much as his instinct was to protect and control what he loved, he had concluded that love itself demanded vulnerability. He never loved his wife more, or felt more able to express his love for her, than when she was under him, naked and soft, trustingly opening her most sensitive places to him. And she had looked at him with great tenderness when he had finally stepped back and let her go. He let her go. She was leaving. This, here, now, might be the last he'd see of her in years.

"I wanted to choose you," he said hoarsely. "And I wish I could turn back time. Forgive me."

She blinked, and tears fell from her lashes. "Lucian."

Lady Lucinda tugged at Harriet's arm.

"Hattie," he said in a low murmur.

She shook off the commanding hand. She closed the distance to Lucian and rose to her toes. Vanilla scent brushed his nose, then her lips moved against his cold ear. "I have forgiven you," she breathed. "And I do love you. Please remember that."

She did not look back when descending the stairs on her friend's arm, while he stood on the same spot long after her carriage had pulled away from the pavement and vanished in the London fray.

Chapter 36

April 1881, Southern France

Spring days in the Camargue had the same warm, treacle-slow feel as August afternoons in England. The classroom's sheer linen curtains billowed lazily whenever the salt-infused breeze blew across the plain through the open windows. Summer here at Mytilene Ville would be sweltering hot.

She turned her attention back to her class. Fifteen expectant pairs of eyes were on her, an eclectic group of young and older women hailing from all corners of Europe was waiting for her next instruction.

She pointed at the blackboard. "Take a few minutes to copy the formula, please, then we shall have a discussion about the process."

As fifteen pens scratched onward, her attention, almost habitually now, strayed to the nearest window again. The brown dirt road winding its way through the marshland was empty. It always was. The sun was high in the sky and the ponds below glittered like mirrors. Yes, sweltering. She would stay until the lavender fields were in bloom, then she'd move on to Paris, or perhaps Italy. Or perhaps, Scotland.

She cleared her throat. "Now," she said to the class. "What do we do once we have the brominized collodion? Miss Esther?"

"We drop it into the solution," Miss Esther said shyly. "One drop at a time, and we mustn't forget to stir."

"Like rum essence into batter," said Mademoiselle Claudine, who had not a shy bone in her body. Giggles erupted.

"Quite right," Hattie said when silence was restored. "And what is the result?"

"Silver bromide?"

"An emulsion of silver bromide. How long until it can be used? Mademoiselle Claudine?"

"There is no set time, but it has to sit until the consistency is like cream, which usually takes fifteen hours."

"Bravo."

Seeing her pupils' heads bent in concentration and watching their pens fly filled her chest with warmth. She knew now why they called it getting a big head, or getting too big for one's boots—with every swell of teacherly pride, every elation over a small success in her makeshift laboratory, she could feel herself stretch and grow beyond her old delineations. Old fears were relinquishing their hold on her; ever since her word blindness might have saved her life by pointing Lucian the right way, the terror associated with academic learning had begun to ease. She had simply recruited Miss Esther for checking the numbers in her formulas so she didn't accidentally teach instructions for explosives, and her pupils never remarked upon it. Very few questions were asked here at the enclave. Most of the women arrived under a false name, and personal information filtered through only as mutual trust grew. It was freeing, not being known. She was a blank slate, and could sketch whatever she wished.

Life slipped by pleasantly in Mytilene. She taught from morning until noon, and in the afternoons, they set out on group walks through the marshlands with their cameras and tried to capture the wildlife. The most popular subjects were the wild white horses that freely roamed Camargue and the flocks of flamingos dotting the shallow waters. The bright pink of the birds inspired Hattie to keep experimenting late into the night with different carbon pigment ratios in bichromate gelatin to bring out the color on the plate.

On Sundays after chapel, she read novels and essays and drank dry cider in the walled orchard. She wrote many letters. To receive mail from Scotland took unnervingly long. *In case you wish to pursue your plans of becoming a soap maker, the women's trade union office in your region now offers business loans for female entrepreneurs*, she had informed Mhairi soon after her arrival in the Camargue. She knew this because she had put part of her separation settlement to good use. *PS: Can you forgive my hasty departure?* The answer came weeks later on thin paper: *Rosie Fraser says all will be forgiven if you return and finish what you started. Madam, I won't be a soap maker. Hamish Fraser asked my hand in marriage and I accepted. . . . I'll be a miner's wife . . . or a novelist's wife, should he ever finish his edits. . . .*

Now and again, she wondered how Lucian's political machinations and his plans to communalize the mine progressed. She tried not to think of Lucian himself. And during her busy, laughter-filled days, he let her be. At night, when she was alone in her spartan chamber, he claimed his space—in her dreams and in her bed, and she would wake with the lingering sensation of his hard body against hers and an echo of his whispers in her ear.

Easter approached, and her class was stenciling Easter eggs, which she planned to use for a study of contrasts and texture. As she wrote instructions on the blackboard, the class was restless behind her.

"Madame," said Claudine. "There is a man."

Alarmed, Hattie looked out the window. Indeed, there was a rider on the dirt path, moving in a cloud of dust. A sharp, quick emotion squeezed her heart. The broad set of the man's shoulders was recognizable even from a mile away. She realized she had her hand pressed over her chest, dusting her green bodice with chalk. Brushing at it made it worse.

"Worry not," she said, her voice sounding thin. "I know him."

Relief rippled through the room, then the women crowded around the windows, speculating whether he was handsome.

"*Allons-y.*" Hattie clapped her hands. "*Mesdames*, attention on the blackboard, if you please."

By the time the class was finished and the students dismissed, her face felt feverish. She stood next to the teacher's desk with its scattered papers and the riotous collection of flasks and jars and pieces of chalk and waited. How she had waited.

Elize appeared at the doorjamb, her face stern beneath her security officer cap. "There is a visitor for you, madame, a man who says his name is Blackstone."

The sound of his name settled hotly in her belly. "Yes," she said. "I wish to receive him."

Elize contemplated her. "Monsieur is keen to see you at once. Here."

She could only nod.

When he entered, solemn and with his hat under his arm, the classroom vanished like Scottish hills into mist. She felt lifted from her own body as she watched him approach.

He halted at a respectful distance. "Good morning, Mrs. Blackstone."

His clothes were dusty. His dark hair was curling into his collar. "Lucian." It came out as a croak.

He stepped closer, and she smelled horse and travel, but mostly she smelled everything she loved the most, and her knees trembled.

"I apologize for my appearance," he said. His gaze moved over her face, his gray eyes appraising. "You look very well."

So did he, more handsome than in her dreams. But this was real. He was here.

He took in the formulas on the blackboard, her collection of chemicals on the table, and the results of her color photography experiments on the wall across.

"Your classroom?" He sounded impressed. Looked it, too. Impressed and proud.

"Yes," she said. "I teach photography. And painting, but mainly photography. I built a lab, too."

His crooked smile brought back the memories of the red-hued mountain slopes, of a day by the sea, of lying naked and safe in his arms on a creaky mattress in an inn.

Her mouth turned dry. "What brings you here?"

He placed his hat onto her desk. "I've had something on my mind ever since we last saw each other."

The dreary courthouse steps. She shuddered involuntarily.

Lucian looked her in the eye. "When you left, you said you loved me," he said.

"Yes."

"And the last time I had seen you before that, you said you wished to be courted and wooed by the man you love."

She nodded, her pulse drumming a hopeful, fateful beat in her ears.

He hesitated. "Are you presently spoken for?"

She thought of the dark-eyed French boys who brought her flowers and chocolates and competed over who would be allowed to carry her camera equipment, no matter where she wished to take her class in the marshlands.

"I regularly correspond with a Monsieur Louis Ducos du Hauron," she said. "He has greatly widened my mind."

Lucian's face looked set in stone. "Du Hauron," he repeated.

"An inventor," she said. "I have decided to work on color photography, and he is the pioneer in the field. However," she added, "I don't consider this being spoken for."

The tension he had been holding in his shoulders since he had walked in eased.

"And what of your captor?" he said, watching her closely. "Still unwillingly attached to him?"

"No," she murmured. "But I still have tender feelings for the man I once married."

Lucian let out a shaky sigh. "Then I wish to court you," he said hoarsely. "And woo you."

"I'm so glad you have come." It had burst from her like a sob. She had hoped he would, though not expected it, despite the lifeline she had extended on the court steps. "Now I notice how much I wished you would."

He gave her a wary look. "It took time to locate you. And you were very clear that you wanted to be let alone, so I didn't think you'd appreciate me showing too soon."

How had he spent the past six months? Had he been lonely? Flirted with other women?

"How did you do?" she asked, suddenly anxious.

"Well," he said. "I now own a dog."

"A dog! What kind of dog?"

"A small whippet," he said, looking harassed. "A prissy thing. Not sure she knows she's a dog."

She couldn't help but laugh. "Lucian, why a whippet?"

"I thought you might like her," he said. "Well knowing you were gone." He shrugged. "It wasn't rational."

A lump formed in her throat. "How did you do?" she repeated softly.

His gaze locked with hers and hid nothing, not an ounce of his raw, deep yearning. "I did all right," he said. "Half agony, half hope."

She blinked. "You . . . read *Persuasion*?"

"I've read them all," he said, his tone faintly amused. "I like *North and South* best, but either way I've learned many fancy words for properly courting a lost love."

She moved closer to him, until the tips of their boots touched and she could breathe him in. "How," she whispered, "how would you say it in your own words?"

His eyes bore into hers. "I miss you," he said. "Come home."

She buried her face in her hands.

Through her fingers, she saw his still starched and folded hand-kerchief. She took it and pressed it to her nose just to gorge on his scent.

"I'd wait another eight years and a half for you, too, ye ken," she heard him say.

Her head whipped up. "No. Please, begin wooing me posthaste." She pulled at the silver necklace she never took off, lifting the wedding ring and the love spoon from her bodice.

Lucian's eyes widened.

"Posthaste," she repeated.

"Well then," he murmured. "There's a tavern at the road junction. It's romantic. There's flowers in baskets and carved hearts on the window shutters."

The first tear was already rolling down her cheek.

He held her face and brushed gently with his thumbs. "*Mo chridhe.* Would you accompany me to a lunch?"

She clasped a hand around his nape. Felt his warmth and strength beneath her fingers, and the loosening of some tension at her center which would forever come with touching him. They could not turn back time, but they could begin again.

"Yes, Mr. Blackstone," she said, and leaned in.

Epilogue

⬥

I t's . . ." Professor Ruskin hesitated; he was making a production of studying the projector apparatus Hattie had installed at the center of the darkened exhibition room. "I say, it's . . ."

If he said *lovely*, she'd defenestrate him right out of the upper floor of the Shoreditch gallery, no matter that it would be witnessed by two dozen of London's most influential people and a hundred visitors with an interest in photography. As predicted, her opening day had attracted a crowd. Entry was free of cost for workers, but the expensive tickets had sold out like hot scones the same date her exhibition had been announced in the papers. "They come to see the scandalous Greenfield-Blackstone, not your photographs," Mina had assured her, but her sister's eyes had sparkled with good humor.

Mina and her knightly husband were studying the children's photographs on the east wall, where each picture was illuminated by a miner's safety lamp. The lighting was low enough to not interfere with the heart of her installation: on the north wall, tapestry-sized portraits of the people of Drummuir flashed and lingered in tireless rotation thanks to the small coal-fueled engine turning the cranks in the magic lantern. The coal fumes were transported out a window through a metal pipe, but the air still smelled faintly of colliery. Reporters circled the small engine with notebooks in hand.

"Modern," Ruskin finally pronounced. "Very modern."

"Thank you," Hattie said, distracted. Somewhere in the crowd were her friends.

"A terrific concept, Mrs. Blackstone." Ruskin added, "We are pleased to have you back at Oxford this term."

She should have felt ardent elation at his words, but it was at best a lukewarm glow. Ruskin's opinion had lost its teeth. She was no longer working for his praise. She was no longer working for praise from a nebulous audience, either. Her work here was dedicated to people she knew, and hopefully it contributed toward the changes she wished to see in Britain. She was quite content with her execution, too. These were the things that mattered.

"Are you all right, dear? Are you too warm?"

Annabelle had appeared by her side with a drink in hand, her feline green eyes searching Hattie's face. Hattie touched her heated cheeks. "I'm fine. Does my face look red? How could you tell? It's so dark in here."

Her friend smiled. "Your expression was very wistful, when you should be rejoicing," she said. She leaned closer, filling Hattie's nose with a delicate jasmine scent. "Apparently, the director of the Royal Academy is interested in acquiring your work."

"Oh my."

Just then Lucie joined them, her arm linked through Catriona's. "Fantastic work, Hattie," she said. "I understand nothing about art, but some of the dullest people in attendance here are muttering disapprovingly under their breath, which means you did well."

Hattie sipped her tepid champagne. "I just wish Mhairi and Hamish Fraser could be here."

After her return from France, she had settled in the Drover's Inn for two months. Lucian had stayed with her the first weeks, to discuss a possible communal mine ownership experiment with Boyd and to oversee the new railroad tracks designed to improve the mining infrastructure of Fife. Hattie had spent her days with Rosie Fraser's family, and on the coalfields and in tunnels to understand what she needed to know. In the end, Hamish had directed her lens as much as her artistic intuition. "You should take a few," she had told him after the first week. "I shall teach you." He had laughed and said he'd rather pull out his eyeballs and pickle them than squint at wee upside-down images all day long. He had taken his mother's portrait, however, and it was comforting to know that the original plate currently graced Rosie Fraser's kitchen wall. Perhaps one day a representative from Drummuir would follow her invitation and come to London. Perhaps when Hamish sent his finished novel to London Print. Apparently, he was still editing.

Catriona was watching her with her usual quiet attentiveness. "Don't you think they would approve?"

They would say no one in this room would be able to tell their arse from an ax.

Hattie giggled. "They approved all content," she said. "I'm certainly hopeful that they will approve of the substantial sum that I shall deposit in Drummuir's community account."

"If you wish to sell the work at a good price," Annabelle said, "I think the duke would be an interested buyer."

The Duke of Montgomery was near the refreshment table, his straight shoulders and the glint of his white-blond hair in the shadows unmistakable. As was Lord Ballentine's remarkably tall form, next to the duke. Lucian had joined them, and Hattie would have loved to be a fly on the wall next to the unlikely trio—the men's icy, smug, and brooding temperaments, respectively, had to make for terrible company. But enabling people who had little in common to cross paths and influence one another was one of the most important side effects of events such as this exhibition. Lucian certainly had to speak to Montgomery about his strategy for the Married Women's Property Act.

Tenderness stirred in her chest as she watched Lucian in conversation. A few days ago, he had gone down on one knee and had asked her to marry him again. She had relished her *yes* like a luscious piece of nougat.

"Behold," came a faintly mocking voice, "it's the artist herself."

Aoife Byrne. Lucian's friend had company; a young blond woman in pink taffeta hung on her arm. Aoife placed a protective hand on top of her companion's. "This is my friend Miss Susan Patterson," she introduced the lady, and to Hattie, said, "Miss Patterson is a grand admirer of your work."

Miss Patterson smiled shyly. With her finely drawn mouth and perfect blond ringlets, she looked angelic.

"Your work is remarkable," she said. Her voice was cultured and soft. "I attend quite a few of such exhibitions, and to see hope and grace instead of only misery is good. And the juxtaposition of portraits and hands—very good."

Hattie felt her heart swell a little. "Thank you. The concept was inspired by Mrs. Rosie Fraser."

"I read her name on the poster," Miss Patterson said.

Aoife took two champagne flutes from a waiter's tray and handed one to Miss Patterson. "What she really wants to speak to you about is your charitable projects."

"Which one?"

"I understand you and Mrs. van der Waal have created an ethical investment committee," said Miss Patterson.

"Word has spread fast, it seems," Hattie said, feeling pleased.

The committee used rooms in one of Lucian's surplus houses as a headquarters. Julien Greenfield had offered his assistance, keen to make amends because he wished for Hattie to return to the dining table on Fridays, but she had chosen Zachary instead. Her brother, who would forever feel guilty over keeping secrets from her, had eagerly committed himself to the task. He was even warming to Lucian now that she had chosen him.

"We are still in the process of defining the criteria for ethical investments," Hattie told Miss Patterson.

The young woman looked curious. "And how do you do that?"

"We are currently in close exchange with the Quaker community in Oxford—we noticed they don't invest in enterprises linked to arms production or arms trade."

"I'm intrigued," said Miss Patterson. "I come from cotton; perhaps my experiences could be of use."

Hattie's eyes grew round. "You are of the textile Pattersons?"

"She was," Aoife murmured, "she was, until she joined her father's workers' union."

The sentence contained a whole story, and Lucie had sensed it, too. She planted herself in front of the pair. "Could I interest you in joining the suffrage movement, by any chance?"

"What I'm interested in is whether one can improve the ills of the world with the same system that's been causing them," Aoife Byrne said. "Reform or revolution, that's the question."

"I like her," Lucie said to Hattie, looking keen. "Where did you find her?"

Hattie sensed a familiar presence at her shoulder, and when she turned, she met Lucian's calm gaze. He raised his pocket watch. "Time for your speech," he said. "Five minutes."

Her heart dropped for a beat. Then she remembered to breathe. She had taught chemistry to a full classroom. She had stared into the eye of a pistol. She was wearing a new favorite outfit: an adorable little hat and a snugly fitted, elegant one-piece in purple satin, hemmed and trimmed with pearl-embroidered velvet. Her speech would be utterly fabulous.

Lucian leaned closer, teasing her nose with hints of his shaving soap. "You need anything?" he murmured. "A glass of water?"

He was distractingly handsome, with his shoulders perfectly filling his navy-blue coat. "Thank you," she said with a small smile. "I have all I need."

Pleasure lit his eyes. Briefly, his attention lingered on the thistle she had pinned over her heart. "The representative of the Chinese Legation has requested an introduction," he said.

"Oh?"

"I told him it was my wife's influence that saw a certain pair of vases returned into his keeping."

A quiet joy passed between themas they stood close with their hearts and little fingers linked, one year after their first encounter in Chelsea. The turmoil of those early days had given way to learning how to love each other well, and at its core, their new union felt warm and safe. At first sight, they were still an unlikely match—opposites in looks, upbringing, and temperament. But on the artist's color wheel, two opposite colors were considered complementary. Their high contrast caused high impact, and they looked their brightest when placed next to each other.

Hattie brazenly slipped her whole hand into Lucian's. "I am the orange to your blue," she said.

He gently pressed her fingers. "My fanciful lass."

"It means we are fine on our own," she said. "But side by side, we're brilliant."

Author's Note

The accident that killed Lucian's family was inspired by a pit disaster in Silkstone's Huskar Pit in 1838, which was one of the events prompting the 1842 Mines and Collieries Act. The public then seemed most concerned about female nudity in the mine tunnels, with the miner-friendly *Labor Tribune* fretting, "A woman accustomed to such work cannot be expected to know much of household duties or how to make a man's home comfortable." For a while, people traveled to mines to take pictures of women in trousers for commercial purposes, and the miners received a share of the proceeds. Female miners frequently defended their work and evaded the law because they needed their wages to feed their families. They very much embodied the conflict between Victorian notions of ideal womanhood (the dainty angel in the house) and the reality of women depending on manual labor for survival.

Pit-brow lasses played a strong role in the fight for women's suffrage in the Edwardian era. In the Victorian era, the organized British suffrage movement consisted overwhelmingly of middle- and upper-class women; British society was rigorously stratified along class lines, and working-class women had low personal incentives and high practical barriers to join the movement for the vote. However, British suffragist leaders were long aware of class-based double standards—in 1872 Millicent Fawcett noted, "It is a small consolation for Nancy Jones, in Whitechapel, who is kicked and beaten at discretion by her husband, to know that Lady Jones, in Belgravia, is always assisted in and out of her carriage as if she were a cripple." Suffrage and women workers's rights movements increasingly overlapped toward the end of the century, particularly in the industrialized North. The full integration of the two movements was frequently hampered by the narrow focus middle- and upper-class suffragists kept on a woman's right to vote rather than wider social reform including the rectification of wage inequality, which was a priority for female workers. On many occasions, aristocrats and factory workers did stand side by side, notably when the suffrage struggle entered its militant phase in 1905. It still took until 1928 for low-income women to vote, while their monied or university-educated counterparts were given the vote in 1918.

Art as a vehicle for change

In the late 19th century, many Victorians turned to art to address societal ills. Artists began viewing their work as a charitable endeavor and a driver for social reform, often by creating either romanticized or shockingly realistic depictions of poverty to move the public. Social photography did play a part in raising awareness about dire working conditions and the continued use of child labor in Victorian Britain.

Wedding nights

I included the artifact *The Art of Begetting Handsome Children* in this story to show that some Victorians acknowledged both the existence and the importance of female pleasure in a marriage. As a rule, however, middle- and upper-class women in particular were kept ignorant about sex until it happened to them. Inspiration for Hattie's wedding-night discussions came from novelist Mimi Matthews's blog post "Ether for Every Occasion":

> *The 1897 edition of* A Manual of Medical Jurisprudence *reports the case of a newlywed Victorian lady who went into hysterics whenever her husband tried to initiate sex. As a result, the consummation of their marriage was "long delayed." According to the report: "The difficulty was at length overcome by the administration of ether vapor. She recovered consciousness during the act of coitus, and there was no subsequent difficulty in intercourse."*
>
> *German philosopher Friedrich Nietzsche, who spent much time with German suffrage leaders, pondered in* The Gay Science *(1882): "There is something quite . . . monstrous about the education of upper-class women. . . . All the world is agreed that they are to be brought up as ignorant as possible of erotic matters, and that one has to imbue their souls with a profound sense of shame in such matters. . . . They are supposed to have neither eyes nor ears, nor words, nor thoughts for this. . . . And then to be hurled as by a gruesome lightning bolt, into reality and knowledge, by marriage—precisely by the man they love and esteem most! To catch love and shame in a contradiction and to be forced to experience at the same time delight, surrender, duty, pity, terror. . . . Thus a psychic knot has been tied that may have no equal!"*

It also exacerbated the power imbalance between men and women on a most personal level. Since contentions around female pleasure exist to this day, I made it a point in the story. I believe romance novels play their part in undoing this legacy.

On leaving a marriage

Divorcing in Victorian Britain was possible but not easy in 1880, especially if the instigator was a woman. An upper-class wife usually had the means to pay for it, but she also inflicted scandal upon herself, and simply living separate lives was not so simple: until 1883, the "abandoned" spouse could petition for a *writ of restitution of conjugal rights*, which obliged their partner, usually the wife, to return to the marital home. If the partner served with the writ refused, they were imprisoned until they changed their mind. While Hattie trusted Lucian not to revert to such measures, I felt it was crucial for her to feel free from any legal hold a man might have over her for once in her life, and to only relinquish this freedom at a point of her own choosing. The legal separation she proposed gave her that option.

Artistic license

While Trollope's novel *The Way We Live Now* was published in 1875, the line cited in this novel is actually from his autobiography, which was published in 1883, three years after the events of this novel.

John Dewey published essays on aesthetics throughout the 1880s, but the full theories about art as experience as discussed by Hattie were printed after 1900.

"They look too lovely to be clever" was not uttered by Professor Ruskin, but his contemporary Professor Henry Sidgwick. He said it in reference to the first cohort of women students at one of the women's colleges he had cofounded at Cambridge.

Acknowledgments

Half of this book was written during a pandemic that changed the world as we knew it. I more than ever relied on an amazing group of people to make it to The End, and I'm incredibly grateful for their generously given time, advice, cheer, and patience. In particular, I would like to thank:

Matthias, for stoically sharing me with all these people inside my head.

Bernie, Montse, and Kate, because that first draft wouldn't have left the building without you.

The LMH squad: Paula (your "pedantic read" was invaluable) and Helen (your cheer is so appreciated).

Dr. Alex Boyd, for his expert advice on Victorian photography and the ways of a Scotsman—find his brilliant photography of the Scottish Isles at alexboyd.co.uk.

My fabulous fellow authors Rachel van Dyken, Jennifer Probst, Lauren Layne, Amy Reichert, Emily Henry, Roshani Chokshi, Eva Leigh, Stephanie Thornton, Chanel Cleeton, Susan Dennard, Jodi Picoult, and the Lyonesses: for squeezing my work onto your towering TBR lists, your blurbs and shout-outs; you are as talented as you are kind.

Isabel Ibañez, Christine Wells, and Kerri Maher—your critique reading was everything.

The Berkley team, especially Jessica Brock and Jessica Mangicaro, for always doing a brilliant job of bringing The League to readers.

Special thanks to my fantastic editor, Sarah Blumenstock, for always giving me the time and space I need to do my best; and to my agent, Kevan Lyon, who is both the fiercest as well as the most supportive agent I could wish for.

Portrait of a Scotsman

EVIE DUNMORE

Discussion Questions

1. *Portrait of a Scotsman* is inspired by the Greek myth of Hades and Persephone. Hades, god of the underworld, is enchanted by Persephone at first sight, but Persephone's protective mother forbids marriage. Hades leaves his dark realm to abduct Persephone, then tricks her into staying by his side below ground for half the year. Sheltered Persephone is unhappy at first but eventually falls in love with her husband and her powerful position as queen of the underworld. Considering that our sensibilities about proper courtship have changed since Ancient Greece, why do you think this myth continues to inspire retellings?

2. The *ideal woman* in the Victorian era belonged in the domestic sphere, where her role was to be a pure, gentle, and mood-lifting presence. The majority of women at the time, however, worked hard outside the home to make ends meet, and their income was required to keep their families fed. Why do you think such an unattainable image was promoted, and do you see any parallels to society today?

3. Poverty, combined with traditional demands on a woman's time in the home, formed a real barrier between working Victorian women and conventional political participation. Working-class suffragette Annie Kenney wrote in her 1924 memoir, *Memories of a Militant*: "After a hard day's work in a hot cotton factory you have very little life left." Can you think of comparable examples today or in recent times? How and where do you see this explored in *Portrait of a Scotsman*?

4. Lucian struggles with his position as a self-made man and feels ambivalent about both his roots and his new social class. Why do you think he feels torn? Do you think he handles his new power well? Why or why not?

5. Lucian believes a governance system can be reformed from the inside out. Do you agree or disagree? Why?

6. Hattie argues with Lucian that a woman is always more disadvantaged than a man regardless of their socioeconomic status because in the power structures of the 1880s, any woman was at a held back on the grounds that she was a woman. Do you agree or disagree? If you agree, how have things changed since?

7. When she first explores married life, Hattie clearly prefers to be submissive in the bedroom. Do you think this preference is at odds with being an emancipated woman? Why or why not?

8. There were two ways of thinking about art in the late Victorian era. The Decadents, led by Oscar Wilde, rebelled against societal constrictions by focussing on beauty and refusing to model *moral* behavior in their work. Other artists began to understand their work as a political tool that could be used to bluntly address societal ills and raise awareness. Do you think art has a moral or political role to play? What are potential risks when expecting artists to create in accordance with particular political ideologies?

9. Hattie demands a separation and leaves Lucian to live on her own for a while, despite his willingness to literally put his life on the line for her. Why do you think taking this step was important to her? Do you agree or disagree with her decision?

Photograph by the author

Evie Dunmore wrote her *USA Today* bestselling series inspired by the magical scenery of Oxford and her passion for romance, women pioneers, and all things Victorian. In her civilian life, she is a consultant with a M.Sc. in diplomacy from Oxford. Evie lives in Berlin and pours her fascination with nineteenth-century Britain into her writing.

CONNECT ONLINE

EvieDunmore.com
EvieDunmoreAuthor
EvietheAuthor

Ready to find
your next great read?

Let us help.

Visit prh.com/nextread

Penguin
Random
House